Drink deep
or taste
not.

EX LIBRIS

Other books by Ben Behunin

Remembering Isaac
Discovering Isaac
Becoming Isaac
Forget-Me-Notes
Borrowing Fire
Put A Cherry On Top
The Lost Art of Wooing Rabbits and Other Wild Hares
The Disciple of the Wind
How to Seduce a Sasquatch
Authentically Ruby
Splendidly Ruby
Pleasantly Ruby

Ben's books are available from his website,
www.potterboy.com, www.amazon.com and
wherever above average books are sold.

PERSUASIVELY RUBY

The Pursuit of Joy

Book 4 in a series

by Ben Behunin

Persuasively Ruby
The Pursuit of Joy

First printing, November 2021

Published by
Abendmahl Press
1150 East 800 South
Salt Lake City, Utah 84102

ISBN 978-0-9838025-4-9

Designed by Bert Compton and Ben Behunin
Illustrations by Ben Behunin
Layout by Bert Compton
Editing by Sharon Ellsworth-Nielson

I ASK NOT
FOR ANY CROWN
BUT THAT WHICH
ALL MAY WIN,
NOR TRY TO
CONQUER ANY WORLD
EXCEPT THE ONE
WITHIN.

—LOUISA MAE ALCOTT

To Nettie,
and our children,
Isaac and Eve.

Table of Contents

Prelude

I don't know if writing is ever easy for anyone. It's work to chip away the dross and then sift through what's left in search of both the nuggets and the small grains of truth. In some sense, it would be far easier for me to give up writing and pursue my gold through other veins, but as I've mentioned in previous Preludes in this series, Ruby and Pops and the campers from Harmony Hill have been reminding me of the claim they staked on my time many years ago. They often don't allow me to sleep much. In fact, I'm writing this bit at least a few hours before sunrise, trying to keep up with their demands.

This is the fourth book in the Ruby Series, but the first to be entirely written during a global pandemic. Two dear friends passed from this life within the last week, both of them having fallen to the microscopic virus that has changed the world in innumerable ways. In addition to the pandemic—hate, depression, discouragement, hopelessness, anxiety, fear, inflation, war and threats of war, homelessness, forced migration, catastrophic storms, mediocrity, and politics are dividing nations, communities and families. So much has changed in just the three short years since Ruby's first book was released. We've all been witnesses to these monumental changes. We've all been touched by them. But how we decide to deal with them, as Ruby is keen to suggest, is entirely up to us.

When Pops and Ruby first reminded me of the keys of joy, I found they felt awfully familiar. Maybe you had the same reaction. They're basic enough for even children to understand, while also offering a lifetime of challenge to absorb and integrate. Perhaps, like me, you've learned that knowing what they are is one thing; putting them to work in our daily practices and interactions is quite another.

For the past fifty-six years, Pops and Ruby have shared these keys, hoping their efforts can offer an alternative path to the rising tide of mediocrity and hopelessness. If there is gold to be found at the humble farm on Harmony Hill and among the citizens of Niederbipp, these keys are it. They've been tried and tested for more than three centuries at the farm, and perhaps since the beginning of time, rewarding all who embrace them with hope, light, and joy.

I recognize that this is more than a novel: this is an invitation. No matter who you are or where you live, I join my voice with Pops and Ruby and invite you to practice the keys of joy and join the growing chorus of Protopians and Candlelighters who are anxiously engaged in flooding the world with hope.

Let's try what love can do!

Viva Niederbipp!

Ben Behunin, September 2021

CHAPTER 101

Bruised But Not Broken

In the middle of every difficulty lies opportunity.
-Albert Einstein

Even though she'd gotten to the point where she knew she should expect surprises, Genevieve Patterson was completely blown away by Ruby's offer. And this—coming on the heels of the longest two weeks of her entire life? She had only just recently begun believing that Ruby and Lorenzo might have some secrets and wisdom she could benefit from. But the old woman's offer felt nothing short of ridiculous, calling all of her *wisdom* into question.

The color under Genevieve's eyes had not yet completely faded; her nose was still tender after being head-butted by Carlos, the sheep. And though the dozens of wasp stings from the previous Sunday had all but disappeared, the memory of her imprudent ride to Tionesta still clung to her pride like a soggy, itchy woolen blanket. This memory might have been easier to carry if it hadn't been close to three weeks since she'd had a drink—over three weeks since she'd had her nails done—and close to the same amount of time since she'd had a truly hot shower. The comforts and perks of her life in the city felt millions of miles away. In just sixteen days she'd experienced a huge range of difficult emotions— betrayal, shame, insecurity, aggression, surprise, fatigue—and more physical distress than she ever could have guessed she was capable of enduring. But as she walked slowly back to the women's bunkhouse by the light of the stars, Genevieve could feel the presence of another emotion—an emotion she was not prepared for—an emotion her head refused to acknowledge, but one which her heart refused to silence: Possibility. She wasn't even sure if that was technically an emotion at all. But there it was, dancing around in her heart to some foreign, primal music that she couldn't silence.

After enduring two weeks of deprivation, humiliation and deep feelings of betrayal, Ruby—the woman Genevieve had come here to expose as a fraud—had just offered her the top job: a lifetime appointment, a commitment of unfathomable proportions.

Did that really just happen? Genevieve wondered to herself as she paused to look up at the stars, or was this just another unexplainable and unbelievably quirky surprise in this ongoing, entrapping nightmare?

She laughed to herself at the absurdity of it all. *Become the next matchmaker of Niederbipp!?! Really?* The entire idea was laughable. She didn't know the first thing about matchmaking. Her own dating experience had been so disappointing and discouraging that she'd almost given up hope of ever having a meaningful relationship that might turn into anything beyond a short-lived tryst or an awkward flirtation that would unavoidably implode in drunken flames and embittered name-calling.

Despite her nearly thirty trips around the sun, she'd been unable to decide what she really wanted in a man—or even if she wanted one at all. It had occurred to her from time to time that her lack of interest might be part of the problem—if that was a problem. And she had to admit that her long list of things she didn't want in a romantic partner was probably longer than her list of things she desired.

That list of turn-offs, no-goes and dealbreakers had grown long and wide over the last decade. Men, after all, were mostly pigs. Or so she'd told herself as she'd wound her way through the gauntlet of soirées, parties and other social gatherings. She'd met only a few men who she'd considered to be true gentlemen. And chivalry—she'd convinced herself—was a dying art if not all together extinct among the male population of her generation. She knew it probably didn't help that she was smarter than any man she'd yet met, was more successful than most, and wasn't about to fall prey to the ignoble and ignorant fools who'd witlessly attempted from time to time to woo her with pomposity and bombast. If marriage was in her future, she'd told herself and anyone else who might ask, it would have to hold an undeniable promise of a life that was a hell-of-a-lot better than what she already had. And that, she knew, would be nearly impossible to find. Her job, her perks, her travels—they not only defined her life, they had become her life—a life that suddenly, *somehow*, had begun to lose its luster.

The happy sounds of women's laughter escaped through the screened windows of the bunkhouse, interrupting her thoughts. Part of her wanted to join them—these women who had somehow all become closer to Genevieve than many people she'd known for years. She'd already shared things with them—individually and collectively—that she'd never shared with any other humans. And each of the women had in turn shared things with her that she never could have guessed by looking at their polished exteriors. Vulnerabilities. Weaknesses. Dreams and aspirations. They'd been honest and real with each other. And they'd also been accepting and encouraging in ways that felt both natural and surprising. It had been frightening but also refreshing. Terrifying, but also disarming. Uncomfortable while also somehow being comforting.

Genevieve paused on the path, looking at the pale yellow light which defined three sides of the bunkhouse's doorway, straining to decipher the distant voices and giggles that were softened if not drowned out by the rhythmic lullaby of a chorus of crickets. She was tired, but she knew she wouldn't be able to sleep before she'd read the contents of the letter Ruby had given her. She also knew the women's curiosity would make it impossible to read that letter in their presence without blowing her already thin cover.

She considered the laundry shed, trying to remember if she'd seen a light switch in that primitive space. She quickly dismissed the possibility, however, when she turned to see that the shed's proximity to both of the bunkhouses would likely draw attention and suspicion should she find a light. She turned to the big house but was disappointed to find that all the lights had been turned off save a dim lamp in the second floor window. She was just thinking about saving the letter for morning when she remembered the bare bulbs hanging from the ceiling of the creamery behind the milking stalls.

The milk barn was silhouetted against the backdrop of the starlit sky as she carefully made her way over the dirt path. She pushed the heavy door open into the darkness and hesitated for a moment, waiting for her eyes to adjust to the sudden absence of all light. The blackness may have been enough to make her turn around had it not been for the curiosity which compelled her to move into the dark space, inching her way forward with outstretched hands, groping her way toward the creamery doorway.

But before she reached it, her left hand brushed against a spider silk, causing her to recoil. Holding in a yelp, she jumped backward, kicking over a milk bucket that sent her nerves skittering through the roof. Off balance, she threw herself forward, tripping over an unknown something, desperate to reach a doorknob as the deafening sound of her own heartbeat echoed through her entire frame.

Finally, she found and turned the polished knob, pushing the roughhewn door open and nearly falling into the darkened space. Again, she groped along the wall, feeling more desperate than ever to find a light switch. She scuffed her hand against a rough beam before hitting her forehead on a low-hanging something. She jumped backward, hitting her head again, this time creating a deafening sound as hanging pots and lids clanged against each other, drowning out her curses, but leaving her feeling panicked as her heart raced.

She closed her eyes, trying to drown it all out and reclaim her composure while the ringing and crashing of the pots slowly diminished. But when she opened her eyes again she was surprised by the faint light in the room. She wondered what had happened. Was she dreaming? Was she going insane? The light grew brighter as she frantically looked from side the side, looking for a place to hide. With the unnerving sound of a creaky door opening behind her, she moved quickly, but without knowing where she was going and unable to see the obstacles at her feet, she tripped again on her way back to the doorway. Stepping into a bucket that seized her shoe, she fell hard, cursing loudly as she hit the concrete floor with her elbow and knee.

CHAPTER 102

Snail Mail

---

*Change will not come if we wait for some other person
or some other time. We are the ones we've been waiting for.
We are the change that we seek.*
—Barack Obama

A re you all right?" a male voice asked from somewhere beyond
the blinding beam of a flashlight.

"What … ? Who . . .?" Genevieve muttered, shielding her eyes as the light approached before it turned toward the wall, the overhead pots still swinging, casting ominous shadows. The light moved to the wall and immediately the room was aglow with the light of three overhead bulbs.

"Genevieve, what are you doing?" Matt asked as he turned and squatted down to look at her, a broad smile on his face as he extended his hand, obviously trying not to laugh.

She reached for his hand, too stunned to respond and he quickly pulled her to her feet before either of them noticed her shoe was still stuck in the metal milk bucket. Laughing, Matt moved a stool behind her and helped her sit before prying the bucket from her foot, her shoe coming with it. With no small effort he pried the shoe from the bottom of the bucket and handed it to her before stooping back down to pick up the mop that had tripped her up. When he turned to look at her, he was smiling even more broadly than before.

"Did you have a late night craving for some cheese?" he asked, not even attempting to hold back his laughter.

Genevieve shook her head, rubbing the goose egg that was forming on her forehead while trying to smile.

"You're bleeding," Matt said, pointing to her knee as he reached for the handkerchief in his back pocket and stepped toward the utility sink to wet it before returning to Genevieve. He knelt on the floor in front of her and wiped the blood from her scuffed kneecap as he examined the wound.

"It's not too bad," he said, looking up into her eyes with a playful sparkle in his own. "You freaked me out there for a minute. I thought you were a raccoon, on the prowl for cheese. I was imagining having to fight you off with a ladle and a mop." He looked to his right. "It's a good thing the trap door was closed. You could have fallen into the cheese cellar and broken your neck. There has to be easier ways to get some cheese, especially on a moonless night."

"Cheese?" she asked, looking into his questioning eyes. "Is that what brought *you* here?"

He laughed. "No, I was working on some...research," he said, nodding to the backdoor.

"In the dark?"

"No, I know better than to be walking around in the dark," he said, nodding to the old flashlight at his knee.

"Were you translating the German words?"

"I was trying. I found another one—Barmhertzigkeit"

"Wow! Is that actually a word?"

""Yeah, and a pretty good one too."

"Let me guess—does it mean barking at the moon?"

Matt smiled but shook his head as he stood, walking to the sink to rinse out his handkerchief before rolling it up from one corner to another to form a long, narrow strip. He returned to Genevieve and wrapped the cool, wet cloth around her knee, tying it on the backside.

As she watched him work, she noticed his hands were gentle but confident. The thinning spot on the crown of his head and the reading glasses that displaced patches of hair near his ears made him look more than a little silly, but she bit her tongue, grateful for his help and compassion.

"Were you a Boy Scout?" she asked as he finished up.

"Yep, an Eagle Scout, actually. I thought about med school for about ten minutes after I earned my First Aid Merit Badge, but I decided I didn't like blood."

"Oh, right, so you became a dentist instead. Totally makes sense," she teased.

Matt smiled good-naturedly as he pulled up another stool and sat down next to her, gently lifting her hand away from her forehead to reveal the small goose egg. "Compassion," he said confidently.

"Oh...and with a smile, no less. Thank you," she responded awkwardly.

He laughed. "No, compassion—that's what Barmhertzigkeit means."

"Oh. Right! From the stones," Genevieve smiled, looking embarrassed.

Matt nodded as he continued to examine the bump on her forehead. "Tell me, are you normally prone to accidents, or do you just enjoy playing the damsel in distress?"

"No, I…maybe I just like giving you a chance to play the hero," she said, glancing out of her eye awkwardly as he slid his glasses onto his nose and leaned in to take a closer look.

He smiled, but said nothing, his focus on the goose egg. "I'd say we should put some ice on that, but considering all the bruises you have on your face I'm guessing no one would even notice. Are there any other wounds that need attention?"

She felt around the back of her head where another small, tender goose egg was hiding in her hair. He followed her fingers, taking a closer look, then examined the scuffed bruise on her elbow.

"I honestly can't believe how many times I've gotten hurt in the last two weeks. I never get hurt. Never!"

"That's good to hear, but a little hard to believe. I'm running out of handkerchiefs," he responded, moving his glasses back to the top of his head and sitting back down on the stool. "So, if you didn't come for cheese, why are you here?"

"Are you running an inquisition?"

"No, not yet," he responded, smiling disarmingly. "But you have to admit it's a curious thing to be tripping around in the dark creamery without a flashlight."

"If I had a flashlight I wouldn't have come."

He nodded. "That's right. You didn't get the packing list, did you?"

She smiled and shook her head. "I didn't get a lot of things that might have made this experience different." She pulled the letter from her back pocket and showed him.

"What's this?"

"Oh, I thought you knew. Ruby says it's what my generation calls snail mail. I think your generation just calls it a letter."

Matt forced a smile, playing along. "Was it delivered by the Pony Express?"

"It might as well have been." She looked down at the letter for a moment before looking back to Matt. "It's from my boss. I was hoping for a private place to read it when I remembered this room had lights and...stumbled in."

Matt nodded. "Sorry to interrupt your privacy," he said, making to get up.

She put her hand on his knee, stopping him. "Do you mind... staying?"

"Uh, sure. What's up?"

She paused thoughtfully. "Matt, you're the only one of the campers who knows who I am and why I'm here. I couldn't open this in front of the women and risk them asking questions."

Matt nodded thoughtfully. "What do you think it says?"

Genevieve shook her head. "I honestly have no idea, but there better be an apology in there somewhere for throwing me into this, completely unprepared."

"Well, what are you waiting for? Why don't you open it?"

She nodded, looking down at the envelope. She turned it over, sliding the tip of her index finger under the edge of the flap, her hands shaking visibly, making the task difficult to accomplish.

"Are you sure you didn't hit your head anywhere else?" Matt asked, looking concerned.

"Yeah, I'm just...nervous I guess."

"Can I help you?"

Without hesitation she handed him the envelope, still only half opened.

He quickly tore through the remnants of the seal and freed the pages of the stationary inside, handing them back to Genevieve.

"Do you mind reading it?" she asked, forcing her eyes tightly shut.

"Is your head hurting?"

She took a deep breath. "Not any more than normal. I'm just feeling...anxious, I guess."

Matt nodded, sliding his glasses back onto his nose before unfolding the stack of taupe colored papers.

Dear Genevieve,

You have every reason to be angry with me for the curtness of my communication regarding this assignment. My intent was never for you to feel like you'd been cast out or abandoned, but I could think of no other way to get you to Niederbipp and have you experience the farm without blowing your cover or influencing the story you are there to write. Please accept my apologies and try to understand that with time constraints and potential authenticity concerns relating to yourself and the other campers, my actions required speed and confidentiality. I recognize now that the fast track of your assignment meant that you were unprepared, both physically and emotionally, for this most important story. I've spoken with Ruby regularly over the last two weeks and I've been comforted to hear that you've rolled with the punches and have acclimated well to life on the farm. I assure you that you will be duly rewarded for your work on this assignment, and hope this experience will lay the foundation for many new opportunities for you in the future.

As you now know, I too spent a summer on Harmony Hill with Pops and Ruby. Those five months, as well as the following months they allowed me to stay on to write my dissertation, were the most life-altering and life-affirming months of my entire life. All of my happy moments since then—all that is good and right in my life—my marriage, my family, and my career—have deep ties to the time I spent on the farm. I can honestly say that not a week has gone by in these last twenty-seven years that I have not thought about the people I met and the numerous lessons and truths I learned during my time there.

The farm, if you have not yet recognized it, is a magical place. At its very foundation are many truths that seem to be in rare supply around the rest of the world. I'm convinced that those precious truths, principles and values have the ability to hold our aching world together by strengthening marriages and families, and offering hope, light and peace to a world in dire need of such things. Largely void of these stabilizing truths, our world is coming apart at the edges and splintering into chaos as the winds of sensuality blow ever harder and the rising tide of mediocrity and apathy threaten to overwhelm all that is good.

For these past several years, Lawrence and I have been waiting for the day when we would be in a position to instigate a change at the magazine and begin a revolution that will hopefully, in time, offer an alternative to the unprincipled race to the bottom and the world's collision course with bad karma. Just last month that change began to become a reality when we emptied our retirement accounts and purchased an additional twelve percent of the ownership of the magazine, making us the largest shareholders and shifting full editorial power to Lawrence and myself. We have big dreams, and we feel an even bigger charge to do our best to become a force for good in this crazy world.

Nearly a decade ago, we were warned by the stockholders that our plans to bring decency and civility back to the magazine would result in cancelled subscriptions and huge losses in advertising revenue. We wish we'd had the money to purchase a bigger portion of the stock back then as our small, more subtle moves toward our goals have proved their predictions wrong, more than doubling our circulation since then. Just as we suspected, we've discovered that people are hungry for something different than stories and advertising that rides the line of all that is offensive, coarse and indecent. We feel we are standing at a crossroads, anxious to adopt a new culture at the magazine—one that will provide our readers with a positive alternative to what's currently available.

Genevieve, I recognized your talent and promise when I first interviewed you seven years ago. And I recognized you then as I do now as a critical part of our transition to a higher, more substantive and hope-affirming platform.

When I sent you to interview Ruby, I had high hopes of using your story to create a photoessay that would form the foundation for our new direction. 10,000 words is longer by at least triple than any story in the history of our magazine. But I knew you would need at least that much space to begin to capture the essence of Ruby and Lorenzo's goodness and passion, the majesty of the farm, and the humble nuggets of truth and wisdom that have been passed down to innumerable generations of campers and their posterity. You are writing the story I always dreamed I would. I have no doubt it will change your life and your trajectory in unpredictable ways.

The germ of this idea began nearly twenty-seven years ago during the winter I worked on my dissertation there on Harmony Hill. Women's roles and opportunities had already changed dramatically over the course of my first twenty-three years, and more opportunities were becoming available to women every year. I remember well, imagining a world with unlimited possibilities for women and girls. And in many ways those dreams have become a reality. The young girls of the First World will never know the same glass ceilings my generation knew. But over the years I have also been troubled as I've witnessed the degradation of honor and dignity that women once demanded. Instead of inspiring the men they interact with to become better, more respectable creatures, women too often become complacent, stepping down from the higher ground while trading their virtue, self-respect and loveliness for something significantly less valuable. Acting contrary to George Bernard Shaw's warnings, we've wrestled with the pigs, but we've only gotten dirty—and the pigs have liked it.

In addition, I fear that in the process of scraping away the prejudices, attitudes and confining traditions, we may have scraped too deep, tossing out the roots of truths and principles that have formed the foundation of civilized humanity since the dawn of enlightened history. Too many of us, in our efforts to be equal to men, have traded our diamonds for common stones, losing the luster and deeply innate beauty that makes us different. Today, more than ever, I feel there's a critical need to restore hope and a solid foundation to families and societies.

Matt glanced up at Genevieve, scanning her emotionless face before turning back to the letter.

As I suggested before, I learned many things during my summer on the farm, but the keys of joy were a true revelation to me. They ultimately taught me that the truest, boldest power we can possess is virtue, and that if we are embrace that virtue with a determination to live by the keys' ennobling principles, we can experience freedom, happiness and joy everyday. Unfortunately however, these secrets of life are not widely understood or practiced. Truth, light and soberness are too often set aside, called old-fashioned, and largely ignored when the masses of men turn their attentions toward selfish pursuits and the crooked paths of immediate gratification.

By now it's likely that you've met a woman in town by the name of Hildegard. I spent many afternoons sitting at her feet during the months I spent in Niederbipp. I will forever be grateful for her insight. She challenged me, in her bold, no-nonsense way, to develop and use my gifts and talents to not only provide for myself, but to make the world a better, kinder, more gentle place where truth and virtue might thrive.

Over the years as I've corresponded with both Hildegard and Ruby, they have promised me that if I was determined to choose the higher ground, the hand of Providence would bring others to help me. Though there have been many times that I've wondered and even doubted, these promises have repeatedly proven true. As I've watched you progress in your craft of writing, I've found myself feeling hopeful that you might learn these same truths and eventually share my desire to change the world in positive ways.

Genevieve, in the years since leaving Harmony Hill, I've continued to learn many lessons by living the keys of joy that have made me a better human. Exercising reverence for God and all living things, and patiently putting my trust in that hand of Providence will always be ranked among my most cherished lessons. In the years that have followed, things have rarely worked out exactly the way I envisioned, but they've always worked out—and always significantly better than my small mind could ever have imagined.

When space opened up for you on the farm this summer, it felt like years of preparation and millions of prayers were coming together. Ruby and I have often discussed the possibility and opportunity of sharing the farm's truths with a wider audience. I've imagined how the power of your experience this summer—shared in the pages of our magazine—could have the potential to change the lives of millions of readers throughout the world. You have the talent, voice, and platform to do immeasurable good if you choose to do so. I have long hoped to offer you an opportunity to use your gifts for greater good. I've imagined you being an even bigger contributor to the magazine's future efforts as we move forward. You've accepted some difficult assignments over the years and you've always delivered. I knew this assignment would be the most challenging of your career, but I also knew that of all my writers, you have the talent to deliver the most impactful story.

I thought I had things figured out, but I see now how my vision was shortsighted and limited.

When Ruby told me earlier this week that I had underestimated you, I worried at first if she was upsetting the foundation of everything I've spent the last three decades building. But further conversations and explanations have opened my eyes to even greater insight and understanding. I quickly recognized that my hopes for you have actually been myopic. When Ruby told me that she and Lorenzo were considering making you an offer to become the next matchmaker of Niederbipp, it didn't take me long to recognize the wisdom in their decision...

"Wow!" Matt said, looking up. "This sounds serious."

"Is that it?" she asked, pointing to the pages.

"No, there are a couple more pages. Should I continue?"

"Yes, please. This is crazy!"

He nodded, looking back to where he left off.

...There was obviously a bigger picture that I'd been unable to see. I was interested in a 10,000 word article. Ruby and Pops are interested in a lifetime of incredible possibilities for you, your future family, and untold numbers of people you might influence—both on the farm and through your writing.

By now, if all went as planned, Ruby has extended that offer to you. I have no doubt the idea of it must be overwhelming for you, but I hope you will give it some serious thought.

My hopes for you have only increased as I've considered the ramifications of Ruby's ideas. Should you choose to accept her proposal I would like to offer you and your writing an expanded platform. I honestly don't know what that would look like. We would have to discuss all the possibilities. Things would obviously be different for you as you would have to balance farm responsibilities with deadlines. Travel—something I know you've enjoyed—would obviously have to change. I imagine this would be a major sacrifice, requiring permanent relocation and a serious adjustment to your pace. But as you consider your choices and Ruby's offer, I hope you will also consider the potential good your contributions to the magazine can make in the lives of countless women, girls and families.

For the last several years, readers have turned to your articles to become informed and educated about the latest trends and fashions. They've relied on you to keep them in the know in an ever-changing industry. You've done what's been asked of you, and you've done it well. But I've often found myself wondering what more you may be capable of. How might things be different if what you wrote could have more staying power than the latest trends? How might your influence be expanded and inspired if reverence, charity and hope were the foundation of everything you wrote? How could your powers of persuasion be used to inspire your readers to focus on those things which beautify and uplift the entire soul rather than focusing primarily on outward appearances?

Genevieve, since spending a summer on Harmony Hill, I've been ceaselessly concerned about helping women recognize and claim their honor and value as daughters of God. This has always been a challenge in an industry that has largely been designed to champion the unbounded, impossible pursuit of youth and beauty. But youth, despite our best efforts, cannot last forever. And true beauty will forever be far more concerned about those things that will remain long after time, gravity and oxidation have irreversibly changed our shapes and figures. None of us can escape the challenges which arise with time. But by learning to focus on those things which transcend time and fashion, and through developing the beauty of the soul, the passage of time can be celebrated and valued instead of being met with dread and foreboding. How might our world be different if we would choose to spend our time only on the concerns we can control and the good we can influence?

You will be surely be aware by now of the scripture posted above the doorways in the bunkhouses: "Except the Lord build the house, they labour in vain that build it."

My generation has done much to scrub religion and spirituality from the fabric of society, but we have been slow to recognize that by so doing we have created nothing more than a thin and ragged cloth, incapable of offering either comfort or warmth. By cutting God out of the structure of society we have labored in vain. We have sown the wind and we are now reaping the whirlwind.

Genevieve, I believe the answers to many of society's problems lie in returning to a sure and solid foundation, to time-honored principles of dignity and virtue, and again connecting with the great and noble truths which our modern society has largely neglected. I don't know what the future looks like, but I believe in that order for it to be happy—

for ourselves and for our children—we as a people—as humanity—must be determine to follow a much greater god than the imitations and idols we've cobbled together out of our pride and indifference. Spiritual apathy has availed us nothing and cost us dearly, separating us from the one true source of all goodness, mercy and grace.

Whatever you decide to do with the options Ruby places before you, please know that Lawrence and I will be praying for you. We hope for you the very best as you experience all the enlightenment and joy that the farm has to offer. Soak it up. Write it down. Make these months count. The time will quickly pass and the November issue is already being designed, awaiting the fruits of your assignment. I just reviewed Patrick O'Brien's photographs and was thrilled with what he captured. He should be returning in the next few weeks for more. No pressure, but I hope by then you can send me at least a preliminary outline for your story.

Please forgive me for not better preparing you for this assignment. I trust that with time and experience you will come to understand my reasons for leaving so much of this undefined. But for now, enjoy yourself! Make good memories and even better friendships. Success will be yours if you'll remain passionately curious and keep your head and heart open to all truths. I can hardly wait to see what you come up with.

All my Best!
Julia

PS. I've contacted your parents to let them know you've taken an assignment and may be difficult to reach over the coming months. You might consider dropping them a note to mitigate worry. We have also moved your cat and her litter box to the office. She's a feisty one, isn't she!? Your apartment has been secured and will be waiting for you to decide your direction at the end of the summer.

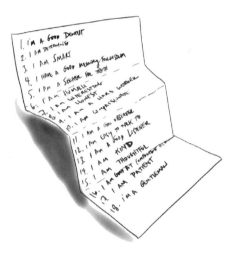

CHAPTER 103

Grit in the Oyster

The only person you are destined to become
is the person you decide to be.
-Ralph Waldo Emerson

"What the…heck?" Genevieve said.

Matt laughed, looking up from the pages as he shuffled them back into order. "Those are some mighty strong words, little missy.

Who woulda thunk...the next matchmaker of Niederbipp! Has Ruby actually offered you the position?"

"I think so, just tonight. This is absolutely insane!"

"You think so?"

She studied his face as if she were looking for sarcasm. "You don't seem to be nearly as surprised as I would have guessed you'd be."

He shrugged, sliding the pages back into the envelope. "You're a natural choice."

She stared at him blankly. "What the heck are you talking about?"

Matt shook his head, but smiled. "Genevieve, we all see it."

"Who? *What*!?"

"All of us campers. As far as I know I'm still the only one of us who knows you're not here for the same reasons we are, but we've come to feel like you belong here. You'd make a great matchmaker."

She raised her eyebrows as if she were awaiting the punchline of this impractical joke.

"Just look at yourself," he responded "You're the obvious choice among our group of campers. You're not afraid to speak your mind. You're good at reading people. You've got no trouble calling a jerk a jerk. We've all been watching you—watching as you stood up to James; watching as you've listened to each of us, watching as you've bounced back after being beat up by Carlos and stung by hundreds of angry wasps on top of facing the challenges we've all faced. Instead of giving up, you just dig in deeper, and all the while you're able to share advice and wisdom like it's no big deal."

Genevieve laughed as if she couldn't believe what she was hearing. "Advice? Wisdom!? Common sense and smart aleck comments—maybe, but I'm sure I don't have the slightest idea what you're talking about."

"Sure you do. Susan. Holly. Spencer. Crystal. Even James. We've all talked about the things you've told us and the advice you've given us."

"Hah!" Genevieve responded. "I can't think of anything I've said to any of you that's worth giving a second thought, let alone repeating. And for sure nothing that should ever be considered *wisdom*."

"Then you don't know the power you wield. I've recognized it as well. I told Ruby what I've observed. We all have."

"*What?*" she asked, laughing.

Matt nodded. "Remember that day up in the garden—how you took my sorry list of strengths I'd been working on and added ten or eleven that I hadn't even considered?"

"Yeah, so?"

"Genevieve, I'd been working on that list for a couple of days and had only come up with one." He pulled the folded paper from his back pocket and handed it to her, pointing to her handwriting. "I've been carrying this paper around with me everyday since then and I still haven't thought of even one more strength. You wrote down two through thirteen in just a few seconds and we'd only spent a few minutes talking to each other by then."

She looked up from his list, reaching for the pen in the chest pocket of his overalls. "I missed a few obvious ones," she said, uncapping the pen and resting the paper on his knee as she added to the list.

14. I am kind.
15. I am thoughtful.
16. I am good at comforting people when they're hurt.
17. I am patient.
18. I am a gentleman.

"I wasn't fishing for compliments," Matt replied as she handed the list back to him.

"I know you weren't, but we both overlooked some important ones. You shouldn't forget those. They're very rare."

He looked over the items she'd added to the list before shaking his head.

"You disagree?" Genevieve asked.

"Yes. No...I don't know," he said, flustered. "All I see is my brokenness and all the things I'm lacking. And you look at me and see...

good things. That's a gift, Genevieve. Don't you see that? Most of us are only critical of ourselves and others. Somehow you see the good—even in James…and Spencer…and Crystal…*even in me.*"

Genevieve shrugged. "I'm a writer. I've trained my eyes to see things quickly so I don't waste my time chasing the wrong story. It's just an exercise of cutting through the crap and getting to the good stuff. There's really no magic to it."

"Sure there is. That's a talent—a gift. Most of us don't see things like you do. I mean we can probably all see the crap, but finding the good… most of us can't even see it in ourselves."

"You're just not looking in the right places," she responded dismissively, contorting her arm so she could see her swollen elbow.

"Well, you obviously don't recognize it, but I for one think you'd be a great matchmaker."

She looked at him and shook her head. "You're crazy, Matt. I'm a writer, not a farmer. I wouldn't last ten minutes around here by myself. You were right—I probably am an indoor girl. I had a standing appointment every Tuesday at 12:30 to have my nails done. I used to wear high heels at least six days a week. You said it yourself—Paris, but never Nepal."

"That was before a lot of things…the bees, the river, being head butted by that sheep and bouncing right back. I totally underestimated you. We all did."

"No, you nailed it, actually. I'm way too soft for any of this. I'm used to being pampered in business class and five star hotels. I hardly own a thing that isn't dry clean only. Life on a farm?…Yeah, definitely not for me."

"Oh, I thought you were getting used to it."

Genevieve laughed out loud. "I guess those lessons I learned as a drama minor have stuck with me."

"I don't believe it," Matt responded, shaking his head.

"Oh, really?"

"Yeah, maybe in the beginning you were acting, but I'd like to think

I know you well enough now to say you're finding your stride and getting used to farm life."

"There's a big difference between knowing you only have to endure this for another four and half more months and the impossibility of enduring it for...what...fifty-seven years!"

"Actually..." he said thoughtfully, "It could be longer than that."

"How?"

"Well, if you were to accept the position, and you were to live as long as Ruby, it could be closer to sixty-seven years. She didn't get started until she was forty. You're not even thirty yet."

Genevieve closed her eyes and shook her head. "Have you seen Ruby's fingernails?"

"Uhhh, I can't say that I..."

"I have, and I see no signs that that woman's ever had a manicure. I don't think I've seen her wear more than four dresses in the past two weeks, and two of those were to church."

"So...what's the point of having a big wardrobe around here? I don't think the chickens or cows would be any more impressed."

"Okay, but she knows how to cook, and bottle food, and milk cows, and grow a garden. I don't know how to do any of those things."

"*But you know how to read people*," he spoke softly. " I'm not sure if you can teach someone that. You can learn how to cook and garden and do all those other things, but that ability you have to read people and boldly say what they need to hear—that's no small thing."

Genevieve looked surprised or confused or both. "I'm an East Coast girl. We all can do that."

Matt laughed but shook his head. "Maybe that's true, to an extent, but not many people can do it without sounding harsh and nasty. People don't change for harsh or nasty people. They just become defensive and resentful. But look what you're able to do—look at Spencer and James. They've taken what you've told them and turned it into a catalyst for change."

She looked incredulous.

"You not only hugged James, you got him to gallop around with you on his back after he was ready to call his attorney to get him out of here. You turned him around—totally changed his attitude."

"That *was* pretty cool, huh?" she admitted. "James is such a blowhard. He just needed to redirect his energy into something more productive."

"Yeah, but you were the one who made him see it. You were the one who made him finally realize he was being an ass."

Genevieve laughed. "We don't say that word anymore, remember?"

"Oh, right. We'll call him a butthead then. The point is that you made it happen. Not even Ruby had been able to tame him. Everyone was afraid of him. And you strode right into the lions' den and treated him like he was kitten."

"I guess I kinda did, didn't I?"

"You totally did! I thought you were nuts when you told him he just needed a hug, and then gave him one."

"You hugged him too!" Genevieve reminded him.

"Yeah, but I never would have thought that might be a cure for anything. I never would have guessed that would have the power to turn him around."

"Sometimes people need exactly the thing they're pushing away."

"What do you mean?"

"Well, James obviously wants to be loved and accepted, but he spends most of his time building up walls and repelling anyone who gets too close."

"Yeah … why do you think that is?"

"That's easy. He's afraid."

"Are we talking about the same James? The outspoken, loud, arrogant brute who's quick to point out everyone's inadequacies? What could he possibly afraid of?"

"You don't see it?"

"Uhh…I'm pretty sure I don't. What am I supposed to see?"

"Isn't it obvious? He's afraid of being weak among other things."

"Oh, right, that totally makes sense," Matt responded sarcastically. "SO afraid of being weak that he's trying to be the opposite, right? As far as I can tell, there's nothing weak there. You saw what he's capable of. He totally *wrecked* that bike. He yelled and screamed at you in the laundry and made a complete...*butthead* of himself with Crystal and everyone else. I honestly worried that he'd hurt her. I couldn't believe Ruby made them work together for who knows how many days."

"What would you have done?"

"I probably would have just sent them to opposite corners of the farm and told them to avoid each other. I don't get it."

"I thought what Ruby did was brilliant!" Genevieve admitted.

"Wait...what? You did?"

"Sure. I mean I thought it was insane at first, too, but it totally makes sense now."

"Uhh, I'm pretty sure I missed all of that," he admitted. "What makes sense?"

"If I had to guess, I'd say Ruby thinks they need a chance to see how the negative power of their weaknesses—weaknesses they both share—are only repelling those around them and perpetuating their problems."

"Okay, but how does that make things better? As far as I can tell it only makes things louder."

"Maybe, but it can't go on like that forever, right? Everybody—if they're sane—they have to calm down at some point and take an honest look at the trouble they've created for themselves. And when you see in someone else a mirror image of your own issues, maybe that helps you develop a desire to do different and be different. It seems to be working. There's obviously a long way to go, but we've already seen a major change, haven't we?"

Matt nodded, but he still looked confused.

"Yeah, it took me a while too, but I can totally see now how perfect they are for each other."

"Uhhhh...*James and Crystal?*"

Genevieve smiled and nodded.

"You can't be suggesting…?"

"That they'll be married or at least engaged by the end of the year? Yep, I am."

Matt laughed. "How's that even possible? They despise each other."

"I don't think so. They despise their own weaknesses—weaknesses that they've identified in each other."

"So wouldn't it be better to run as far away from that as they could instead of making them look at each other?"

"What, and have two dysfunctional, unhappy, volatile relationships?"

"Oh, so…are you suggesting that if they got married they'd save two other people the pain and suffering of having to live with them?"

"There's always that!" She said with a little chuckle. "But they've both learned to get what they want by getting louder rather than listening and compromising. I'm sure they've probably come by that honestly."

"I'm not sure I follow."

"You've heard them talk about their parents' messy divorces. I don't know if it's possible to live through that and not be effected by it negatively. I'm sure they're both carrying the burdens and scars of listening to years of ugly interactions. When that's all you see and hear, you can't help but begin to think everyone communicates that way—that that's normal."

Matt nodded slowly. "So, how do you fix that?"

"Well, it seems like you'd have to recognize there's something wrong with that behavior and then be willing to work your way through it. And maybe there's no better way of working your way through it than having to figure out how to communicate with someone who's as broken as you are. I'm sure it hasn't been pleasant. But despite James's outbursts and narcissistic conniptions, you've got to admit he's making *some* progress, right?"

"Okay, I'll admit things have gotten a little better. But there are some things I still don't understand."

"Like what?"

"You said he was afraid of being weak."

Genevieve nodded. "It's all a show, Matt. He's totally afraid of being weak—of being vulnerable. So he tries to operate on what he supposes is the opposite end of the vulnerability spectrum. I honestly believe he's just a scared little boy who's incapable of expressing his true emotions without losing status. You've heard him talk. It's all about decorum and keeping up appearances. He's afraid of letting his true colors show. He's scared to death."

"I guess that's the part I don't get. What is he afraid of?"

"Of failing. Of being alone. Of going through all the hard work of this summer and still not finding a woman who'll look past his attitudes and outbursts and love him. I'd guess that's why he wants to leave—get out early so he won't have to wait to be disappointed."

"I thought he just wanted out because he's losing so much money. That's what he's been saying."

"Yeah, I don't believe it. I mean, sure, that probably plays a part, but probably only a small part."

"Really? He's always telling us how much his time is worth—how much money he's losing."

"Yeah, but you're all losing money being here. Susan rolls her eyes every time James opens his mouth about it. She bills out for just as much as he does. I really don't think it's about the money as much as it is about this head game he's used to winning by controlling every detail of his life. And the fact that there are thirteen other people on the farm with opinions and agendas of their own is driving him crazy. He's lost control. And the money that has always made him feel powerful and accomplished has been replaced with chicken eggs and homemade bread." Genevieve laughed. "We've all had to adjust to a different economy, haven't we?"

Matt nodded.

"Yep, I've never really thought that much about it before coming here, but money is generally much more cooperative than people are, especially women with our own opinions and agendas that he can't belittle or push around. But he met his match when he challenged Crystal. She's no pushover."

"No, she's not," Matt agreed. "I knew she was strong the first time I worked with her, but I've gained a whole new appreciation for her strength in the last few days as I've watched her work with James."

"Me, too."

"So, how do you know all this stuff?"

"What *stuff* are you talking about?"

"You know...how to make sense of people's idiosyncrasies without going totally insane yourself."

"Pfff, maybe it's just being able to see myself in them. That, and I've spent a small fortune visiting more than a handful of therapists over the last fifteen years. You pick up a few things in that amount of time, whether you care to or not. How about you? Do you have a shrink?"

"Yeah, a really small one who lives inside my head."

Genevieve smiled. "He must be pretty smart."

"Why do you say that?"

"Well, it seems like he's helped you figure out life pretty well."

"As long as you don't look very close," Matt muttered.

She reached for the folded paper he still held in his hand, taking it from him. She looked over the list before handing the paper back to him. "Maybe it's you who needs to look closer."

"Is that right?"

"Sure. Look at all the great things about yourself that you've overlooked."

"And if I acknowledged any of them, I'm sure I'd become an arrogant jerk."

"I doubt that?"

"Why?"

"Because there's nothing in you that's arrogant. You're a humble guy, Matt. I don't see you ever turning your strengths into cockiness. That's not who you are."

He nodded slightly, but didn't looked convinced. "Well, I know this isn't a democratic institution, but if I had a chance, I'd vote for you. I think you'd be a great matchmaker."

"Matt, this is insane. You know I can't do this."

"Actually, no, I don't see why you couldn't."

"You're as insane as Ruby, and my boss! I don't…this is way beyond my skill set."

"Well, you wouldn't be doing it alone, right?"

"What do you mean?"

"Well, look at us. You'd have twelve campers every year to help you, and I *assume you'd get married.*"

Genevieve moaned, closing her eyes as she shook her head.

"I don't know. Maybe you could do it alone. The old photographs and portraits above the shelves in the library—you know the ones of all the matchmakers over the years—they all have husbands, but I don't know if there's a rule that says you have to be married. Of course, it might be tough for those seven months out of the year when you don't have the campers here. I suppose you could go to the laundromat, and buy your flour during the off-season so you could just focus on your writing, but it would probably get pretty lonely up here by yourself."

"This is impossible," she replied, rubbing her hands over her farm-tanned face, stopping at the tender spot on her forehead.

CHAPTER 104

Not So Bad

The moment you doubt whether you can fly,
you cease for ever to be able to do it.
– J.M. Barrie

Marriage is just a hurdle—and really not a very big one," Matt suggested.

Genevieve looked at him with questioning eyes, one eyebrow raised. "Really? You're one to talk."

"Okay, so maybe it is a big-ish hurdle," he admitted, backpedaling. "But excluding myself for obvious age-related reasons, there are still five eligible bachelors here on the farm, and probably at least dozens more in the county—men with experience and know-how who could help you run the farm. It wouldn't be so bad."

She laughed. "*So bad?* You'd make a terrible matchmaker."

"Really? Is it that hard?" he challenged.

"How would I know? But I do know that marriage has got to offer something better than *not so bad.*"

He smiled. "Fair enough. I obviously don't know much about either love or marriage, but I'm sure you'd have options if you chose to accept Ruby's offer. Ruby and Pops have made it work up here for fifty-six years. And all those other matchmakers in the library, too. It seems like it would be a pretty good life and give you plenty of time to write during the off-season, free of distractions and interruptions and… "

"Culture, humanities and civilization," Genevieve said, cutting him off. "It's impossible to think of this as an upgrade from anywhere else in the world. No concerts, no museums, no theatre."

"That's not entirely true. Don't you remember that museum we saw last week, down in town?"

"The *pudding mold* museum?" she asked, laughing. "That hardly counts."

"Okay, so it's a far cry from the all the offerings in the city, but you told me a week ago that you don't take advantage of many of them anyway."

"Did I?"

"Yep, you said you're too busy working or too tired to enjoy most of the offerings of the city. You might as well live here."

"Oh, really?"

"Sure! The air is clean, you can swim in the river and spend your afternoon chasing dragonflies. I have yet to see a traffic jam…or even a traffic light. The people are friendly and they seem anxious to tell you stories and share sourdough bread. And if you don't get along with the campers you choose, well, they'll be gone at the end of the summer and you'll have seven months of peace and quiet to help you choose better next time. It kind of feels like a no-brainer, not to mention there will be a friendly dentist just a short bike ride away if you ever need your teeth cleaned or a cavity filled, or find yourself in need of a chat."

"I almost forgot you're sticking around at the end of the summer. How do I know you're not just trying to con me into staying so you won't be lonely?"

"Oh, I don't plan to be lonely."

"No?" she asked playfully.

"You forget sometimes that you and I are here for very different reasons. I want to get married. I know that's difficult for you to understand, and obviously even more difficult for you to understand why someone would be interested in a man of my advanced years. But unlike you, my hopes and dreams of marriage are the reasons I've sacrificed my summer to be here. By next summer I hope I'll be happily married, living the dream as the dentist of Niederbipp, and looking forward to the arrival of a child."

"A child? Already? You're not wasting any time!"

"Well, thanks to you I'm constantly reminded that I don't have any time to waste."

"Constantly? Really?"

"Maybe I'm just sensitive. But I'm guessing it takes a few years to create a marriage like Pops and Ruby's, and the sooner I get started the better off I'll be."

"They're pretty cute, aren't they?"

"Cute is really just the beginning. You've watched them, right? You've seen the love they have for each other. I can't even imagine what Pops is feeling right now, knowing he's going to lose her. Fifty-six—almost fifty-seven years of marriage—good marriage! He'll be absolutely lost."

"Yeah, well, just think of all the pain and suffering you could avoid by staying single."

Matt smiled, but shook his head. "There's no joy in avoidance. I'm old enough to know that. You don't think about that so much when you're thirty, but when you're almost forty-four, it becomes a bigger part of your long list of regrets. From my observations I've come to believe that happiness and joy in marriage only comes when two people are willing to jump in with both feet and figure things out together—with however much time you've got left."

"That's fair," Genevieve said, conceding, but not looking totally convinced.

"*But?*" Matt asked, sensing one was coming.

"Yeah, so, how do you take a *not so bad* marriage like any of us here might be capable of creating and turning it into the kind of marriage Ruby and Pops have? Theirs is inspiring. I'm pretty sure that *not so bad* would never inspire anyone."

"Okay, but we're looking at a marriage that's been tried and tested and had fifty-six years worth of renovations and improvements. Do you really think their marriage inspired anyone in the beginning?"

Genevieve furrowed her eyebrows as she considered the question.

"I'm sure they had all sorts of kinks and bumps that had to be worked out," Matt continued. "I can't imagine that any two people as different as Ruby and Pops have ever created a union that was inspiring from the very beginning. Plus, they had seven months up here on the farm by themselves before they had to dazzle any campers. I would guess you could figure out a lot of things in seven months if that was all you had to focus on."

"Yeah, maybe, but I'm definitely not patient enough for any of that."

Matt snickered. "So you're looking for a ready-made husband who has everything figured out, huh?

"Isn't that every girl's dream?"

"I wouldn't know. But it seems like a woman like you has the ability to mold a man into what you want him to be. It seems like your boss recognizes that ability, too, right?"

Genevieve looked confused.

"You know...that part about returning to virtue and spreading the keys of joy. She wants you on her team! She obviously sees you have the potential to be a force for good, right?"

"Yeah, I didn't understand that part at all. I'm hardly a force for virtue and goodness."

"Oh, I think you've underestimated yourself and your power to change people's hearts and minds toward the good and the virtuous."

"What are you talking about?"

"Spencer told us what you told him the day you guys worked together at the farm stand."

"Spencer? He's one self-centered, chauvinistic, son-of-a-gun. I pity the poor woman who falls for his charms and discovers how shallow and conceited he is."

"So it's true then?"

"What is?"

"That you straight-up told him just like that?!?"

"What was I suppose to say? He needed to hear it!"

"I don't disagree with you, but if I'd have told him just like that I don't think it would have gone over the same way as it did for you."

"How would it have been any different?"

"Let's just say I don't think men like Spencer like having their manliness and swagger questioned or attacked."

"But he needed someone to call him on his crap!"

"Yes, and you weren't afraid to do it. You haven't been afraid of telling any of us what we needed to hear. That's gutsy. That's chutzpah!"

"*Chutzpah?* Are you in cahoots with Ruby?"

Matt laughed. "That's not a bad idea, but no. I wish I could have been there in person to see you ream Spencer, but he seemed pretty impressed and humbled when he told us that night how you called him out. And the crazy thing is that he took it—took it all as far as I can see, and he's been chewing on it ever since—making changes—taking a deeper look at himself. You recognized the root of his problems and you fed it to him in a way he could see how his life needs some major remodeling. We were all in awe of what he told us you shared with him. Haven't you noticed how different he's been in just few short days?"

"Pff, that guy's still got a long way to go!"

"Sure he does. We probably all do. But you got him started. You got him to see it. You obviously don't know your own power. If he stays humble and keeps working on himself he'll be a totally different person by the end of the summer."

"Well, for the sake of women everywhere, I hope he is."

Matt laughed. "You can totally do this job, Genevieve."

She shook her head. "There's a huge difference between kicking someone's trash by telling them they're not a decent human being, and sticking two people together for the next fifty to sixty years. That's way more responsibility than I'm willing to accept."

He shrugged. "It's a good start, though, right? Honesty..."

"Honesty means nothing if the person you give it to isn't willing to accept it," she responded, cutting him off. "Besides, I'd imagine that a matchmaker has to have a lot more than just a few blunt honesty arrows in her quiver. Matt, I don't know the first thing about dating or courtship or relationships. What if the best I could do is to make people into the mess that I am? I'd be screwing up twelve campers every year who might go and get married and then screw up their kids. That could be hundreds of screwed up people in just a decade! Plus, I'm clumsy and pissy and I already mentioned I'm not the least bit patient. I would be a complete disaster."

Matt smiled.

"What?"

"I won't argue with you that you were a complete disaster, but look how far you've come in just two weeks! By the end of the summer you could be a completely different person. Confident. Wise. Experienced. Knowledgeable in the ways of chickens and cows... It could be fun, right?"

"Fun? *Fun!?!* To spend the rest of my life helping people like you and me realize how inept we are? Oh yeah, that's more fun than a barrel of monkeys. Don't you see how stupid crazy this is?"

He nodded but looked doubtful. "So what did you tell Ruby?"

She shook her head, straightening her knee so she could take a closer look at the damage. "I told her I needed to think about it," she muttered.

"So there's a possibility?"

Genevieve closed her eyes and shook her head but she couldn't hide the slightest of smiles on her face. "This is nuts!"

"Which part?"

"Maybe all of it. Maybe this whole farm and everyone on it— everyone who's ever come here. What if you're all raving lunatics?"

"Maybe we are."

"You're not going to argue with me?"

Matt shrugged. "What's the point? We all have to want something bad enough to work for it. Marriage—especially a happy marriage—it's worth fighting for, isn't it? It's worth sacrificing a summer for if it means fifty or sixty good years, right? Isn't that worth something? You have to recognize that it's worthy of your time or you would have jumped ship the first week."

"You know I can't jump ship. My job, my loft in SoHo, my entire *life* is riding on this summer—on this story."

"So, that's all this is then?"

She closed her eyes and took a deep breath before blowing it out loudly.

"I call bull," Matt responded.

"What do you mean?" she responded, obviously not liking his challenge.

"You know there's something here that you want—that you need. You've felt the magic of this place—of the farm—of the town. These past two weeks have been the most difficult but meaningful weeks of your life and you know it. You've discovered things about yourself that you never knew, not the least of which how much pain you're able to endure. You can't blow off Ruby's offer because you know there's some part of you that would love to accept it, that would love to put down roots right here and make this your home for the next sixty years. I know it scares the heck out you, but there's a part of you that is secretly craving the challenge of making this your life."

"Matt, you're nuts! She's nuts! I feel like I came to a nut farm. Am I the only sane one here?"

He shrugged, but laughed at her response.

"I mean, how would you feel if you showed up this summer and were greeted at the front porch by *me*? ME! Hah! You'd take one look at me and run all the way back to the bus station and tell all your friends that I'm a fraud—that the matchmaker of Niederbipp is a thirty-year-old, ignorant, single chick who's been on maybe three successful dates in her whole life. Yeah, not a great way to increase applications. This is crazy. Writing a 10,000 word essay is going to be hard enough. I wouldn't even know where to start if twelve campers showed up at my door, ready to dedicate a full summer to learning how to farm and cook and milk cows in exchange for matchmaking services. We'd starve! The chickens would probably all die and cows would start giving sour milk within a week. And that's saying nothing about sharing any wisdom and advice. Even if I could eventually learn how to do each of the farm chores, matchmaking is a total non-starter. The whole idea of me taking over is absolutely absurd."

He smiled and nodded. "So, why didn't you tell her no?"

"Aghhhh!" she shouted, her voice echoing off the walls and floor as she shook her head.

Matt laughed, causing her to smile then to break into laughter of her own.

"You, of all people, know I'd be terrible at this. I'm a poser, a fake. You told me so yourself."

"Stop! That was so a week ago. Look at all that's changed since then! Look how you've become invested, how you've traded all your baggage for the good stuff—the real stuff. Don't you see it?"

She paused for a moment before shaking her head. "What am I suppose to see, Matt?"

"Genevieve, you may not be ready today, but we've still got more than four months left of this summer. You've got a boss and Ruby who seem to think you're the only woman for the job, and eleven campers and Pops who've rubbed shoulders with you for the past two weeks and have seen enough to believe you *could* do this."

She shook her head again and laughed. "Matt, this still feels so crazy."

He laughed in kind, nodding. "Yes, probably because it is. But if you don't do it, who will? We both know Ruby's days are numbered. She chose you, right? That's got to mean something, doesn't it? Of the hundreds of women she's worked with over the last fifty-six years, she chose you."

Genevieve shrugged. "I don't know if that makes me feel any better."

"Why not?"

"Matt, I've never been less qualified for anything. I'm a pretty good writer, but I write…okay…mostly fluff. How to you pivot from that to… to something of substance."

He nodded slowly, looking concerned. "Is that why you haven't made much progress?"

"Probably. Where do I even start?"

"Well, what about the things we've already learned, the keys of joy, the secrets of this farm and the good people of Niederbipp?"

"But that's so…*not me.*"

"You can't tell me you haven't connected with all of this," he responded, incredulous. "No, I mean … yeah, I have, and I'd be lying if I said it doesn't speak to me, but it's all so…new…untried…unproven! I feel like I'm just beginning to wrap my head around most of it. How in the world am I suppose to write about any of it with any sense of conviction? I'll sound like a total fraud. I don't think you understand how big of a pivot this is. I've basically spent the last seven years writing about all things fashion—interviewing the biggest designers, models and retailers. In those seven years I don't know if I ever even heard the word *reverence*. *Charity* came around once or twice a year in the form of fancy fundraising balls and galas for the rich and famous to show off their newest gowns. And *hope*...yeah, the only hope I've heard of that is hope that the Botox will work, or that the augmentations will make a girl look younger, or that a model won't be laughed off the runway in the ridiculous avant-guard costumes the designers try to push as the latest trends."

Matt laughed. "Sorry, but you sound more than a little jaded. Why are you still there?"

Genevieve shook her head thoughtfully. "I'm doing exactly what I always wanted to do. I'm traveling. I've got a sweet loft. I have an expense account and a corner office and I get to work in and influence a multi-billion dollar international industry...." She paused, shaking her head.

"But?"

She took a deep breath, exhaling loudly. "You asked me why I didn't tell Ruby no."

He nodded.

"I never considered any of this before coming here, but what if... what if I have everything I don't really need, and I'm short on everything that really matters—everything Ruby and Pops and so many other people around here live by? *What if...maybe...I got everything wrong?* Does that make any sense at all?"

Matt nodded thoughtfully.

"I hated this place two weeks ago. I hated everything about it; most of all, the torture of having to spend five months here. But...I don't know...somewhere along the way I started wondering if five months is going to be enough."

"Me too! Now you know why I'm excited to be able to stay around here indefinitely!"

She nodded.

"Genevieve, look, I know the idea of taking over for Ruby feels crazy and huge right now, but maybe your boss is right?" he said, pointing to the envelope.

"Which part?"

"That part about how our broken world needs these things. How would things be different if everyone could experience the hope that's hovering all around this place—the hope that's been filling our lungs with every breath we've taken since we stepped off the bus and into this parallel world where life and time have more meaning? I've never experienced anything like this, where strangers—filled with some wild spirit of generosity—are anxious to share their joy-filled secrets. This is a special place—a place where there's time to think and feel and experience the gentle, quiet bits of life that most of us are too busy and stressed and rushed to take the time to even notice."

She nodded solemnly.

"People need this, Genevieve. They may not recognize it yet, but we all need it! The world beyond the river and these hills—they don't know what they're missing. We don't even know the last two keys of joy, but we've seen what can happen when people choose to practice the principles of reverence, hope and charity. People are in need of light and hope, and I can't think of anybody who has the experience and platform that you have who is more capable of sharing it with the world."

Genevieve closed her eyes and shook her head.

"Look," Matt said, wresting his hand on her forearm, "You don't have to make this decision tonight. You have months to figure this out."

"Ruby told me she needs to know in the next couple of weeks so we can get started with training!"

"Then you have a couple of weeks. That's plenty of time to think about it and consult the universe, right?"

She forced out a long, airy breath before turning her head to look right at Matt. "I think I'm afraid to ask."

"Why?"

"Because what if I don't like the answer?"

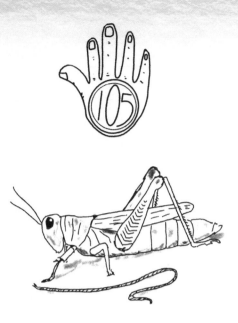

CHAPTER 105

Green Lightning

Listen to the murmur of water and you'll hear Mother Nature.
Listen to the stillness beneath, and there you'll find God.
—Donald L. Hicks

They all seemed to sense it. There was something different about the rhythm and cadence of the farm starting with the new week. Monday began the same as the previous Mondays had: early and loud with the cock's haughty cry. But the chores went faster somehow, and the flight of the sun across the sky felt quicker than it had before despite the fact that the hours of daylight were still growing longer.

Chore rotations continued for ten of the campers; James and Crystal continued their work in the kitchen to help them learn to work together without becoming unhinged. It wasn't hard to see their improvement with each meal, both in their skill in creating food that was better looking and tasting, but also in the decreased volume with which it was created.

It might have been forgotten that the regular chore rotations excluded kitchen patrol for the rest of them but for Josh's complaint on Tuesday that he was doing laundry for the fourth time in three weeks, which, he protested to the others, didn't seem fair. The complaints were varied but persisted with each passing day as the other five chore rotations continued on with only ten participants.

Some of the campers made no objections to James and Crystal taking the kitchen rotation indefinitely. Kitchen Patrol, was after all, the most time consuming of all the chores, leaving little time for other activities. With one team gone each day to the farm stand, and James and Crystal sequestered in the kitchen, the remaining eight campers and their elderly hosts made great use of their free time as they explored the farm's many options for extracurricular activities.

Upon finding a few fishing poles and lures in one of the sheds, Spencer spent Friday afternoon at the pond with Holly and Susan, attempting to teach the women the dying art of angling. He had a few bites but no real success, and the women were obviously losing interest by the time Pops checked on them an hour later. When Pops heard they'd been skunked, he walked into the tall cattails on the far side of the pond and returned a moment later with his hands cupped around something. Then taking the end of the line from Holly's pole, he ran a hook through the thorax of the large, green grasshopper and told her to cast the bug out on the water. Immediately, the surface of the pond erupted as what looked like every fish in the pond lunged for the fresh meal.

Holly squealed with delight, lifting the rod above her head as she attempted to reel in the first fish she'd ever caught in her life. It took her the better part of five minutes to bring the giant close to the shore, and in the meantime, she had made so much noise as the fish jumped and stripped line from the reel that seven of the other campers gathered around her to watch the fish come ever closer to the shore before running again and again. Spencer, perhaps a little too anxious to redeem himself after his own poor performance that day, removed his shoes and had just stepped into the water when the fish ran hard into the deep, snapping the line and leaving all of the campers disappointed.

Pops explained that the fish Holly had hooked was likely Oscar, a brown trout Ruby had brought home from the river in a bucket at least fifteen years earlier. He'd been caught at least once each summer for the past several years, but had, in each case, snapped the line, producing many disappointing endings to what had certainly become scores of incredible fish stories.

When the campers learned that there were several other fish in the pond that were nearly as big as Oscar, there was an immediate rush for the four fishing rods. It was Holly who suggested they could work together and all be involved if they took turns holding the fishing poles and hunting for grasshoppers. Soon all four lines were in the water, while the eight remaining people, including Pops and Ruby and the kitchen staff, were chasing through the tall grass and cattails, trying to keep up with the demand for fresh grasshoppers. Seven fish ended up being caught that afternoon, all of which were returned to the pond after Pops unhooked them.

The farm's fishing pond doubled as the farm's swimming hole that afternoon when Pops, who had stooped over on the dock to release the seventh fish, was playfully nudged from his precarious perch by Ruby's hip. But almost as if Pops had been expecting this, he turned, and in the very act of falling, caught hold of the hem of Ruby's apron, pulling her in behind him.

Though the campers were at first alarmed to find their elderly hosts bobbing in the pond, the joy on their wet faces was both convincing and inviting. Chasing grasshoppers had left them all hot and sweaty, and the cool water of the pond was a refreshing break; all of the campers jumping in, fully clothed.

A mud fight ensued, and soon dark, rich, stinky mud was being scooped off the bottom of the pond and being flung in every direction. Susan, the normally affable and well-mannered attorney, surprised everyone with her expertly lobbed globs of slime which she landed again and again just inches from her various targets, splashing muddy water over the faces and hair of each of the campers. Laughing at each other and their dirty faces, the rest of the campers retreated deeper into the pond. Here they stayed, treading water, until Susan had joined them. But the gathering in the deepest part of the pond was short-lived when Crystal began screaming that a fish had just nibbled her toe.

Laughing and awkwardly frolicking, they rushed back to the shallows where they stayed, floating on their backs as they watched scores of dragonflies performing aerobatic stunts overhead. It wasn't until James and Crystal excused themselves to get back to the kitchen for dinner preparations that the soggy campers broke for the showers.

Porch games that evening were memorable when a card was drawn from the game file: *Green Lightning*. Holly read the instructions which sent the day's teams back to the pond in search of grasshoppers. Greg and Rachael, who had been at the farm stand during the afternoon shenanigans and had missed the grasshopper-catching tutorials, were slower than the other teams and needed a little help. But soon they were all gathered back on the porch, one member from each team cupping his or her hands around a live and wriggling grasshopper. Holly read the rest of the instructions as Ruby handed each team a six-inch long piece of brightly colored yarn. These were to be gently tied to around the abdomen of each grasshopper before the race was to begin.

Spencer and Holly had to return to the tall grass a second time when the knot Spencer was tying around their grasshopper slipped and accidentally severed its tiny, green body. But soon all seven grasshoppers were lined up on the bottom step of the porch and the final instructions were given.

At Ruby's whistle, the string leashes would be let go and the grasshoppers were to be encouraged and cajoled to jump, hop, or walk to the gravel drive, thirty feet away, which would serve as the finish line. No participant was allowed to use their hands to lift, scoop, or throw the grasshopper, and only words of encouragement could be spoken to the tiny, green contenders. Once the winning grasshopper crossed the finish line, the leashes of all the grasshoppers could be picked up by each team. Then, after linking arms with one's partner, each team, by means of either skipping or galloping, would race their grasshopper to the chicken yard where it would be fed to the chickens. The first team to return to the porch with an empty leash would be declared the winners.

All of the campers were already laughing before the game even got started, but the laughter quickly became raucous as team members got down on all fours to utter their encouraging words to their miniature flag-bearers.

Genevieve and Ephraim were off to an early lead when their grasshopper launched itself nearly ten feet off the front step. But Greg and Rachael's little friend quickly overtook the leader and might have won had it not been maimed by the edge of Josh's shoe as he and Susan were enthusiastically coaxing their own little critter.

Greg and Rachael did what they could to rehabilitate their grasshopper, but when it became apparent that his remaining minutes were numbered, Greg heroically took their grasshopper's leash in his teeth and ran past the finish line for an unconventional yet bonafide win.

With a head start, Greg and Rachael were halfway to the chicken yard before the other teams realized what was happening. The rest of the teams, including Ruby and Pops, chased after them, their grasshoppers dangling from yarn leashes as they galloped and skipped the best they could with their arms linked together.

The chickens, anticipating a meal, rushed the fence, eager to accept the six tasty grasshoppers that the teams flung into the enclosure. Pops and Ruby, having the upper hand in the know-how department, silently fed their grasshopper to the chickens who reached their beaks through the fence, and then quietly slipped away while the others were distracted by the mayhem within. The chickens, for their part, made quick snacks of the grasshoppers, leaving behind most of the leashes. But the campers watched as one leash was swallowed whole—along with the grasshopper—by one of the largest hens.

Retrieving the empty leashes proved to be a little more difficult than anyone anticipated as the chickens stood by, waiting for more offerings. When Susan, Genevieve, Josh, and Holly entered the enclosure, several of the chickens tried to escape and likely would have if Rex, the noisy but loyal farm dog hadn't shown up just in time. With the sound of his bark, the chickens ran to the far end of the yard, leaving five trampled leashes in the dirt. The teams regrouped on the outside of the enclosure and raced back to the porch, galloping, skipping and laughing so hard that they collided and careened off each other, unable to steer straight.

The leaders, Greg and Holly, made it all the way up the stairs before realizing they'd grabbed the wrong partners. But as the others fell in close behind them, they found Ruby and Pops with their feet kicked up on the wicker table, sipping tall glasses of chilled peppermint tea, Ruby holding aloft their grasshopper's leash, proudly for all to see.

Grasshopper fans might have considered the whole activity a morbid genocide, but as Ruby explained, this game needed to be played at least a couple of times each summer to help keep the hungry grasshoppers from overtaking the garden and the fields.

Returning to the afternoon's fish story, Pops relived in detail for those who may have missed it the great lesson to be learned by Holly's fishing success. Though they'd been fishing for some time prior to the introduction of the grasshopper, it was not until the desired bait was offered that success was found. He concluded that what was true for the fish was not dissimilar for a spouse: if you're fishing with the wrong bait, success will always be elusive. Find the right bait, he suggested, and hopeful contenders would be lining up for a chance to date and eventually marry.

While most to the campers nodded in thoughtful agreement, this analogy did not sit well with Susan and Rachael. Rachael expressed that the whole analogy was fundamentally flawed, suggesting that offering bait that would eventually lead to either the demise or release of the fish, was a poor simile for a lifetime commitment in marriage. And Susan's protest included the thoughtful explanation that in her experience, while the shallow, superficial baiting of men might be easily accomplished through the wily application of sex appeal, she wished there was a better, more efficient way to help men recognize that a woman's merits and value run much deeper than her cleavage.

When the other women agreed with Susan, Pops humbly acknowledged that most analogies, similes and metaphors had both flaws and limitations, and invited the others to weigh in.

As the campers rearranged the assorted porch chairs into a circle to face each other, a spirited discussion followed in the which it was unanimously conceded that both Susan's and Rachael's objections were valid and the analogy was indeed flawed. Spencer, however, explained what he had learned about fishing with artificial flies from Thomas, even admitting how the older man's insights had caused him to take a long, hard look at his own practices of meeting and interacting with women. He admitted his traditional weakness for sex appeal. But he also divulged how he, in recent days, had come to the conclusion that shallow appeals to his carnal appetite had only clouded his senses and complicated his sincere desires for deeper connections and understanding.

All of the women seemed genuinely surprised when the conversation blossomed among the men, each of them sharing tales of discomfort and embarrassment related to their interactions with the fairer sex and the amount of skin some women chose to expose. Each of the men spoke of struggling to understand the general protest and uproar among women for the level of respect they were receiving when the clothes many wore—or didn't—seemed to suggest that they wanted men to focus on their bodies rather than their talents, intellect or other important virtues.

This was met with a collective bristling from the women, turning the finger of blame back on the men who were ultimately responsible for their own thoughts and actions. To the women's surprise, the men fully accepted and acknowledged their accountability. But each of them cautiously wrestled with their words as they tried to express the awkwardness they felt when speaking to women who were wearing tight or revealing clothing, either in public or in the workplace. With the combined voices of all seven men acknowledging that the distraction was real and nearly impossible to avoid in the modern world, the women— somewhat reluctantly at first—took pause to listen. The open and candid discussion seemed to be a revelation for many of the campers as they listened and shared their opinions and experiences with each other with open, unpretentious honesty.

Genevieve found herself wishing she had her notebook or better yet, her digital audio recorder. But for a lack of both, she found herself listening perhaps closer than she ever had before. It was real and raw, and as she looked into each of their bright faces, illuminated by the glow of the carnival lights strung overhead, she felt a growing connection to each one of them. She watched as Pops and Ruby smiled to themselves as they basked in the warmth of the virtual fire they had kindled with their discussion. And before anyone seemed ready, the distant sound of the church bells marked the time—eleven o'clock. They reluctantly left the porch and turned in for the night with promises to reconvene the next evening.

Saturday's chores and activities separated the campers between bike trips to town for grocery items and the farm stand. But there was also time for conversation and letter writing, hammocking and solo time on the benches for those who desired it. Spencer, Ephraim and James spent a couple of hours that afternoon trying to fix the bike James had smashed, each of them getting thoroughly greasy before they acknowledged that the rear wheel was beyond repair, at least with the time and tools they had at their disposal. They reluctantly put the bike back in the shed, promising to keep their eyes open for other solutions.

Saturday evening's porch games brought ice cream again, along with a new game called *Snot-Nosed Monkey*. It was a silly game that pitted player against player. Two people would face each other, only three inches apart, with a piece of cardboard between their noses. Then, with everyone else looking on, the cardboard was removed and each of the players were to pull a face with the object of trying to make the other person laugh first. James quickly became the clear leader, holding a straight face while getting all of the women and many of the men to laugh at him. Scores were kept for each success, while those who laughed first took a turn on Bessie, the pedal-powered ice cream machine.

In the final heat, it came down to James with ten points and Crystal with six in a winner-takes-all prize which included bragging rights and a necklace with the crude face of a very ugly monkey carved into a peach pit. With all of the campers huddled around them—the men behind James and the women behind Crystal, the cardboard was lifted.

It took Crystal less than five seconds to break James's stoicism. With exaggerated puckered lips, and an overplayed wink, Crystal became the Snot Nosed Monkey champion of the summer, claiming her prize with an exuberant victory dance that had everyone in stitches.

The discussion for the evening turned naturally to the merits of being able to laugh at one's self. Like the night before, things quickly became personal and vulnerable. And for the second night in a row, Genevieve found herself leaning in, listening intently to the campers sharing their weaknesses and painfully awkward experiences with each other. And even though many of the stories shared were met with uneasy laughter, it was clear that sharing them threw open windows and doors that had been vigilantly sealed and guarded. Each of them recognized that their difficulty with laughing at themselves had held them back from enjoying themselves more fully. But they each expressed how being able to share so freely here felt liberating.

A few of the campers including Susan, Matt and Rachael went so far as to say they'd never felt comfortable enough with anyone to share these things. Several others spoke about their natural tendencies of hiding behind facades and trumping up their strengths in an effort to plaster over their weaknesses and social phobias. Even James admitted that he was recognizing that this behavior only made him unapproachable and callous to the emotional needs of others.

As many of the campers shared their reactions to these new, honest revelations, Genevieve's analytical mind kicked into overdrive. And before she could stop herself, she found herself verbalizing a long, beleaguered personal history of avoidance of such intimate details. Silence and evasion had traditionally served her well in avoiding emotional entanglements, but to what end? She was surprised to be able to be so open, and even more surprised to be both heard and validated by the others. And as she walked back to the bunkhouse with the women that night she couldn't imagine ever feeling closer to a group of people— people who had been total strangers only a few weeks before.

The church services on Sunday were somewhat less inspiring than they'd been the first three Sundays. Edward Mackey, the town's very elderly mortician, had been asked to give the sermon. It was difficult to extract his message from his name dropping—mostly of dead people he'd embalmed along with his long genealogical narrative tying himself to not only many of the town's most notable historical characters, but to a long list of dukes and earls and "other people of importance and note."

Many in the congregation were napping before his sermon was over. And many of the campers later admitted that the whole church experience for the day may have been a bust had it not been for the lively organ postlude music that turned into a mini-concert. The organist, apparently deciding that the congregants needed to go home with something more than a very boring sermon, spontaneously pulling out all the stops. With unprecedented vigor, she blasted the chapel with a thrilling medley of what sounded like mostly Bach's organ concertos, interspersed with a few show tunes including a piece from Phantom of the Opera and *One Day More* from Les Miserables. By the time the concert ended, everyone had awakened from their slumber and the entire chapel felt like it had been electrified by at least a gigawatt of electricity.

The energy of the concert flowed out of the chapel and into the churchyard with the congregants, and even accompanied them to the courtyard behind the pottery shop where Jake and Amy's social experiment, Sourdough Sunday, drew a crowd of nearly fifty people.

Some late-comers missed out on the bread, but they still appeared grateful for the opportunity to mingle and connect with neighbors.

As they had the week before, Matt and Genevieve stayed on to help clean up. The previous tension between Amy and Genevieve had all but completely dissipated as they washed and dried the dishes in the studio's small sink while the men stacked the benches from the courtyard. While Matt helped move the various pieces of wood that had formed the benches, he noted the five small symbols, one on each piece of wood, that had been burned onto the surface like a brand. But the ongoing conversation between Thomas and Jake did not allow for questions regarding their meaning.

Dark, ominous clouds blew in from the east on their way out of town and began to drop dime-sized drops of rain before Matt and Genevieve had made it half way up Harmony Hill. They sought refuge under a tree until they believed the worst of it had past. But after pushing their bikes another hundred yards, the rain came down again, even harder than before. With no shelter in sight, they pushed their bikes as fast as they could, but were drenched to the bone in less than thirty seconds. When they reached the summit, they ditched their bikes next to the phone booth and crowded in together, listening to the rain fall all around them and the thunder rolling across the valley. The windows soon fogged up and they laughed together as they imagined James finding them once again in an awkward position. But to their relief, the rain kept any would-be telephone users away.

They waited until the downpour had turned to a drizzle before they left the shelter, walking out into a cloud that had parked itself atop Harmony Hill, making everything dreamlike. Enchanted by the beauty of their surroundings, they stood and watched silently as the cloud passed before their eyes, hiding the farm and everything beyond twenty feet from their view. And then, as fast as it had come, the cloud moved on, peeling off the mountain and ascending, trailing wispy, white tails that evaporated in magical swirls. Like curious, playful children, they chased the clouds, jumping over puddles that had formed in the potholes and depressions on the old road. And shortly after the clouds lifted beyond their reach, they broke open, filling the valley with sunbeams that raced across the golden landscape. They moved to the bench behind the phone booth and silently watched the colors change across the valley. Matt listened attentively as Genevieve shared her list of growing concerns about taking over for Ruby until they were too chilled in their wet clothes to endure any longer. But as they walked down the long, muddy drive, she had to admit that her concerns felt less monumental than they had the previous Sunday.

They returned to their bunkhouses to change into dry clothes before joining the rest of the campers in the big house where everyone had gathered in the music room and library. James, in an unusually good mood, was playing the Steinway while Holly played the fiddle and Greg plucked around on the guitar. Several others sat in comfy chairs, enjoying the music while a few of the campers looked through a stack of scrapbooks that had been piled up on the coffee table. After an hour, Ruby led a group of five campers to the barn for evening milking while Pops took the rest of the campers to the kitchen to make grilled cheese sandwiches and tomato soup. A round of wisdom cookies opened a lively discussion about fear. This continued among some of the campers long past sundown while others returned to their music or books.

Tired and ready for bed before the others seemed ready, Genevieve walked from room to room, saying goodnight to all of the campers before heading out into the cool, damp air. She hoped to journal before going to bed, but words failed her as she tried to remember the details of the fastest week of her life. Instead, she fell asleep with the pen in her hand, waking to a round puddle of black ink that had absorbed onto the open page of her journal.

CHAPTER 106

The Bobbinator

*A mediocre idea that generates enthusiasm will go
further than a great idea that inspires no one.*
—Mary Kay Ash

Teamed up with Josh in the laundry the following morning,
Genevieve quickly realized that even though she'd been rubbing
shoulders with him for more than three weeks, she had yet to really learn
much about him. Porch games and discussions from recent nights had

opened doors which had previously been walls, and the discussion at the pedal-powered washing machine quickly proved to be one of the most insightful conversations she'd had with any of the men.

Josh, she learned that morning, was a man who had struggled his whole life to define himself. The son of a "recovering-Catholic" mother and a "semi-devout" Jewish father who'd discovered too late that religious beliefs could be divisive, Josh had learned early to choose the more peaceful path of spiritual avoidance. He'd admittedly spent most of his life feigning apathy for most things of any consequence, while in reality he had deeply-seated questions about life's meaning and purposes. These questions, Genevieve learned, had largely gone unanswered, and as a result, left him feeling pensive and subdued. He admitted how the events and discussions of past few weeks had pulled open the curtains on windows in his soul that he had not even known were present. As a result, he acknowledged becoming more empathetic and engaged in social interactions than he'd ever been before, especially towards women who'd typically scared him. As a former, short-term member of an online InCel group, he admitted that he'd often felt women were so enigmatic that he'd spent many years questioning how he'd ever feel comfortable marrying one.

Genevieve bristled when Josh told her he was a former InCel member. She had once been trolled by a man who claimed membership in an InCel chapter based in Atlanta. After researching the group of Involuntary Celibates, she had come away from the experience feeling more disgusted than threatened by the man and his group who believed they were somehow entitled to sexual intimacy regardless of their alienating and misogynistic ideology and behavior. She had concluded they were nothing more than a group of losers and reprobates, but she was forced to take a second look when Josh—the gentleman she'd come to respect—admitted his former affiliation. She even found herself empathizing with him when he explained how his connection to the group had begun years before when a friend from his Dungeons and Dragons group had invited him to join.

Genevieve was relieved when she learned that Josh's affiliation with the cultish group had been short-lived. He'd left when he recognized that none of the other members in the group were going anywhere, nor using their time and energy to do anything productive. Not only had he turned his back on his InCel friends, but had also distanced himself from his Dungeons and Dragons League, charting a different course that would eventually lead him to the farm, and ultimately, he hoped, to a marriage filled with love and possibility.

Before the laundry had been hung out to dry, Genevieve had a new respect for Josh. She admired his ability to recognize what needed to be changed in his life and his fortitude in pursuing it. And though he was handsome and sensitive enough to be attractive, there was something that stopped her from seeing him as anything more than a friend.

The need for a few items from the grocery store opened the morning for the possibility of an excursion into town. After breakfast the group packed the pickup truck with items for the farm stand. Leaving James and Crystal to continue with their KP duties, the remaining ten campers took to their bicycles for a carefree descent down Harmony Hill. After helping Ephraim and Susan open the farm stand, the other eight campers turned their bikes toward town.

Matt and Genevieve offered the rest of the group a guided tour of the Englehart Ebenezer, telling them what they'd gathered from Thomas's book. While a few of the campers seemed genuinely intrigued by the details of what Genevieve and Matt had to share, the others were restless and obviously far more interested in exploring the town or feeling the wind in their hair. The tour was cut short, and Genevieve and Matt tagged along behind the others, wending their way indirectly to Niederbipp's main street, Hauptstrasse.

The bright morning had invited a flurry of foot traffic on the cobblestone streets. They parked their bikes at the bike rack near the upper fountain, drawing the eyes of the locals as their eight colorful bikes quickly overwhelmed the rack built for four. There was an air of careless excitement as they made their way into the cool shadows still engulfing the otherwise vibrant lane lined with shops. For the first time since arriving here, Genevieve walked the street with her eyes wide open to the beauty all around her. She wondered how she had missed the multi-colored geraniums which cascaded from window boxes above the quaint shops. She slowed her pace when she saw the men putting up the bright yellow umbrellas over the tables in the small courtyard adjacent to Mancini's Ice Cafe.

Catching her shoe on the uneven surface of the cobbled street, she remembered the ruined heels of her Christian Louboutins—one of them now serving as the very expensive finial on the farm's eclectic fence. The sting of the now-crucified shoe paled in comparison to the sting she felt at the memory of the very pretentious, entitled ignoramus she'd so recently been.

Looking up at the Tudor-style architecture, she was charmed by its dark, exposed, wooden framework filled with various colors and textures of masonry and stucco that reminded her of her many European jaunts. She had missed all of this too, stuck in her own small head.

Distracted by the surrounding charm, Genevieve's left shoe slipped off the edge of the street's wide, central gutter and into the running water, quickly filling her shoe and soaking her sock past her ankle. She would likely have fallen had Matt not caught her elbow and kept her upright. With the others twenty paces ahead of them, Matt waited patiently for her to catch her breath while doing his best to hide his charming smile, saying nothing. While the others shopped for the items on Ruby's list, Matt sat with Genevieve on the stone-slab bench just outside the store, gallantly ignoring the ever-growing list of bumps and bruises she'd endured.

But the wait on the bench somehow felt fortuitous when Susan, the woman who had given the Sunday sermon ten days earlier, approached the front doors of Braun's Market wearing her distinctively sassy, red-framed glasses. She smiled at Matt and Genevieve cordially and was just pulling open the door when Genevieve spoke up, thanking her for her thoughtful sermon. Susan stopped and turned to them, glancing down at the puddle of water at Genevieve's feet before introducing herself. Pegging them as Ruby's recruits by their mismatched socks, Susan welcomed them to Niederbipp. Genevieve quickly explained that she, too, was a writer and hoped out loud that Susan might be willing share her publishing experiences.

Susan pulled a receipt from her purse and scrawled her address and phone number on the back, telling them to drop in whenever they had the time. The conversation may have lasted longer were it not for the lively noise of the six campers exiting through the door Susan was standing in front of. She smiled at all of them and disappeared into the store.

Remembering their promise to be back by lunch, the troop circuitously worked their way back to the farm, stopping briefly at the farm stand before ascending Harmony Hill.

After lunch, served up on the front porch, Pops led the men to the shed where they'd stored the washed wool a week earlier. They loaded nearly half of the bulky sacks into three wheelbarrows along with a wooden box filled with assorted tools and headed back to the front porch. In the meantime, Ruby and the women had rearranged the furniture on the front porch and added an ancient looking spinning wheel. Additionally, Bessie's modified ice cream churn was swapped out for another handmade contraption made up of two wooden cylinders, one eighteen inches in diameter and the second about three inches in diameter. Connected horizontally to a wooden frame, their exposed surfaces were covered with thousands of tiny silver tines like a dog brush.

It took a minute for the campers to catch on to the purpose of the afternoon's activity, none of them having any experience with the tedious process of turning raw, washed wool into yarn. But before long they were all involved in the activity. They learned that the carding contraption connected to Bessie's hind end had been created by a couple of enterprising campers several years earlier who decided there had to be a faster way of carding the wool than the ten sets of hand-held carding brushes.

To help them appreciate the value of the carding machine, Ruby sat all of them down to teach them the art of hand carding. After loading a brush with a handful of the wool, she demonstrated the tedious process of brushing the wool between the brushes, over and over again, to align the fibers and eliminate any additional debris left in the wool after the washing. Then she turned the campers loose to try their hand at it. Some got the hang of it much quicker than others, but soon they were all producing small roll logs as Ruby had taught them, piling these small, fluffy logs on top of the wicker table.

When the stack of roll logs reached about twelve inches high, Ruby invited Genevieve to take a seat on Bessie's saddle and encouraged her to pedal, making a few adjustments before she invited Josh to set his brushes aside and join her at the back of the machine. Here she instructed him to feed the raw wool under the slowly rotating tines of the smaller cylinder. Within seconds, the more quickly moving tines of the larger cylinder began picking up the virgin wool. The hundreds of silver tines from both drums interacted in the middle, combing the wool smooth, much as the hand-held carding brushes had done. In only a couple of minutes the larger drum's tines were loaded with the soft, brushed wool. Ruby showed them how to free the fluffy mat from the tines with a long, pointy rod connected to a wooden handle, the mat unfurling from the large drum as Genevieve rotated Bessie's pedals. They repeated their efforts twice more, and in less than ten minutes had carded more wool than the rest of the campers had in a half hour.

The rest of the campers, along with Pops, took turns either powering Bessie's pedals or feeding the machine on the back end. Soon the carded wool was piled high on the wicker table and several of the chairs.

While Spencer and Holly continued to keep Bessie producing, Ruby started the other campers on the next step of turning wool into yarn: spinning. With only one spinning wheel however, and many hands to keep busy, Ruby pulled several items identical from the wooden box the men had brought up from the shed, handing one to each of campers. These, she explained, were drop spindles and would be used to spin the roll logs into tight, strong yarn. The spindles looked much like elongated toy tops, only with a central dowel that about twelve inches in length. A small, brass hook extended from one end of the dowel while a smooth wooden disk, about three inches in diameter and one inch thick was secured to the opposite end of the dowel, two inches from the bottom. While the campers examined the darkly patinated wooden objects, Ruby handed each of them one of the roll logs.

Standing in front of them with the same tool and materials, she showed them how to pull one end of the log to thin it out. Pinching the narrower tuft of wool between her thumb and fingers, she twisted it quickly before attaching it to the brass hook at the top of the spindle itself. Then, suspending the spindle by the tuft of wool, she gave the dowel a quick twist with her fingers, making it spin quickly. The weight of the spindle, along with its rotation, quickly produced twelve inches of fairly uniform yarn, drawing wool from the roll log she held in her hand above the spindle. The campers oohed and aahed at the alchemy that was taking place before their eyes. She spun the spindle again between her thumb and finger and the length of the yarn continued to grow.

When the length of yarn extended to about thirty inches, Ruby wrapped the new yarn around the dowel on the underside of the disc, coming back around to the hook at the top when only a few inches remained. She spun the spindle again, continuing to draw wool from the roll log, allowing it to twist and turn into beautiful yarn as gravity slowly pulled the spindle closer to her feet. Ruby wound this new yarn around the dowel also before hooking the last few inches onto the brass hook as she had done before. Again and again she repeated these motions, encouraging them to watch closely as she joined a second roll log to the end of the first one, seamlessly continuing the creation of new yarn. Mesmerized, they all watched her spindle magically turn four roll logs into beautiful yarn before Ruby invited them to pick up their spindles and follow her lead.

It quickly became clear that following her lead would be more difficult than Ruby's skilled hands had let on. Josh's first attempts produced a short strand of very chunky, uneven rope before his spindle broke loose and fell to the floor with a loud smack. James's first results weren't any better, but he did manage to hang onto his spindle. After twenty minutes of practice and a lot of pointers from Ruby, all of them began to catch on. It would take another twenty minutes before any of them would create anything resembling usable yarn. By then, Spencer and Holly had carded more than half of the wool that had been brought up from the shed and were ready for a break, trading places with Rachael and Matt.

The afternoon work continued on like this, the campers taking their turns on Bessie as the rest of them practiced the fine art of yarn making using the spindles. But even with all their improvements, and with all of them working, they couldn't keep up with Ruby's yarn production on the ancient treadle spinning wheel. Bobbin after bobbin were loaded with beautiful yarn while the others did their best to create much smaller collections on their spindles. But there were no feelings of competition. On the contrary, a unique sense of harmony existed as they worked together in this common goal of turning the farm's harvest of wool into usable yarn.

Before all the bobbins were filled, Ruby took a break from the spinning wheel and pulled two more tools from the wooden crate. Looking somewhat similar to nautical anchors, these niddy noddies, hand reels for yarn, were made of three pieces of wood: two bowed pieces, each about eighteen inches long, were drilled through the middle and attached to opposite ends of a central dowel, the two end pieces oriented at ninety degrees to one another.

She handed one of the contraptions to Pops who demonstrated how it worked. Holding the niddy noddy by the middle dowel with his left hand, Pops slipped the end of the yarn from the bobbin under his thumb.

Then after looping the yarn over one end of the bowed cross arms, he stretched it to the cross arm on the opposite end of the dowel. He continued to stretch the yarn back to the opposite end of the first cross arm, and then back again to the second arm. He repeated this slowly at first so they all could see what he was doing before picking up his speed, turning the yarn and the niddy noddy into a blur of motion until he had counted to twenty five lengths which, he explained, equalled about fifty yards of yarn.

While Pops demonstrated how to tie off the ends and secure the skein with a couple of figure-eight hitch knots, Ruby explained that each pair of socks required about 400 yards of yarn or roughly eight skeins. Hundreds of skeins would need to be made and dyed over the coming weeks to prepare the wool for future socks.

After removing the long loop of yarn from the niddy noddy, Pops stretched the loop between his hands and twisted it again and again until it was tight. Then, bringing his hands together, the skein twisted around itself. He tucked one end through the other and set it aside on a chair before moving on to create the next skein.

With each of them rotating through the different steps of creating the skeins, no one was bored. In fact, James and Crystal lamented having to leave to get dinner started when Ephraim and Susan returned from the farm stand on their bicycles. But the work continued as Ephraim and Susan took their places in the rotation, quickly learning from the others.

At six-o'clock they broke for the evening milking and to take in the laundry, while a group of four campers went to the berry patch to see what they could find for dessert. The dinner bell brought them all back to the big house where James and Crystal fed them waffles with buttermilk syrup and bottled peaches brought up from the cellar.

After sharing in a round of wisdom cookies, they all went into the kitchen to clean up before reconvening the party back to the front porch for more work on the yarn. Ephraim took his turn on Bessie, but he quickly became distracted, closely watching the mechanics of Ruby's spinning wheel. When his feet slipped from the pedals for the third time, causing him to fall off the modified bike completely, he turned Bessie over to Spencer and found a place in front of Ruby where he could better examine the spinning wheel's mechanics, tracing the power from the treadle through the big wheel, the flyer, and the bobbin.

They all watched and listened as his curiosity and imagination churned, and before long he asked if he might be excused to visit the tool shed and see if he might come up with a modification for Bessie that could mimic the spinning wheel. After Susan reminded them of Ephraim's time-saving success with the wool-trifuge, it was unanimously decided that he should be given a chance.

Matt and Susan volunteered to help him, and soon, the sounds of power tools, hammer blows and tinkering could be heard from the distant shed. Within an hour, they returned to the porch with a strange-looking contraption. Nuts and bolts, leather straps, bicycle parts and bits of recycled farm implements had been welded together to form what they called The Bessie Bobbinator.

It took only a couple of minutes for them to detach the carding machine and install The Bobbinator. Then with all of them looking on, Susan sat down on the saddle and began to pedal while Matt and Ephraim began drafting yarn through the orifices on either side of the machine. With the click of a lever, the bobbins engaged, turning slowly while the two flyers made of modified horseshoes circumnavigated the bobbins in a whirling blur. Yarn, smooth and consistent, began filling up both of the bobbins as the campers looked on with both amusement and awe. Ruby tried to keep up with the new machine on her spinning wheel, but even at her top speed The Bobbinator was producing yarn at least four times as fast. With so much wool drafting through the two orifices, everyone's help was soon needed to either feed the machine or empty the quickly filling bobbins onto the nitty noddies. When those working the nitty noddies couldn't keep up, Ruby turned two of the porch's straight-back chairs into of spontaneous substitutes by turning the chairs upside down and wrapping the yarn around the outsides of their four legs.

The campers continued to rotate, moving through each of the stations, pausing only when the bobbins were filled and had to be switched out. It wasn't until Holly discovered that by pedaling Bessie a little slower, they were all able to keep up with the production. To keep the tempo correct, Greg took himself out of the rotation and picked up the guitar, playing classic 60's rock and roll songs. Several of the campers sang along, turning the yarn production into a dance concert.

By the time all the carded wool had been consumed by The Bobbinator, the dancing and fun had magically created four-hundred and seventy-four skeins of beautiful, creamy yarn. As they ate strawberries bobbing in fresh cream, Ruby and Pops explained that the production of this much yarn often required one full week of work. And though more than half the wool remained in the shed, they suggested that if the team could keep up the pace there would be plenty of time for another afternoon at the river.

The energy the campers had gone to bed with rose with them the next morning. Chores were accomplished quickly and Genevieve and Matt reluctantly took their turn at the farm stand, promising to try to sell out as quickly as possible so they could get back and help with the yarn production. But the traffic on the highway was slow and it was nearly three o'clock before they were able to sell all the goods they'd taken to the stand. They discovered upon their return that while they'd spent their day discussing Ruby's offer to Genevieve and reading through passages of Thomas's book, the rest of the campers—along with Pops and Ruby— had carded the remaining wool and had been able to turn two-thirds of it into yarn.

Two additional sets of hands were a welcome addition, and before the animals needed attention, all of the year's yarn had been processed and divided into twelve different groups for dyeing.

Pops and Ruby were overjoyed with the speed and efficiency of the campers. Ephraim, Matt and Susan were praised for their ingenuity on their work on The Bobbinator, but they humbly reflected the praise back on each of the campers and the work they'd accomplished together.

That sense of accomplishment went with them as they broke for evening chores, and no one but Pops seemed to notice Ruby's fatigue. He sent her up to take a power nap while he joined the milking team. By the time they gathered for dinner, fatigue had settled into the bones of all of the campers, leaving them much less exuberant than they'd been the night before. After cleaning up the kitchen, they gathered back on the front porch, too exhausted for ice cream or a dance party but still wanting to be together. When the yawns began an hour later, one by one the campers excused themselves to return to the bunkhouse until only Pops, Ruby, and Genevieve remained.

CHAPTER 107

The Merits of Sass

All you can do is all you can do, and all you can do is enough.
–A.L. Williams

It had been more than ten days since Ruby had offered Genevieve the farm's top position, but no opportunity to speak privately with her had presented itself. Genevieve had a million questions, but she had realized in the last few days that they all boiled down to one main question: Why her?

She had just posed the question to Ruby and Pops when the door of the big house closed behind them and the three of them turned to see Matt walking away from the house with a book in his hands, his head down, already reading by the porch's carnival lights.

"Oh, I'm sorry," Matt said, looking startled to see he was interrupting something.

"That's quite all right," Pops replied. "What are you reading?"

Matt looked embarrassed. "Uh, *Pride and Prejudice*."

"Not a bad choice," Ruby replied with a gentle smile. "You've decided it's time to check out your competition, eh?"

Matt looked even more embarrassed. "I figured it's better late than never."

"Good for you," Pops affirmed. "I personally started by sizing up John Knightley, but Mr. Darcy proved to be a worthy opponent as well."

"Sounds like I have my work cut out for me," Matt said, offering a charming but tired smile.

"Perhaps you could pass that on to James when you're finished with it," said Ruby. "He's made a lot of progress in the last few days, but there's not a man alive who couldn't benefit from taking on a little Darcy charisma."

"And when James is done with it, see what you can do about passing that on to Spencer," Genevieve suggested.

"I'll do my best," Matt responded. "Have a good night."

"You, too," Genevieve replied.

"Actually, do you have a minute?" Ruby asked of Matt.

"Uh, well, I was kind of in a hurry to read this book so I could pass it on the other guys."

"They've got all summer. Join us," Ruby encouraged, patting the arm of the wicker chair at her side.

Matt glanced sheepishly at Genevieve before taking a seat.

"Genevieve, here, was just asking us why we offered her the position as the next matchmaker of Niederbipp," Pops reported. "I have a hunch you may have heard something about that."

"Just a little," he acknowledged. "What'd you tell her?"

"We were just getting to that when you joined us. But as a member of this year's team, and one who suggested Genevieve should be considered, perhaps you could offer some insight to her question as well," Ruby suggested.

"Oh, uh, yeah…what can I tell you?" He responded awkwardly.

"Why don't you tell her what you told us," Pops prodded.

Shyly, Matt looked Genevieve in the eye. "I…uh…I told them you had grit—grit and sass."

"Uh, yeah, that hardly qualifies me to match socks, let alone matching people for something as consequential as marriage," Genevieve responded.

"No, you're quite right," Ruby confirmed. "But without grit *and a little sass*, you wouldn't have what it takes to learn the hard-earned skills of matchmaking, nor the ability to properly deploy them."

"The fact that you don't recognize these apparently natural gifts has only confirmed that we have chosen the right person," Pops added.

Genevieve smiled, but shook her head. "I don't understand any of this. Why would you want a person who was ignorant of her own *apparent* gifts or skills to continue a legacy you've worked so hard to keep alive?"

"Oh, would you suppose it better to choose someone who was confident that she had *all* the necessary skills to match a couple for life and beyond?" asked Ruby.

"Well, yeah, isn't that obvious?" Genevieve responded, looking confused. "Why would you want to turn the farm over to someone who has no discernible skills?"

"I'm quite certain I had no discernible skills either when we took over," Ruby admitted.

"Really?" Genevieve asked, looking very surprised by this revelation. "Then why were you chosen?"

"Because by the end of that first summer I was about as meek and humble as I've ever been, while still somehow being able to maintain my natural sass."

"Sass? You?"

Pops laughed. "Mom may look like a cool-tempered, well-mannered specimen today, but under that gentle exterior she's quite a firecracker—always has been. As you might imagine, we've seen our share of sass over the years, but you're in a league of your own. Mom recognized a kindred-sass in you from that very first day, but when each of your comrades began recognizing it too, we knew we were indeed dealing with a rare talent."

Genevieve blinked several times, looking confused. "Uhh, talent? Really? I know a lot of people who would call it a character flaw. It seems counterintuitive that sass like mine would somehow make me eligible for such sensitive work?"

"In its unfiltered rawness, you'd be right," Ruby admitted. "I had to learn to temper my own sass before I could become an effective matchmaker."

"She's still working on it," Pops concurred. "Few things are as volatile and potentially destructive as untempered passion and excessive zeal. Our best selves usually require the application of self-awareness and the harnessing of our more base characteristics before they can positively effect the lives of others."

"It's true," Ruby responded, nodding her head. "Passion and zeal—if properly employed—can prove empowering and ennobling. Left in their natural state, however, and allowed to run wild without regard for either accountability or the welfare of others, these potential strengths can be corrosive, explosive, and ruinous."

"Uh, right, which brings me back to my question: why would you want someone who's so...all of those things...to get anywhere near what you've worked so hard to preserve?"

Ruby smiled kindly. "We attempt to share many principles on this farm—principles, which if embraced and implemented, have the ability to positively change patterns, lives and outcomes. But despite our best efforts, we have yet to be able to teach even one camper passion. Every person with a pulse has some degree of passion. We each were born, as the poet Wordsworth says, "trailing clouds of glory." But the brightness of that innate glory tends to vary from person to person. And rare is the person whose passion and glory have the ability to inspire the awakening of the same in others."

"Are you suggesting that I..."

Ruby nodded. "Have what it takes to inspire others to discover and nurture their portions of glory? Yes! That's exactly what I'm saying."

Genevieve's face went still before breaking into laughter. "I'm flattered, really, but I think you've got the wrong girl. I'm just a..."

"No, that's only who you are now!" Ruby protested. "There is still great potential that's been left untapped within you."

"How do you know?"

Ruby tapped her chest. "You get a feel for these things after so many years of practice."

"I don't understand."

"Nor will you until you open your heart to it. That's the way all truth works. It requires that you give it room to swell and grow. And if you'll nourish it with hope and reverence, it has the ability to push out all doubt and fear, chasing out all darkness until only light remains.

Genevieve nodded slowly. "I...I have to admit I really don't know much about truth."

"Maybe not, but you've been here long enough to know that truth is light, right?" Pops replied.

"I guess I've never really considered that..."Genevieve responded thoughtfully.

Matt leaned forward. "So, that light...truth...is that what makes you and the rest of the people around here so different?"

Ruby smiled. "I believe the good people of Niederbipp are somewhat unique, at least in today's world, in their interest in truth and wisdom, and in their desire to share it with others. Light is happiest when it's allowed to fulfill the measure of its creation and burn bright, offering hope and possibility to all that it touches."

"Okay...so why does it feel like most places outside of Niederbipp are only growing darker and more cynical?" Matt asked.

Pops glanced at Ruby before turning back to Matt. "Where the hearts of mankind are set on darkness, light and truth are generally shunned and abandoned. But where the hearts of mankind sincerely seek for truth and light, darkness is quickly pushed out by the brightness of hope and the aspiring harmony of reverence and truth."

"You've just described the farm," Matt mused.

"Thank you," Ruby said with a smile that filled her whole face. "Our first goal, when we decided to take over from the Smurthwaites, was to not mess up the feeling of light and hope we had grown to appreciate here."

"*Uh, and now you're offering all this to me?*" Genevieve asked, trying to smile. "I don't know if I can handle that kind of pressure."

Pops laughed. "I remember feeling the same way, fifty-seven years ago...and at the beginning of pretty much every summer since then."

"Is that really true?" Matt asked, looking quite surprised.

"Absolutely!" Pops declared as Ruby nodded.

"We've often said that as long as we don't get in the way, the farm will teach you kids most of the lessons you need to know," Ruby added. "Our job, as we've come to understand it, is to simply facilitate the transfer of clarity that this farm has to offer. That clarity follows a rather precise recipe, but as long as we've stuck to it and complied with the design put in motion more than three-hundred years ago, things tend to work out nicely."

"Part of that recipe has always prescribed having a passionate woman at the helm," Pops added. "We've seen several potential candidates since we began considering stepping down eleven years ago when Ruby had her first cancer scare, but none of them have had the same level of sass and passion you have, Genevieve."

"But I'm so...many things that aren't...you."

"Oh, honey, there've never been two matchmakers who are alike in every way. Millie Smurthwaite had far more patience than I could ever dream of having."

"But Ruby's always been a better cook and a faster knitter, and she leaves more room for fun than Millie ever put up with."

"The truth is that each matchmaker has come to the farm with different strengths and gifts. And each one of us has benefitted from a summer's worth of refining or polishing."

"And the keys of joy, if you haven't already observed, have the ability to set us on a course of refinement and advancement," Pops added.

"Okay, but…really? In five months?"

"These five months are really just the beginning. Much of what we get started here requires the better part of a lifetime to complete. Perfection has obviously never been a requirement to be a matchmaker. We're far more interested in a willing and humble heart and a hunger to learn and grow. Despite our best efforts to filter out those who are ill-prepared to take advantage of the light the farm has to offer, occasionally someone slips through."

Pops laughed and nodded. "Yep, but in each of those cases, some bit of magic has come into play, which, not unlike your own experience, tends to bring about a change of heart. Of course, to my recollection, none of our campers have had to endure quite as much as you have."

"No, I'm quite certain that's true, which is indeed a compliment to you."

"A compliment?" Genevieve asked, looking confused.

Ruby nodded. "That the hand of providence thinks enough of you to not only offer you large servings of humble pie, but also to trust you enough to know you can endure it. There has yet to be a camper who has come to this farm who has not had to endure the refining chrysalis of adversity on their way to becoming graceful butterflies, but you, my friend, have taken the cake."

Genevieve shook her head, but smiled. "I swear I was never this accident-prone before coming here. I'm just out of my element."

"Yes," Ruby said, "but if you consider the spirit you came here with nearly a month ago, compared with the spirit you carry with you today, it's not hard to begin to recognize how your accidents may have been far less *accidental* than they now appear."

She nodded slowly, looking very thoughtful. "Are you saying the accidents ...?"

"I'll leave the interpretation of those things for you to decipher, but I will say that in my ninety-four years, I've lost my belief in coincidence while gaining great confidence in the hand of providence and the power of miracles. And when miracles line up in such ways as they have in these past weeks of your life, I've found it's usually best to embrace the wonder of it all rather than to curse the yet-unknown reasoning behind them."

"I don't believe we've ever met a camper who has not been changed in innumerable positive ways by the end of the summer," Pops added. "Some changes come quickly, and some require months to bloom, but if your heart is tuned to the vibrations of truth, and your eyes are open to the light which offers understanding, you can't help but grow and learn and become a new creature. And the more you generously offer of yourself to the process, the more you gain in the things that matter most. By making room and giving permission for a softening and refining of all things, and throwing your head, heart and hands into the light of your new truth, magic happens."

"You wouldn't believe the miracles we see every summer," Ruby added. "Amazing things happen at the intersection of sincerity, humility and truth. Collisions occur there that produce otherwise impossible outcomes, full of deep and abiding change brought about by new understandings full of hope and grace."

"That all sounds good," Genevieve admitted, glancing quickly at Matt. "But there's a big difference between the commitment of one summer, and the commitment of who knows how many years."

"You're quite right," Ruby agreed. "That's why I suggested you take some time to think about it."

"And pray about it!" Pops added. "If it hadn't been for the answers we both received, there would have been many times it would have been easy to throw in the towel and call it quits."

Ruby chuckled. "And even with those answers, we've had our share of moments when we've wondered what the heck we were thinking."

"So why do you do it?" Matt asked.

Pops looked at Ruby and waited for her to speak.

"Being the matchmaker of Niederbipp for these past five-and-a-half decades has been the source of my life's greatest trials and difficulties. I've cried and labored and sweat far beyond what I ever could have guessed I was even capable of. But I've also laughed and loved and known deeper joys than I ever knew were possible. We know that what we share here—the experience—the secrets—the keys of joy—they are needed in this world, now more than ever. At a time when common sense is becoming altogether uncommon, and families everywhere are under attack, we have trouble believing there's anything we could be doing that's more important than the work we're doing here."

Pops nodded thoughtfully, placing his strong, farm-worn hand on top of Ruby's. "It probably sounds strange that we'd choose this life, and have continued to choose it for so many years, but there's nothing much better than watching kids like you transform from doubtful creatures into people who are filled with hope and joy—who know how to love and know they're worthy of love. Watching you kids go on to build marriages and create families where the lessons this farm imparts will be shared with the next generation, and hopefully many more..."

"But don't you ever wish you were...I don't know, somewhere else, relaxing, enjoying your Golden Years?" Genevieve interrupted.

"We've talked about it," Ruby confessed. "The winter months can sometimes feel a little long and lonely, but we decided several years ago we'd rather wear out than rust out. We've got stuff to do here, and the majority of it has meaning and purpose to it. Bingo is a fine game, but if that's all you're livin' for, you ain't really livin'. Nope, we've stayed on, probably long past our prime, but it's a beautiful thing to feel like you're still making a difference, especially at our age."

Genevieve took a deep breath and subconsciously exhaled rather loudly. "So, if I were to say yes, which I'm not prepared to do today... what would I be saying yes to?"

"Well, I'll tell you what the Smurthwaites told us when we asked them a very similar question," Pops offered. "You'd be saying yes to a life of hard work and low pay, but it's work that comes with a clear conscience with the bonus of well-earned sleep, 365 nights a year. You'd be saying yes to a stewardship that you would carry until you die or retire, whichever comes first. You'd be committing to the abandonment of mediocrity and selfish desires, and working instead for excellence and the greater good."

"And don't forget about saying yes to being willing to be a caretaker of the keys of joy, 200 acres, a menagerie of untold numbers of animals, a farmhouse and twelve outbuildings, and the legacy of accepting twelve new recruits every summer," Ruby added. "I'll warn you that it won't be glamorous, and your abilities and motives will be questioned on a regular basis by the very kids you're trying to help, and even by outside reporters."

Genevieve flinched, looking embarrassed. "Look, I'm sorry. I didn't know you then."

"No, you didn't," Ruby responded with a gentle, disarming laugh. "You can fight against a lot of things in life, Genevieve, but until you learn that only the best battles are fought *for* something, your battles will always be in vain."

Genevieve looked confused. "Tell me what you mean."

"As I recall from what I've learned from the porch games, your parents are still together, right?"

Genevieve nodded. "They're still married, but I'm not sure if that's the same thing as being together."

"That's an astute observation. Unfortunately, it's also a common one. Tell me, what have you learned about working with a partner over these last few weeks that you failed to learn from watching your parent's marriage?"

She considered the question for a moment in the context in which it was asked. "That unity and harmony are worth fighting for...that it's really the only way to get stuff done."

Ruby's blue-grey eyes sparkled with the reflection of dozens of carnival lights. "You learned that in the fields with the harrow and planters. You learned that by working the flour mill.

And, if you're open to it, your appreciation of balance, order, rhythm and harmony will grow every time you do the laundry. If you can learn to focus your energies in the pursuit of all things good, bright and hopeful, you'll be much more likely to create and maintain a marriage and a family where there's no room for disharmony and discontent."

Matt stirred, remembering the verse written on the beam above the flour mill. "We are, each of us, angels with only one wing..."

"Exactly!" Ruby responded. "And the only hope we have of flying... of elevating ourselves and our families above the deafening din of mediocrity, is to fiercely embrace each other with love and mutual respect, and work together for a glorified vision of the future."

Matt shook his head. "Why don't more people know about this?"

"There was a time when more people did," Pops responded. "But things change. The world turns. And unless we hang onto the most precious truths and passionately teach them to our children and our children's children, important truths quickly become lost forever."

"And I guess a lot of that depends on the next generation being willing and interested in carrying on the old ways," Matt suggested.

"Indeed," Ruby replied. "Every generation, since the very beginning of mankind, has had its idols that have distracted humanity from the simple truths of God. Though the keys of joy have been present since the beginning, humans are generally quick to search out alternatives to work and shortcuts to success. And when they find that the shortcuts often lead to dead ends and the many alternatives to work are only unfulfilling lies, they are generally slow to admit their folly, and generally even slower to warn their children and neighbors. Instead, many set up camp in the wasteland to which their choices have led them. They set aside their dreams of grandeur, surrender their hope, and embrace the tepid comfort of mediocrity and apathy which quickly engulfs them."

"Since our first summer here, we've held onto the burning truth that God intended mankind to know more and be more than mediocre," Pops reported. "We've done our best to endow each camper with the increasingly rare truths and hope for a better life which are embedded in the keys of joy."

"That has to feel like a huge responsibility," Matt suggested.

"Indeed, it does," Ruby answered. "But the responsibility has its own rewards. To watch the light go on in the hearts and minds of kids like you two—to help you see that life can be rich and filled with unspeakable joy—that you can leave mediocrity in your past and reach for excellence instead...I can't imagine a more fulfilling life."

Pops patted Ruby's hand again, turning to face Genevieve. "We know that the decision to become the next matchmaker of Niederbipp won't be an easy one to make—and you'll receive no pressure from us. We are fully aware that it's a commitment that requires great sacrifice, and we'd never want you agreeing to any of it if you weren't comfortable with its challenges and obligations."

Ruby nodded, smiling serenely. "It will likely be the most difficult thing you'll ever choose to do in your life. But I'll tell you this, Genevieve: the joy that comes from sharing these ancient truths with kids like you... to see lives change and hearts grow full and healthy...to watch families form and the lives of children be blessed through the light that comes from living according to the recipe of joy...beyond my own marriage, I've known nothing more rewarding in my life."

Genevieve forced a smile, but said nothing, looking up into the night sky for a long moment. "I'm not saying no, but I have to say the idea of saying yes scares the heck of me."

Ruby chuckled. "We'd be worried that you didn't understand if it didn't scare you. There are four months left. We welcome your decision, either way, at any point."

"But I thought you said you'd need to know right away."

"Yeah, well, what do I know? The way I see it, you're already in training. I can't think of anything I'd teach you different if you'd accepted the position yesterday. Let's consider this summer on-the-job-training. If you decide you want it at the end of the summer, the job is yours."

"And if I don't?"

Ruby turned to look at Pops, winding her fingers through his and smiling at him before turning back to Genevieve. "Then we'll go to sleep in peace, knowing we've done our best with the stewardship with which we've been entrusted. That's all that was ever asked of us. What you and the others choose to do with what you've been given, is, and always will be, entirely up to you."

CHAPTER 108

Big Picture

It does not matter how slow you go as long as you do not stop.
—Confucius

Ruby's decision to keep James and Crystal working in the kitchen for at least a few more days after a particularly loud interaction on Monday morning in the cellar began to affect the morale of all of the campers. Fairness concerns, laundry fatigue, and a limited menu all played a role in the growing grumblings among the rest of the campers. Rumors that

James and Crystal's "problems" were little more than a ruse to avoid sharing responsibility made the disgruntled campers decide something needed to be done.

It was covertly decided before dinner on Thursday evening that the problem should be discussed at the porch gathering that night, with nine of the ten campers selecting Susan to bring it up. Susan wasn't thrilled with the idea, but Holly volunteered to start the conversation in a way that might lead to the problem at hand.

"So, I know you warned us almost two weeks ago that time would begin to pass quicker, but I never could have guessed time, *and the chores*, could fly quite like this," Holly admitted, once they'd gathered on to the porch.

"Yeah, these last two weeks have honestly been the fastest of my life," Crystal added. "It's hard to believe James and I have already been cooking for two weeks."

"Almost three," Josh grumbled under his breath, as the campers passed furtive glances between themselves.

"We hear this every year as the kids fall into the patterns of work and farm activities and further forget about the distractions you've all left behind," Ruby said, either not hearing Josh's complaint or ignoring it.

"This is the longest I've ever gone without watching sports," Spencer admitted.

"Yeah, and it's been a week longer for the rest of us," James reminded him. "I like watching a good game as much as the next guy, but there's no game worth biking twenty miles to see."

"I don't know about that," Spencer replied.

Susan rolled her eyes as she changed the subject to a more pressing matter. "So, I didn't think I'd ever say this, but I actually miss working in the kitchen. When do you think we're going to start the regular chore rotations again?" she asked bluntly before the men could lose their focus any further.

Many of the others nodded as if they shared her question.

"I suppose that depends on James and Crystal," Ruby responded. "What do you two have to say for yourselves?"

James and Crystal, who'd been sharing one of the wicker couches with Holly, turned to look at each other, smiling sheepishly.

"Uh, I don't know if putting us back into the rotation is such a good idea," James replied. "It seems like it would be foolish to put an end to a good thing so soon."

"Yeah, I agree," Crystal replied. "We've finally gotten used to each other. You never know what ugliness might happen if we have to go back to working with everyone else. It seems like our bad attitudes and difficult personalities might be best contained by just keeping us together for at least another week, or maybe even the rest of the summer."

Genevieve made eye contact with Matt and smiled quickly before looking away.

Ruby chortled. "Is that right?"

"We've discussed this and we both agree that we really wouldn't mind," James added. "It's probably better than having any more blow ups like what happened before you forced us to work together."

"Well, I'm not sure if that's a good idea," Ruby responded. "There are ten other campers who've each lost at least two opportunities to learn how to cook and create with their partner in the kitchen. That hardly seems fair."

"And some of us have had more than our share of laundry duty over the past two weeks," Ephraim protested. "I'd much rather have extra days in the kitchen than extra days in the laundry."

"Well, maybe James and I could be assigned to the laundry for a week or two to make up for it," Crystal suggested, almost sounding like she was grasping at straws.

Pops chuckled. "I was born in the night, but it wasn't last night," he said as his chuckle broke into full-on laughter.

"I think what Pops is trying to say is that we've been around the block a time or two and we know how this goes. James, Crystal, I would like to congratulate you both on your work at overcoming the attitudes and behaviors that caused us to ground you to the kitchen."

"Does this mean we're being grounded to the laundry?" James asked, looking almost hopeful.

"No, it does not. It means that for the sake of harmony, you'll both be rejoining the regular chore rotation tomorrow."

"But that means we'll only get to work with each other once a week?" Crystal protested.

"That is correct," Ruby confirmed.

"But I was finally getting James trained just the way I like him."

All of the campers glanced quickly at each other with knowing smiles.

"Yes, well, it's time for the other five women to see what magic they can perform to keep James moving in the right direction. And I'm sure the other five men will be happy to learn the lessons you've imparted to James."

"But..." Crystal said.

"Sorry, I'm not interested in hearing any buts. The decision is final," Ruby replied. "We have far too many months left for any two of you to be monopolizing, exclusivizing, or otherwise diverting time and attention away from the harmony of whole farm."

"Are you suggesting your decision might be different if we only had a few weeks left?" James asked.

"No, I am *not* suggesting that," Ruby responded firmly. "If you were looking for romance, James, you should have tried out for the *Bachelor*. You will recall from the contract you each signed, page three, paragraph five, that there will be no pairing off or eclusivizing in ways that could make others feel uncomfortable, left out, or playing second fiddle to your assigned daily partner. Fifty-seven years of observations at the intersection of Hormones and Close Interactions on this farm have taught us that if ever this rule is bent, kinked, pretzeled or broken—or any other creative adjective like unto it—things don't go well.

"James and Crystal, you're fondness for each other has been duly noted and will play into my decisions at the end of the summer. But I'm warning you, *don't push it!* We're far too early into this year to even think about the emotional mess of romance, which has been known from time to time to very quickly turn a good thing into a place of strategy and chaos. We've worked hard to maintain the distinction of the farm's earliest settlers who called this place Harmony Hill, and I'll be pickled and put up in the cellar before any two campers turn this into *Dis*-harmony Hill for the rest of us."

James nodded, but didn't look settled on the matter. "So, hypothetically speaking, if this were, say, September 20th, would romantic advancements be acceptable then?"

Pops laughed. "James, let me put it this way: You try to make any romantic advancements toward me and I'll pop you in the nose, no matter how or when you may feel compelled to express it."

James looked flustered as the rest of the campers hooted and applauded.

"The short answer is no, James," Ruby offered by way of clarification. "I'm just gonna nip it in the bud and say no—both hypothetically and literally. We have way too much at stake for any two of you to be getting fresh with each other. But I will assure you, as I do campers every year, that learning how to control your passions and emotions, and adhering the time-honored rules of the farm will help you establish a stronger foundation of self-discipline and mutual respect. Any questions?"

Ten of the campers looked quite pleased with the decision, and only a few noticed Josh and Spencer's stealthy fist bump.

"Very well," Ruby responded with a resolute nod. "Tomorrow morning, we will begin again with all six chores in rotation. Now, what shall we discuss tonight, and more importantly, will there be dessert?"

"The kitchen staff is on strike," James responded, looking bent.

"And we've run out of ideas for desert," Crystal added.

"Then I'm glad we've made this change," Ruby replied, looking disappointed. "I'd like to publicly thank you both for your efforts in the kitchen. I'm sure we can all agree that we've seen a marked improvement in both attitudes and the edible results of your efforts to work together. Congratulations for being the first team of the summer to endure grounding. I hope you'll be the last."

"Mom and I discovered decades ago that there are many ways to inspire excellence. Grounding teams has never been our favorite, nor has it been the most productive. Our hope in still employing the penalty is to give you kids a chance to learn how personal interactions are generally far more pleasant and effective when mutual respect and love are present. You will discover, if you haven't already, that harsh words, name calling, and bullying are contrary to all the keys of joy.

"Uh, are you referring to what's happened in the kitchen over the last two weeks, or are you sharing wisdom in general," Ephraim asked, looking confused.

"Both. Most of us have to suffer our way to wisdom. But if we'll learn to observe both good and bad examples around us, we will enable ourselves to forgo much suffering. You will hopefully someday learn, if you haven't already, that love and mutual respect reduce friction in every interaction, while opening the possibility for boundlessly meaningful connections."

Ruby nodded. "There are many powerful motivators in life—money, greed, duty, fear… but the greatest of all motivators is love. And until we learn that truth and practice it in our own lives, joy will forever be elusive."

"I object," James replied.

"I'm all ears, Counselor," Ruby responded, opening her hands, motioning for him to speak.

"It's too simple. It's too weak. There's no way love has any more power to motivate than, say, money, or fear."

"Is that right?" Ruby answered.

"That's the way I see it."

"Okay, then I have a question for you, James. As you've worked with Crystal over the last couple of weeks, what evidence have you gathered as you've improved your relationship with her that supports your position?"

"Well, I…" he began boldly, but suddenly looked like he'd lost his courage. He was silent for a moment, thirteen sets of eyes fastened upon him as he struggled to find his voice. "I…I'd like to withdraw my objection until I've heard more of your evidence."

"That might be a wise thing to do, Counselor."

"But I'd like to reserve my time and right to argue to the contrary."

"Of course you would, and your request will be granted if you still require it," Ruby responded.

Turning away from James, she reached for Pops's hand and squeezed it firmly before looking into the faces of all the other campers. "I appreciate James's enthusiasm to learn new things. And I appreciate that his questions create openings to share the things I've learned over these many years. My predecessor, Millie Smurthwaite, taught us that no sincere question should ever be avoided or set aside. Sincere questions, she taught, are the doorways to great understanding, knowledge, and even revelation. As this relates to James's challenge to my argument, I will add that some understanding, revelation and knowledge cannot be quantified, diagramed, or categorized in ways that can be understood with the mind alone. In order to understand many of the universe's greatest truths, one must often lean heavily on the grace, understanding, and intuition of the heart."

"So, are you suggesting that love is either the second or fourth key of joy?" Josh asked.

"No, but I am suggesting that in order for joy to become a part of one's life, love ultimately must play a role in every aspect of that life. Love may be more closely aligned with the key of charity than any other, but I'd like to suggest that unless and until love becomes the ring that runs through each of the keys, tying them all together, joy will forever remain an elusive ideal."

"You can't possibly be suggesting that a person who doesn't love isn't capable of experiencing joy," James challenged.

Ruby smiled. "No, I am not suggesting that."

"Wait. You're not?" Holly asked, looking confused.

Ruby shook her head. "We are all children of God. We were created out of joy and I don't believe we can properly fulfill the measure of our creation without ultimately becoming partakers of joy. But there's a mighty big difference between *experiencing moments of joy* and *living in joy*. The first, by the grace of God, can be enjoyed by all people from time to time. I believe this is by design. It offers to all people, regardless of how they may be living their lives, subtle reminders of their connection to something bigger and brighter. The second requires a very different level of commitment, sacrifice and love."

"I'm not going to lie—these keys of joy…it's beginning to feel like a lot of things to keep up in the air at the same time," Rachael said, moving her hands as if she were juggling.

"I remember feeling the same way when I first began learning them," Pops admitted. "But you need to remember that each of the keys support each other and build on each other. In the beginning, when these principles and practices are new, they may feel intimidating or even overwhelming. If they ever do, try thinking of each element of each key as a piece of a jigsaw puzzle. The image will become more clear as each piece is connected, giving you confidence and helping you see the bigger picture.

"It almost sounds easy when you describe it like that," Sonja admitted.

"I agree," said Genevieve. "So why does it still feel like a challenge?"

Josh nodded. "I can obviously only answer for myself, but the keys almost feel like a game with objectives and purpose rather than just running around, willy nilly, without any direction."

Many of the campers nodded.

"We hear similar things every year," Ruby admitted. "It's an imperfect metaphor, but there are many similarities between assembling puzzles and discovering one's own big picture. I think most people probably have a desire to see the big picture, but they're often surprised when they realize it's been around them all along, unassembled."

"Oh, man, that's bad news for me. I hate puzzles," Spencer responded, drawing the laughter of many of the campers.

"Why?"

"Because they're just so tedious and time consuming. My mother always has one out on a card table during the holidays. She's always trying to get me to sit down and help her put it together."

Many of the others nodded.

"Sounds about right. I've observed that people have all sorts of different responses to puzzles." Ruby continued. "Some, like Spencer, choose to avoid them. Some are excited as they help turn all of the pieces face-up, and maybe stick around long enough to find a corner or connect a few pieces before they decide they've seen enough."

"Nailed it!" Crystal said, raising her hand and pointing it at herself.

Several of the other campers nodded their head in agreement.

"And I'm sure we all know those who'll keep working on a puzzle for days and even weeks until every piece has found its home," Ruby continued.

"That's my Momma," Spencer said.

"So, are you suggesting we won't see our big picture until we buckle down and put all our pieces together?" Holly asked.

Pops smiled, but shook his head. "If only it were that easy. If we could do it on our own there'd be no need of marriage and families. People would be content with being alone, going about their lives without having to worry about anyone else."

"That doesn't sound much like joy." Greg said.

"Why not?" asked Pops.

"Because…shoot, I've been down that road, only worrying about myself and my interests and issues. It doesn't give you a bigger picture of anything except for maybe the inside of your own head, and I don't know how healthy that is for anybody."

"Are you suggesting that life is somehow better when you have to worry about everyone else's issues in addition to your own? James asked.

"No, but look at what's happened here in the last month," Greg responded, looking around at all of the campers. "We were strangers when we got here; strangers fixated on our own small, sad pictures."

"My picture wasn't that sad," Holly protested.

"And I'm glad that it wasn't," Greg replied. "No offense to any of us, but what I'm saying is that over the last month as we've talked and shared and opened our lives and hearts to each other, I think we've each begun to see that maybe we're actually small parts of a much bigger picture."

"Yes!" Ruby exclaimed. "Exactly! There are many people who will cross our paths, and if we're open and willing, will expand our insight and understanding of how our pieces fit together. The way of joy is nearly always contrary to our natural propensities to be self-centered and uncharitable. Everyone who has ever learned the keys and committed to live their lives according to their precepts has had to wrestle with fear and the elimination of our natural, selfish inclinations in order to make room for new thoughts, a new heart, and a new way of life."

"You almost make it sound like following the keys of joy requires a total overhaul," Greg suggested.

"In many ways that's true," Pops admitted. "We've heard many of our kids compare following the path of joy to a kind of rebirth—a new beginning—a new way of life that offers new insights and understanding. In many ways this new life will feel familiar. It will remind you of the time when you were children and the world was new and uncomplicated, when curiosity fueled all your interests."

"I've felt that way pretty much every day since being here," Sonja said.

Many of the campers agreed.

"Yes, well, you're each discovering new pieces of your puzzle, aren't you? Pieces you didn't even know you were missing. And your big picture is getting much bigger than you anticipated it ever being."

Susan nodded. "But, weirdly, that doesn't seem scary..."

"I was just thinking the same thing," admitted Sonja. "I've usually had all sorts of anxiety, trying to protect my little corner and the five or six pieces I knew went together. And then I come here and suddenly... the world got a lot bigger."

"I guess I feel much the same way," Genevieve admitted. "What kind of strange magic is this?"

Pops smiled. "I think what you're referring to is the magic that comes when the light of truth collide with love and joy. We might experience bits of this on our own, but that magic has exponentially more power when people come together in the spirit of sharing and a willingness to express love and concern for one another. And when that happens, as it has here over the last couple of weeks, it's like everything falls into a state of swing—a place where all things begin to work together like cogs in a well-engineered machine, and time passes as if it were a dream."

"So how do you stay in this place forever?" Josh asked.

"Forever?" Ruby asked, shaking her head. "I don't know if that's possible in this life. Things change. Distractions happen. We fall into bouts of selfishness and pull ourselves away. We forget the small and simple joys we once relished, and complicate our lives as we pursue the sparkly and glittery things of the world."

CHAPTER 109

Geschwisterkeit

Man is lost and is wandering in a jungle where real values have no meaning. Real values can have meaning to man only when he steps on to the spiritual path, a path where negative emotions have no use.
—Sai Baba

And what's wrong with the sparkly and glittery things of the world?" James challenged.

"Well, that all depends on what you want out of life," Ruby answered. "Some people are able to be surrounded by the glittery things of the world and still maintain their integrity and charity. But it's been our observation that sorrows often follow those who let those sparkly, glittery things become their gods. And too many of these folks allow their treasures to define them, not as children of God, but as self-important "better-thans" who are often quick to scrub even the memories of the simple joys they once knew."

"You must be careful with glittery things. If left unchecked, they can quickly turn innocent interests and admiration into lust. And once glittery things have their hooks in you, it's difficult to shake them off and ever return to joy's uncomplicated simplicities. Too many hearts turn cold in the pursuit of status and riches. Too many children and grandchildren of the rich, raised without the merits of work, and sheltered from the natural consequences of their choices by their parents' wealth, clothe themselves in the golden robes of narcissism and believe they are entitled demigods—depraved, selfish, and disobedient to the laws of God and man," Pops said.

"Hey, I know lots of rich people who aren't any of those things," James responded defensively.

"As do we, James," Pops confessed. "As do we. But we also know many more who have abandoned their virtues, turned their backs on the poor and needy, and lost their souls in their pursuit of sparkly things."

James pursed his lips but remained silent.

"So…" Susan spoke, hesitating as she formed her question, "How do you maintain a trajectory of joy while also pursuing your career and your treasure?"

Ruby nodded. "Do any of you have any answers for Susan?"

They looked around at each other for a moment before Holly slowly raised her hand. "Uh, I seem to remember some advice about that from the Bible."

"Well, that's always a good source for answers. What have you got?"

Holly smiled nervously. "It's been a long time, but they were some of my Mom's favorites verses. I think it's from the Sermon on the Mount."

"A very good source, indeed," Ruby said with a smile, encouraging her to continue.

"I don't know if I entirely understand it, but I think it basically says that if you seek first for the kingdom of God, for the intent of doing good, you don't have to worry about the future because all the good things that you want in life will come to you."[1]

"Pfff," James responded, turning away.

"You disagree, James?" Pops replied.

"Yeah, I guess I do. It's ludicrous. That's not the way the real world works."

"No?" Ruby asked.

He shook his head. "Look at me for example. I came from a poor, broken, blue collar home. I could have stayed in that hole and been stuck with the circumstances I was raised with, but I didn't want that life. I have no shame in saying I want to be rich. I want to drive nice cars and own vacation property. And I want my kids to be able to do all the things I never was able to do when I was young. I don't see anything wrong with that. If life, as you say, is about finding joy, I'm going to find as much of it as I can, and fill up my bank account, and buy a big house so no one will ever wonder if I found my joy."

"And then what?" Pops asked.

"And then I'll retire and enjoy traveling."

"And then what?" Pops asked again.

"Well, if the market treats me right and things turn out as well as I hope they will, I'll donate some of my money back to my alma mater. Maybe they could name a building after me or something."

Pops nodded slowly. "And then what?"

James looked flustered. "Is that not enough?" he asked, rather loudly.

Pops shrugged, unruffled. "We each have to decide what is enough. If you're lucky you'll have someone by your side to help you make that

---

1. Matthew 6:33

decision. But I'd like to point out something about your plan there that you may have missed."

"Okay?"

"Forgive me for saying so, but most of what you just shared was about ego—even down to the end when your name lives on long after you're gone in the form of a building dedicated to your honor."

"Is there anything wrong with that?" he challenged.

"Beyond the fact that it lacks creativity? Probably not," Ruby suggested.

"Creativity? What do you mean?"

"James, every university is supported in part by its alumni. Loyalty to one's school is commendable. But considering a man with your background and upbringing, I guess I'd just hope for something more?"

"More? *My background...*? Buildings aren't cheap. I don't know what you're saying."

"I guess I'm suggesting that maybe you shouldn't sell yourself short. A building with your name on it would certainly draw the attention of your classmates and colleagues, but I'm not convinced it would be the best way to make sure you would be remembered, if that's what you want."

James looked confused, like he didn't know how to respond.

"Look," Ruby continued, "the last thing Pops or I want to do is to tell you how you should spend your money. But considering the challenges you faced in your youth, perhaps your sensitivity and compassion for others might be better applied to supporting a Boys and Girls club, a counseling center, or even a hospital in a low-income neighborhood. You could offer scholarships to kids who wouldn't otherwise have the chance to go to college. And instead of working hard just to feather your own nest, you could put your skills and talents to work in different ways, helping the poor settle their differences with landlords and bill collectors. You could give back to the community that gave you a reason to want more."

"Pfff. Where's the glory in that?"

"There may be no temporal glory in it at all, James, other than the satisfaction of knowing that you did something for someone they couldn't do for themselves. If you do everything solely for the recognition you might receive, you may find validation—even happiness, but it will likely be difficult for you to find joy."

James scratched his head, staring back at Ruby. "Why?"

"Because pride, arrogance, vanity and narcissism are all contrary to the rules of joy. You cannot tangle with any of them for long without becoming blind to the plight of others and losing your sense of compassion and charity. And without charity and compassion, joy can only be an unreachable dream."

"So...is compassion one of the keys of joy then?" Ephraim asked, looking hopeful.

"Not exactly," Pops replied, "but compassion, like love, is an element that winds its way through each of the keys. Without compassion, reverence, charity and hope are all starved of some of their power. Developing and exercising compassion is an essential part of finding joy."

James shook his head and looked away.

"I suppose I shouldn't be surprised, but you disagree, James?" Ruby asked.

"I don't understand any of this. It's basically against all of my education and training. Compassion? Really?! You can't argue the law and expect to win if you're more concerned about such frivolous things as compassion and charity."

"I disagree," Susan reacted. "Practicing law without either one is tantamount the unholy imbalance of justice run amok. I know plenty of lawyers who'd agree with you, but I don't have much respect for any of them. They too often lose their heads, if not their souls, in the slicing and dicing of pedantic technicalities and nonsensical loopholes which only leads to morally bankrupting everyone involved. As far as I can see, it's a dirty game, James. And yes, it's a game that often goes to highest bidder. But at what cost to society and true justice? At what cost to integrity? I'll admit I've been intrigued by money too, but there has to be more to live for than money, right? Money has no soul, nor any end to its ability to starve virtue and canker the very hands that hold it."

"Pfff, says the girl who bills out at three-hundred bucks an hour," he said haughtily.

"Three twenty-five, for the record, thank you very much. But James, where does it end?"

"Well, hopefully a good portion of it ends in my bank account, right?" He looked around into the faces of the others, looking for support, but he didn't find it. Even Crystal appeared unimpressed.

Susan shook her head, looking disappointed. "And then what?"

James rolled his eyes.

"No, I'm serious," Susan pressed. "And then what? I'm sure we all know professionals and executives who have it all: houses, yachts, medallion status travel if not their own private jets, along with all the perks and privilege of the upper crust. But so many of them don't have a lick of charity, reverence for anything other than themselves, and zero compassion to speak of."

"And your point is?" he challenged.

"My point is I've spent my entire career helping rich people get richer, and I can't think of even one of those clients who has even a visible ounce of the joy I've felt here. What if we missed the point of life? What if it's not about making as much money as you can, as quick as you can, so you can live in the right neighborhood and send your kids to the best colleges. What if there's more to life than kicking back at the country club, living a selfish life of leisure while you watch the other half struggle to just feed and clothe themselves.

"Isn't that why we went to school? So we don't have to be like *them*?

Susan shook her head as the others watched on quietly. "This is pointless."

"What's pointless?" James asked. "You're an upper-middle-class woman. Are you telling me you'd be willing to give it all up in pursuit of some intangible magic keys that may or may not have any power to make life even one iota better for anyone?"

"James, I'm grateful for my education and the many doors it's opened for me, but you've met the people of Niederbipp, right? As far as I can tell they have none of the perks I thought were important when I went to grad school, and none of them seem to be the least concerned about it."

"Maybe they're just too ignorant to know what they're missing," James suggested.

"Do you honestly believe that's true?" Crystal asked.

James shrugged.

"Dude, didn't you learn anything from your conversation with that Amish guy, David?" Ephraim asked.

"Like what?"

"You asked him something about getting ahead, remember?"

James looked blank.

"His response surprised me, but I've thought about it almost everyday since then," continued Ephraim. "He was way less concerned about getting ahead of anything or anyone than he was about being a good member of his community and serving his neighbors and family. I thought capitalism and social and financial independence was a good thing until I witnessed what life in a communal setting could be. I'm not under any delusion to think what the Amish have created is perfect, but you saw what they were able to create together—each of them using the skills they had to support a common good."

James nodded, looking truly thoughtful.

"We saw the same thing with the Amish women," Genevieve offered. "There seemed to be a total lack of competition and one-upmanship. Instead, there was a unique but genuine sense of complimentary cooperation. No one was jockeying for position. Instead, they made everyone feel important and needed."

Many of the campers nodded their agreement as James quieted down.

"So how do we create something like that in our world?" Sonja asked.

They watched as Pops and Ruby smiled at each other. "You apply the keys of joy to every aspect of your lives and continue to ask yourself that very question every single day," Ruby offered.

"What the Amish and the people of Niederbipp have created was no accident. I don't know of any culture or community in the world today that enjoys a sense of Geschwisterkeit spontaneously. It requires work and sacrifice, and not only the *ability* to share, but the *desire* to do so. It requires a change of heart," Pops explained.

"Uh, there was a word there I didn't understand," Holly admitted.

"Sacrifice?" Pops asked

"No, it almost sounded Yiddish, or maybe German," Sonja suggested.

"Ahh, yes, Geschwisterkeit—one of my favorite German words," Pops replied.

"What does it mean?" asked Holly.

"I suppose it's something similar to family," Pops reported.

"Yes, but it's even more than that," Ruby added. "Geschwister means sibling, and keit is something like—a mutually nurturing bond—a state of being close—sharing a close connection and understanding."

"Like a fraternity?" Spencer asked.

"Well, yes, but better. It's more fully inclusive of both genders," Ruby explained.

"*Sounds like my kind of fraternity*," Spencer reacted, his voice heavily laced with swagger, drawing the laughter of most of the campers.

"Oh, I assure you it's much more than a cheap attempt at romance, Spencer," Ruby said with a smile. "There's no selfishness in it. In fact, it's much more about what you're willing to give than what you might receive. It's a recognition of a shared state of being, an awareness and embracing of a those things which have the ability to unify, and a rejection of divisions and alienating distinctions."

"That almost sounds like socialism," James replied.

"Yeah, I suppose in a way it is. But socialism generally restricts rights, individuality and freedoms. Geschwisterkeit, on the other hand, recognizes the strengths of the individual, her gifts and talents, and invites the sharing of those gifts through charity, compassion and understanding rather than demanding the indiscriminatory expropriation of them."

"Okay, but I still don't see what keeps people from abusing the system for their own personal gain," James argued.

"Geschwisterkeit can be difficult to understand in a world ruled by selfishness, greed and individualism. And I'm not sure if it's possible to truly understand it or embrace it without first committing to live by the keys of joy."

"You almost sound like you believe the keys of joy are a panacea to all the world's problems," Rachael said.

Pops shrugged. "Knowing what you know about the keys of joy, what do you think?"

"Well, I don't know. I mean I see the potential power they might have in my own life. And I've seen what they've done around here. But we're only a handful of people. And the world is big, and often dark, and so...not like Niederbipp."

Pops and Ruby both nodded knowingly.

"We each have natural tendencies and inclinations that pull us away from what can be," Pops admitted. "Like Mom said, our selfishness and greed are usually the first culprits. But fear, envy, pride, lust and laziness—among other vices...they can hold us back from finding joy."

"You'd only have to add anger, gluttony and pride and you'd have the seven deadly sins," Josh reported.

"I've heard of those," Spencer said. "What are they again?"

All eyes fell back on Josh. "I had to learn them in school when I was a kid. Pride, greed, wrath, envy, lust, gluttony and sloth. They're basically all the vices that are suppose to lead to sin."

"And those are like the Catholic don'ts, right?" Spencer asked.

"I think so. I learned them in Catholic school."

"Yeah, I was gonna say I didn't learn those at my school," Genevieve admitted.

"Do you know their history?" Pops asked.

"The history of the deadly sins?" Josh clarified.

Pops nodded affirmatively.

"Uh, I should. Did they come from Moses?"

Pops smiled. "I'll give you half a point. The commandments certainly influenced them, and the men and women who identified them also spent a lot to time in the desert, seeking wisdom in prayer and meditation. You might be interested to know that these early Christian hermits also identified a list of seven heavenly virtues. Do you happen to remember those also, Josh?"

"Uh, pffff, I...I seem to remember the sins much easier than the virtues."

Ruby smiled. "Funny how we all get caught up on the 'shalt-nots' and forget the beautiful simplicity of the virtuous 'shalls'. I'll give you a hint: you already know three of them."

Josh looked confused.

"Uh, it wouldn't be reverence, hope and charity, would it?" Matt responded, looking uncertain.

"Very good," Ruby responded. "And to those three, the desert fathers and mothers of early Christianity, perhaps borrowing from early Greek philosophers, identified the virtues of temperance, wisdom, justice and courage. They put their own spin on the old ideas of course, but since the beginning of recorded wisdom—and likely long before that—there has been a set of guidelines and commandments that have inspired humanity toward an upward and productive trajectory. There have been, of course, in every generation, those who have challenged the wisdom of the ages and attempted to write their own rules and raise up their own gods. But time and time again, the skirting of eternal laws has reaped only the difficulties and calamities promised those who flout God's laws."

"So, the five keys..." Holly said thoughtfully, "it sounds like they're not only designed to bring us joy, but to help us avoid the challenges that past generations have faced."

"Absolutely," Pops responded. "If you'll look at the greatest challenges of the past century alone you'll quickly discover that each of them has come about through the disregard of eternal laws. Wars, sexual revolutions, financial depressions, the rise of divorce and the collapse of families, environmental degradation, drug abuse, abortions, and even racial and political strife all have at their roots the abandonment of virtues and the entanglement of vices. The details may vary from century to century, but the results of vice have remained much the same over the history of the world—depression, despair, and the loss of freedom."

Holly shook her head. "This is really depressing. How do we get off this crazy train?"

"Well, you already know some of the keys that will free you from the entrapments of the world," Ruby replied. "That's certainly enough to get you started."

"Okay, that's all well and good, but with only twelve of us…"Sonja asked, trailing off. "There are more than eight billion people on this earth and I can't imagine many of them have even heard of the keys."

"Not to mention the fact that we only know three of them," Ephraim added.

Ruby held up her wrinkled hands, silencing the growing murmur among the campers. "I believe there will come a time when the corruption and despair of the world will grow to a point when more people will long for hope and peace. And being unable to find it in any of the philosophies of men, they will turn their eyes toward heaven in humility, and search out the old ways—the ways of eternal truth and wisdom."

"That could take forever," Crystal protested.

"Yes it could, but I don't believe that's likely. Humanity has been itching for answers for a long, long time. Many are already looking for light and hope. Knowledge, when coupled with humility, compassion, charity and reverence—tends to burn bright, offering hope and possibility to all who see it. What you are learning here this summer will give you the potential to light the way for others. Yes, there are only twelve of you, but in the history of the world, far greater wisdom and hope has been spread by the humble hands and hearts of only a few."

"You're speaking of religion again?" Ephraim asked.

"Perhaps in part, but what we're really talking about is hope," Pops replied. "Religion is little more than the practice of hope—the dedication of exercising hope and making it real. Reverence has taught us to seek for wisdom and light in all exercises and expressions of hope. We've discovered that wherever humanity seeks the light and is willing to exercise charity and compassion to share it with others, there will be something of God in it—some beauty to observe and some light to be gained.

"We've found fellow seekers and sharers of hope in many places, and we've heard from others whose travels have taken them far and wide, that humble and sincere seekers are scattered through every sect and religion across the globe. But we've also found seekers in unlikely places, at the end of dusty roads and in humble hovels; people desperate for the light and hope you have to share. Our world is not dark because there is no light. Our world is dark because many of those who have the light are too afraid to let their light shine, afraid of getting hurt, afraid of alienating others, even afraid of losing the humble light they have under the scrutiny of naysayers and critics.

"For the past fifty-six years, Mom and I have been grateful for a chance to share the light we've been given. And we've discovered something along the way—something that, looking back, feels obvious and silly to have even worried about. We worried that first year that it would be difficult to share our little lights with our first campers. But we discovered something beautiful happened each time we did. In quiet moments like this, when the time was right and the questions were sincere, sharing became natural. Every year since then we've watched lights turn on in the eyes and hearts of our kids. For some of them, it's been the first time they've ever known this kind of light. For others it's been more of a relighting of a candle that was snuffed out by fear or doubt or indifference. But we have yet to know anyone who leaves this farm at the end of the summer without an increase of light—light that has grown as they've discovered their connections to God and their own true natures."

Ruby nodded. "If the conditions are right—and somehow the conditions are always right here on the farm—magic happens. Every summer. Without fail."

"Is it the same for everyone?" Josh asked.

"Oh, heavens no," Ruby replied. "It all depends on how much light and hope you're willing to make room for—how much light you're willing to accept. We've met plenty of kids over the years who've been more afraid of the light than they are of the dark."

"Why? What are they afraid of?" asked Josh.

Ruby nodded thoughtfully. "Change. Light. Experiencing the love of God. It's a funny thing. For most folks, after they've experienced it and recognized that it's real, they want more of it. But there are plenty of people, who, after they experience light, attempt to turn their back on it and deny it exists."

"But if light is hope and truth, why would anybody do that?" Crystal asked.

"Because the light of truth and hope requires something of us," Ruby responded. "It encourages us to change, to sweep out the dust and cobwebs from the corners of our souls and set aside our vices and fears. Being exposed to truth and light always encourages us to do the work to develop greater virtues."

"Why would anybody be opposed to that?" asked Holly.

"Because sometimes…we're not ready for change," Greg offered. "I…it took a long time for me to want this change…for me to be willing to admit that my life of mediocrity was far less than it could be. That required courage…courage to take a hard look at my mess of a life and believe I was worthy of more."

Ruby nodded. "Courage you didn't have at the time, right?"

Greg shook his head.

"Timing is critical in most big changes," Ruby continued, "but so is sincerity. Without a sincere heart and a genuine intent to pursue light and hope, I don't know if our efforts here would amount to much more than amusing triflings. If you don't want to change—if you're not ready to set aside your lesser self to make room for a better, any light will be offensive to you. But if all the elements align—a sincere heart, a desire for positive change, and a portion of God's light to show the way—beautiful things can happen. Miracles are made here every summer."

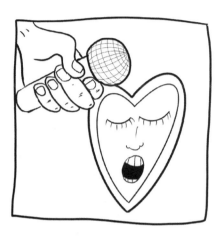

CHAPTER 110

Heartsong

The place to improve the world is first in one's own heart, and head, and hands.
-Robert M. Pirsig

So...what if you're not sure you're ready to change?" Spencer asked.

"Well, I'm not sure you'd be here if that were the case," Ruby responded. "We do our best in the application process to screen out those who are unprepared for change—those who are emotionally and spiritually immature, and those are still under the illusion that they're God's gift to humanity. Those ones are hard to help, and generally require a great deal of tenderizing before they're humble and meek enough to even recognize that there's a light brighter than themselves."

Genevieve shifted uncomfortably. In that moment she knew that the application process would certainly have eliminated her. Things had obviously changed in the weeks since she'd arrived. The tenderizing was real and was taking affect. She realized she hadn't even needed to fake her enthusiasm for at least a week. But as she glanced into the faces of the others she saw that they too were imperfect applicants. They too were going through some process of tenderization. They too were identifying things about themselves that needed work.

"Agency, you will discover for yourself if you haven't already, Spencer," Ruby said, interrupting Genevieve's thoughts, "is a beautiful but terrible thing. There are consequences for every choice we make. Many of those consequences are bitter, but fortunately a great many of them are sweet. It often takes us many years before we learn that we cannot know the sweet without having experienced the bitter. And we certainly can't reasonably expect our lot in life to turn toward the sweet if our choices are incapable of producing sweetness."

"Kinda like that thing Einstein used to say, right?" Greg suggested.

"What are you referring to?" asked Josh.

"You know, that one about insanity—how it's doing the same thing over and over again, but expecting different results."

Ruby nodded. "It can be maddening to watch the insanity of others, but in reality, the insanity Einstein describes seems to be a universal plight of all humanity. Despite the fact that all religions and civilized societies offer proven wisdom in selecting good choices over bad ones, most of us ignore the wisdom of those who've both failed and succeeded, opting instead to set it all aside and exercise both our ignorance and our freewill."

"I represent that remark!" Greg said with a little laugh.

"I think we all do to some extent," Matt admitted.

"Yes, I think we all do," Pops agreed. "The blessing and the curse of mortality is that we all have to figure it out. And we all have to decide what to do with our freewill and the truths we encounter along our way. We all get to decide how much light we can endure, and how much of it we'll choose to hold onto."

"Okay, but the problem, as I see it, is that most us are slow learners," Sonja offered.

Ruby nodded. "Yes, for most of us, it would be far easier and wiser to trust the warning signs posted by others than to ignore or question everything, and have to receive our own licks in the usually painful process of discovering truths that have already been discovered, deciphered, and documented. We could all save a lot of time and trouble if we'd seek wisdom from the heavens and from those who've walked the path before us. But most of us—in our impatience, pride and egotism— toss out the wisdom of the past, ignore the warning signs, and even curse the heavens, determined to go for broke as we blindly beat our heads against the walls rather than using the doors that would open for us if we were sincere about seeking truth and open to change."

All of the campers grimaced sympathetically at the picture Ruby painted.

"So...how do we stop the insanity?" Susan asked.

Ruby glanced at Pops, patting his knee before looking back into the camper's expectant faces. "Well, it's probably easier than you might think. Beyond the application of the keys of joy, you have to determine if the road you're on is going in the direction you want to go."

"But what if you can't tell?" Crystal protested. "How are you supposed to know if you can't see where it ends?"

Ruby smiled, her kind eyes sparkling. "I'm not sure if it's possible to exercise reverence without developing the side effect of longer vision. When we are mere mortals, our view will always be constrained by what is right before our eyes, and it will always be myopic when compared to the view we gain when we begin to recognize that we are eternal beings and children of the creators of the universe. Most of us would be thrilled with a bird's eye view of our lives. But God offers us much more than that, and if we're patient and humble and ask the right questions, He will also give us all the why's."

"The why's?" James asked.

"Yes. Science and the learning of men can answer many of the how's, but it usually falls short when it comes to the why's. Especially as they apply to the details of our own lives. Reverence opens the windows to the wisdom and understanding of eternal answers. It replaces our natural limitations with infinite possibilities. It not only allows us to see the big picture, but it helps us to recognize that the picture is far bigger than we ever imagined, and that the few pieces we've been able to put together are needed in a much bigger whole."

"Uh, I'm not sure I can even handle understanding my little picture," Crystal admitted.

"And yet you still wish your vision could reach further?" Ruby teased.

"Yeah, I know, it's just...scary to give up control."

"I hear you!" Pops replied. "I remember feeling much the same way my first summer here, wondering how I could possibly let go of my own steering wheel and let God direct my future paths."

"So how did you overcome those fears and hesitations?" asked Ephraim.

"Putting your trust in an unseen power—I suppose it's different for everyone, isn't it? But you can't know until you try—until put your trust in God that as long as you do your part, He'll do his."

"That's the first lesson of the farm, isn't it?" Sonja mused. "Except the Lord build the house, they labor in vain that build it."

"Yes," Pops said with a warm smile. "You've probably noticed that that keeps coming up, as important truths always do. Mom and I know from personal experience, and from watching hundreds of kids like you over the years, that things change in miraculous ways when reverence turns into faith and trust. Until then, we are left to our own devices to try and figure things out and make the most of what we've got."

"So, you expect us to just pick up our lives and drop it all into God's hands, and what…wait for magic to happen?" James asked.

Pops laughed. "Not at all, James. First off, Mom and I have no expectations. We'll admit that we *hope* you'll accept our invitation to get to know God better, but as Mom is keen to say, what you do with what you learn here is entirely up to you. And second, it sounds like I need to make it clear that Mom and I are not at all suggesting that dropping everything in God's hands is the answer to anything. Where's the learning, growth and understanding in a response like that?"

"So what are you suggesting then?" James replied.

"We're suggesting that God is interested in partnering with you to create your house," Ruby responded. "There's a big difference in building a house in a partnership and just turning things over entirely to a contractor to make all the decisions. If you partner with God, He expects you to work along side Him. He expects you to show up and give it your best self everyday, to be all in—your intellect, your heart, your passion, your personality—everything. If you're humble enough to let Him, He'll help you identify both your strengths and your weaknesses. And if you'll invite Him to offer suggestions and work with what you've got, He can help you turn your weaknesses into strengths."

"I don't know…it sound's too…easy," James admitted.

"Then forgive me," said Ruby. "From the moment you decide to let God be your partner in building your house, life will never be same. From the demolition of your old, sorry attempts, to digging a new foundation, to building up walls and cutting in windows, through all the fixtures and details—it's work. It's work, and change, and sacrifice, and if there's an easy part, I wouldn't know what it was."

"I don't know either," Pops admitted. "But when compared to the endless, unproductive attempts and disasters that come of building a house with no foundation and crooked lumber…maybe the hard way is actually the easy way. I don't know of anyone who's opted for the foundationless plan and ever found it easy in the end. Do you?"

James squirmed, looking uncomfortable.

"I never really thought of it that way," Matt said, "but I can't think of anybody who's taken the shortcut and found much happiness either. I used to believe that wealth could make things easier and provide an accelerated path to happiness, but it doesn't take any more than a stroll past the newsstand to see that those with money aren't without their challenges."

"No, they certainly aren't," Ruby confirmed. "Over my nearly hundred years I've wondered many times about the fairness of life. Of course, there isn't any, as I'm sure you're all aware. You can choose be angry about that, but anger and bitterness will only consume precious energy and do nothing to make things better. Too many folks waste valuable time worrying about who's who and how the grass appears to be greener across the valley or even on the other side of the world. The truth is, we've only got one life—one chance to make this time as awesome as possible, and there ain't no sense in wasting even a minute of it on the bullpucky you can't control or the hogwash that has no relevance to your life. We each are capable of great things, but it all has to start by getting your own house in order. Spend your time and energy in your own gardens, pulling your own weeds, and then go lift the world."

"Well said, Mom," Pops declared.

"Darn tootin'! Ultimately, there's only one person in the entire universe that you can control or change. There are plenty of good ways to influence others in positive directions—primarily with encouragement and love, and through leading by example. But everyone has their choice what they'll decide to do with any of it. That's one of the least understood realities in the world today: choice and accountability. Too many folks from y'alls generation have been sheltered from the natural consequences of their own choices by well-meaning but misguided parents and society at large. Despite the good intentions of many parents, sheltering their children from the natural consequences of their own choices only robs them of the wisdom which may come as they learn to better navigate their lives. If we're allowed to be fully accountable we soon learn for ourselves which is sweet and which is bitter."

"That's how things changed for me," Greg responded. "My addictions and my stupid choices eventually alienated all of my friends and every member of my family except for my mother. It was only when I began to see how my choices were killing her—after all she'd been through to help me—that was my rock bottom."

"Rock bottom is a fine place to begin building a new foundation," Pops replied.

Greg nodded, thoughtfully.

"Until we decide to be accountable for our choices, to learn to decipher the bitter from the sweet consequences of our choices, and determine to seek the sweet, joy will remain elusive." Ruby declared. "Alcoholics and drug addicts hide from consequences by staying drunk or stoned. Shirkers and rascals attempt to avoid work and accountability by borrowing money from friends and hiding from bill collectors. Masterminds of Ponzi schemes attempt to avoid accountability by continuing to fudge records and telling lies that even they begin to believe. But sooner or later the bill is called due, the bubble bursts, and the piper expects to be paid, exacting his toll from somewhere that will always hurt, especially when it's been dodged or procrastinated for any significant length of time. Even the most loyal drinking buddies and unscrupulous lawyers will abandon you when the money's all gone and the party is over. But sometimes being left alone with your own conscience is the best impetus for change. It invites reflection in ways few things can."

Many of the campers nodded thoughtfully.

"As you know, Pops and I don't have any kids of our own, but we've watched closely and taken careful notes as we've watched fifty-five graduating classes leave the farm to pursue the creation of their own families. Many of the children of our first classes now have grandchildren of their own. Time marches quickly, and from our observations, joy always favors those who focus their efforts on making their world brighter, happier, kinder, and more compassionate. If you'll choose that course, you'll discover that people of all ages will seek your companionship, and the sun will always warm your face as the shadows fall behind."

"That's what you and Pops have created here, isn't it?" Susan suggested.

Ruby shook her head, but smiled. "To some it is given to create. To others it is given to nurture that which has been created. Pops and I inherited much of this, and our hope has been from the beginning that when it's our turn to pass it on it will be at least as steeped in joy as it was when it came into our keeping.

"If the light you gather this summer is to do you any good in your world back home, it must be given room to shine. Just as a candle gains strength and resilience when it's surrounded by other candles, you'll need to surround yourself with others who'll stand by you and support you, people you can trust to help shelter you from the wind, people with whom you can be mutually encouraging and supporting when your lights are threatened by life's doubts and fears."

"I don't think I know any people in my world that could be mutually supportive of any of this kind of stuff," James spoke solemnly.

Ruby nodded. "We thought that may be case when we read your application. And yet we also sensed within you a desire to gain a greater light."

James pursed his lips before nodding slowly.

"We heard your heartsong, James," Pops responded sympathetically. "It cried out above a din of doubts and fears. That's why you're here. That's why we chose you."

James looked at Pops and Ruby as if he were searching for any hint in sarcasm or insincerity. When he couldn't find it, he looked down at his hands. Crystal and Holly responded, simultaneously reaching out to touch his arms as James exhaled loudly, this breath mixed with a torrent of emotions too big for him to control or hide. As tears began to roll down his cheeks, the other campers gathered around him in a tight, awkward huddle, embracing this often loud and obnoxious brute who'd made life difficult for each of them. They held onto him for a long moment until he spoke.

"I can't breath," James uttered, drawing laughter and bringing an end to the huddle.

The campers returned to their seats, and James wiped his tears, looking embarrassed.

"I hope you all know you've all blown my decorum," he said, trying to laugh as tears continued to flow.

"Hallelujah!" Ruby responded. "We've been waiting for this day since we first read your application. We're glad you're here, James. We're glad you came."

CHAPTER III

Harmony and Duct Tape

Free will, though it makes evil possible, is also the only thing that
makes possible any love or goodness or joy worth having.
—C.S. Lewis

Sleep was slow in coming for Genevieve. Her mind continued to circle around the evening's conversation. There was something there, something big that had happened. With more than mild shock she'd watched the tears flow down James's cheeks. Tears. Real tears!

Big, fat, ugly tears. But she had to admit it had also been strangely and uniquely beautiful. Somehow the farm and an untold number of unidentified elements had conspired to soften the heartless James to the point that real tears had dripped freely from the hard head of one of the most difficult men she'd ever encountered.

There was something about those tears that seemed to surprise everyone present; everyone, that is, except Ruby and Lorenzo. Genevieve had caught a glance of the old couple's faces as the campers broke from their awkward group hug. It was only a second, really only a peep that was quickly obscured as the campers shuffled about, finding their seats again. But that peep had burned an indelible image on Genevieve's memory. In that quick glance she had seen light, almost like the halo around a photographic negative. The porch was otherwise dimly lit; night having fallen as they'd been talking. But in that dimness the old couple's faces had shone with light. She couldn't remember if they'd been smiling or not. But they were definitely surrounded by a peaceful aura and an undeniable radiance.

As Genevieve stared up at the stars through the skylight, now several hours later, many other images paraded through her head. There was the crushed bike at the top of the drive surrounded by white dust—the last of the fifty pound sack of flour that James had biked into town to buy when he had refused to work with Crystal. And Genevieve couldn't help but smile to herself when she remembered the gargoyle-like expression on James's face when he'd chased her around the laundry shack as he cussed and yelled and did his best to hurl soggy laundry in her direction. But there was also the memory of the fear she'd felt at his unmistakable anger, the bulging veins on his face and neck as he'd confronted Ruby on the front porch, demanding that he be released from his summer contract. It would have been impossible for any of the campers not to recognize that James had a short fuse and was quite possibly disturbed in addition to being a bigheaded jerk, a tyrant, and a bully. He'd made life difficult for all of them, not the least of whom was Ruby.

But Genevieve couldn't deny that things had changed dramatically over the past two weeks. James was still mouthy and cynical, and had continued his futile attempts to ruffle feathers with his contrary provocations; provocations which had repeatedly fallen flat, ignored by Ruby and Pops and an increasing number of the campers. And as his attempts to arouse contention had increasingly been ignored, James had begun to lose his nerve. Somehow in the last week as he'd worked in the kitchen with Crystal, most of his spit and venom had become diluted to the point that it had lost its sting.

Retracing her memories from the evening's conversation, Genevieve tried to remember the words Ruby and Pops had spoken, the words that seemed to have served as the pivot point for James's emotional breakdown—or breakthrough. There'd been something said about his application that had caught her attention, a word Genevieve had never heard and could only guess its meaning: heartsong. His heartsong, they'd implied, had convinced them that he needed to be here this summer.

Despite her first dozen negative interactions with James and the ugliness he'd espoused among all the campers, something big had changed that evening for all of them. As she considered their collective and rapid dramatic transformation towards James, Genevieve was surprised by a feeling of guilt for the negative emotions she'd been silently harboring toward him. He'd been a jerk. A brute. A sexist, egotistical, arrogant, unpredictable wild card. She'd never really asked herself why he was the way he was. It had been far easier to label him a heartless jerk and write him off. But what if she'd missed something? What if they all had? What if this heartsong thing was legit and the stoney-hearted porcupine had only been protecting a soft, vulnerable underbelly?

As she listened to the soft breathing of her sleeping bunkmates, Genevieve found herself wondering what she would do if she were the matchmaker of Niederbipp and James's application arrived for her consideration. Would she be able to see through his prickly exterior and recognize his heartsong—*whatever that was*? Could she see past his obvious flaws and imagine him as a sensitive and eligible bachelor, or better yet, a kind and doting husband? Bringing it even closer to home, could she ever take the risk of lining him up with any her girlfriends without fearing for their sanity—or even their lives? How did Ruby do it? How did she make these choices? How did she make sense of any of this? But she *had* made sense of it. Several hundred successful marriages had stemmed from her efforts here on Harmony Hill. And in order to do that, she not only had to make sense of it for herself, she had to convince twelve new campers every year that they could make sense of it.

Thinking about her fellow campers, Genevieve recognized them all as strugglers in their own way; odd, quirky, flawed. She couldn't imagine any of the men or their female counterparts being natural or obvious fits for each other. Even Crystal and James, who'd expressed an interest in each other, seemed like an impossible pairing of attitudes and character flaws. And she struggled to imagine how Ruby, such a simple woman, could see anything in any of them that prompted her to choose them over the hundreds of other applicants. If these campers truly represented the best of hundreds of applicants, what did the rest of the applicants look like? Who had been left out so these weirdos could be here this summer?

 Her thoughts came back around to James. What had happened to him? One minute he was playing it tough, and the next he was a blubbering mess. It felt so out of character for the rigid, heartless persona he'd worked so hard to maintain. But it wasn't just James who had cracked. His tears had triggered some strange, innate sense of compassion in all of them. Even Genevieve had felt it.

Confused by her reaction, she asked herself why she'd felt compelled to embrace him. She'd done so before, just two weeks earlier at the phone booth when he was spouting off, threatening to sue Ruby and jump ship. But this time the others had done so too. It had been so spontaneous, but also intriguingly inclusive—all of them apparently feeling the same primal urge to connect in a platonic yet intimate way; to comfort and reassure the same guy who'd made life difficult for all of them. Why? She couldn't remember ever feeling that way.

Over the last eight years she'd been exposed the plenty of tears.

The fashion industry was often heartless, and though the models and designers she'd rubbed shoulders with were generally unsentimental and professional, tears were not uncommonly seen backstage. But she'd never once felt an urge to embrace any of those emotional strugglers. As she thought about it, Genevieve wondered if her concerns for professionalism and objectivity might have jaded and clouded her humanity. Had that professionalism served her in the same way as James's decorum served him, keeping each of them aloof, apathetic, even callous to the needs and emotions of others? It didn't take her long, pondering this question, for her to begin to wonder if she was slipping. Was she too close to her subjects on this story to be fully objective? Was it even possible to write about any of this while being imbedded in the middle of it and still maintain any sense of professionalism or objectivity?

But her questions continued to come back to James. The evening's conversation left her with the sense that Ruby and Lorenzo's choice to invite James to come this summer had been somehow inspired, a strange, extraordinary part of some master plan. But still Genevieve wrestled with the cold reality that if the choice for this year's team had been up to her, she undoubtedly would have rejected him. She didn't like trouble, and the idea of taking on any more than was necessary seemed like a really stupid idea. Life was already hard enough without having to deal with a selfish, cantankerous, pigheaded lawyer. And yet Ruby had also accepted Crystal, and Spencer...and her.

But why? What did Ruby have to gain from any of this? Surely hiring out the labor that needed to be done would be ultimately cheaper and far less hassle than taking on twelve soft-handed ignoramuses and training them to work the farm. What were she and Pops getting out of this? There was no money exchanged for their services. There was no social media fame or influencer status that was motivating them or stroking their pride. And there was certainly no reason to believe a sense of duty motivated them to keep this up, year after year, decade after decade, occupying all of their golden years with what surely must be endless headaches. But after exhausting all other potential motivations, in the wee hours of the morning, Genevieve's reluctant mind fell on the last possible motivator—love.

Love? Could that really be it? Could love motivate a couple to give up fifty-six years to helping strangers find happiness in marriage? Could love possibly be enough to keep them going through so many painfully difficult times, watching patiently as each of the hundreds of campers they had invited to the farm struggled through their own unique challenges and quirks? But it wasn't just a reprieve to their individual challenges and quirks that Pops and Ruby were offering their campers. They were offering time-proven secrets to happy marriages and happy lives. They were offering a trail map to uncommon treasure. They were offering an understanding of the keys of joy, as well as day-to-day coaching for each camper who progressed toward that distant reward. Was love enough of a motivator to keep two people who were older than dirt anxiously engaged and interested in spreading hope to yet one more generation of young people?

The idea that love had that much motivational power felt absurd to Genevieve, and yet from all that she had learned over the previous weeks, love, she knew, was the only possible answer. How many times had she heard Pops's explanation of the first and the last keys? As she thought about it she realized they'd been dropping clues to their motivation since the very beginning. Reverence and charity—the love of God and the love of humankind. They weren't just teaching the precepts of joy—they were living them. And their lives, their happiness and contentment, and the unity and strength of their marriage were all billboards for love's power when applied to every aspect of a life well lived. Why had it taken her so long to see it?

Somehow sleep came, but it didn't last long. What felt like only ten minutes after finally closing her eyes, the rooster's crow welcomed the new day. Tired but strangely motivated by the night's epiphany, Genevieve rose from her bed and made her way to the bathroom to splash water on her face.

Staring at her own wet face in the mirror, she felt like she was looking into the face of a stranger. The highlights in her hair had had three weeks to grow out and fade, leaving nearly a half inch of darker colored roots. It had been more than a decade since she'd seen this much of her natural brunette color, her regularly scheduled appointment at the salon had made sure of that. Her nose and eyes were no longer swollen, but the small freckles she'd been trying to conceal since she was an early teens appeared to have been growing in both numbers and hue, having been kissed by the same sun which had darkened all of her exposed skin by many shades. It had been so long since she'd gone anywhere without putting on her face, even to the gym, that she'd somehow forgotten what her natural, unadorned face looked like. It wasn't exactly scary, just new and different. But as she stared into her own green eyes, almost an emerald color against her tanned skin, she was surprised by the strange sense of confidence she felt.

"Write it on your heart that today is the best day of the year!" Holly said as she approached the sink next to Genevieve.

"Huh?"

Holly pointed to the note taped to the upper corner of the mirror.

Genevieve read it before nodding. "It seems like you've taken that to heart."

"I hope I have. How about you?"

She looked again at her own reflection, offering herself a smile. "I'm working on it."

Remembering that she'd been assigned to kitchen duty for the first time in more than two weeks, Genevieve realized that if she hurried she might have a chance to chat privately with Ruby without any interruptions. She dressed quickly and rushed to the big house, almost in a jog. Dropping her muckers at the back door, she glided silently over the dining hall floor in her hand-knit socks, trying to locate the source of the faint and garbled conversation. The kitchen was empty, but she could hear Pop's voice coming from somewhere near the front of the house. The big front door was open and the screen door whistled softly as a morning breeze passed through it.

She approached the porch, expecting to find her elderly hosts there, but her attention was quickly diverted to the library, Pop's gentle voice filling that space with a calm and gentle sense of reverence. Genevieve paused quietly at the door and looked in, finding the old couple kneeling on the rug-draped floor, their heads bowed across from each other, and their elbows resting on the old, leather ottoman on which their clasped hands rested.

Feeling like a voyeuristic interloper, she bowed her head, listening to Pop's words as he thanked God for another day to live and love. He prayed for each of the campers, naming them by name, praying that they might learn to know the love God had for each of them. And with emotion hanging from his gentle words, Pops prayed for Ruby, that she'd be able to endure the challenges of her cancer with grace and strength, that she wouldn't have to suffer, and that her concerns and prayers would be met with answers and opportunities.

As he concluded, Genevieve watched as they both leaned forward and kissed each other. She'd seen them kiss before, but not like this. In spite of their age there was a tender yet passionate connection between them, leaving Genevieve in the strange position of feeling like an inspired intruder. She shifted her weight and immediately wished she'd held still, the oak floorboards creaking beneath her.

Pops looked up and smiled. "I thought I heard someone. Please, come in."

"I didn't mean to disturb you. I'm sorry."

"Nonsense," Ruby said, moving her body until she sat on the ottoman, facing her. "What can we do for you?"

"I...uh...I didn't sleep very well last night."

"Oh, that's too bad. Did you have a mosquito in your room? It is the season for those things, you know. It's amazing how much disturbance one little insect can ..."

"It wasn't a mosquito."

"No?"

"No, I was thinking about you."

"*Me?*" Ruby asked, looking concerned.

"You and Pops both, actually."

"Sounds serious. Is everything okay?"

"Yes, it's just that I found myself wondering what would motivate you to spend fifty-six summers trying to help hundreds of ungrateful campers."

"Oh. And what have you come up with?" Ruby asked with a coy smile.

"Well, the only thing that makes any sense is...love. There's obviously no money in this, and no fame. And I can't imagine you having any joy in this if duty were your only motivation. I feel like you do this because of love. Am I right?"

Ruby turned to look at Pops, reaching for his hand. He struggled to get to his feet before walking around to the other side of the ottoman, sitting down next to Ruby.

"Would you like to sit down?" he asked, pointing to the adjacent craftsman-style chair with soft leather cushions.

She moved across the creaky floor sitting down in front of them.

"Tell us," Pops said when she was comfortable. "What prompted this question?"

Genevieve took a deep breath, looking up into their kind eyes. "I guess it was...James. I feel like I'm at a loss for understanding what happened last night."

"You were there. You witnessed what happened. What more can we tell you?" asked Ruby

"Yeah, I saw it happen, but I don't understand it. It was like he... broke...right there in front of everyone. He broke wide open. I never would have guessed he even had a heart, let alone a soul. But there he was...about as emotionally exposed as you can get."

"It was beautiful, wasn't it?" Pops asked.

"Well, yeah, in a strange and surprising sort of awkward way. How did you know that was even in there?"

Ruby leaned forward, taking Genevieve's hands in hers. "Pops and

I learned many years ago that everyone has a soul, even though some may be difficult to find. What happened last night happens every year in one way or another. It's one of those quiet miracles of the farm. You don't always know when it's coming, so you have to be ready for it when it happens."

"But...I guess *that's* my question. What happened?"

Pops chuckled. "Love happened. Like Mom said, it happens every year. Some feel the love and recognize what is it is right away. Others discover it as they sit on the benches, minding their own business, and suddenly come to the realization that love has been there all a long, waiting for them to open their eyes and see it. And then there are kids like James, kids with a chip on their shoulders who've been working their whole lives to try and avoid love's light."

"But...I don't understand why anyone would want to avoid that."

"That's because you know what love is," Ruby suggested. "Sure, it may be a different kind of love than you've been experiencing here, but somewhere along the way you had someone love you—love you for who you are, or who you were at that time. There's a sense of joy that comes from experiences like that. And that joy finds it way deep into your soul where it waits, hopefully, for another dose of love and light."

Genevieve nodded, but looked confused. "Does that have anything to do with...what did you call it? Heartsong?"

Ruby nodded.

"So what was it about James's heartsong that caused you to invite him here this summer?"

Ruby glanced at Lorenzo before turning her kind eyes back to Genevieve. "I believe you already know that we received more than eight hundred applications to spend this summer on the farm."

"Yes, that's why I'm confused."

"Tell me what's bothering you."

"Well, if he's the best of the applicants, how terribly awful are the worst?"

Lorenzo laughed. "I think maybe you're looking at it the wrong way."

"Then please, tell me how I should be looking at it."

Pops nodded, looking thoughtful. "Sending rejection letters is one of the worst parts of our jobs. For every acceptance letter we sent this year we had to send nearly seventy letters that we knew would be met with disappointment. Because of this, we spend a lot of time reading the applications and praying, weighing things out in both our heads and our hearts, not only searching for those we know need to be here, but figuring out how to encourage those we have to turn away."

"Wait, are you saying you send letters of encouragement to everyone you reject?"

"Every one," Ruby confirmed. "It takes us the better part of the month to handwrite a meaningful letter to every man and woman who applied to be here. Some years require more work than others. This year was a big one."

"But why? That's so much work. I don't remember the last time I wrote a letter by hand, let alone eight hundred of them."

"Yes, it is a lot of work. But even though we can't bring all those kids to the farm for the summer, that doesn't mean we don't want to help them. Greg applied three years in a row. The fact that he did proves that our long-handed approach helps at least a few of those who don't make it in their first try. Like many other letters we've written in the past, we offered Greg a few suggestion and encouraged him to apply again once he'd taken those suggestions to heart."

"We had one young woman apply five years in a row before we finally felt she was ready," Pops reported.

"Okay, so, I guess that's part of my confusion. You rejected Greg two years in a row, but you accepted James his first time? Why? What does he have that Greg didn't have? And for that matter, what does Spencer have that Greg doesn't?"

"That's hard to say," Ruby admitted. "We've learned to trust our gut. Some things like consumer debt and addictions are quick disqualifiers.

We've never felt like it's fair to bring someone here for the summer who hasn't learned to control his or her spending, or whose habits would make it difficult for them and their future spouse to find success in marriage. Drugs, gambling, pornography—those are all challenges we encourage folks to be rid of before they come here. We can do a lot in five months, but we can't take an addict and turn him into the perfect candidate for a successful marriage if he hasn't learned to control his appetites. We've got bigger fish to fry than having to drop what we're doing on the farm to pick kids up along the highway from here all the way to Tionesta."

"Uh, I'm sorry about that. I…obviously didn't think that through."

"You weren't the first, and it's doubtful you'll be the last," Pops said with a wry smile. "If there ever was a perfect kid who came to the farm, it was long before our time. Everyone who comes here is working on something."

"Or they find out very quickly they *need* to be working on something," Ruby added. "Our job, we learned early on, is to set you kids free in green pastures and encourage you to ask the right questions so God can help you become the men and women and future marriage partners you can be."

Genevieve nodded, but she felt confused.

"We didn't answer your question, did we, dear?" Ruby asked.

"No…well, not exactly. I guess I still don't understand what you saw in James that made you know that all of his baggage and difficult attitudes would somehow be worth it."

The old couple looked at each other before turning back to Genevieve.

"It sounds as though you may have discovered your foetidum mediis soccus?" Pops said with a smile.

"My what?"

"Your foetidum mediis soccus. It's an ancient Latin term. You've never heard of it?"

"Uh, I don't think so, and it's been way too long since my last Latin class to even give it an educated guess. Can you say it again?"

"Foetidum mediis soccus," Pops said with an exaggerated accent that made Genevieve smile.

"What does it mean?"

"Literally translated, it means *stinky sock*."

"What?"

"Yep," Ruby confirmed. "Stinky sock. It sounds like you found yours."

"I'm not even sure what that means."

"It means you found the fly in your Jell-O, the rabbit in your arugula, or, my personal favorite, you've found a louse in your armpit hair."

Genevieve looked more confused than ever. "Uh, yeah, all of those things sound like unpleasant things."

"They can be if you'll let them. A stinky sock is never a pleasant thing, is it?" Ruby asked.

"Well, no."

"Of course not. You've been around here long enough to know that we collectively produce at least twenty-eight stinky socks each and every day. That makes for a whole lotta stink. That's why we do the laundry every day—except Sunday—and hang them out to dry where the sun and the breeze have a chance to carry off whatever stink might remain after the soap suds and Big Bertha have had a chance to neutralize things."

"Okay. But what does that have to do with Jell-O, or arugula...or armpits?

"It depends." Pops replied

"On what?"

"On what you're looking for," said Ruby. "If you're looking for answers and solutions to your questions or problems then you know that moaning about stinky socks will not do any more to change your situation than complaining about the fly in your Jello, or the rabbits in your arugula, or even the lice in your armpit."

Genevieve nodded slowly, but she still looked confused. "I'm not sure if I follow."

"I'll give you a hint," Ruby said. "How do you keep a rabbit out of your arugula?"

"Uh, maybe put up a better fence?"

"And what about flies in your Jell-O?"

"Well, I try not to eat Jell-O, but I'd guess that putting a cover on it and storing it in the fridge might help."

"Not a bad idea. And what about the lice?"

"That sounds dreadful, but I suppose that if you shaved your hair, the lice wouldn't have any place to hide."

Ruby nodded at Genevieve as she turned to Pops. "That's three out of three. Do you think she's ready?"

"There's only one way to find out," Pops said.

"Ready for what?" asked Genevieve.

"The most important question of the day."

"Uh, I'll give it my best shot."

"Very well. I'll need you to close your eyes for this one and try to imagine the scenario."

Genevieve nodded, closing her eyes.

"So this problem is a tough one. I'd like you to imagine for me that you've thrown a birthday party for your eight year-old nephew. All the guests have begun arriving when you notice one little boy is having a bad day. He's angry and upset and doesn't want to participate in the all the fun and games, choosing instead to hide behind the garbage cans on the side of the house. You let it go for a little bit, letting him have his space, but before long you begin to wonder if this little boy is trying to sabotage the whole party. You just caught him a with pocketknife, trying to cut a hole in the side of the bounce house. And the next thing you know, he's licked the frosting off of four of the cupcakes. You try to talk to him plainly, try to get him involved and direct his attention in a more positive direction, but it only gets worse when you discover some of your nephew's gifts have already been unwrapped and tossed behind the garbage cans. What do you do?"

Genevieve furrowed her brow, her eyes still closed. "Oh, man, that's a tough one. He's too young to call the police, right?"

"Yes, quite. This is a problem you're going to have to solve yourself."

"You mean I can't call his mom to come pick him up?"

"No, I should have mentioned that earlier. His mom dropped him off on her way to work, and his father recently abandoned the family and has been missing in action ever since. His siblings are all away, and his grandparents live in New Mexico. It's all up to you. Go."

Genevieve pressed her eyes even tighter together as she shook her head. "This is an impossible scenario."

"Yes, but, it's your nephew's party, and you don't want to disappoint him or any of your other guests. Somehow you've got to get him on board so he doesn't torpedo the whole experience for everyone. Time is of the essence. The next activity is making tie dye T-shirts, and after that the kids will be swimming. I don't want to put any extra pressure on you, but if you don't figure out a solution, I'm afraid there will be a dozen screaming kids, covered in bright dye, drowning in the pool. "

Genevieve's mind raced as her palms began to sweat. "Oh man, I'm really bad at this, and I'm afraid of children. What am I supposed to do?"

"I'm not sure, but it seems critical that you do something, and soon."

"Uhhh…can I use duct tape?"

Ruby snickered. "Nope. No children may be harmed or restrained in the calming of this situation."

"Can you give me a hint?" She asked, opening one eye slightly.

"Well, if I were you, I would draw on your knowledge of what you've learned in the last few weeks on the farm."

Genevieve pressed her eyelids together tightly, focusing all her effort as she imagined the growing storm of a dozen hyperactive children and one rogue misfit who has the ability to ruin the fun for everyone. It seemed so unfair. Why did she have to deal with this? Who put her in charge of this party? And who decided duct tape couldn't be employed to help even the playing field? She tried to push those thoughts out of her head, knowing they would not help her, trying to open her mind instead to the lessons she'd learned on the farm. And suddenly in the darkness, almost like a distant light at the end of a tunnel, there was a glimmering bit of hope. It grew brighter as she imagined a scenario in which she could somehow trick—or better yet convince—the little boy that she needed his help.

He seemed surprisingly willing, ready to be helpful with a long list of things that needed to be done; handing out rubber bands for the tie dye, helping the other kids put on their plastic aprons, gathering up the pool toys.

"He needs to be needed." Genevieve said softly after she'd compared the idea to the things she'd learned from her first few weeks on the farm.

"Not a bad place to start. I can imagine him finding that amusing for at least a few minutes. What else does he need to keep him from burning the place down?"

"Oh, uh…he needs to hear that he's doing a good job."

"Praise and even gratitude will go a long way in helping him feel like he's a part of the party. What else?"

Again Genevieve turned her thoughts inward, considering the keys of joy. "Uh, this doesn't seem like a really great time to try to teach him anything about either reverence or hope considering everything that's going on, but maybe…charity?" Somehow the light grew even brighter in her mind as she mentioned it.

"That feels like a positive direction. What can you tell us about that?" Ruby encouraged.

"He…he's just been dumped by his father, and his mother…she's probably too busy working and trying to pick up the pieces to give him much of her time. He's got to feel abandoned and lonely. Maybe… maybe its not that he's a bad kid…maybe he's just acting out, crying out for attention. Maybe he just needs…maybe he just needs to be loved."

She took a deep breath, filling her lungs as her vision was suddenly drenched with light. She smiled to herself as she opened her eyes, finding smiles on the faces of her elderly hosts.

"You found it," Pops replied.

"What did I find?" Genevieve asked, wanting to make sure she hadn't missed anything.

"You found the master answer."

"The *master* answer?"

Pops nodded. "The answer upon which all correct and true answers are based. The answer to which all other answers should be compared."

Genevieve nodded slowly, thoughtfully.

"You can look at James—or Spencer, or Crystal or any of the others—as the stinky sock—the problem—the annoyance," Ruby suggested. "Or you can look for the answer instead. But you really can't do both. James is a tough one. We knew he would be. But each of you learned something last night—an answer to all of the Jameses you'll ever encounter. There are countless ways to deal with the Jameses in your life—avoidance, shunning, *perhaps even duct tape*. But there are better ways. And the best way will always include a generous application of love."

Genevieve nodded again as lights continued turning on inside her head and heart. "It was the same for me, wasn't it?"

"The details were different, of course," Ruby responded, "but the answer was the same. Each of you required some tenderizing before you could see or feel the love. But when the time was right and the questions were sincere—when you were willing to sacrifice what you were for a hope in what you could become—magic happened."

Genevieve shook her head. "I didn't understand why you could let someone like him...someone who threatened to blow this all apart... why you would bring him here on purpose."

Ruby smiled kindly. "Not one of us is without the ability to blow it all apart, Genevieve. We each wrestle with our own wolves. Some are just louder and more ferocious than others. I was the James of my year."

"You?" Genevieve asked in disbelief.

"Oh, we all took our turns as each camper does in their own way. But I was the one who was poking the inflatable bounce house and threatening to ruin the party for everyone. I was the prickly porcupine trying fiercely to protect my soft, vulnerable underbelly. Yes, the details are different. But if the only kids who ever came to the farm were the easy ones, the Matts or the Hollys, what a terribly unhelpful, predictable, and unfruitful farm this would be."

"Ruby and I were taught by the Smurthwaites that we should seek for balance in the personalities and histories of the campers we bring to Harmony Hill," Pops inserted. "It took us a couple of years to understand what they meant. In hoping to make life easy for ourselves in those early years, we probably accepted too many folks who were polished and refined, and not enough of those who were humble enough to know they still had work to do; and the work suffered. Many people believe they'll be happy if they can marry the perfect, refined, polished spouse. Many of those wait in vain to meet that person. The fact is that we need each other, our strengths and our weaknesses, to complement and encourage and refine us."

"And to bring us down or lift us up as needs be, and make us all both a little more tolerant and tolerable," Ruby added. "There are many virtues that can inspire a person to change for the better: humility, patience, kindness, reverence, and compassion to name a few. But none of these have the same power as love. James's journey, like yours, and like every camper who came here this summer, is far from over. And there are still many wolves who need both feeding and taming. But if you'll choose love, Genevieve; if you'll choose it first and often in all your interactions with these crazy kids, and everyone you meet along your journey, things will be good for you. Change will happen, both within and without. Your first reactions will turn away from duct tape, apathy and enmity, and lead you toward harmony, understanding, mutual respect and charity."

"That sounds really good, but also…impossible," she admitted.

"Without a little help, you're right," Pops concurred.

"Yeah, I mean…how?"

Ruby leaned forward, taking Genevieve's hands in her own before looking deeply into her eyes. "There's only one source of miracles. And it's really quite a waste of time talking to anyone but the miracle maker."

Genevieve nodded solemnly. "That's what you were doing when I came in, isn't it?"

The old woman smiled and nodded. "Pops and I have made it our habit and tradition to spend the best part of the first hour of every day right here, balancing the world."

"You mean like the Ebenezer?" she asked, connecting the dots.

Pops nodded. "I continue to stack those stones every time they fall as a personal practice of patience and self-discipline. But the real balancing of my world—of *our* world—happens here, together, as we counsel with God and with each other." He held his hands up, forming a triangle with fingers touching fingers and thumbs touching thumbs. "All things that balance rely on three points of contact."

Genevieve nodded. "Like hope, charity and reverence, right? And the milking stools, and like the triangle around the Ebenezer down behind the milking barn?"

Pops nodded again. "And like the yoke that hangs over the dining table."

Genevieve thought about it for a moment before nodding.

"When a man and a woman come together and commit to form a marriage," Pops continued, "and they invite God to be a part of their union, a beautiful balance is created, offering happiness, stability and joy. If marriage partners will continue to strengthen and nurture their union by continuing to nurture and strengthen each other, and by continuing to invite God to be a part of it, life's greatest joys will flow toward them, refreshing and renewing them with reverence, hope and charity. That's our hope for you, Genevieve. That's our hope for every camper who will ever come to Harmony Hill."

CHAPTER 112

Thomas's Bench

The one who plants trees, knowing that he will never sit in their shade, has at least started to understand the meaning of life.
—Rabindranath Tagore

There was a shift that occurred that morning as Genevieve got to work in the kitchen with Spencer. As they ground the wheat into flour, she shared with Spencer the things she'd been discussing with Pops and Ruby when he found them in the library.

Spencer, having witnessed the change in James the night before, was intrigued by what she shared with him and the power love had to generate change like that. Spencer in turn shared with her how the men had powwowed the night before at the bunkhouse, staying up late to discuss sensitive matters, memories and vulnerabilities, each of them sharing things that they'd never felt comfortable sharing before. As she listened, Genevieve was impressed by the change these events seemed to have triggered in Spencer, somehow reforming his attitude from one of sarcasm and cynicism into one of hope, humility and even respect.

They set no time records on the flour mill that morning, nor did they produce a breakfast that was exceptionally noteworthy. But they spoke with each other peaceably, respectfully and more friendly than they'd ever been able to manage. The fiascos of their outing to Tionesta and their difficult, inflamed assignment at the farm stand shortly thereafter were set aside and referenced only non-confrontationally as a mark of the things they'd each learned from these experiences.

Due to the warmth of the day, the bread dough rose more quickly than normal, enabling lunch to be served early. And when Ruby and Lorenzo encouraged the campers to spend some of their free time journaling or writing letters before the evening's activities, Genevieve was quick to respond, grabbing her journal and heading to the bench overlooking the orchard. Because her escape was swift, she was surprised when she came out of the woods to find the bench already occupied. Disappointed, she was about to turn around, hoping not to disturb its occupant, when the man on the bench turned to face her. Dressed in his typical black clothes, Thomas smiled at her, encouraging her to join him.

"I didn't expect to find you here."

"Well, I'm sorry to intrude on your space," Thomas apologized, standing and moving to the far end of the bench while motioning for her to take the other end. "Ruby and Lorenzo have been kind enough to let me use this bench from time to time when I'm working my way through my own thoughts."

"Then I should leave you in peace," Genevieve said, backing up.

"No, please, I insist," he said, motioning to the bench. "There are eleven other benches scattered across this farm, but this one has always been my favorite." He waited for her to sit down on the opposite end of the bench before sitting down himself. "There's something special about this one, isn't there?"

"I've felt the same way."

The older man nodded, looking out past the orchard to the river that cut its way through the Niederbipp valley. The bright blue sky was dotted with billowy, white clouds, casting their moving shadows on the woods and farmland below. "I've often wondered if this bench isn't the center of the universe," he mused. "Some of my best sermons have been inspired up here, as well as many of the best thinks I've ever thunk."

Genevieve smiled as she took in the beauty all around her, her mind and heart once again filling up with awe for this unique place. "Are you working on your sermon?" she asked, pointing to the small, black notebook sitting on the bench next to him.

"No," he said, patting the book. "Fortunately Jake agreed to cover tomorrow's sermon, giving me a chance to work on some of my own thoughts."

"Jake? T*he potter*?"

The old priest nodded.

"Is that something he does regularly?"

"Oh, I'd say probably at least once a year."

"So, like the florist, and the professor…and the mortician from last week?"

"That's right. There a many members of the community who take a turn at the lectern."

"But doesn't that cut into your pay?"

Thomas smiled. "It's been more than fifty years since I made my living as a paid cleric. There is no paid ministry in Niederbipp."

"But…" she looked at his dark shirt and pants, obviously confused.

"It's a long story," he said with a little laugh. "I may look like a priest, but after spending most of my life in Niederbipp I'm probably a much better Quaker than I am a Catholic. The town decided years before I got here that Sunday services would be something of a spiritual hybrid. Niederbipp, as you may know, was settled by Quakers, but many other religions and spiritual traditions have influenced our beliefs and ideology. It was decided many years ago that though we would focus our messages on Christian values, we would be open to the truths of other faiths as well."

"And you're not at all threatened by that?"

Thomas shook his head. "When we come to a place where we realize that there's far more that unites us than divides us, we can be better neighbors and citizens, more compassionate and inclusive. Reverence and charity becomes far easier to practice when we begin to see that there's really only one team. And instead of becoming distracted by the minutia that makes us different, we can choose to see each other as brothers and sisters in the family of God."

Genevieve nodded. "I guess I've never given any of that much thought, at least not before coming here. But you really believe it, don't you?"

He smiled. "There are always those who make you wonder, but we're all made of the same eternal stuff. And we've discovered that our lives and our community are far better and stronger when we are free to share the truths we hold dear. That's why we invite people of all stripes and walks of life to share the truths that resonate within their souls. And we invite the congregation to take home whatever new truths resonate within them. We know it's an unorthodox approach to worship, but I've found myself becoming a better listener, a better citizen of the world, and a better Christian than I ever was when my dogma closed the door on all different truths."

He turned and looked out at the glorious view before them before continuing. "So much is missed when we build of our hearts a fortress, and send away those truths who come knocking simply because they might look, smell or taste different than we're used to. I've come to the conclusion that God, in His infinite love and wisdom, distributes His truths among all people across the earth, and we cannot come to know Him without seeking and embracing the greatest truths that are scattered among us. Perhaps you'd like to give the sermon sometime?"

"Me?"

"Sure! I'm certain there would be things we could learn from you—truths you've discovered along your journey that could benefit all of us."

"Uh," she laughed nervously. "I'm sure I wouldn't even know where to begin."

"Well, if I may be so bold, I'd like to suggest that it all begins in your heart—those truth seeds that sprout and send out roots and branches, and eventually fruits. You may not recognize them for what they are at first, but they're the truths that offer you hope and vision, and inspire greatness within you. Those are the truths we look for when we ask folks to share their sermons. You wouldn't be the first of Ruby's recruits to share a message of hope and faith."

Genevieve laughed nervously. "I'll keep that in mind. I don't know if I've ever considered myself a person of faith."

"Until now?"

She looked at him, surprised to find him smiling.

"You've felt it, haven't you?" he said, pointing to her chest.

"What have I felt?"

"Oh, it goes by many different names, but there aren't many people who come to Niederbipp without feeling a sense of peace and warmth—regardless of the season the year or the presence of the sun."

"Then yes, I've felt it. Do you know what it is?"

"There's only one thing that can be so many things to so many different people and leave each of us feeling nourished, uplifted and inspired. You've experienced the love of God, manifested through the Holy Spirit."

"Are you sure?"

"Absolutely."

"How do you know it's not just…I don't know…some kind of cosmic vortex or transcendental mojo?"

Thomas chuckled. "I've heard it described in just those words many times before by people who are willing to admit they've experienced something mystical, but aren't yet ready to bring themselves to admit that there's a God. There are plenty of people who demand some sort of physical or scientific corroboration before they're willing to believe in the very things you've felt and experienced. Others might enjoy the mystery of it for a time, but leave it all behind in their pursuit of other things."

"So…what have you done with it?"

"I've done my best to become a student of it and pursue it, the best I can without scaring it away."

"*Scaring it away?*"

"Sure. Like many of the good things in life, the Holy Spirit is influenced by our patience and attitudes, and the rightness of our desires. We are all capable of catching glimpses of it as we go about our day if our eyes and hearts are open to it. I've discovered that chasing it like you might on an old-fashioned fox hunt has never been very productive— at least not for me. But I've also learned in recent years that if you'll simply be still and wait in watchful expectation, the Holy Spirit will light upon you like a butterfly, filling your heart and even your very soul with wonder and enlightenment."

"Be still and know that I am God," Genevieve spoke softly, running her thumb over the tile embedded in the backrest of the bench.

"Yes," Thomas said. "Of course in our noisy, busy world, stillness is usually the farthest thing from most people's minds. That's why every time I've found myself in need of stillness over the last few decades, I've been coming to this bench, and this farm."

"Uh, yeah…my experience with Niederbipp is obviously limited, but it seems like it's one of the *stillest* towns I've ever visited."

"Maybe, but not on a weekend when it's swarming with curious tourists. But even on the best days, it's difficult not to become distracted and forget to take the time to be still. There's something about turning my back to the noise and making the effort to ride—or push—my bike up Harmony Hill that opens my soul to inspiration. This is a magical place, you know?"

Genevieve nodded slowly. "I'm beginning to understand that."

"Yep, I've been watching the magic happen up here for more than fifty years now," Thomas admitted. "Kids who've never taken the chance the contemplate the things of God often find themselves confronting Him for either the first time ever, or for the first time in many years. I'm not sure if you can spend much time here without recognizing the hand of providence. And if you know what you're looking for, and know the right places to find it, this can be a beautiful place to rebalance your world."

"*Rebalance your world...*" Genevieve repeated thoughtfully. "That's what Ruby was just saying this morning about prayer...and what Pops called it when he was resetting the Ebenezer behind the cowshed."

"Yes, those are both beautiful ways to create and find balance," Thomas affirmed. "I believe there are probably innumerable other ways to find it."

"Like yoga?"

"Sure. And being outdoors, and attending church or synagog, and fasting, and serving others. With all of those things, when done in an effort to unify and harmonize our physical and spiritual selves, balance can be obtained.

"But it's so short-lived. At least that's the way it was for me and yoga. It felt like any balance I achieved wore off within a few blocks of the studio."

Thomas smiled and nodded. "That's why I come here at least once a week. It's why Lorenzo is quick to reset the Ebenezer every time if falls. It's why I pray daily and why I attend church services once a week. Balance is always in flux and rarely lasts for long. I've learned and relearned that truth over the course of my lifetime. Balance is both a physical and a spiritual game with a million moving parts, all of which have the ability to fall apart at any time if you're not constantly watchful and mindful, and even then there are plenty of surprises."

"It almost sounds like a lost cause."

"Yes, balance can certainly feel that way sometimes. But the joy one can experience during those moments of balance and peace—it can make you feel—however fleeting—that all is right with the world."

"And the next minute, everything falls apart and crumbles into a mess," Genevieve said, laughing.

Thomas smiled, nodding knowingly. "Sometimes it feels like that, doesn't it? But I've learned from my own experience, and from watching the lives of others over many years, that it's quite rare for *everything* to fall apart. Sure, things come lose from time to time, and they can certainly be unwieldy and unbalanced. But accepting Christ's invitation to build on His sure foundation keeps things from falling apart completely."

Genevieve sat silent for a moment, thoughtfully considering the older man's words. "So, that foundation…it's the three keys, right? Hope, charity and reverence?

"Can you think of a more sure foundation?" Thomas asked.

"You mean besides concrete and rebar?" she joked.

"Funny you should say that."

"Why?"

"Because it feels like it's basic human nature to turn away from many of life's simplest truths if they push against our pride or bruise our egos. But even the strength of concrete and rebar are limited if the ground they're built upon is in anyway unsteady. Without tapping into bedrock, even the world's finest building materials are of little consequence when subjected to life's biggest storms and negative forces. Without the bedrock foundation, all things, both physically and spiritually, fall apart."

CHAPTER 113

Gentle Persuasion

Neither family, nor privilege, nor wealth, nor anything but Love can light that beacon which a man must steer by when he sets out to live the better life.

— Plato

Thomas excused himself, and wandered back through the woods to find the farm's elderly hosts, leaving the bench that overlooked the orchard to Genevieve.

With her mind filled with inspiration from the morning's conversations, Genevieve set about recording in her journal the many things she'd been learning and experiencing. In the quiet of that special place, surrounded by beauty and stillness, she thought things she'd never "thunk" before. With nothing to distract her, and birdsong and the hum of the insects to serenade her, she quickly filled nearly seven pages with her thoughts and ideas before she remembered why she was there on the farm.

The article she'd been sent here to write loomed large on her mind. She set aside her journal and looked out at the valley below, wondering how what had once felt like the opportunity of a lifetime was beginning to feel like the heaviest burden she'd ever carried. In that moment she envied the other women who had little more to worry about over the next four months than the regular chore rotation. She, on the other hand had 10,000 words to write—words that would require more thought and meaning than anything she'd ever attempted to write in her life. And the more she learned about this farm, about Pops and Ruby, and about the keys of joy, the more intimidated she felt to even begin. But she also knew that continuing to put it off would only cause her more angst. She opened her journal again to a blank page and stared at it for at least five minutes, frozen, unable to proceed with even one word.

Somewhere in those five minutes, another question arose, one she hadn't asked herself, one that had the potential to change everything she was doing here. She mulled over the idea in her mind, trying to understand it in a way that made any sense. Why hadn't she thought of this before?

Julia had sent her here to do a story on Ruby. Sure, the farm was part of that and would certainly make for some great photos. But Ruby was the reason for all of this. She was the one with the secrets and the legacy. And Ruby was dying—the protagonist of her story, the heroine of her narrative—she was dying.

Julia was certainly aware of this by now, right? Genevieve tried to remember any mention of Ruby's imminent death in Julia's letter, but she couldn't remember anything that suggested Ruby had told her.

The story Genevieve had been sent here to write would make sense if the Ruby planned to be around for at least the next five to ten years, but would it make sense to publish this story if she were to pass away within months or even weeks of it going to press? What if, after reading the article, people were to head out to find Niederbipp and the magical farm on Harmony Hill? What would happen if instead of a vibrant farm, they found a distraught old man, the farm in shambles, and a fresh grave in the orchard? Genevieve knew that wouldn't be good press for Niederbipp, or the magazine, but it also wouldn't be good press for her as the writer. There would be rumors and slander, and things would go poorly and potentially get very messy. If she were going to go to all the trouble of enduring these five months, writing the longest, most compelling thing she'd ever written, it would only makes sense if the farm still had a resident matchmaker to uphold the legacy and tradition. Without it, these five months would be…

Genevieve shook her head, closing her journal, and suddenly felt ill. If this article were to have any relevance at all, there had to be a matchmaker on Harmony Hill. There simply had to be!

Ruby had offered her the top job, but the idea of taking over still remained completely preposterous. She didn't know any of this farming stuff, and she doubted she'd ever be ready to sort through hundreds of applications, accept twelve of them, and then teach them anything of any real value. Discouraged, she got up off the bench and wandered back toward the big house to begin dinner preparations.

With each step she took, the challenges before her felt increasingly daunting. Oblivious to the world around her, she slipped into a brain fog, walking right past Matt who sat on a bench, just ten feet from the trail that cut its way through the woods.

"Is it really that bad?" Matt asked, startling her. She jumped, dropping her journal. He sprung from the bench, picking up the fallen book as she caught her breath.

"Don't scare me like that!" she said firmly, slugging him in the shoulder.

He looked like he was trying not to laugh. "You look stressed," he replied, handing her the journal.

"What's it to you?"

He looked at her closely as if he were trying to read her. "I'm sorry. I didn't mean to frighten you. Do you want to sit down for a minute?"

She nodded, walking to the bench.

He moved his journal and encouraged her to sit. "Is everything okay?"

She forced a smile and shook her head. "I was actually having a pretty great day until ..."

"Don't tell me that all changed when I accidentally scared you?"

"No." She shook her head, but didn't speak for a moment.

He watched her closely, waiting.

"Do you ever feel like you have no idea what you're doing, where you're going...or even how you got here?"

Matt thought for a moment before shaking his head. "Never, actually."

She looked incredulous, causing him to laugh.

"Yes, all the time. In fact, those are probably three of most commonly asked question in my long list of existential conundrums. You're having one of those days, I take it?"

She shook her head, turning to face the woods. "Maybe."

"You're not sure?"

"Pffff. Why me? Why now? Why here?"

"Well, those are fairly broad questions, but if I had to guess, I'd say why *not* you? And *when* would the timing be *any better*? And I'd probably add that this place seems like as good a place as any. You've been considering Ruby's proposal, I take it?"

She looked surprised, but nodded. "I don't know how to do any of this, Matt. I'm a hot mess—a hot, clueless mess. Why would she pick me?"

"Because you're smart, and capable, and incredibly resilient, and recently humble, and you're not afraid to call a spade a spade, and you look pretty cute in overalls. Why wouldn't she pick you?"

"Because I'm no good at this—any of this?"

"Then you seem to be a pretty good faker."

She rolled her eyes. "You already know I'm a bad faker. You called me out on it weeks ago."

"Oh, yeah, sorry about that. You've gotten a lot better."

"At faking it?"

He turned his body to look at her. "I don't think you need to do that anymore, do you?"

She shrugged.

"Maybe you should just accept that you're smart enough and prepared for this—or you will be by the end of the summer. You've totally got this!"

She shook her head but couldn't hide her smile. "Why are you doing this?"

"What?"

"All of it! Why are you nice to me? Why are you there to comfort me every time I do something stupid...or I need a reality check...or I feel hopeless and lost?"

"*You're feeling hopeless and lost?*"

"I don't even know anymore. One minute I feel like I have all the clarity in the world, and the next minute I'm feeling completely overwhelmed. I've made exactly zero progress on my article. I was just feeling lost and alone. And then I bump into you—*again*—and it feels like there's ... hope, like things aren't as bad as all my crazy insecurities want me to believe. Are you spying on me? Are you somehow able to read my thoughts?"

Matt laughed. "You caught me."

"What? You *can* read my thoughts?"

"Of course. Right now you're thinking you better get back to the kitchen and work on dinner before the rest of us get hungry."

"Pfff. That was an easy one. I'm on kitchen duty and it has to be late afternoon. Of course I'm thinking that. What else have you got?"

He closed his eyes, looking quite serene as he pondered her question. "Mmmm. Interesting."

"What?"

"You've decided to accept Ruby's offer, but you're not sure how you could possibly manage this farm and twelve green campers every year by yourself."

She didn't answer, stunned into silence.

He opened his eyes and watched her shake her head. "Maybe I could help."

"What do you mean?"

"Well, I was just thinking this afternoon that it would be a shame to see 300 years of history, tradition and learning fall apart and fade away at the end of the summer. As a concerned *soon-to-be* citizen of Niederbipp, I...well...I can't imagine I'd be busier than a few days each week at my new dental practice. Maybe, on my days off, or in the afternoon...if you and your future husband don't mind, I could be of some service up here."

"How would I pay you?"

"Mmmm. That mesquite French toast you made the first week wasn't half bad," he said licking his lips.

She shook her head, but smiled. "Matt, even if I did accept this job, there's no amount of French toast—mesquite or otherwise—that I could pay you to help me. There's no money in this. I've been doing the math. Pops and Ruby barely make enough to pay the taxes and keep the lights on, and that's even with the proceeds from the farm stand and whatever Ruby makes selling her socks. As far as I can tell this whole farm runs on little more than love. I stayed up most the night thinking about the fifty-six years they've given to this farm and the hundreds of kids who've spent a summer here with them. There's nothing about any of this that makes any financial sense at all. They've basically sacrificed the best years of the their lives to give hope to people like us, all for the purpose of spreading a little joy in the world. It's insane."

Matt nodded slowly. "But isn't it also beautiful?"

"Well, sure, but is beauty and a few good feelings enough to keep you going—for basically free—for who knows how many years? If I lived to be as old as Ruby, I could be here for almost seventy years!"

Matt nodded again. "I get that it's a lot of work, and basically no pay, but you gotta admit it's also at least a little bit exciting, right?"

She blinked her eyes as if she were waiting for the punchline. "Matt, in the past fifty-six years, Ruby and Pops have been away from the farm for a total of three days! Three freakin' days! You can just barely get to Europe and back in three days. *Three days off in fifty-six years!* I bet Ruby hasn't had a manicure in at least a decade, if she's had one at all. I mean, shoot, how would you milk a cow or bake bread, or slop the pigs, or even weed the garden and maintain a decent manicure?"

"Okay," Matt said with a shrug. "I mean I don't know anything about manicures, but I'd guess a lot of things would have to change."

"Yeah, like basically everything! They do their laundry by bicycle power, for crying out loud! And I have yet to even see a dry cleaner. There's absolutely *nothing* about either ease or comfort around here!"

"No, I guess not."

"That's it? That's all you've got to say?"

"What do you want me to say? I mean, yeah, it would be a big adjustment. It already has been. But have you really missed anything from your old world that hasn't been made up for here?"

His question seemed to surprise her, leaving her without words as she considered the question. "Yes," she began. "I've missed long, hot showers, and my choice of a hundred different clubs, live theater, museums, thousands of choices for things to eat, the ability to hop on a subway and be across town before my podcast is half over. I've missed having my nails done every other week and my hair done once a month. And I've missed Starbucks, and jogs around Central Park, and knowing that I'm living in the world's most-happening city."

Matt nodded. "That's not what I asked."

She looked at him blankly. "What was your question again?"

"I know it's obviously different—Niederbipp versus New York. But hasn't most—if not all of your loss—been made up for?"

"Matt, you didn't hear me...I haven't been to a salon in over a month!" she said, pointing to her roots.

"I know. But does it matter?"

She looked at him blankly.

"Does any of that *really* matter?"

She turned, resting against the back of the bench, slowly letting out at least a month's worth of pent-up breath. "So, if I'm hearing you correctly, you're basically asking me if my whole world matters ... my travels ... my job ... my industry ... "

Matt nodded innocently. "Does it?"

They sat in silence for a long, awkward moment.

"I think I might hate you right now," she finally said.

"Me, or my question?"

"Pffff. Maybe both."

"Yeah, well, I've been asking myself the same question I just asked you. Does any of it matter? I mean, yeah, I like what I do, helping people have better teeth and making them look better when they smile...maybe fixing a toothache now and then. But I've been sitting here for the last hour or so wondering if any of it really matters. And the only affirmative answer I've come up with so far that's really felt meaningful is the chance I've had over the years to help people who can't possibly pay me for my services. I don't know, Genevieve. When it comes right down to it, it feels like maybe there's a lot less in this life that really matters."

"I never expected to hear that kind of cynicism from you."

He shrugged. "I don't know if it's really cynicism. I just feels like maybe I'm discovering that most of the things I've been spending my time on don't really mean much. And maybe I've been paying way too much attention to the stuff that really doesn't matter at all."

She shook her head. "You, *of all people*? Really?"

"What does that mean?"

"Matt, I feel like you're way ahead of me and most of the rest of us in understanding what life is all about. How many days have you spent traveling the world in the last year, doing charity work?"

He shrugged. "Never as many as I'd like."

"Okay, but you're doing it! You're making the time and effort—on your own dime—to help people live better lives. The rest of us…" She shook her head. "The rest of us are more concerned about our own bottom line, feathering our own nests, and trying to get ahead of some imaginary line that just seems to keep moving."

"So, what really matters in life?" he asked, nodding thoughtfully. "What really matters?"

She turned and looked into the woods. "Maybe I don't know anymore. What answers have you come up with?"

"I keep coming back to a quote that's been stuck in my head for years. I think it's from Gandhi, or maybe Einstein. It says something like, 'Only a life lived for others is a life worth living.'"

"I don't know if I agree with that," she admitted, after taking a moment to mull it over.

"No?"

"Maybe I don't understand it, but it seems like that could get you into a lot of trouble—always living your life the way someone else wants you to."

"I don't think it's so much about living the way someone else wants you to as it is about choosing for yourself to make other people a priority."

"I don't know if I like that, either. How is that any better?"

"I'm not sure, but … isn't that what parents do, at least for the first eighteen years of a child's life? I've been around enough young parents in my dentistry work to know there probably isn't a parent alive who doesn't have to give up at least a small piece of who they are in order to be a decent mother or a father. And women, for the sake of bringing children into the world, exchange their trendy wardrobes for maternity clothes, knowing they may never regain their former shapes and figures. But they do it—everyday around the world they do it—most of them knowing their sacrifice and investment will take them to the verge of death to produce a life that will only require additional sacrifice, work, sweat and tears for the rest of their lives."

"Yeah, you make parenting sound super duper attractive," Genevieve teased.

"Right?" He laughed "But the thing is, I have yet to meet one empty nester who wasn't glad—even grateful—that they made those sacrifices and raised those unthankful kids. I don't know how it changes, or how it makes any sense at all, but somewhere along the way, it seems like most parents discover that raising kids becomes a joyful experience."

"Do you really think that's true?"

Matt shrugged. "Maybe not in the middle of raising teenagers, or changing a dozen diapers each day. But unless a whole lot of parents are really good at just pretending to be happy in order trick the next generation into starting their own families, I have to believe it's gonna be an ultimately joyful experience."

She shook her head. "I don't know. What if it all just … sucks?"

He laughed.

"I'm serious! What if parenting totally blows? You can't just throw in the towel and say, 'Just kidding, I don't really want to be a parent anymore,' and send your kids to foster care so you can get back to living your own life."

"Yeah, no," he said with a little laugh, "you can't really do that."

"No, I mean, I know it happens, but I can't even imagine getting into the whole parenting thing and feeling … stuck … hopeless … and not have any reasonable way of getting out of it. What do you do then?"

Matt nodded slowly. "So this fear of feeling stuck, hopeless, and unable to get out of it … I can't tell if you're only talking about parenting, or if maybe you're also talking about taking over the farm, too."

"Am I that transparent?"

"Maybe."

"Matt, the whole idea of it just sounds so … *nuts!* I came here for what I thought was going to be a weekend, maybe four days, tops. It was going to be a quick story, in and out. I … I'm ashamed to admit it but

I thought it would take me about ten seconds to poke enough holes in Ruby's story for everyone to know she was a fraud."

"And now?"

Genevieve shook her head. "And now she wants me to be the next link in this long chain of matchmakers and carry on the 300-year-old legacy. Do you have any idea how crazy this is?"

"Is it?"

She rolled her eyes. "Matt, you know as well as I do that I'm no matchmaker. I don't the first thing about any of this stuff."

"So why can't you just tell her to find someone else?"

She shook her head after a moment.

Matt laughed. "It sounds like that's exactly the question you need to be asking yourself."

"Why do you have to ask such annoying questions?"

"If I don't, who will?"

"You almost make it sound like it's an unavoidable question that, come hell or high water, has to be asked."

"Maybe it does."

She shook her head, looking unconvinced.

"Look, this my job, right? You're the one who gave it to me."

"What job is that?"

"To be a megaphone for that little voice in your heart that you've been trying to ignore?"

"Pffff…" She shook her head again. "What if I didn't?"

"What if you didn't what?"

"What if I didn't tell Ruby…I mean…what if I…what if I decided to reinvent myself as the next matchmaker of Niederbipp?"

"Then I'd guess you'd have a lot of things you'd need to figure out between now and the end of the summer."

"Yeah, I know, right? Like so many … like … what kind of things would you be most concerned about?"

Matt laughed at the strangeness of the question. "Are you serious right now?"

"I don't know!"

"Yeah, I mean we were just talking about what's real, and how you hated me for even questioning the value of your job, and the next thing I know you're acting like you're seriously considering Ruby's proposal. I guess I'm just wondering where you really are with all of this?"

She looked down at her feet, kicking a small rock down the earthen path before turning to look at Matt. "This is nuts, right? All of this is totally nuts."

He shrugged. "Yes and no."

"So...which part of this is *not* totally nuts?"

"I'd say it's that piece of possibility in your heart that's standing in the way of you telling Ruby that she asked the wrong girl."

"How did you know about that piece of my heart?" she whispered softly.

"That's my job, remember? To be hold up the megaphone...?".

"So what is it trying to tell me?"

"I think you already know."

"Remind me."

"I believe it's trying to tell you there's a reason you can't turn Ruby down. And even though it feels scary, and overwhelming, and you have a million questions, there's a reason you can't let it go."

"Even though everything about it is way out of my comfort zone?"

Matt shrugged. "It doesn't seem like any of the best things in life ever happen in our comfort zones."

"Okay, but this is totally scary."

"Which part?"

"The unknown. All of it. I know how to write—at least short articles about fashion and trends. I know nothing about dating or farming or matchmaking. I would be a total fiasco."

Matt nodded. "If you were to take over today, yeah, you're probably right."

"Thanks for the vote of confidence! Matt, I feel completely overwhelmed!"

"I hope so."

"Why do you say that?"

"I'm not gonna lie. This is a really big deal. As your friend, I'm not going tell you it's all going to be roses and pixie dust if you choose to accept Ruby's offer. It's going to be hard—undoubtedly the hardest thing you've ever done in your life. And the reality is that you may never get another pedicure, and your roots will probably just grow out to become your natural color, and your travel will be mostly curtailed to a five mile radius.

"Then, while you're learning to overcome the changes to your grooming habits, you'll have to deal with cantankerous men like James, and difficult women like Crystal, and old, desperate, dried-up duffers like me. And you'll have to learn and remember all the different nuances of the farm, working with all the animals and the garden, and who knows how many acres of grain. I'm sure there'll be lots of days that will suck, really, really suck. And you'll still have to put on your game face and get to work and maintain some sense of dignity even when you want to spit and cuss and tell all the campers to go to hell, or send them back to wherever they came from.

"And you'll have to learn to cook with enough confidence to be able to teach twelve campers every year how to make meals using the stuff you grow and bottle and raise on the farm. At the same time you'll have to learn how to live on a super tight budget and save for taxes and surprise expenses. And if you and your future husband decide you want kids you may have to do all of the above while you're pregnant, and puking, and nursing, and changing diapers, and trying to raise babies among an ever-revolving set of twelve strangers who'll look to you to help them solve their problems, and for wisdom and comfort and sage advice. Oh, and because of the farm's location and the county's strict teetotalism, you'll have to do it all sober.

"And except for the annual rock skipping contest, your biggest social event of the week will usually be church down in Niederbipp. And you'll have to be okay with date night consisting of porch games played with twelve weirdos. And your hands will always be calloused. And your laundry will always be perfumed with a trace of manure. And for the rest of your life, or until you decide it's time to pass the farm and the crown on to the next matchmaker, those cute freckles on your nose will always be shining through the dust, and the grit, and the sunburn."

Genevieve rubbed her nose unconsciously, looking as though she'd been scared sober. "So you think I would definitely have to be crazy to take it?"

"I never said that. I maintain, like I told Ruby, that you'd probably be good at it, once you got past the hard realities and the personal sacrifices that'd be required. I just don't want you or anyone else to step into those shoes without having a really good idea of what this is going to be like. It's fun sometimes as a participant, but I have to believe it's a very different animal when all the burden and responsibility is riding on your shoulders."

She nodded slowly. "But if I were crazy enough to accept this job, you said you'd come up on your days off to help?"

Matt looked out at the trees for a moment. "I'd hate to see this end—something that has meant so much to so many people for so many generations. But ... "

"But?"

He smiled shyly. "But I think you'd be good at it."

"Really?"

"I mean, yeah, it would be a huge adjustment and change of pace, but yeah, I don't know anyone who might be better suited for this."

"Are you sure you don't just say that to all the girls?"

He smiled, shaking his head. "Don't think this won't be the toughest thing you'll ever choose to do."

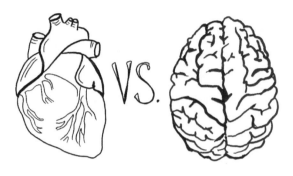

CHAPTER 114

Swing

*Nothing in life is to be feared, it is only to be understood.
Now is the time to understand more, so that we may fear less.*
— Marie Curie

With excitement and anticipation for the evening's activities, dinner was served at six o'clock, shortly after Crystal and Josh returned from the farm stand. An extra plate was set at the table for Thomas who'd spent the afternoon fishing—unsuccessfully—for Oscar, the pond's resident gargantuan, brown trout. His lack of success was quickly forgotten, however, with the half-dozen polished fish tales he shared with the campers, leaving them all in stitches, and with a new appreciation for this man in black.

After and hour or so, they broke for evening chores, Pops and Thomas leading the milking team to the barn while the laundry team gathered in the dried laundry from the line. Several of the others stayed and helped with the dishes and kitchen clean up, making light work of the duties. Fresh raspberries were picked from the garden while Bessie was loaded with ice, and everyone converged on the porch to bring it all together.

Instead of a game, the campers decided to take advantage of having someone new at the farm, and even though he'd entertained them during dinner, they spontaneously and unanimously decided the pseudopriest/plumber/baker/librarian would be the evening's designated fun. Thomas was a good sport about it, answering as many questions as he could. But with twelve interviewers and only one interviewee, it made for a disorganized mess until the topic of marriage was selected and the discussion broadened to include everyone. To help keep them from talking over each other, it was decided that the person on Bessie's saddle would have as long as they needed to share the best bits of marriage advice they'd ever heard.

This quickly proved to be entertaining with things like: 'If you have to fight, do it naked,' to 'Always hold your wife's hand in the mall: it's both romantic and economic.' But considering that the company included a priest and a geriatric couple, the things that were shared tended to be more on the tame side than they might have been had the company been different.

When it was Ruby's turn to peddle Bessie, she surprised everyone by being significantly less shy than the others had been, suggesting that it takes a lot more than sex to build a great marriage, but that building a great marriage is nearly impossible without it.

Pops talked about the importance of being on the same page with your partner, not necessarily in small things like political opinions or which team to root for, but for sure on matters like finances and how to raise and discipline the kids.

More than one of the campers talked about the importance of giving way more than just fifty percent to a marriage. Fifty percent might be worthy of divorce, but for a happy marriage, it was agreed that each partner needed to give one-hundred percent. This was a new concept to a few of the campers, but they all agreed it made sense.

Rachael suggested the importance of continuing to flirt with your spouse, while committing to never flirt with anyone else. This spawned additional conversation about continuing to date after marriage, keeping things exciting in the bedroom, and expressing gratitude in both word and reciprocative deed.

There were good recommendations regarding finances, holidays with the in-laws, keeping marriage alive through quick getaways, compliments and honesty, and communicating through challenges even when you didn't want to. Before the ice cream was done, they realized that most of the things they'd been sharing were the nearly universal desires of their hearts.

As the ice cream was served, the discussion continued with all of them recognizing they shared the same basic desires: harmony and love.

Thomas shared that in his years of watching marriages, lasting love did not come as a result of luck or compatibility, but rather from mutual commitment and fighting for each other rather than against each other.

Thomas's comment turned the conversation down a different path, focusing around the emotional, physical, and spiritual commitment of marriage. This commitment, for some, especially those who'd come from broken homes, had been a daunting hurdle. They believed in the idea of marriage enough that they were still pursuing it, but they expressed fear of jumping in, fear of getting hurt or hurting someone else, fear of choosing the wrong partner, and fear of getting stuck in a relationship that was neither fun nor nurturing.

It was quickly recognized that these fears were universal among all of the campers, regardless of the examples for good and bad that they'd had in their lives. Pops, Ruby and Thomas all agreed that from their experience and observations, the only thing that was more problematic than fear, as it related to the commitment of marriage, was the lack of respect for that commitment. They encouraged the campers to begin transitioning their fear of marriage into reverence for marriage. This, they suggested, could best be accomplished by applying the practice of reverence, hope and charity to every future love interest until they found the one they were interested in committing to, and then applying those same keys throughout their marriage to bolster and secure their commitment to their spouse.

Even though they'd been discussing the keys for several weeks, this suggestion seemed to be a revelation to all of them. As they began discussing specifics of how the application of the keys may have saved previous relationships and their parents' marriages, a different respect for the keys grew. They weren't just a good idea—they had real world applications—applications that had the ability to strengthen, deepen, enhance, and even save all relationships, especially the one many of them feared the most.

Reverence, hope and charity: they were on the surface so simple, yet they had the ability, when properly applied and practiced, to change everything—everything! For the first time since they'd first begun learning the keys of joy, their eyes began to open to their vast applicability. From environmental concerns, to financial, to political, to medical, to the challenges of homelessness, mental health, and the degradation of the families, the keys offered a balm and potentially a cure to everything. It was almost as though the proverbial false ceiling had been suddenly lifted, and the light of truth was scattering the fear and darkness many of them had been harboring for years.

Reverence, Hope and Charity…it could change the world, if they could only remember to keep them alive and activated.

There was something different in the air Sunday morning. Before the campers even met on the lawn between the bunkhouses, they all felt it. It was almost as if the sun somehow shone a little brighter, the grass was somehow a little greener, and the farm, somehow a little more harmonious.

As they made decisions about who would do what for the morning chores, there was a different sense of unity, mutual respect, and even understanding that seemed to permeate the space between them. While some went with Pops to the barn to work on the milking, and another group divided to feed the chickens and pigs, Genevieve went with a group of three others to help make breakfast with Ruby.

In the cellar, the flour mill seemed to create flour without any of the usual drama. The stove and cast iron skillet created pancakes without burning even one of them. Bottles filled with beautiful pears and peaches were brought up from the cellar. And fourteen people sat down to breakfast, sharing a sense of unity and family that few of them had ever known.

"What happened last night?" Holly asked as two giant stacks of pancakes were passed around the table.

"I've been wondering the same thing all morning," said Josh.

Ruby smiled from her end of the table. "How would you describe what you're feeling?"

"It just feels like…like we're together."

"I wasn't even grumpy this morning," Crystal added. "I've been trying hard not to be grumpy in the morning since I got here, but today I didn't feel like I had to try."

"Yeah, and we didn't even burn one pancake," said Genevieve .

Ruby nodded. "It almost sounds like you kids have reached the state of swing."

"Swing?" James asked.

"Yes. I hesitate to even suggest it, being that it's so early in the year, and because it's so rare."

"Swing? You really really think so?" Pops asked from the far end of the table.

Ruby pointed to the plate of pancakes that were coming his direction.

"You take a look at that plate of pancakes and consider the events of the last few weeks, and try to tell me it's not swing."

He pulled a few pancakes from the pile, turning each of them over before taking a closer look at the others in the stack. With eyebrows raised, he looked back down the table at Ruby. "This early? We've never had kids hit swing in the first month."

"No, but then we've never had kids plant grain on the first week either, or wash all the wool in one day and card it in another. And two days for spinning? Two days?" She laughed, shaking her head. "Remember that year it took almost two weeks to get the wool turned into yarn? I thought we'd never finish.

Pops nodded thoughtfully. "That was hard to forget. But swing already?"

"What exactly is this *swing*?" asked Rachael.

"It's a little bit difficult to define," Ruby admitted, "perhaps, at least in part, because it's so rare. Some years, our kids never come to the place you kids have just described, and those that do don't usually find it until the last few weeks of the summer. But swing...it's almost like slipping into a parallel world where everything is balanced and harmonious without continual effort to make it or keep it so. I'm sure you've each ridden on a swing before and enjoyed that beautiful sense of flying that, once it's been reached, can be maintained with very little effort."

Many of the campers nodded.

"So, kind of like falling into a groove?" Matt asked.

"Yes."

"Then yeah, it feels like we've kind of reached that point," Sonja suggested. "I don't even feel like I need a nap any more, and Josh and I had no trouble with the flour mill this morning, even though it's been more than two weeks since either of us have practiced that rhythm."

"It was the same way with me and James in the laundry yesterday," Rachel reported.

"Then I'd say these perfect pancakes are something more than a fluke," Pops admitted.

"So, this swing thing," Ephraim said, "is it like homeostasis?"

"Yes, in many ways its similar," Ruby acknowledged.

"Sorry, but what's homeostasis?" Crystal asked.

"It's basically the balance that happens when all the systems and functions in a body are in alignment with each other, balancing and counterbalancing and complementing each other in ways that allow everything to function as it should," Ephraim explained.

"And something like that can happen with a group of people?" Susan asked.

"It's uncommon," Ruby admitted, "and it takes work to both achieve it and maintain it among a group of disparate characters and personalities."

"It happens sometimes in sports teams," Spencer suggested.

"Yes, and sometimes in work groups, or church organizations, or circles of friends where a common goal is shared and people are willing to set aside their own agendas, egos and selfishness for the benefit of creating oneness," explained Ruby.

"So...if this is really swing, how do we maintain it?" asked Genevieve.

"That's a great question. And I believe that if more people could experience what you kids seem to have created here, more people would be interested in doing all they could to find it and maintain it. But swing, as far as I know, never happens on it's own. Like homeostasis in a body, it requires all systems to be functioning and working together."

"So, it's kind of like those geese we saw a couple of weeks ago?" Matt said.

"Exactly," Ruby confirmed. "I don't know much about the personalities of geese and other birds, but somehow they are able to unite their different personalities to create something that benefits each of the different members of the flock. Such displays of unity and oneness are far more rare among people today. We tend to be independent and self-centered and more concerned about our own comforts than we are about sharing and uniting with others."

"It's just easier that way," Crystal said.

"You think so?" Ephraim challenged.

Crystal thought for a moment. "Whatever it is that we have here has been really nice, but it seems like a pipe dream for anything on a bigger scale, or for anything that can be maintained for more than ten minutes."

"Our experience with the Amish would prove otherwise, wouldn't it?" suggested Matt.

"Oh...yeah." Crystal responded, looking a little embarrassed. "I forgot about that."

"Forgetting is one of the easiest things to do," Ruby replied. "That's one reason there are benches scattered across the farm—to provide places for you to think and remember the important things in life."

"So, there's an obvious common element in both what we're experiencing today and what we all felt and observed when we were with the Amish," Susan reported thoughtfully.

"Are you thinking the keys of joy?" asked Greg.

Susan nodded. "The Amish know them too, right? And it seems like they live them more fully and openly than anyone I've seen."

"That's true," Ruby replied. "And what else did you observe that the Amish had that day?"

"Swing!" responded Ephraim. "They built that huge barn in one day!"

"Yes, but it wasn't just the barn. The women had it too in the kitchen," Holly recalled.

"I've been thinking a lot about something David told us while we were—what felt like—lamely carrying wood to the Amish men who were doing all the work," said Matt. "He pointed out that if we weren't there, some of the more skilled guys would have to be doing our job, and the whole machine that was building the barn would be slower and less efficient. He pointed out that you ladies, along with the other women, were also building the barn. Even the young boys who were making sure we had water and the young girls who were tending the children—

everyone was needed and important in turning a few big piles of lumber into a finished barn by the end of the day."

"So, if that's the power of swing, why don't we just stay in this mode all the time?" Josh asked.

Pops smiled. "That's a great question, Josh. I think that in order to answer it, you all need to close your eyes for a moment."

The campers looked at each other and smiled before closing their eyes.

"Now, I want you all to imagine you're at your favorite park you went to as child. You've finally learned how to pump the swing all by yourself, and you start off slow, sticking your feet out in front of you, and bringing them back, starting a motion and a rhythm that begins to push you higher and higher. The wind begins to rush past your ears and through your hair. You lean back and pump, higher and higher until you begin to experience the momentary sense of weightlessness every time you reach the peak of the ascent before gravity pulls you back down to earth, before gliding you backwards where you feel that same sense of weightlessness and ease as you glide back and forth, again and again."

Pops smiled to himself as wide grins formed on the faces of each camper, some of them swaying with the memory of the simple joy Pops described.

"Before you open your eyes," he continued, "I want you to consider why you got off."

Greg laughed after a moment. "Because I learned how to launch myself off!"

"Because I wanted to join my friends on the slides and merry-go-round," Sonja added.

"Because I got bored," Rachael admitted.

"Very good," Pops said. "Each of you will have a reason to get off. Life is short, especially when you're a kid and you want to fit in as much fun as you can."

"Or when you're old and your days are numbered," Ruby added.

Pops nodded. "Maybe life is always short. But Mom and I were fortunate to discover that any time spent in swing is not deducted from life, and in most cases, it's time that gets added on somewhere in the middle of life, adding a richness and joy that is rarely found in any other source."

"So…I was going to ask how we get more of that…but we already know, don't we?" Rachael asked.

"If you've been paying attention, you're three-fifths of the way there," Ruby confirmed.

"And all of this comes back to the metaphor of building a house, doesn't it?" asked Josh.

Ruby nodded. "If you can build your house using God as your architect and foreman, and incorporate the keys of joy as you work on yourself and with your spouse, it will almost be difficult not to have fun, to find joy, and to fall into the glorious rhythms of swing."

"Then I propose we make a unified effort to stay here and swing," Greg suggested.

"Do you really think that's possible?" James asked.

"Why not? We know what tools are needed, and we're learning how to use them," responded Susan.

"And it feels like we all want it," Crystal added.

Many of the campers nodded.

"Then the only thing that's holding you back is you," Ruby responded.

"So, where do we go from here?" asked Greg.

"You practice what you know," Pops said. "You consult the architect, sign on to be His apprentice, and begin digging your foundation."

"If we work hard, do you think we can we finish our houses by the end of the summer?" Holly asked.

Pops looked down the table at Ruby. "For all of your sakes, I hope not."

"Why not?" Holly asked, looking confused.

"Because building your house was intended to take a lifetime. If you try to rush it, I'm afraid you'll cut yourself short and deny yourself the full extent of all the beautiful details God has in store for you."

"By the end of the summer," Ruby added, "we hope your footings will be laid and your broad and strong foundations will be firm and ready to accept all the good that will come to you as you begin laying your first course of bricks."

"Am I the only one who thinks that feels discouraging?" Greg asked. "It just feels so…long."

"Patience is hard for most of us," Pops admitted. "But remember why you're here. Most of you applied this summer because you recognized that your hasty, impatient attempts at creating a suitable home on life's shifting dunes have amounted to something much less than your heart's desires."

"Divine discontent," Matt mused.

"Exactly. Mom and I recognize that it takes a lot of trust to step away from what you know and have always done and try something new. But we hope that the things you've felt and seen and experienced over the last month will allow you to see that there are more possibilities and greater hope when the architect of the entire universe stands waiting to help you build your house, and write a very new and different story, filled with endless possibilities and eternal perspectives."

CHAPTER 115

In the Potter's Hands

*We are either in the process of resisting God's truth
or in the process of being shaped and molded by His truth.*
—Charles Stanley

The morning's discussion, though illuminating and inspiring, was ill-timed for twelve campers and their elderly hosts who planned to attend church. The previous evening's porch gathering had also gone late, the campers' discussions in their respective bunkhouses making the night even later. Showers that had been postponed the night before were now rushed, and the joyful calm that had attended the farm that morning was unwittingly swept away in the hustle and bustle of rushing off to church.

Pops and Ruby, along with Crystal and James, departed in the pickup truck well ahead of the others. In their haste, they left the basket of butter, jams and jellies—their offering for Sourdough Sunday, on the steps of the front porch. While Matt and Greg arranged these items in the handlebar baskets on a couple of the bikes, Josh, Ephraim, and Spencer paced impatiently, waiting for the women to finish getting ready. After ten minutes they decided they'd waited long enough. Leaving Matt and Greg to accompany the ladies, they left the farm, looking incensed.

Susan, Holly and Sonja arrived at the bike shack just as the three men were cresting the drive. The women, still complaining about the cold showers, were not impressed by the men's impoliteness in leaving them. Greg, hoping to make things better, agreed to ride with the ladies, leaving Matt to wait for Genevieve and Rachael. And wait he did, his own patience being tried with each passing minute.

Finally, after what felt like an hour but couldn't have been more than a few minutes, the last two women arrived, out of breath and definitely miffed.

"Are you girls finally ready?" Matt asked, sounding not quite as impatient as he felt.

"You should have just gone without us," Genevieve responded, matching his tone while avoiding eye contact.

"I'm sorry I didn't," Matt said, kicking his kickstand up. The sudden jolt altered the balance of his bike, and the heavily laden basket on his handlebars caused the whole bike roll out from underneath him. He grabbed for the handlebar, but it was too late, his whole bike crashing to the ground and the contents of the basket spilling out onto the lawn. "Shi...crap!" he managed, looking down at two broken bottles of jam and fresh cream slowly dripping from the butter church.

"Just go!" Matt said, stooping to examine the disaster.

"No, we'll help," Rachael responded.

"GO!" Matt shouted.

His response was so unlike the calm, gentle man they'd become accustomed to that both of them jumped and didn't require any further encouragement. They grabbed their bikes and moved out.

As quickly as he could, Matt began separating the glass from the sticky, gooey disaster, but he hadn't gotten very far when Rex, the farm dog, showed up to examine the mess and claim his share of it. Matt tried to shoo him away, knowing the sweetly flavored, broken glass would be problematic if not dangerous. Rex, mistaking Matt's actions as an invitation to wrestle, quickly decided this would be fun. After several minutes of trying to work around the dog and clean up the mess, Matt decided he couldn't do both. Luring Rex into the empty bike shed with a healthy chunk of grape jelly, he closed the door behind him before rushing to the kitchen for a washcloth and a container for the glass.

Within minutes, the glass and jam had been mostly cleared away, and he ran it all back into the kitchen, leaving it all on the counter before descending the stairs into the cellar to procure two fresh bottles of jam. But his speedy descent was not without peril, and he hit the crown of his head on the overhead beam he'd previously, under normal circumstances, been able to narrowly avoid. In pain, but undaunted, he rushed to the shelves of jam and selected two new jars before rushing back out. But the rush did not bode well for his ascent either, and he caught his foot on the second to last stair, bruising his left shin and sending him sprawling across the kitchen floor, trying to protect the bottles by taking the brunt of the blow to his shoulder while narrowly missing the island.

Bruised but not broken, he got to his feet, trying to decide if he should laugh or cry. But he pushed on, and before he reached the top of the drive, the church bells tolled ten times, marking both the hour and the beginning of Sunday services.

He considered calling it quits and going back to bed, but something pushed him on, not wanting to miss out or be alone when the rest of the family was together. The winding descent down Harmony Hill did not afford much opportunity for speed, but as soon as the road leveled out, he pedaled hard, coasting into the courtyard just less than ten minutes later.

"I'm glad you made it?" Genevieve said from the shadows of the tree-lined courtyard, startling Matt as he dismounted. He forced a smile as he leaned his bike up against the others.

"Why aren't you in there?" he asked.

"Oh, yeah, well..." she stammered, looking up at the open chapel doors, "It just didn't feel right going in, knowing you weren't in there because of me. I'm sorry to make you late."

Matt nodded. "I'm sorry I yelled at you. I..." He shook his head. "I thought I'd gotten over my temper, but...yeah, I'm sorry."

She stopped him, holding his forearm until he looked at her. "I also need to thank you."

"For what?" he asked, looking surprised.

"For being kind to me, even when I was anything but deserving of your kindness. The whole ride down here I found myself thinking how you've been there for me when I needed a friend—at the pond, and the river, and basically at every turn. I haven't been very grateful, and then I was short with you this morning and...I'm sorry. Thank you for being my friend."

Matt took a deep breath as if he'd been holding it since he left the farm. He looked around at the empty courtyard before turning to face the chapel. "You're welcome," he said softly. "Do you want to go in?"

"I do now."

Instinctively he offered her an arm as they climbed the stone steps, and she took it without even thinking about it, not fully recognizing that she was holding his arm until they were standing in the oversized doorway. Looking in, they were both surprised to hear not a sermon, but the last few notes of a string quartet playing an unmistakable tune, Pachelbel's Canon in D. They waited for the musicians to finish, finding two seats on the second to last row as the hall erupted into applause.

"Thank you, Niederbipp Strings!" Thomas said as the silver-haired musicians cleared away from the chairs near the lectern. "We're fortunate to have them." Another round of applause echoed through the chamber. "We are always looking for supplemental music to enrich our worship services. If you have a talent you'd like to share, please let me know. We'd love to get you on the schedule.

"For today's sermon, I asked our resident potter, Jacob Kimball, to share his insight on the workings of God in his own life. I think most of us probably know Jake, but for those who've not yet had the privilege of meeting him, I'll offer a short introduction.

"Jake just recently turned thirty, and has been with us here in Niederbipp for just over eight years, which is nearly as long as he and his wife, Amy Eckstein, have been married. Jake and Amy are excited to be welcoming their first child to their home in August—an event, I know, that's been anticipated and prayed for for many years. Amy and Jake live just above the pottery shop on Zübergasse.

"Amy, I might add, is a painter of no small renown in these parts. Over these past eight years we've been fortunate enough to hear from Jake and Amy many times. And I believe I can speak for all of us when I say how refreshing it is to hear from young people with faith. We are fortunate to have more than our share of such young people here in Niederbipp, but I'd publicly like to commend Jake and Amy for their fine examples of Christian love and service. We're always happy to have people move to Niederbipp, but it's even more appreciated when those who put down roots do so with a desire to embrace and understand what makes Niederbipp so unique. So, thank you, Jake, for sharing your light with us today."

Thomas motioned to Jake before taking a seat on the end of the second pew.

Jake stood, a black leather Bible in his hands as he approached the lectern. He laid the Bible down before looking up and smiling at the congregation. "Public speaking has never been one of my strengths. The opportunity to exercise this weakness however, has helped both Amy and me to recognize our reliance on God as experiences such as these call on us to lean into our faith, ask hard questions, and seek guidance and illumination. That being said, I'd much rather be in any one of your seats, grateful to be listening about *your* walk with God.

"As Thomas mentioned, I have the good fortune of being able to make my living with my hands. I arrived here eight years ago, answering a want-ad in a ceramics magazine. As you may recall, Isaac Bingham, my predecessor, had recently passed away, leaving the responsibility of finding a new potter in the hands of four of his friends, all of whom I see are with us today.

"I came here on a whim, not even knowing how to pronounce the name of this town. I was on my way to spend the summer in Greece, to apprentice with a potter there, when the hand of providence nudged me way off course, to the exact place I needed to be, and at just the right time I needed to be here. The author, J.M. Barrie, said, 'The life of every man is a diary in which he means to write one story, and writes another; and his humblest hour is when he compares the volume as it is with what he vowed to make it.'"

"Amy and I have had many years to reflect…and sometimes laugh… about the plans we've made for our lives, and compare them with the reality that's come our way. Admittedly, sometimes these realities have felt painful. But as we've put our trust in God and worked our way through the distractions and challenges, we've become increasingly aware of the hand of Providence that brought us here and has continued to nurture us and provide opportunities for us to learn and grow in patience and charity, while teaching us to value friendship and honor interpersonal connections. Emerson once said, 'All I have seen teaches me to trust the Creator for all I have not seen.' These words, shared with us at a time of loss and heartache, have humbled us, reminded us of the great value of patience, and helped us remember the goodness of God.

"Amy and I both appreciated Susan's words from her sermon two weeks ago. We, too, were inspired to start a gratitude journal many years ago after a visit to the Swarovski's farm on Harmony Hill. And like Susan and her family, we have discovered the fingerprints of God, even in the hard times, as we've remembered to practice gratitude." He paused for a moment to smile and nod to Susan and her family, and also to Amy who sat on the front row.

"As I've sought inspiration in some of my favorite quiet places, I've felt inspired to share some thoughts about a subject I happen to know a little bit about: pottery. I know you may be thinking that pottery is a mighty strange subject to be discussing in church. But I hope that these thoughts may help us better understand our place in the universe, as well as the love, patience and grace of God.

"There's an old Native American proverb I first heard when I was in art school that says, 'In the beginning, God gave to all people a cup of clay, and from this cup they drank their life.' I don't know when man first discovered that exposing clay to fire changes it into something that can last millennia, but pottery is not only one of the oldest forms of creative expression, it is also one of the longest lasting. And I can imagine that in an era void of plastics, metal and glass, pottery must have been a revolutionary game changer in the storage and preparation of food.

"Many years ago on a beach in Italy, I found this potshard," Jake said reaching into his pocket, then lifting the item, about the size of a fifty-cent piece, for them all to see. "It had been buffed by the sea and the sand for who knows how many decades, softening the edges while still preserving both the glaze color and the intricate carving beneath it. Most folks would probably consider this little nugget nothing more than garbage, but for close to ten years I've carried this shard in my pocket nearly everyday to remind me that the work I'm making, day to day, will long outlast me.

"That may sound like a presumptive ego thing, but knowing that my medium—by its very nature—will basically last forever, at least in shard form—it reminds me of the responsibility I feel to make my work say something about my values, my desires to make and spread beauty, and my hope that my pottery will enhance the lives of its owners for generations to come. Maybe even future potters will be as inspired by my shards as I've been by this one.

"For many millennia, clay tablets were used to record transactions, laws and even scripture in one of humanities earliest forms of written language: cuneiform. In our modern world, filled to overflowing with plastics, glass and metal, we often forget that for the majority of humanity's history, pottery served as an umbilical cord between the earth and our bodies; a conduit for food and water and other nourishment. As I work with clay, I often reflect on the mercy and goodness of God who provides us with matter unorganized, that we might also—if we so desire—come to know the beauty and joys of creation.

"Amy and I, as we work alongside each other in our shared studio—she with her paint and me with my clay—we often speak of this joy, this primitive and innate desire to take raw materials and create beauty, purpose and meaning from them. I would be remiss if I didn't express our gratitude to you for finding joy in our joys and supporting us in our dreams to live out our lives as artists. Thank you! Thank you!

"Many years ago, shortly after I arrived here in Niederbipp, Thomas shared with me a passage of scripture that has never left me. It's found in the Old Testament, in the eighteenth chapter of Jeremiah." He paused for a moment to flip through his Bible before looking up again.

"I ask you to forgive me for taking a prophet's words from more than 2600 years ago and paraphrasing them in language that might be more easily understood today. I've learned from my years of conversation with Thomas that scripture really only has meaning as we make it our own; as we put it in our pockets—if you will," he said, holding up the potshard once more, "and discover the richness and truth of those who wrote it so many years ago.

"Jeremiah, as you may know, was a prophet who lived in Jerusalem around 600 BC. He lived in a difficult time when the city was filled with hypocrisy and vice, when people flouted God's laws and indulged in the diverse lusts of the flesh. And in the middle of all this, Jeremiah was commanded by God to go out into the busy streets and tell his neighbors and even his friends that their sinful ways had attracted God's ire, which would, unless they changed their ways, lead to the destruction of their beautiful city and the captivity of its people."

Jake laughed nervously. "Tough job, right? I've tried to imagine the inner turmoil Jeremiah must have felt as his friends abandoned him, calling him an extremist and a fanatic while their parties raged on. Surely his mission and the convictions of his heart must have felt challenging as all his world seemed to turn against him. And yet day after day he felt compelled to go and do these really hard things, declaring a message no one wanted to hear.

"I can imagine him going back to God many times in prayer, saying, 'Are you sure, God? Are you sure I shouldn't just pick up and leave? The people hate me and my message. I've already lost all of my friends by telling them what you've told me to tell them. Are you sure this is how you want me to be spending my time? It just feels like a really unproductive way of winning friends and influencing people.'"

Many in the congregation laughed softly.

"So, one morning, Jeremiah goes to God in prayer, needing strength to go on in this difficult cause. And to his relief—and perhaps adding to his confusion, Jeremiah is told to get off his knees and go visit the village potter—that it was there that he would hear God's words and receive more light and understanding.

"I can imagine him making his way through the cobbled streets of Jerusalem, probably grateful the direction he'd been given was something other than making people mad with his usual condemnation schtick. But a potter? Really? What was he supposed to learn from a guy who made mudpies all day?"

Many in the congregation chuckled softly.

"But despite the strangeness of his inspiration, Jeremiah follows through, arriving at the potter's studio anxious to hear whatever it was he was there to receive.

"Now, if you haven't ever watched a potter work, I invite you to drop by the studio sometime. It's difficult to describe, but suffice it to say that watching pottery being made is something akin to alchemy, almost like watching straw being spun into gold. At least that's the way it usually goes—on a good day. But on this day, the local potter was not exactly having the best day of his life. In fact, as he's working, Jeremiah is a little disappointed when the big vase the potter is turning on his wheel suddenly crumples into a sticky, gooey mess.

"I can imagine Jeremiah looking at the mess and thinking, 'Yep, that's about how my life feels right now. I had a good thing going. I had friends. I had a nice little business. I used to get invited to dinner with friends. And now look. My life is really hard. I listened to the voice of God and my life only got harder.'"

"But just as he's thinking this, he hears another whisper say, 'Watch and learn.' So he turns his attention back to the potter who has cut the messy clay from the wheel and has carried it to a table where he's wedging that mess, vigorously kneading it back into shape while improving its consistency. Then, with firm but gentle hands, the potter puts the clay back on his wheel. In a flurry, the potter's skilled and experienced hands work the clay to the center of the wheel, bringing it gracefully into conformity with what he had in mind for it.

"Once the clay is centered he begins to pull—or *lift* the clay into a tall cylinder. This is where the magic really begins to take place as the clay rises from the wheel, growing taller with each rotation, leaving the marks of the potter's connection to it as well as his hopes for what the clay can become.

"When the desired height is reached, with the wheel still spinning, he begins to work from the inside, shaping the cylinder into something both more voluminous and shapely. With a tool called a rib, he bellies out the midsection, forming a graceful curve while continuing to add to the pot's volume and value, as well as its eventual ability to both preserve and distribute sustenance for years to come. When the body of the vessel is formed and aesthetically pleasing, he moves on with the rib, forming the neck and shoulder, leaving an ample lip at the top. Then, before cutting the beautiful vessel from the wheel, he forms a graceful pour spout to remind the pot that it was not meant for beauty alone, but was intended to fulfill the measure of its creation as a vessel that was built for service.

"As the potter finishes his work, the voice of God again comes to Jeremiah saying, 'Behold, as the clay is in the potter's hands, so are you in my hands—you, and all the people you've been called to love and help and serve.' And with this message of hope and responsibility, Jeremiah takes courage, and once again goes out into the streets of Jerusalem to declare the message of God's mercy, love and grace for all people."

Jake paused for a moment as he looked out on the congregation. He smiled warmly before continuing. "As I've pondered the hopeful message of these verses many times over the last several years, I've looked at it almost like a parable that may be understood by many different people of many different stripes and in many different ways. But as a potter, some of these meanings stick out to me. I assume that once I have children, and teenagers, and as I progress through life, there will be different understandings that will come as I attempt to be open to them.

"Near the beginning of this story, Jeremiah watches as the first pot fails and is reduced to a worthless mess. Now, we should assume because of the potter's success with the second pot that this was not his first rodeo. He'd probably been making pots for many years. He knew what he was doing. He was skilled and creative and working on becoming a master of his trade. So what happened? Why was his first attempt so pitiful?

"Well, again, as a potter, my experience has been that clay often has a mind of its own. Sometimes it's too hard. Sometimes it's too soft. There are occasionally bumps and air bubbles and inconsistencies in the clay that offer challenges to the potter. But a potter—perhaps more than any other person on earth—knows the potential of a lump of clay. And despite the difficulties the clay may offer him, he's not about to give up on it without a wrestle. He is going to work with it, again and again if necessary, trying to help the clay understand that its highest value and potential comes only after it has been worked by the master's hand.

After that, the pot must be exposed to the heat and further refinement of the kiln, changing even its molecular structure before it is enabled to last centuries, and quite possibly eternities.

"A potter, looking at clay, can see the beautiful potential from its very humble beginnings. Clay, on the other hand, is usually happy just being a lump of clay—not expanding, not improving, and without any ambition of becoming anything more than a humble lump of clay."

"Amy and I have had the great privilege and honor of sharing a beautiful friendship with Ruby and Lorenzo Swarovski. For the past fifty-plus years, the Swarovskis have invited twelve individuals each summer to their farm on Harmony Hill for a little help in the matchmaking department. Though Amy and I were married before we were aware of the magic that takes place each summer on Harmony Hill, our friendship with the Swarovskis has inspired each of us, individually and in our roles as husband and wife, to take a look at our lives and recognize the value of enlisting the help of an architect who knows what He's doing. One of the most important themes we have learned from Ruby and Lorenzo is actually scripture, from Psalms 127: 'Except the Lord build the house, they labour in vain that build it.'

"Inspired by what we learned on one of our early visits to the Swarovski's, Amy, with the help of her aunt Bev, created a cross stitch of this scripture for our first wedding anniversary. It hangs near our front door to help us remember its truths everyday as we come and go. I recognize that this verse is very similar to the message given to Jeremiah and many others throughout scripture. With God, all things are possible. Old things can become new. Broken things can be mended. Sick things can be healed. Blind things can be given vision. And even sticky, muddy messes that may appear hopeless and worthless can be turned into beautiful vessels. With God, there is hope, even in the darkest, most discouraging moments of our lives."

Jake pursed his lips, nodding to his wife on the front row. "As many of you know, Amy and I have had our share of disappointments and heartache. In another month, we will be married eight years. Our hearts have swelled with big emotions as we've watched children being born and grow over that time. We, too, have desired children of our own. We've prayed for a family. We've dreamed fabulous dreams about our future children. We've painted the nursery and bought a crib. We've spent endless hours discussing how we plan to balance kids and work. And since our first miscarriage, more than five years ago, we've been praying for a miracle. With each additional miscarriage, our prayers have intensified. We've hurt and we've cried and we've been loved and comforted by so many of you as we've worked our way through our heartache. In many ways, you have shared those heartaches with us as extensions of our family—family not by blood, but by choice. You've cared. You've reached out. Some of you have said some really difficult things to hear. But as we've worked our way through these things we've decided that the only thing worse than hearing difficult things is to hear nothing at all. We've heard your words, but more importantly we've felt your heart as you've reached out in love and charity and compassion.

"We really haven't understood it until the last month or so, but we've come to recognize that this child that's growing in Amy's womb is not our child alone. Your prayers have mingled with ours as we've walked this difficult path. You've cried with us. You've rejoiced with us. And we know you'll soon be smiling with us as baby Isaac's healthy, bellowing voice echoes off the walls of this chapel, interrupting our worship and reminding us all of the great mercy and grace of God.

"Shortly after our last miscarriage, we received an anonymous handwritten note that was slid under the Pottery's front door. Its message was brief, but deafening. It read simply, "Faith in God includes faith in His timing."[1] I have to admit we hated that message. It felt callous and insensitive. But with time and understanding, we've recognized it as truth. Faith, we've learned, is for the good times. But it's for the hard, no good, terribly painful and awful times too. And maybe it's especially for those hard times.

"Our faith has been tried. It's been tested. It's been shattered to bits and then gathered up and assembled in beautiful ways we didn't know

1. Neil A. Maxwell

were possible. In many ways we know what it feels like to be that broken down pot that Jeremiah saw—hopeless, wasted, defeated. And we have become all too aware of the fact that there is a dark and hopeless force that would like us all to believe that if ever we look like a mess of sticky, broken down, mucky clay, that we can never be anything better.

"Like the sign 'Abandon hope all ye who enter here,' that hangs over the entrance to Dante's Hell, this dark force is anti-light, anti-love, anti-hope. And we've discovered that if you wallow in that mire of all things dark and miserable, it will suck all the joy from your heart and mind and limit your ability to see the light of hope that is always near if not seen, even in the darkest and coldest of nights.

"We were tempted to shred and burn that note that had been left at our door, but instead, after a couple of weeks, we hung it on our fridge where it has been hanging ever since. What felt like a slap in the face when we were already reeling with pain and disappointment has come to serve as a daily reminder that we are not in charge of the universe. If we truly believe in the powerful, merciful, all-knowing God we claim to believe in, we must also put our faith in His timing.

"As we've learned from our difficulties, we've also learned that the truth has the ability to eventually set you free, but in most cases it first ticks you off, throws you off balance, and often forces you to rethink half your life before you allow that truth to resonate and grow into something more beautiful and palatable, softening into something you can chew on, and eventually swallow.

"The trick, as we've come to understand, is learning how to sip from the bitter cup without becoming bitter. In our journey through post-naïveté, and on the far side of the desert of criticism, we found hope again. I believe that the truth Jeremiah was supposed to see that day in the potter's studio was the hope and love that God has for His children. But what he may have missed in that representation was the truth that God's hope for His children has no end, no limits, and it never tires.

"Like a potter who is bound and determined to help the clay reach its greatest potential, God is infinitely more interested in helping us attain our greatest potential. His love for us is eternal because we are eternal beings. And so no matter how many times our hopes for the future implode, we forget who we are, or we fall into the traps of apathy, God is there to lift us up, dust of off, knead us back into shape, and recenter us with His firm but gentle hands of compassion and love.

"Yep, life is hard. I have yet to meet anyone whose life is without many challenges. But it's those challenges—we've learned from watching all of you—that bring us to our knees, helps us to see clearly, and teaches us that with God's help, we are capable of infinite growth. Amy and I are grateful for your kindness and patience with us as we've navigated our way through hard times. We are grateful to you for sharing the wisdom and truths of your hearts. Like the wise and kind hands of a potter, your kindness and wisdom have nudged us and shaped us, pushing us back into center—into balance—helping us, with each rotation, reform, adjust, and refine.

"In both my work with clay and my observations of people, I've discovered that those people and pots who are most at peace are those who have managed to avoid the extremes, who have willingly allowed themselves to be moved to the center where balance can be achieved and maintained, where the greatest growth and refining can occur, and where, with trust and hope, the hands of the Master can shape lives into beautiful, functional, successful masterpieces.

"It's a hard thing, I know, to allow that Master to mold you and shape you, especially when you believe you know what's best and what timing is most appropriate and convenient. But we have learned the truth of the Yiddish proverb, 'Man plans, and God laughs.' Just as a potter is with a lump of clay, He can see the end from the beginning. And though some apathetic clay might be quite content being turned into ashtrays or dog bowls, a wise and kind potter can look at that same clay and recognize the potential for greatness and glory within it.

"Each of us is somewhere in the process of becoming. We are, each of us, wet clay, capable of becoming vessels that range from mundane to extraordinary. Though God recognizes our greatest potential and can help us get there, we cannot sit by, complacently waiting for Him to perform his magical work of immaculate transformation. We must instead be active collaborators, communicating our hopes and desires, as well as listening to God's hopes and desires for us. God, I'm convinced, has much bigger hopes for us than mediocrity. The Parable of the Talents suggests that despite our lot in life, each of us is expected to build something glorious on it.

"God's grace is sufficient to fuel our efforts and provide for our happiness, but none of us can be truly happy until we have given it our best, until we're committed, until we are *all in* and have experienced a conversion away from the habits of mediocrity and an embracing of the ways of self-discipline and excellence.

"Until then, our wheels may be spinning—to use a potter's metaphor—but we are only cranking out ashtrays and dog bowls. That, I believe, was never God's hope for us. While we limit ourselves with our own choices of embracing mediocrity, doubts and fears, and buying into a scarcity mentality, God goes right on operating within the paradigm of abundance, love, compassion, grace, and excellence. Until we develop a desire to know the true nature of God and His purposes of creation, I don't believe we can come to a true understanding our own natures and purposes.

"I arrived in Niederbipp with a reverence for God and a hope of eternal possibilities. Eight years later, having tasted both the bitter and the sweet of life's offerings, I feel like the limited vision I had before has been expanded. Amy and I have grown together as a couple and our marriage has been strengthened as we've both individually and unitedly sought out deeper spiritual understanding and eternal perspectives. Our conversations with each other and many of you have enlarged our appreciation for this town and its undertones of eternity that help us remember who we are and the true purposes of life.

"I shudder to think of where my life would be today without those perspectives. I came here a headstrong, impetuous vagabond, determined to see the far corners of the world before I settled down. I remember imagining my eventual home would be a lot like this—a place where children still build tree forts and neighbors truly know their neighbors. I'm grateful such places still exist—that people like you have nurtured and maintained this sense of acceptance and tolerance, faith and hope, virtue, integrity, kindness, generosity, and above all, love of God and love of neighbor. While the rest of the world is embracing godlessness, corruption, vanity, pride and an indifference to all things of an eternal nature, you good people of Niederbipp—you Candlelighters and Protopians—you are holding tight to the principles you preach in word, and more importantly in deed. Amy and I are grateful to live among you and we aspire to become like you."

He nodded thoughtfully as he scanned the congregation, looking into the faces of many individuals, his attention flitting quickly from person to person.

"I had a couple of visitors in my shop a few weeks ago—tourists who said they'd been to visit our town several times over the course of the last few years. When I asked them what it was that kept bringing them back, they talked about the quaintness of the nearly-European architecture, Sam's bread and pastries, Robininto's Alfredo Parmigiano, and of course *the world's largest pudding mold museum in the world*."

Many of the congregants laughed softly.

"It wasn't until they were leaving that they mentioned the sense of calm and peace that exists here. Typically this is something I find my customers mentioning at first meeting them. There are often lots of questions about this church and the faith of the people here. Because of this I was anticipating some mention of the spirituality, but I never got the chance. They mentioned they'd visited with a couple at breakfast at their B&B who enthusiastically told them that the reason for the peace they found here was because of the faith and spiritual convictions of the people who live here. When I tried to confirm this was true, they left my shop looking put out, claiming they were atheists and were not interested in the fanatical proselytizing of yet one more apparent zealot."

Many in the congregation chuckled.

"I don't know if that couple will ever be back after discovering what we all believe is the source of Niederbipp's inherent peace and calm. But I'd like to imagine that in a quiet moment, somewhere down the road, they will feel something unexplainable sneak through their secular lockbox that might remind them of the unique aura of this wonderfully unique town and the esprit de corps of its unique citizenry.

"Though we are each unique individuals, I've been struck since I first arrived here that we are united in a bond of that beautiful German word we've come to appreciate—Geschwisterkeit. We are family. We are children of God. We are connected to each other in profound and beautiful ways which transcend all trappings and limitations of the terrestrial sphere.

"Thank you for accepting Amy and I into this beautiful Geschwisterkeit. We feel your love and thank you for sharing in both our griefs and our jubilations. We look forward to introducing you to baby Isaac in the coming months and rejoice that each of you, as part of our village, will help raise him.

"There is much of faith and reverence that I'm still trying to wrap my head around, but I know enough to say I believe in God. I believe He cares for His children and has great desires that we find happiness and joy in this life and in the world to come. I believe He and His angels, both mortal and immortal, desire to help shape our lives in meaningful ways that will help us to both know our potential and achieve it. After watching all of you for the last eight years, I believe our greatest hope of reaching that potential is to develop and then maintain a daily connection to God through the practice of humble prayer and making time to discover Him in expectant stillness.

"Thank you for your influence for good in my life, for helping me to see more clearly and listen more closely. Our lives have been truly blessed by your examples of faith and fortitude, your kindnesses and compassion, and your trust and hope that you've extended to us. Amy and I feel like the richest artists we've ever known. Thank you!"

CHAPTER 116

A Second Temple

As I lived up to the highest light I had,
higher and higher light came to me.
—Peace Pilgrim

Matt glanced sideways at Genevieve as Jake took his seat. He recognized that she'd been as engrossed in Jake's sermon as he had been. The message had been honest and clear, vulnerable and trusting. The life of the village potter and his artist bride had not been easy, and yet Jake claimed to recognize that they'd been blessed as they'd witnessed the firm, yet gentle hand of Providence shaping and molding their lives for the better.

The congregation rose from their seats to sing a closing hymn before an elderly woman came to the lectern to offer a benediction. The prayer was short but sweet, thanking God for the hope and peace that comes from faith, and included a quick petition to bless Amy and her growing child, that all would be well.

"What are you thinking?" Genevieve asked, as they watched some congregants moving forward to talk to Jake while others made their way out into the bright light of the courtyard.

Matt sat silent for a moment, watching the congregation. "I was just thinking that I'm grateful I came."

Genevieve nodded. "Are you talking about to church, or to Niederbipp in general?"

"Both, I guess," he said turning to her. "I considered staying home after the jam fiasco." He rubbed the top of his head, noticing the goose egg was recognizably smaller than it had been immediately following his connection to the cellar's doorjamb. He smiled to himself, turning back to the front of the chapel. "I needed to hear this today. It would have been a shame to have missed it."

"Yeah," she agreed thoughtfully. "I'm ashamed to admit that when I heard Amy had married a potter, I...I imagined she must have married some high school dropout who made ceramic ashtrays and smoked a lot of marijuana."

Matt smiled. "It looks like you got that totally wrong."

Genevieve nodded. "I got a lot of things totally wrong about this place."

"We hear that from campers like you every year," a small voice with a rich accent said from behind them.

They turned to find the old German woman smiling at them. "I'm glad you kids could make it today to hear the story of one of my favorite young friends."

"You know Jake?" Genevieve asked.

"Of course I do. When you live in a small town, everyone knows everyone. Good boy, that one. Amy is lucky to have him. But then he's quite lucky to have her as well. They are a handsome couple, but then you two make a handsome couple also, don't you think?"

Matt and Genevieve looked at each other and tried not to laugh.

"It's not like that," Matt replied. "Genevieve's far too smart to get tangled up with a guy like me."

"*A guy like you*? I've been watching you two. You're often together, no? I've seen you on the streets of town. I've watched you in the courtyard and in the graveyard. You," she said pointing to Genevieve, "I saw you fall into the gutter this week and get all wet. When I saw that you were all right, I couldn't help but laugh." She paused for a moment to giggle. "Yep, you two have been fun to watch, trying so hard not to let on that you're crazy about each other."

Matt and Genevieve smiled at each other again before laughing awkwardly.

"What? Us?" Genevieve replied.

"Just look at you! It doesn't take much of an eye to see that you fit."

"Fit?"

"Sure! You know...he's the yin to your yang," Hildegard said, nodding to Matt. "And it's obvious to everyone with eyes that you're fond of each other. It's a beautiful thing to find love—to be able to watch it blossom before your very eyes and grow day by day. That's the way it was for me and my husband. It seemed the whole town knew before we did. We found out later some had even placed wagers we'd get hitched before we even began courting. When it's right, it seems everyone knows it."

Matt smiled. "That's kind of you to think a young girl like Genevieve would be attracted to an old man like me. What I mean is that's kind to me, but not very nice to her."

"Oh, what's the fuss? Sure, you're a few years older. Who cares? Your pants are still dry, aren't they?"

Matt laughed. "Last I checked."

"Then what's the big deal—a few years here or there? Far too many people lose out on a chance to love and be loved because they let silly things get in the way. And age is one of the silliest of all. A few extra trips around the sun ought to be appreciated rather than feared."

"How has that worked out for you?" Genevieve challenged.

"Oh, not as well as I hoped, but better than some."

"What does that mean?" asked Genevieve .

"I married only once, October 10th, 1943, and my husband was killed less than a year later in France. You don't soon get over that grief. There were six of us young brides who lost our husbands that year. None of us remarried. There weren't many options around here, you know. I am the last of those women on this side of the turf."

"You never fell in love again?" Matt asked.

"Oh, no, I did. Many times, in fact. But in a town as small as this one, most of the men are already taken, and the ones who aren't...well, let's just say most of them have a good reason to still be single."

"There've been many times I've felt that way...like I have a good reason to be single," Matt admitted.

She nodded. "But you realized you were wrong, didn't you?"

"Why do you say that?"

"Because you're here—you're still trying. You agreed to spend the summer on Ruby's farm because you wanted to be married and you hoped you were still eligible. That, and you're still grooming yourself like a man who cares. Too many men—and I suppose women too—once they've decided they're either no longer worthy of love or have lost hope in the enterprise, tend to go to seed. They stop caring. They give up hope. Somehow they get discouraged and forget they were made to love and be loved. It's our purpose, you know? To love! Actually, our purpose, I'm quite convinced, is to learn to live in joy. But unless there's something I missed, you must carry love with you or joy will forever elude you.

"I never gave up the hope of love, and neither have you," she said, patting Matt on the shoulder. "I am ninety-eight years old and I still dream of love and companionship. You don't get to my age and maintain a cheery disposition without believing in love, without looking for it in the faces of strangers, and sharing the hope of it with anyone who'll listen. There's no other fuel that can keep a woman as old as me going. I still believe in the miracle of love. And I still encourage it to grow wherever I see it sprouting."

"And you see it sprouting here?" Genevieve asked, motioning to the space between her and Matt.

The old woman smiled. "I only have so many breaths left, and I would not have wasted one in saying so if I hadn't seen the small bits of love growing between the two of you. Granted, it's only a seedling now, but it certainly has promise. If you'll both nurture and encourage it, you two have the potential of inspiring the entire world with your love."

Jake and Amy glanced sideways at each other, each of them forcing an awkward grin.

"You'll have to excuse me," Hildegard continued. "I have an appointment, and unless my eyes deceive me, the eyes of many of your comrades are upon you. Don't disappoint them. Love, *real love*, always inspires and uplifts, even those whose hearts are filled with doubts and fears," she said, nodding to their left.

Matt and Genevieve turned to catch the awkward stare of James, sitting six rows ahead of them and off to the left, next to Susan, Crystal and Greg. Genevieve waved at him playfully, but he quickly turned away, looking embarrassed. They turned back to the old woman, but she was gone.

"Hey, what are you doing right now?" Genevieve asked, turning to Matt.

"Oh, I was thinking I'd catch a movie, or maybe take a long drive through the countryside with the top down. How about you?"

She looked over her shoulder quickly before turning back. "Follow me." She grabbed his hand and pulled him to the doorway. With many of the congregants still moving forward to speak to Jake, the aisle and doorway were mostly clear.

"What's up?" Matt asked, shading his eyes with his free hand as she pulled him out into the sunlight.

Genevieve stood on her tiptoes, looking out across the courtyard where a few dozen congregants were visiting in scattered groups. "There she is," she said after a moment, pointing to a thin figure dressed in black on the far side of the courtyard, half obscured in the shadows. "Come on," she said, grabbing Matt's elbow as she went bounding down the stairs.

"Where are we going?"

"I'm not sure," she said, turning back to look at him, a mischievous twinkle in her eye.

They paused at the top of the stone staircase that dropped down to Hauptstrasse, watching as the thin woman, dressed in black, finished her descent, turned right and disappeared beyond their view.

"Isn't that Hildegard?" Matt asked.

Genevieve nodded. "Come on," she replied, taking the stairs two at a time.

"Remind me, why are we chasing her?"

"We're not *chasing* her," she responded without pausing. She stopped her mad rush at the bottom of the stairs, stealthily peaking around the corner as Matt caught up to her. He stood behind the wall as well, looking up the street at the old woman who was making surprisingly good time up the cobblestones.

"You got another one of those bees in your bonnet?" Matt asked, wondering what they were doing.

"Shhh," Genevieve replied.

"Is this some kind of a stakeout?"

"Yes. Kind of."

"Okay, tell me what's going on."

"Every Sunday after church, she disappears," Genevieve whispered.

"Uh, like into thin air?" Matt asked.

"Maybe. I don't know," she continued to whisper. "Come on, we can't lose her!" She took off running, hugging the tall retaining wall and looking completely comical as she hurried along through the nearly empty street.

"You know you look ridiculous, right?" Matt suggested, walking down the middle of the street, trying not to call any attention to himself from the handful of strangers who had not yet taken any particular notice of them.

"Shhh," she responded, quickly crossing the street and hugging the corner of the building adjacent the parallel lane, down which the old woman had disappeared. Still making good speed, she was at least thirty paces ahead of them, walking briskly as if she might be late for something.

"Are you going to tell me what's going on, or are you just going to act like a crazy spy?"

"Shhh, she'll hear you."

"So what if she does. She's probably going home for a nap."

"I don't think so. She's told me a couple of times that she has an appointment. It seems suspicious."

Matt looked up at the old lady. "Suspicious or curious?"

"What's the difference?"

"Well, suspicious, I think, implies she might be doing something nefarious. Curious…that's just doing something you don't have an answer for."

"Yeah, this is definitely suspicious," Genevieve whispered. "Let's go. She turned right!"

Matt couldn't help but laugh as Genevieve loped down the narrow cobblestone lane like she was stalking a dangerous killer, hugging the buildings on the right side.

"Is that a crime?" he asked, when he caught up to her. She'd stopped, hiding behind another building as she watched the old woman retreat through a winding, shady allée of trees.

"I'm not sure, but we should probably find out. Follow me."

They followed the elderly lady from a growing distance as the blind corners for them to hide behind became increasingly scarce. They walked through the shaded allée and across the highway before they realized where they were. The top stone of the Engelhart Ebenezer was visible just above the stunted trees and shrubs which lined the highway.

Wandering past the Ebenezer, Matt glanced at the adjacent bench, remembering discovering this place a few weeks ago with Genevieve. A narrow path on the far end of the natural alcove continued on toward the river and they picked up the pace, trying not to lose the elderly woman while also trying not to alert her that she was being followed.

But the path soon opened onto the river bottoms where the grasses and wildflowers grew tall and the hiding places became increasingly sparse. They watched the woman from a greater distance here as she made her way along the narrow footpath that paralleled the river. Finally, a hundred yards ahead of them, she turned to her right, veering off the path, and disappeared behind the curtain of the long, flowing branches of a majestic weeping willow perched at the river's edge.

"Well, that's not what I expected," she admitted, as she lifted her hand to her brow to shade her eyes from the sun.

"Oh, did you expect her to be meeting her dealer for her weekly bag of dope?" Matt asked.

Genevieve shrugged. "I'm not sure what I was expecting, but it was definitely not this."

"What do you think she's doing in there?" Matt asked.

"I have no idea. Do you want to find out?"

"How can we do that without making it obvious that we've been following her?"

"I don't know yet. Follow me."

They took their time covering the distance, bracing themselves for any potential surprises. They soon were standing at the intersection of two paths; the main footpath, and a second, much shorter and less worn path that disappeared into the willow's darkly shaded canopy.

"I don't like it," Genevieve said.

"What don't you like?"

"It's spooky."

"I was just thinking it was beautiful. What are you afraid of?" He stepped closer, closing the thirty-foot gap between them and the first of the cascading branches that hung low enough to touch the heads of the tall grass.

"Where are you going?" she asked, grabbing his arm.

"I just want to see what's up. There's a sign over there," he said, pointing to the far end of the wooden bench, obscured by shadow, which stood adjacent the place where the path disappeared behind the green curtain.

She reluctantly followed him, bracing herself, for what, she did not know.

The bench, similar in structure and design to the benches on the farm, looked as though it was quite old, the graying planks that made up the seat and the backrest worn smooth. The small, ceramic tile embedded in the bench's backrest was also similar to those on the farm, but this one was glazed with a bright blue glaze, its words, BE STILL, AND KNOW THAT I AM GOD, clearly legible through the glaze.

Matt sat down on the bench, leaning against the backrest.

"What are you doing?" Genevieve asked.

"What the sign told me to do." He pointed to the larger ceramic tile that had been fastened atop a four by four standing ten inches taller than the bench's seat, planted next to it in the ground.

She leaned over and read the darkened words. PLEASE BE STILL, AND WAIT YOUR TURN.

"What is this place?" Genevieve asked, straining her eyes to see into the shadows.

"I'm not sure."

She sat down next to him, feeling unsettled and impatient.

While they waited, they discussed the morning's sermon. They had each been around Jake a couple of times. They knew a little about his work as potter, and a little bit more about his heart because of interactions they'd had with him during Sourdough Sunday. Because of this, his faith had appeared to be a vibrant, even vital part of who he was. But neither of them had been prepared for the depth of that faith, for the expressions of hope in both God and Christ that he'd shared that morning.

It was still strange to both of them how prevalent the talk of spirituality was here. They both recognized how limited such talk had been in their worlds back home. Things were different here. People were not ashamed or embarrassed to express their hope and faith in God and a better world. There was a sense of reverence present in even normal, everyday interactions that felt neither forced nor weird. It was simply another natural part of who these people were.

Matt shared with Genevieve how this was both a refreshing and positive alternative to the growing secularism he'd witnessed across the globe. Even among some of the poor communities where faith remained at least among the older set, the younger millennials and teens were commonly distancing themselves from the faith traditions of their fathers and mothers. Being swept up in Hollywood's every-expanding tide of alternative morals, many traditional values and principles which had served to preserve faith and families for generations were being set aside as superstitious relics.

Matt shared his observations of how, in the name of progress and modernization, reverence for spirituality was becoming largely uncommon, hope was giving way to hopelessness, and charity was being swept aside by greed and indifference. He wondered aloud if the magic Niederbipp appeared to have in abundance might somehow offer an alternative path to this apparent race to the bottom.

As Genevieve listened to him talk, she couldn't help but feel at least subtle pangs of guilt for her contributions to the shifting sands of moral apathy. In her heart of hearts she had to admit that her work had done nothing to promote rectitude. In that moment of clarity, instead of there being at least fifty shades of gray, there was a much clearer delineation between what was right and good, and what was not either one.

"Well, I didn't expect to see the two of you here," Hildegard said with curious smile, parting the greenery curtain and interrupting Genevieve's thoughts. "Are you also here for an appointment?"

"An appointment? Yes, I think we are," Matt replied.

The old woman smiled, sweeping the long branches to the side, making room for them.

When Matt saw what she was doing, he stood, his curiosity piqued as he looked through into the darkened canopy, seeing very quickly this was much different than anything he could have expected. Sunlight danced off the water on the far side where the ends of the tree's supple tendrils delicately touched the river's surface, refracting ripples of light into the canopy above his head. Stunned by the beauty of this place, he turned back, taking Genevieve's hand and pulling her into the beautiful space as Hildegard held open the veil.

"What is this place?" Genevieve asked in amazement as she watched in awe the silver coins of light dance across the shady branches overhead.

"You like it?" Hildegard asked with a generous smile.

Dumbstruck, Genevieve walked in further, approaching the gnarled trunk that looked to be at least four feet in diameter. Two branches, extending from the trunk nearly parallel to each other, each about ten inches in diameter, stretched out over the river. The bark on the lower branch was smooth and worn, offering a comfortable seat, while the branch above offered stability and a rest for visitors' arms.

She sat down before pivoting, lifting her feet over the lower limb so she could face the river. As she stabilized herself with her hands on the branch above, she noticed the surface of the limb had been carved. The bright sunlight reflecting off the river and into her eyes made it difficult to see the carving until she lowered her head into the shadow cast by the limb.

She traced the rough, scarified letters with her finger, making out the letters as untold numbers of visitors had done before her. BE STILL AND KNOW THAT I AM GOD.

Any other words would be inappropriate in a place like this, so full of natural beauty and charm. Holding on to the branch above her, she leaned her head way back, watching the light dance all around her to the gentle purr of the branches ruffling the river's surface.

"Is this heaven?" Genevieve asked, turning Hildegard.

The old lady smiled. "It's certainly a window into heaven, isn't it?"

"Do you come here every week?" Matt asked

"Yep, at least nine months out of the year, if circumstances permit. As pleasant as it is today, winter is not nearly as enjoyable."

"And…Sundays…you have a standing appointment?" Genevieve asked.

She nodded. "Every Sunday at eleven. I often come on other days, too, if I find myself in need of a pick-me-up. This has been my special place for more than seventy-five years. It's a place where heaven and earth are not very far apart."

"Seventy-five years," Matt said, doing the math in his head. "That must have been about the time you lost your husband."

She pursed her lips, nodding solemnly. "This is called The Crying Place."

"The *Crying* Place?" Genevieve asked, looking quite surprised. "But it's so beautiful. There doesn't seem to be any sadness here."

"That's exactly why I come. If you think it's beautiful now, you should see it the first week of October when all these leaves turn to gold."

"The sign by the bench…do many people come here?" Matt asked.

"There used to be many. There were times we had to wait a half an hour or more for our turn. But people die, or move on, or their griefs have become…less than they were."

"And you? Is it grief that still brings you here?" Genevieve asked.

"In part, yes. Grief is part of loving, or rather, proof that you have loved. But everyone needs their quiet place, their temple or their haven where their souls can be still for a moment and the truths of your heart can reconcile with the truths in your head. This is where I come to rebalance the world."

Genevieve pivoted on the lower branch, turning back around. "So, balance…that's what you come here looking for?"

"Oh, that's certainly a big part of it, yes! Our world is so easily turned upside down. There've been times over the years that I've come ten days in a row, trying to find my bearings."

"And how does being here change things for you?" Matt asked.

Hildegard took a deep breath, looking up into the tree. "Our spirits crave silence and reverence, don't they?"

Matt nodded before shaking his head. "I know what you're saying is true for me, but I'm not sure if that's true for everyone. It seems like lots of folks don't know what to do with reverence or stillness and are often frightened of silence."

"No, you're quite right. And the younger generation hardly knows what to do with it. It's no easy thing to make time for expectant stillness, if you can even find a place that will provide it. I think you both know that I am Jewish. My people are known throughout the history of the world as temple building people. Even in the wilderness they carried their temple with them as they moved, providing a place to be holy even in the desert. Why? Because what my forefathers knew is that mankind is incomplete without a recognition of that part of him that is not of this world. And not unlike the food and water that is required to keep our bodies nourished and strong, our spirits require sustenance of a different kind to stay strong, nourished, and resilient. Just as you cannot neglect the nourishment of the body without suffering, you cannot neglect the nourishment of the spirit and maintain balance. This is why I come here, and go to church, and pray, and love my neighbors. All these things are reverence and worship and points of balance and good will."

Genevieve nodded slowly."But, you're Jewish, and the people here are Christian. Do you ever have a conflict?"

Hildegard laughed. "What, and miss out on joining myself to a community who shares all my core values? No, my people are still waiting for the Savior. These people already believe He came and will soon return, and are trying to live their lives in a way that will allow them to know Him better. None of us have all the answers. And I'd much rather surround myself with love and light and rejoice in our shared faith and reverence for God and our fathers than allow small differences to close my heart to anyone." She lifted her head, looking up into the canopy. "A temple on the hill, like the one here in Niederbipp, is a fine place to connect with God's children. But a temple like this one, a place where you can connect with God without the distractions of the world, this is also necessary to finding balance.

Matt nodded, looking contemplative. "So...if balance requires at least three points of connection, we have a temple on the hill...the church—or Charity. And then a temple like this one where we can practice our own reverence. That leaves the third point of connection— hope. Where is that temple?"

Hildegard smiled, stepping closer to Matt. "The third temple is here," she said, laying her hand over his heart.

He nodded slowly. "Of course. Why didn't I think of that?"

"Many people don't. But Jesus told you where to find it...'*the kingdom of God is within you.*' Or, '*your body is a temple,*' or one of my personal favorites, '*you will seek me and find me if you seek me with all your heart.*'"[1]

"And balance," Genevieve said, standing and walking to where the others stood near the oversized trunk, "it can't truly happen without all three, reverence, hope and charity."

"That is correct," Hildegard confirmed.

"So that scripture...the one where Jesus is asked which is the most important commandment and He answers: to love God and to love your neighbor...there are only two," Matt suggested.

"You missed one," she said, reaching for his hand which she opened, palm up. "Reverence, the love of God," she said, pinching his thumb softly. "And charity, the love of your neighbors," she said, touching his pinky. "Many forget that it doesn't end there. Jesus said to love your neighbors...AS YOURSELF. There is a hierarchy of importance, but all are necessary for balance to prevail. Without love for yourself," she said, lightly pinching the tip of his middle finger, "there can be no enduring hope, only misery and imbalance."

1. Luke 17:21, 1 Corinthians 6:19, Jeremiah 29:13

"And that's part of why you come here," Genevieve said, "to work on loving yourself?"

The old woman smiled warmly, nodding. "Questions like these... curiosity...seeking for answers—those things are all important parts of finding both truth and balance. I commend you both."

Matt smiled but shook his head. "It just feels like the more I learn, the more I realize I don't know."

"Good!"

"Wait, that's a good thing?" Genevieve asked, as Matt looked puzzled.

"Sure. If you have it all figured out, you stop asking questions. You stop searching for answers. You get cocky and believe you know all there is to know. There's no meekness in that. It's only a meek and humble heart that welcomes new truth and is anxious to change and evolve to fully accept it."

"So, where do we go from here?" Matt asked.

"I don't know."

"You don't?"

She shook her head. "It will be different for both of you, and it will be different for each of you than it was for me. There will be many who will try to tell you which way is best, but those who truly know will always encourage you to go straight to the source of all truth and light, and not be distracted by any of its reflections. Anything less than the real deal will be inadequate and unfit for your personal quest."

Matt glanced at Genevieve, then turned back to Hildegard. "So the keys...the three temples...are you suggesting that's where we should look?"

"If it's truth and balance you're seeking, yes. I'm aware of no other path that will provide you with the answers you desire."

CHAPTER 117

The End of Swing

By three methods we may learn wisdom:
First, by reflection, which is noblest;
Second, by imitation, which is easiest;
and third by experience, which is the bitterest."
- Confucius

Hildegard left Matt and Genevieve at the tree to discover their own connections to the mystical place. The beauty and peace surrounding the tree was beyond anything they'd ever experienced in the natural world, leaving them to wonder if it truly was a window into heaven. As they sat together on the lower branch, their feet dangling just inches above the water, Matt examined the carving on the upper branch, guessing from the scarification of the bark that it had to have been done many years before. They wondered together about the age and history of the tree, and what it was beyond its physical beauty that had endowed it with such an aura of peace.

When the church bells chimed twelve times, they retraced their steps back to town to see what they could do to help Jake and Amy with Sourdough Sunday. But as they walked through the courtyard to get their bikes, they found the rest of the campers in a chilly discussion on the benches, many of them still miffed about the events of the early morning that had made them all rushed. There had obviously been some finger-pointing and the airing of hard feelings, and the happy spirit they'd so recently identified as "swing" had completely evaporated and devolved into something much different.

They learned that Pops and Ruby had headed back to the farm to give Ruby a chance to rest, taking James and Crystal with them since they didn't have bikes. Matt and Genevieve listened for a few minutes as different factions argued their points of who was to blame and why it was unfair. Before much more could be said, Crystal, Josh and Sonja decided they'd heard enough and would rather bike back to the farm than have to endure any more futile rehashing that afternoon.

Hoping to tame the beast that had grown in their absence, Matt and Genevieve invited the other seven campers to join them in helping Jake and Amy get ready. Greg and Holly joined them eagerly, grateful to have a more productive option, but the other five were bent on arguing their points and defending their platforms, saying they might catch up later.

But Sourdough Sunday came and went and the last five of the campers never arrived. Jake and Amy's gathering went fairly well, other than one loaf of bread that slipped from the peel and crashed to the studio's floor, and the fact that in his haste to leave the farm that morning, Matt had grabbed to jars of beets rather that two jars of jam. The butter, at least, turned out well, and others provided jams and honey to cover Matt's mistake.

As the four campers made their way home to the farm, they all recognized a feeling of darkness around them. Despite the day starting well, Jake's beautiful sermon, and Matt and Genevieve's experience with Hildegard at the tree, the negativity of the campers' interactions overshadowed the good. The four of them collectively dreaded what they would find at the farm upon their return. And as it turned out, the foreboding they felt was prophetic. Ruby and Pops were absent, and the eight campers who'd returned earlier were scattered across the farm, unwilling to reconcile or even talk to each other, some even promising that things would never be the same. It all felt melodramatic, especially for Matt and Genevieve who'd missed the earlier brouhaha in the courtyard, and Greg and Holly, who'd left the negativity and name calling for something better and were now being accused of treason and abandonment by those who stayed to fight.

After an hour of assessing the situation, trying not to get sucked in to any one side, they discovered that the spirit of contention had created at least five different factions. From Susan on Team 'Woman have the right to take as long as they want to get ready', to Josh firmly in the 'Church takes up too much of my Sunday' Camp, each of the campers floated between at least two of them, depending on the argument. But for the four who'd separated themselves and claimed neutrality, all of the factions seemed petty and meaningless. This proved to only be more problematic as those with dogs in the various fights fought even harder to win the allegiance of the latecomers, until the neutral four left to make dinner, making the others feel like they'd been abandoned.

By the time the dinner bell rang, only Pops, Ruby and Rachael joined the four in the dining hall. The others, incensed beyond either their hunger or their rational thinking, dug in. Matt and Greg returned to their bunkhouse to find the all bunks re-stacked according to teams, and their beds stacked haphazardly against one wall.

Sleep softened some of the hard feelings, but the next morning's chores were performed without much harmony, both the KP and laundry staff unable to speak to each other when they showed up late for breakfast. The normally affable mealtime discussion was replaced with silence and stink eye. By dinner, the disharmony had produced two burnt pot roasts, five gallons of spilled milk, at least a dozen cracked eggs and a whole lot of hard feelings. Most of the campers went to bed hungry for the second night in a row, porch games having been cancelled due to the ugliness.

Since Ruby had gone to bed early, Matt and Genevieve stayed up talking with Pops, trying to come up with a solution to the challenges and disharmony. It was clear that the problems would not be quickly repaired, but they knew something needed to be done before a mutiny could occur.

Pops seemed less concerned than Matt and Genevieve, suggesting most summer recruits had their hiccups, even after experiencing a close sense of harmony. "You kids have known harmony," he said. "And the fact that you've tasted its sweetness and have even experienced swing will help you all find it again if you'll unitedly seek it out and learn how to work together once more."

That night, Genevieve pulled Sonja aside, and appealing to her expertise as a botanist, invited her to give the family a daily update on the garden. And so, the next evening, after visiting the garden, Sonja stood at that at the dinner table and offered an expert's opinion on the health and progress of the garden. With enthusiasm, she announced that the first of the peas would be ready to harvest that week, that the lettuces and other greens were doing very well and that the pepper and tomato plants were flowering and already producing tiny, green fruits.

The next day, Rachael, the most accomplished visual artist among them, found her way to the garden for other reasons. A bench on the far side of the enclosed space offered a fine view of the garden plot that she'd been enjoying for a couple of weeks, but the growing produce became the subject of several watercolor sketches which she shared with the family that night.

Inspired by Rachael's talent, Holly, Genevieve and Spencer asked her to lead a class for non-painters. And so, the next afternoon, they gathered at the dining table in the big house for the first artistic instruction most of them had had in at least a decade. The flurry of creativity attracted the attention of four more of the campers who joined them, sharing the brushes and paints and producing nearly two dozen paintings of produce in a wide range of quality.

Before class was even over, it was decided that they should attempt to sell the paintings at the farm stand, if for no other purpose than to help pay for more art supplies. But the idea soon proved to be a good one when even the sophomoric paintings began fetching at least a few dollars every day at the stand. Many of the campers, used to earning close to six figures and better, found themselves surprisingly joyful when the paintings they made with their own two hands and requiring an hour to complete, began bringing in five to ten dollars—dollars they didn't even get to keep, but were rolled into the collective kiddy to help support the farm.

With each passing day, the garden grew bigger and greener. This was most recognizable from week to week as they rotated through the chores, but Sonja's daily updates helped to keep the somewhat less-observant campers apprised of the growth and progress of each variety of the seeds they'd planted. She was soon reporting on radishes, beans and potatoes, and the herbs were producing enough to sell their surplus at the farm stand. Her reports on the corn were probably the most exciting; it seemed to almost shoot out of the ground, growing sometimes a few inches in just one day.

The small watercolor sketches continue to sell well, but some of the other creative endeavors to help support the farm were unfortunately not as successful. Pops and Ruby were quick to support most new ideas. They'd seen many good ones over the years, as well as witnessing their share of outright failures. Homemade cookies continued to be a hit, but Josh's idea of Pet Rocks was nearly a total flop, even after he enlisted Rachael's help in painting eyes on each of them. After only three of them sold in ten days, Josh was forced to cut his losses, which, in all fairness, amounted to little more than the time he'd spent scrubbing the rocks and building a *corral* for them to hang out in. James's paper air planes and Holly's origami, both of which were invented the afternoon they were working the stand together, replaced Josh's rocks on the counter and sold surprisingly well, garnering nearly twenty dollars from a handful of tourists who may or may not have felt sorry them.

But Ephraim wasn't ready to give up on the pet rocks. With Josh's help and blessing, he engineered a new idea, repurposing the rocks in his Alexander Calder inspired *Rock Mobile*. Wrapping the stones with common twine and suspending them from the ends of several willow switches, Ephraim demonstrated to all the campers how, with a little creative pizazz, regular, garden-variety rocks could appear to float weightlessly, moving with even the slightest breeze.

At dinner that night, the campers were all impressed with Josh and Ephraim's demonstration of their new product. Josh, with a little coaching from Ephraim, shared how balance could be achieved, even among very disparately sized rocks, by finding the center of gravity. The demonstration led to a thoughtful conversation about the fragility and temporary nature of balance. The next day at the farm stand, Josh and Ephraim's *Rock Mobile* sold to a tourist for a whopping $85 after Genevieve and Greg explained to them the beauty of finding one's center of gravity. The proceeds of the sale of the mobile went to buy other arts and crafts supplies, and Ephraim generously taught all the campers how to build mobiles.

Each of the campers shared hopes that the mobiles would be a great boon the farm's meager coffers, but they never were. Though they made and displayed a couple dozen mobiles of various sizes and complexity, only two additional mobiles sold over the course of the next several weeks, and for far less than $85.

Sensing discouragement in the troops, Pops spent an afternoon teaching them a simple design for making hand-carved Santa Claus Christmas ornaments from the fallen twigs collected in the woods. These, he explained, had been made from time to time by campers over the years and had been met with varying degrees of success. Happy to have a new challenge and an opportunity to work on something which required the work and interaction of all members of the team, they got busy, and within a couple of days had carved and painted nearly sixty ornaments. To everyone's surprise, the ornament sold like hot cakes at $10 apiece. They decided to up the price to $15 each or two for $25. Still, the ornaments continued to sell quickly, perhaps even faster than before. By common consent the price rose to $20, and then $25 before a woman showed up at farm stand to say she'd just bought a similar ornament at a farm stand five miles to the north for only $15.

It was Genevieve and James who examined the counterfeit Santa and found it nearly identical to the ones they'd been making. They returned back to the farm that night full of rage after two more cars from the north stopped by the stand with the same bad news. And what was worse, the competition was reportedly having a difficult time keeping up with the demand.

The discussion around the dinner table was heated among the campers that night. They spoke of sending out spies to discover who these scabs were, and even joked about roughing them up. Though they appeared troubled, Ruby and Pops kept quiet until they were asked for their opinion on the matter.

"I'm glad you asked," Ruby admitted. "As I've listened to you kids talking I've found myself wondering how your response to these *imposters* jibes with what you kids have learned so far about the keys of joy."

When pressed for his opinion Pops responded, "I don't believe you kids have enough information to provide yourselves an adequate view of the big picture." He went to suggest that if they truly had a desire to understand while at the same time applying the keys of joy, more information would certainly be needed.

The campers returned to their bunkhouses earlier than normal that evening, with weighty discussions and constructive arguments taking place under the two different roofs until the men knocked on the women's door and suggested a solution they all could agree with. It was acknowledged that Pops was right: they simply didn't have enough information to form any objective conclusions, and that mercy and charity would need to be applied in order to come to any desired understanding.

And so, the next day after morning chores were accomplished, a small delegation of the farm's two attorneys, along with Spencer and Crystal, left the farm to discover for themselves who these scoundrels were. Five miles north of town, they spotted the dastardly farm stand. They parked their bikes on the shoulder of the highway and approached the rundown stand like they were looking for a skunk. But to their surprise they didn't find one. Instead, they found a cute, little, old woman and her husband, who couldn't have been much younger than Pops and Ruby. The man, sitting in a wheelchair next to a pile of sawed up branches, was busily carving away while his wife painted the Santas.

The sight of the elderly pair took the wind out of the campers' sails. They spoke to them for a few minutes as they looked around at the couple's meager offerings—a few old carrots and some sprouted potatoes alongside two small baskets full of Santas. But when they learned that the elderly couple were making their ornaments to help pay off medical bills, it became clear that no one would be suing anyone today, and the well-polished cease and desist threat that James had rehearsed all morning went without being uttered. Instead, James surprised the others by not only purchasing a Santa ornament from the couple, but by leaving a $5 tip to help with their medical bills.

The delegation returned home silently and humbly, so thoughtfully reckoning their impressions that they didn't even stop at their own farm stand before ascending Harmony Hill. The discussion that night was very different than it had been the night before. Instead of anger and contempt, there was a palpable sense of compassion.

After a lengthy analysis led by Matt, the campers came to a few common conclusions. One, they wanted to keep making ornaments. Two, they'd originally been very happy making them for only $10. Three, they knew that the folks who ran the farm stand to the north, whom they'd once dubbed imposters and scabs, were in need. And four, that they had it in their power to do something to help the elderly couple.

Taking their lead from their barn-raising experience on the Stoltzfuss farm and the keys of joy, it was decided that evening that they would lower the price of their ornaments back to $15 and donate $5 from every purchase to the folks up the road who had copied them. It wasn't fair, but they all agreed it felt right when overlaid with the keys of reverence, charity and hope.

Pops and Ruby were quick to offer their support to the plan without any suggestions for alterations. And so the next day, and every day after that, at least one team would leave the farm in the afternoon, and after picking up cash from their own farm stand, would ride five miles north, purchase an ornament from the couple they came to know as Nora and Ned, and leave a generous tip from the earnings of their own ornament sales.

Something big changed over the course of the next few weeks as they worked together on the Santas. Their work became more than a chore. It had a purpose—a purpose with a heart. And somehow it filled their own hearts with hope and peace and love as they worked and shared and discussed the things they were learning about Nora and Ned.

They learned they had married in their late twenties and been blessed with two sons, one in California and the other in Tennessee. They had five grandkids and twelve great-grandkids, but rarely had visitors, and hadn't made the journey to see their family themselves in many years due to health and finances.

Ned, they learned, was a retired farmer who'd been forced to sell all of their land except the half acre around their humble home when they outlived their meager retirement savings. Hospital bills from a couple of illnesses had quickly evaporated the money they'd made from the sale of their farm, forcing them into a reverse mortgage on their farmhouse. But they just kept living, more than a decade longer than they'd planned for and more than two decades longer than any of their parents. They'd joked with a few of the campers on one visit that love alone had kept them alive and thriving well beyond what they believed was a useful life. They told another group of campers that the ornaments they were making kept them going, both financially and by giving them a reason to live. With another set of campers, they disclosed that beyond the purpose the work gave them, it was also breathing new life into their marriage as their work united them in something far more productive and positive than whiling away their days in front of the television while waiting for the good Lord to call them home.

Ned and Nora were often the topic of conversation at the dinner table over the next few weeks as the campers worked together in their chores and on their own products for the farm stand. And as they stitched together the story of this cute couple, there developed among them a growing sense of compassion and charity to the point that they each looked forward to making the daily trip, five miles to the north on their bicycles. Soon, cookies and other treats from their own farm stand began accompanying the campers as gifts to Ned and Nora.

And then one Monday afternoon the farm stand to the north was closed when the campers arrived at their usual time. It was closed again the next day, and the next. With growing concern, it was decided that most of the campers would make the journey the following day to investigate.

And so it was that ten of the campers made the journey the next morning before lunch. Finding the farm stand once again closed, they split up to begin their investigation. Not far from the shack, half concealed by overgrown shrubbery, they discovered a humble farm house. They ditched their bikes behind a shiny Buick with Tennessee plates, parked in front of a dilapidated garage, and knocked on the front door of the farmhouse.

A balding, middle-aged man answered the door, looking quite surprised by the sight of ten concerned campers. When asked if he might know Ned and Nora, his face fell with emotion. The man's wife, standing behind him, explained that they'd received a call on Saturday night that Ned was not doing well. He slipped into unconsciousness shortly after they'd arrived from Tennessee on Sunday, and had died early Monday morning. Nora, the woman explained, had gone to bed in peace that night and hadn't awakened next morning.

There had been no funeral. With all of their friends having already gone to heaven and their second son unable to come because of health problems of his own, they'd followed their parents' wishes for their bodies to be donated to science. It wasn't at all the news the campers had hoped for, but with tear-filled eyes, the elderly couple thanked the campers for helping to make their parents' final days joyful.

Shocked and heartbroken by the news, the campers left the loaf of bread and plate of cookies intended for Ned and Nora and were tearfully making their way to the highway when they were called back by the couple and asked if they might have any need of the three old bicycles that were in the garage. The folks from the bank, they explained, had already been in touch and given the family only two weeks to vacate the property as outlined by the reverse mortgage contract. It would be doing them a favor, they said, if they could take the bicycles and any tools that might be useful from the garage. Whatever they didn't want would be given to Goodwill or the county dump.

The campers returned to the garage and dusted off the old bicycles. Most of the tools were old and worn, but they gathered up a few shovels and rakes, whatever they could carry on their bicycles, and were on their way out of the garage when they noticed a basketful of half- finished Santa ornaments along with Ned's carving tools and Nora's paint brushes. Knowing these would all go to waste if they didn't take them, they added these to the baskets on the front of the bicycles and thanked the couple for their generosity.

Encumbered with the extra bicycles and tools, it was foolish to attempt to ride. But the long walk back to Harmony Hill was contemplative for each of the campers. Conversation came slowly at first, but it came with rich thought and deep emotion as they discussed the shortness of life and the sense of loss they all felt at losing two friends they'd known for only a few weeks—friends, they were reminded, who had started out as perceived enemies and scoundrels.

The campers stopped by their own farm stand to tell Greg and Rachael what they'd discovered. More tears were shed as they shared the sad news. It was Holly and her emotional reminder of Ruby's tenuous prognosis that opened the floodgates of thoughts and emotions that many of them had been feeling but had been unable to express. Before the ten delegates continued to the farm, it was unanimously decided that they would do all they could to make whatever days remained for Ruby as pleasant and as easy as possible for both of their elderly hosts.

That evening's porch gathering began far more subdued and reverent than any other previous gathering, but things began to change as words came. There was peace. There was healing. There was a depth of understanding of the purposes and joys of life that many of them had never considered. Despite their many difficulties in the final days of their life, Ned and Nora had endured and enjoyed life with grace and love to the very end. And they had been blessed to be able to move into the next life together, separated for only a few hours. It was admittedly the best-case end-of-life scenario for all of the campers. And they learned that night that it had also been the hope of Pops and Ruby for many years that they would be blessed to wrap up this life at about the same time, not knowing how to function very well without the other.

Though the discussion was far more sober than usual, it was accompanied with an undeniable sense of hope. Death, whether they liked it or not, was a critical part of life's story, a part that would ultimately play a critical role in each of their plots. Ruby's gentle spirit touched each of them deeply that night as she openly expressed her humble courage for whatever the future held, and the timing of the Lord in calling her home. She had lived, she explained, in a way that had mercifully allowed for many course corrections over the years, enabling her to reach this advanced age without many regrets that hadn't already been reconciled. Death, she offered, was, after all, the last great adventure, and one she'd been preparing for—at least passively—since she first realized she was mortal, somewhere in her mid-twenties.

Before turning in for the night, Ruby and Pops announced that the town would be celebrating Independence Day the following day. She had committed to bring a cake for the annual cake auction and asked for volunteers. They all agreed to be helpful, but on the heels of losing Ned and Nora, they hesitated making any commitments to participate in any other activities.

They'd all separated to their bunkhouses that night feeling a renewed desire to make however much time they had left in life count for something good, positive and meaningful. And as Genevieve lay looking up through the skylight that night after an hour of thoughtful journaling, she found herself wondering how she could possibly go back to her old life after a summer filled with such variety, color and meaning.

11∞

CHAPTER 118

Celebrations and Promises

---

*our best chance of finding God is to look in
the place where we left Him.*
—Meister Eckhart

The campers rose the next morning with a different spirit in their hearts. Somehow, in the mayhem of producing items for the farm stand and their race to keep up with their competition to the north, a semblance of harmony had been restored. It had taken a month, but somewhere along the way they'd made room in their hearts for the joys that come of teamwork. Pushed far out of their comfort zones, they'd had to work together, each of them taking on a portion of the work, doing things many of them had never done before and coming up with creative solutions they might never have otherwise imagined. And they'd had to be patient with each other, learn to forgive each other, and rediscover the joys of harmony before they all wanted it enough to allow the good feelings to return.

As they worked through their morning chores, there was a sense that a burden had been lifted. Ned and Nora were gone. There was nothing any of them could do about that. There was solace in the fact that they'd gone together, and somehow even greater solace for each of the campers who recognized the path they'd chosen in dealing with the old couple was one that had provided peace instead of anger and regret.

The discussion around the breakfast table that morning was one of gratitude that the keys of joy had given each of them a clearer vision and a better understanding of what life was all about. They each expressed thanks to Pops and Ruby for bringing them back to center when they'd wanted to rage without knowing the details. The discussion was healing for all of them, but it was cut short by Ruby's reminder of the town's Fourth of July celebration and her commitment to bring a cake for the auction. Though none of the campers felt particularly interested in the celebrations, having just spent their emotional budget on mourning for Ned and Nora, it was clear that Pops and Ruby were excited to be there.

The kitchen was crowded after breakfast as all the campers were enlisted by Ruby to help create her famous carrot cake. While the KP team worked on the day's bread, the rest of the campers gathered around the kitchen's large island, helping with one aspect of cake preparation or another. Flour was milled, fresh carrots were brought in from the garden and grated along with cinnamon bark and nutmeg from the cellar. While several campers worked on turning granulated sugar into powdered sugar with the help of a blender and a little cornstarch, four other campers were put in charge of creating cream cheese.

Cheese making had become a regular part of their chore rotation, but cream cheese was new to them. Ruby was attentive as she instructed them to boil two pots of the morning's milk on the behemoth stove and to keep the milk from scalding by constant stirring. The addition of a teaspoon of salt and several imprecise scoops of the plain yogurt, along with the reduction of the heat, caused the milk solids to separate from the whey. And after draining off the whey, they used the blender to break down the cooled curd into a thick and creamy consistency which they put in the fridge to chill.

This was not the first time any of them had made a cake from scratch; Ruby had made sure of that over the last two months. But it was the first time they'd all been enlisted in the process together. With each of the campers accepting a portion of the work, the task went quickly. And after several handfuls of pecans had been chopped, the mixing of the batter began, combining the different ingredients in an ancient stoneware bowl.

As had become the habit when Ruby cooked or baked with only a memorized recipe, Holly took the best notes she could, guesstimating wherever she had to in order to record what she quietly guessed might be the last time Ruby would be preparing the dish. Eggs, spices, salt, baking soda, carrots, applesauce, and crushed pineapple were combined before slowly adding the flour and sugar. Spencer, claiming the need of an arm workout, did the mixing until Ruby was satisfied. Then, when the three richly-patinated twelve-inch round pans had been buttered and dusted with flour, they were filled with the chunky, light brown batter and slid into the huge oven.

As they tidied up the kitchen and waited for their bread to rise, the conversation from breakfast continued. Gratitude for life and the opportunity to know Ned and Nora were the most repeated themes as they recounted details and memories from their interactions with them. Before they knew it, the cake was ready to be tested and pulled from the oven, which was then filled with the daily bread.

When Ruby began using the hand mixer to create the cream cheese frosting, she sent the campers back to their bunkhouses to get ready for the events of the day. While a picnic was being packed in the kitchen, fourteen inner tubes were inflated and strapped into the back of the pickup along with the bungee board. And before church bells tolled eleven times, the troupe of campers were on their way down Harmony Hill, their elderly hosts following closely behind in the overloaded pickup, carefully cradling a tall, frosted cake.

Hauptstrasse, Niederbipp's Main Street, was already crowded with revelers awaiting the beginning of the parade. With the bike rack at the top of the street already full, Pops and Ruby ushered their crew to a vacant bench a stone's throw from the upper fountain where they could lean the bikes against the retaining wall. Children played in the streets and neighbors, old and young, crowded into the space, standing shoulder to shoulder.

Just before noon, the explosive sound of cannon fire erupted from somewhere near the river, and the parade began with Sousa's *Stars and Stripes Forever* performed by a ragtag band of musicians ranging in age from junior high school kids to geriatrics. A flamboyant band leader who looked like he was in his mid-eighties, wearing a tall, tufted hat and carrying a silver-topped baton, led the group slowly down the cobblestones. It was impossible not to smile and at least wiggle, if not dance, as the comical mix of uniforms and the variety of instruments wandered past them. The skill and talent of a handful of the musicians made it fun for many of the others who were lucky enough to hit a few right notes out of ten. But this magnanimous display of kindness, inclusivity and goodwill electrified the musicians and the spectators alike. Genevieve laughed with the others when they spotted Hildegard, trailing the band with her concertina, wearing an uncharacteristically bright and patriotic getup and a three-cornered hat with red white and blue streamers swinging from each corner.

The marching band was followed by a small group of uniformed Girl Scouts who waved to the crowds on either side as they passed out advertising leaflets for their upcoming cookie fundraiser.

A group of seven rather stoic-looking Shriners came next wearing bedazzled maroon fezzes and business suits which looked far too warm for the day. They marched side by side, their flashy scimitars leaning against their shoulders, glistening in the sun.

The Niederbipp Soccer Club, mostly early teens wearing their jerseys and bouncing soccer balls on their toes, knees and foreheads, followed the Shriners, attracting the applause of the crowds.

The mayor, dressed in a large seersucker suit and a straw hat, and his rather rotund wife in a watermelon-print dress and an enormous sunhat rode down the street seated on a whimsical chariot pulled by a team of Shetland ponies, waving to their constituents.

Kai, Molly, their two children, and an older man, dressed in bright Aloha shirts, walked down the main drag, holding a banner which read, "Thanks For Shopping at Braun's Market" and waving to the crowd with their free hand.

Several other shops from the town followed in quick succession, waving flags and tooting horns. There were jugglers and a couple of clowns and a little girl taking her prize-winning rooster for a walk at the end of a leash. And just when it looked like the parade was ending, Pops and Ruby stood from the stone bench, unfurled a burlap banner that read "Harmony Hill Farm Stand" and encouraged the campers to fall in behind. There was a bit of confusion for a moment, but Matt was quick to respond, falling in behind the banner with his bicycle and waving to the crowd. The other campers joined in quickly, and soon all twelve of them were walking along the parade route, waving to the crowd who lined the streets. Many of them looked embarrassed at first, but that emotion quickly gave way to smiles as they realized they were doing something they'd never done before and would likely never do again.

They were halfway down the street before they realized the crowd was falling in behind them, following them and waving to the remaining crowds who in turn joined the parade-turned-procession through the end of the street and out onto the highway. Carnival rides, including a twelve seat Ferris wheel, rose above the trees, where the head of the human snake had already turned off the highway. The music of the marching band continued to play near the entrance of the fairgrounds until the last of the parade revelers had arrived.

Pops handed out ribbons of tickets to each of the campers for rides and games, and dispatched Matt and Holly to return to the truck and drive it to the fairgrounds where they would have easy access to the inner tubes and picnic. After delivering the cake to the pre-auction display tables under a large canopy that had been stretched between four telephone poles, they joined the others. They found Spencer surrounded by many of the village children as he threw baseballs at leaden milk jugs. Several of the children were holding stuffed animals, and many others were waiting in line to trade tickets for prizes which Spencer was generously sharing every time his ball met its mark.

The smell of popcorn filled the air, and children and adults strolled between the rides and games holding sticks of pink and blue cotton candy. The Girl Scouts were trading tickets for tall glasses of lemonade, and the river bank, partially shaded by old growth trees, was dotted with picnic blankets and the village folk milling about, enjoying each other's company.

There was an old fashioned charm and innocence woven through each of the activities, a place where children were safe to roam without supervision, and neighbor could mingle with neighbor in open friendliness.

After a picnic lunch, all of the campers joined Pops and Ruby in floating the river, along with what seemed like four hundred other revelers of all ages. Water fights and horseplay kept the regatta refreshing and entertaining over the course of the three-mile float to the bridge. Four flatbed hay wagons, linked together in a train, met the soggy-bottomed company, offering shuttle rides back to the fairgrounds to anyone who wanted. But the campers stayed and played along with their hosts, jumping from the bridge with the local teenagers and waiting their turn for another try at the bungee board.

By all accounts, the afternoon on the river was magical, and thanks to prior learning experiences, the male campers left the belly-flop competition to the younger lot. When they returned to the fairgrounds, an entourage of kids were awaiting Spencer's throwing arm and he quickly obliged them, graciously playing the hero by sharing his prizes with any kid who'd pay for him to play.

Pops, along with Matt, Genevieve, Ephraim and Susan rode back to the farm in the pickup to take care of the evening milking and the feeding of the chickens. They returned to plate dinners of fried chicken, corn on the cob, watermelon and potato salad which were served up by the ladies of the Junior League under the large awning. A hand painted banner, strung up behind them, notified everyone that all proceeds were going to the maternity ward renovation at the hospital. The campers were surprised when Ruby, who they discovered was a founding member of the Leagues Niederbipp Chapter, slipped on an apron, donned a hairnet, and spent an hour serving dinner with the ladies.

The cake auction started about the same time the ladies ran out of chicken. A large crowd gathered under the tent as the silver-tongued auctioneer took to the raised platform and began showing off his impressive skills of tongue and wit.

None of the campers were new to auctions, but the Niederbipp Annual Cake Auction was different than any they'd ever seen before. All of the regular hysterics were present, but after each cake had been auctioned to the highest bidder, it was taken and cut into as many slices as possible. When all the cakes had been sold and sliced, the auctioneer led all the onlookers in an unusually raucous rendition—especially for such a stone-cold sober gathering—of *For He's a Jolly Good Fellow.*

When they were finished, folks lined up to pay five dollars for a fork, a plate, and as many small slices of cake as they could eat. It seemed like a far more practical idea than sending any one person home with more cake than he should reasonably eat, while raising additional funds for charity. As the campers gathered to eat cake with the citizens of Niederbipp, they recognized a grand sense of sharing. No auction winner seemed at all upset about sharing his or her expensive cake with the neighbors, and no auction loser or spectator was kept from sampling as many of the cakes as they desired.

After the last of the crumbs had been consumed, the campers turned back to the carnival rides until the golden evening faded into night. For the second time that day, cannon fire was heard, only much closer this time. The rides and games quickly came to an end and the campers gathered back together with the townsfolk on the riverbank for a firework show none of them would soon forget.

Staged across the river on the pebbly beach, a small pyrotechnics crew moved about with red flares, illuminating the short tubes pointed heavenward. The marching band, from somewhere near the tent, raised their instruments and played *The Star-Spangled Banner*. Men, women, and children, silhouetted by the starry sky, rose to their feet, put their hands to their hearts and sang the words of the first verse with conviction.

Just as the music ended, a deep thud echoed off the hills as a tumbling light shot skyward. With an enormous boom, a thousand sparkling spiders exploded across the sky, trailing silks of silver sparks as they fell to the earth. The reflection of the light on the mirrored surface of the river doubled the dramatics as the crowd oohed and aahed. Before the last of the sparks burned out, another thud was heard and the sky again exploded in sparks and color flashes. Many on the beach, including the campers, leaned back, making it feel as if it were raining fire directly above their heads.

The campers had all seen plenty of fireworks shows before, but never had any of them been close enough to feel the concussions of the blasts and smell the acrid scent of the explosives or been incapable of holding back their audible expressions of awe. For fifteen minutes the show filled the night sky, culminating in the grandest finale any of them had ever seen.

When the light finally faded, leaving ghostly memories in their eyes, a loud roar of applause rose from the crowd, echoing off the hillside. They were just getting to their feet when the sound of cannon fire once again filled the night air, five deafening blasts in quick succession.

"Remember the keys of liberty," a woman's voice exclaimed in the darkness. "Remember the keys of liberty," many others echoed enthusiastically in reply.

The exclamation, seemingly lost on her companions, had not been lost on Genevieve. Instead, they echoed in her mind, causing her to remember what she'd learned from Thomas's book about the town's Freiheitsbrünnen. This Liberty Fountain, with its statue of Lady Liberty rising high above it, had stood in the heart of Niederbipp for two centuries. She remembered the five lost keys which had gone missing from the statue's grasp, many decades earlier. She remembered that Thomas had read his way through the town archives and interviewed dozens of individuals only to be stymied in his pursuit of answers. She remembered that the keys of liberty were also the keys of joy. And at the close of this day dedicated to the celebration of freedom, the cry, 'remember the keys of liberty,' had just rung out through the crowd as they parted for the evening.

Walking back to their bikes, the five cannon blasts and the woman's cry still echoing in her ears, Genevieve considered how easy it had been to forget the keys. She hadn't purposefully tried to forget them, but somewhere between the madness of the ornaments and busy-ness of the farm, they'd slipped through her fingers and out of her mind. She wasn't alone. All of the campers had forgotten. They'd lost their curiosity and wonder in the pursuit of far lesser things. And in the process, they'd lost a lot of time.

Before the campers left the fairground for their dark ride home, Genevieve determined that she would not allow herself to be distracted again.

"Did you hear it?" Matt asked as he pedaled up alongside her in the dark.

"'Remember the keys of liberty'?" she asked.

"Yes."

"I heard it, too," Ephraim said from darkness behind them. "Was that for us?"

"I was wondering the same thing," Holly admitted.

As they reached the steepest part of the incline and had to begin pushing their bikes up Harmony Hill, they learned they'd all heard the five words that had come on the heels of the cannon blasts. Some wondered aloud about the curious words while others who had not been privy to Thomas's book questioned if the keys of liberty might have anything to do with the keys of joy. Several wondered if the five cannon blasts at the end of the show had anything to do with remembering the keys they'd neglected in their month of disharmony and distractions. They all concluded that in a town where there was meaning and purpose behind everything, the deafening roar of the cannons were intended to be heard by each of them, and others who'd forgotten.

Slowed in their ascent by the thickness of the dark, Matt and Genevieve shared with the group many of the things they'd learned from Thomas and his book. And through the sharing of the things they'd learned, they collectively came to the same conclusion: most of the sites and points of interest around the town of Niederbipp served in one way or another as physical reminders of ethereal concepts and principles.

Several of the campers were quick to point out that it wasn't just the town that offered insightful connections. The farm was also full of reminders, symbols, and connections that might offer, if one were at all observant, regular reminders of the virtues and lessons Pops and Ruby had to share.

They reached the summit realizing that in their month-long bout of contentious disharmony, they'd missed a lot of important stuff. They stood for a moment, huddled together, looking down at the big house illuminated by the festoon porch lights. With each of them acknowledging that they wanted something more for their future and the time they had left, they committed to each other to not allow themselves to forget the keys of joy or the bigger reason for them being there. Tomorrow would be different. With only three months left of the summer, it had to be.

CHAPTER 119

Ünapologetically

Truth is like the sun. You can shut it out for a time,
but it ain't goin' away.
— Elvis Presley

There was a bit of a scramble the next Tuesday morning at breakfast when Ruby announced that the photographer who'd come six weeks earlier would be returning to the farm that morning to record the progress on the farm and to collect more photos. While most of the women ran back to the bunkhouse to straighten things up and try to look their best, Genevieve, along with Ephraim, were sent to the farm stand. They might have missed all the excitement had Patrick O'Brien not stopped by the stand again to purchase a selection of goods as a gift for Ruby. Under a thin disguise of sunglasses and a straw hat, Genevieve bit her tongue and encouraged Ephraim to do the same as they'd loaded him up with berries, cheese, radishes and wild flowers. Having made the same mistake he made last time in showing up early in the morning with only a hundred dollar bill, Patrick lingered a little longer, making sure he saw it all. The small selection of watercolors in the basket on the counter drew his attention, and he flipped through these quickly, choosing a small painting of radishes that Rachael had rendered and two Santa ornaments, obviously trying to make his hundred dollar donation stretch as far as possible.

Ephraim chatted up Patrick as he helped him load the items into his silver Land Rover. Noticing the gold wedding band on his left hand, Ephraim learned that since the photographer's last visit to the farm, he'd gotten married and that the small watercolor was actually a gift for his new bride.

Genevieve knew it was stupid—that cruel twinge of envy she felt as she watched him drive away. Their limited interactions had really only been enough for her to know that she admired his talent, and she couldn't help but appreciate his rugged good looks. But he'd be heading home in the next few hours, home to a marriage and a real life. And she'd be stuck here for the next few months, with no discernible plan after that.

Without a word, she left Ephraim at the stand and walked across the highway to the river. Picking up the biggest stone she could find, she heaved the rock above her head before tossing it into the river's flow. It felt good, so she did it again and again, tossing at least a dozen large rocks and splashing water all over her frontside before sitting down on the stoney bank, drawing her legs up to her chest and resting her chin on her knees.

It had been six weeks since she'd discussed Ruby's offer with Matt in the creamery—six weeks since Ruby had invited her to take her place at the end of the summer. In that time there'd been great moments of clarity, but plenty more of confusion and bewilderment at why a woman of Ruby's acclaim and reputation would not only allow but invite such an inexperienced imposter to fill her shoes. There was so much of it that didn't make sense, and yet over those weeks she'd often caught Ruby looking at her with kind and hopeful eyes.

True to her word, Ruby had applied no pressure. But whenever she was around her, Genevieve felt an ever-present sense of hope that she would accept the offer. She'd come close a few times to turning Ruby's offer down; come close to telling her it was simply too much of a commitment to make. But as she thought about each of those situations now, she recognized they'd all been based on emotional reactions to stupid situations that had long since resolved themselves. And with that recognition came another: that one by one, the pillars of her resistance were slowly giving way to possibility and potential.

Ephraim checked on her after an hour had passed. The traffic on the highway was busier than normal, and things were moving quickly in the farm stand. They were sold out by noon and considered heading back to the farm when an ice cream truck passed the stand, headed north. Thinking it best to avoid the farm with Patrick there, Genevieve talked Ephraim into checking out Mancini's Ice Cafe. And so, after eating the lunches the KP team had sent with them, and closing up the farm stand, they rode their bikes into Niederbipp.

Parking their old Schwinns at the top of Hauptstrasse, they walked down the town's main drag, surprised by the number of people in the streets. The town was still decorated with red, white and blue. Pleated fan flags hung from windows and lampposts, and patriotic pennant banners crisscrossed overhead all the way down the street, creating an inviting atmosphere for tourists and locals alike. They took their time wandering down the street, the memory of the first parade they'd ever marched in still fresh in their minds.

A scratchy speaker hanging above the open doors of the town's pudding mold museum belted out a Sousa march. Genevieve and

Ephraim smiled at each other as a couple, walking just in front of them, stopped to dance a jig before stepping into the eccentric space, its window displays showcasing retro-colored pudding molds donning paper wings, suspended by nearly-invisible monofilament line.

Ephraim looked tempted to follow the couple into the museum until Genevieve pointed out the marquee sign with mismatched lettering. Even with the holiday discount running through the end of the month, the cost of entrance was still $15 for two all-day passes. Looking disappointed, he turned away, but she quickly diverted his attention to the Ice Café where a dozen yellow umbrellas shaded the tables underneath them.

Feeling a desire to splurge using the magazine's expense card, Genevieve insisted they each order a five scoop bowl, suggesting they get a total of ten different flavors so they could try as many as possible. Ephraim was quick to agree, forgetting all about the pudding mold museum when they walked past it again as they continued their stroll through the decorated town. They stopped at the patriotically adorned fountain at the bottom of the street, both its basin and its statue draped in red, white and blue. Having missed most of these decorations in the flurry of excitement on Saturday, they sat down on the fountain's built-in bench and enjoyed their treat under the undulating shadows cast by the patriotic pennants overhead. They were nearly finished with their ice cream when they were caught in the crossfire of a rush of seven kids with squirt guns. Playing along, both Ephraim and Genevieve responded to the attack by dipping their hands into the catch basin behind them and hurling water back at the kids whenever they came within range.

The kids, four boys and three girls ranging in age from probably six to ten, turned their targets away from each other and ganged up on the two adults, dive bombing them with incredible accuracy before retreating, often unscathed by retaliatory attempts. This went on for several minutes until the kids disappeared with loud fanfare down a perpendicular lane.

Wet but refreshed, Genevieve and Ephraim returned to their repose on the bench, finally noticing the dozen or so bystanders who'd been watching their futile attempts with obvious pleasure.

"It's nice to see you finally enjoying yourself," Hildegard said as she approached them from behind. "I was worried about you in the beginning, but I see now my worry was unnecessary."

Genevieve smiled. "Worried? Why?"

"Oh, you know—you were always so serious. But look, you've remembered the simple joys! This is good to see. And unless my eyes deceive me, you have a new boyfriend!"

"No, he's not my...this is Ephraim. We were working the farm stand together today, but we sold out early."

Hildegard smiled. "Yes, I know how that works sometimes with you campers. But you must admit this one is also good looking, eh?"

Genevieve turned to Ephraim, smiling at him before turning back to the old woman. "Yes, he is good looking. Are you looking for a boyfriend?"

"Always," Hildegard said with a teasing wink.

"Well, perhaps we could make an arrangement."

"I am always a fan of arrangements, especially those with the potential for a little fun along the way."

Ephraim looked at the old woman, bewildered. "How do you know her?" he whispered under his breath, turning to Genevieve.

"You mean you haven't met Hildegard yet?"

Ephraim turned. "You look familiar, but I don't think so."

"No, we haven't yet met officially, though I'm sure I've seen you dashing through the streets on your way to the craft shop and the hardware store. It looks as though you kids have been very busy."

"We have! It's been nuts trying to keep up with demand at the farm stand," Ephraim admitted.

"That's what I suspected," she said, pivoting on her cane and sitting down next to him on the bench. "I'm glad to see you, dear," she said, leaning forward to look at Genevieve. "I've been wondering how you've been holding up to the rigors of farm life, but you look quite well."

Genevieve nodded. "Thank you. It's growing on me."

"Yes, I can see that. And your research…how many keys do you kids have now?"

"Wait, you know about the keys too?" Ephraim asked.

"Indeed I do."

"Well, I guess we're still working on hope, charity and reverence," Ephraim offered.

Hildegard pressed her lips together and nodded. "I'm still working on those myself. It's always a struggle, isn't it?"

"Even for you?" Ephraim asked, looking surprised.

"Sure. If they were easy they'd be much more common, wouldn't they? Even the easy ones take more practice than you might think."

"Which ones are those?" Ephraim asked with a little laugh.

"I suppose that's different for everyone, isn't it?"

"I guess so. The ones we know seem hard enough. I hate to even imagine how difficult the others must be."

"Oh, I wouldn't worry too much about that."

"No?"

She shook her head. "If you're working on reverence, hope and charity, you're already working on the last two as well."

"We are?" Genevieve asked, surprised.

"Of course. Those three keys form the foundation for the others to be built upon. You cannot work on any of them without strengthening and improving all of them. Once you have a handle to those three the others will come when you're ready."

"Pfff. I keep hearing that, but I was ready weeks ago," Ephraim whined. "I don't understand why we can't just know what they all are from the very beginning. It all just feels like a bad case of hurry up and wait."

Hildegard smiled. "Ah, patience is a difficult virtue to learn, isn't it?"

"Yeah, it is! And we have less than three months left. I don't know how anyone could expect us to be proficient at any of the keys in only five months, and we still don't even know the last two."

Hildegard nodded thoughtfully. "Tell me, what is your profession?"

"I'm an engineer."

"Ahh, then surely you learned something in school about footings and foundations."

"Uh, well, I'm actually a mechanical engineer, but sure, I learned about that kind of stuff early on in my program."

"Then you know."

Ephraim smiled. "What do I know?"

"That no matter the structure, a significant amount of time and effort is focused on the stuff you don't usually see, the stuff below the ground that will, if done correctly, keep the building square and straight as it rises, and provide stability for it in the years to come as the wind blows and earthquakes threaten."

He nodded, but looked confused.

"It's funny, isn't it, how we expect there to be building codes and standards for houses and structures, but when it comes to our own spiritual and physical lives, people are allowed—even encouraged—to build without plans or patterns, or even vision. In the process, foundations are often neglected and guidelines are tossed aside as superfluous details."

She turned her head to look at each of them before looking back up Hauptstrasse. "When you've lived as long as I have, and have the tendency to stick your nose into everyone else's business, you see a lot of stuff. You learn the value of being rooted and grounded when you observe the difficult lives of those who lack either grounding or rooting. And you discover the benefit of footings and foundations when you watch lives, marriages and families crumble from the lack of things like charity, hope and reverence for all that is sacred."

Ephraim nodded thoughtfully. "Those keys...that's the foundation Pops and Ruby are trying to give us, right?

Hildegard nodded. "Those keys are the foundation of this very town."

"So, the cannon fire—the five of them at the end of the firework show?"

The old woman smiled. "You heard it, didn't you?"

"What did I hear?"

"You tell me."

"Somebody said, 'Remember the keys of liberty,'" admitted Genevieve.

"That's right. Five words, five cannons, five keys that are so easily forgotten in the tangle of lesser things."

"So why even try?" Genevieve replied.

"That's an important question, and one I imagine you've already asked yourself many times since first hearing of the keys. And if you choose to make them part of your life, that will undoubtedly be a question others will ask you as they watch you thoughtfully making efforts others are not making."

Genevieve nodded. "So why do *you* make the effort to remember them? Why do you open dialogues with near strangers about this kind of thing?"

"We all have different callings in life. I learned mine long ago, and I've done my best to not forget it."

"What do you believe that calling is?" Ephraim asked.

"I like to think it's to help people not fall asleep and forget the important things in life."

"So, that's why you hang out in town, and in the cemetery, and at the church, and..." Genevieve replied.

She nodded. "It's where the people are, right? I'm a watcher. Most busybodies are. I could stay at home at watch my cat and help no one, or I can be out here, looking for people who need someone to plant a good idea in their head, or who could benefit from thinking about life a little bit differently."

"It seems like you could also annoy a lot of people doing stuff like that," Ephraim replied.

She shrugged. "It's worth the risk. And it's gotten a little easier over the last twenty years or so. Most people don't mess with a little, old lady, even if I do ruffle their feathers."

"And you're purposely trying to ruffle people's feathers?" Genevieve asked.

The old woman shrugged. "Feathers. Traditions. Fruitless opinions. People get stuck, you know, sometimes without even trying. They get lazy and apathetic and live life as if they're doing it all for themselves. And pretty quick they're going nowhere and doing nothing that's of any positive consequence."

"That sounds about right," Ephraim admitted.

Hildegard nodded. "But that's not the way life was meant to be lived."

"How do you think it's supposed to be lived?" Genevieve asked.

She smiled with a twinkle in her eye. "With passion, and energy, and enthusiasm. If you're not living for the purpose of finding and spreading joy, you're wasting everyone's time."

"That feels true, but it doesn't seem like many people agree with you," suggested Ephraim.

"That's only because they're focusing on the wrong things. You can't find joy if you're only concerned about yourself. And you certainly won't find it if your money is all you're living for. There are a lot of empty hearts out there, folks who have either lost their sense of direction or never had one in the first place because they never learned to focus on anything or anyone beyond the end of their own nose. That's not living! When we forget that we need each other, that we belong to each other, life loses its charm and magic. Folks like that tend to get wrapped up into boring little prickly bundles, sour and narcissistic. And unless they come to themselves and decide to change, most folks who follow that course are doomed to loneliness and despair."

Ephraim and Genevieve glanced at each other, nodding knowingly at the truth the old woman shared.

"So, how do I make sure that doesn't happen to me?" Ephraim asked.

"You learn the keys of joy and do your best to practice them every day. I learned long ago the no one can fully appreciate the value of the keys of joy until they've been applied to the way you live today and plan for your future. There are some who gloss over the keys quickly without truly getting to know them. Many others set them aside as relics of a quaint but bygone era. But no matter how you regard them, they're of little value or benefit until you sincerely choose to embrace them and allow them to become part of who you are."

"Okay, but if we only know the three…" Ephraim protested.

"Then you're either not looking hard enough, or you're focused on lesser things. You've certainly heard by now that the writing is on the wall."

Ephraim glanced quickly at Genevieve, then back to Ruby. "Yes, but what does that have to do with the keys of joy?"

"Surely you've spent some time on the benches, right?"

"You mean the ones on the farm?"

"Yes, the ones on the farm, and across town, and down by the river, and in the church, and basically every bench of any age here in Niederbipp."

"Yeah, I'd say this town has far more than it's share of benches," Ephraim acknowledged.

"Have you ever stopped to ask yourself why?"

"Because y'all like to have a comfy place to sit?" Ephraim asked.

"Sure, but who doesn't? Why does the farm have so many benches?"

"Pops and Ruby told us it was to give each of us time and space to think," Ephraim responded.

"Yes, but there's more to it than that. You can think sitting on a rock or a log. Why a bench made of five pieces?"

"Matt and I were working on this several weeks ago," Genevieve reported to Ephraim.

"And what did you come up with?" asked Hildegard

"Well, we discovered that each of the five pieces of wood on the bench had a symbol carved into them."

"That's good. Why did you stop there?"

"Because we...we got busy doing other things."

Hildegard nodded. "It's a common problem. We all get busy. But if we're not careful we end up giving our best time to things that matter less, and giving us less time for the things that matter most."

Genevieve sat silent for a moment. "So, are you suggesting that making money for the farm is less important that learning the keys of joy?" Genevieve challenged.

"I suppose I'm suggesting the same thing an old Jewish friend once suggested: that where your treasure is, there you'll also find your heart[1]."

"What kind of treasure are talking about here?" Ephraim asked.

"Oh, it's different for everyone, isn't it? Money. Travel. Love. Service. Work. Play. Each of us must decide who, what and where our treasure is. But no matter how we choose, it's certain that our hearts won't be far behind. This is why it's important to choose wisely, for some treasure hunts have blindly led good men and women into dark and forbidden paths where they've been lost forever, giving up their very souls in the pursuit of unsympathetic treasures."

"So...how do you make sure your treasure isn't stealthily leading you into darkness?" Ephraim asked.

"That might be the most important question you ask today. And it's one that we all need to ask ourselves regularly. There is a season and a purpose to all things under heaven, and what is good and right at one season of life may not be right at a different season. Change is critical if we hope for growth to continue throughout life. And if it's joy we're after, we must evolve and progress with the changing seasons, always searching for the truths that will lead us to joy ."

"I hear you say that, but the keys of joy...aren't they supposed to be at least hundreds of years old?" asked Genevieve.

"Probably closer to many thousands of years old," Hildegard mused.

"Really?!?" responded Ephraim.

The old woman nodded. "As a Jew, I grew up learning from the Torah—those first five books of Moses. And as I've continued to study

1. Matthew 6:21

this foundation of many faiths, I often find hidden within that ancient scripture the cornerstones for these principles of joy. The writing is on the wall there, too. You just have to have a desire to see it, and be willing to sincerely ask the right questions as you discover them."

"Okay, but how can something that's thousands of years old still be relevant today?" Genevieve asked.

The old woman nodded thoughtfully, pointing the tip of her cane at the display windows of the clothing store a few doors up. "In a world where fads and fashions change from season to season and rarely hang on for longer than a decade, ancient truths can sometimes feel dated compared to popular trends. But void of expiration dates, true principles and moral laws transcend all time and fashion. They hold true even when no one embraces them, and they continue in perpetuity, independent of bias of popular culture. Yes, they may be old, but if you look closely you will find that they form the bedrock of all relationships, attitudes, and behaviors that not only lead to joy, but to all eternal success and happiness."

"That's a bold statement," Ephraim responded.

"Indeed it is. I would never ask you to take my word for it. Instead, try it out and see if you can come up with any outliers. I believe you will find as I have that the history of the world is filled with stories of men and women who've tried to find shortcuts to joy or exceptions to the demands of its high standards only to fall short of their aspirations.

"You almost make the keys sound like a miracle drug," Genevieve replied.

"No, though there are plenty of quick-fix cures and snake oil solutions sold by the unscrupulous to the desperate and bewildered, I'm not aware of any viable alternative course than the slow, regular work which the keys invite."

"So..." Ephraim said, pausing to gather his thoughts, "What's in this for you?"

Hildegard laughed. "I'm not selling anything, if that's what you're asking. In fact, the truth is that I have nothing to gain other than a brother and a sister who have come to their own understanding of these same truths and can share in my joy."

"That's why you do this?" Genevieve asked.

"What else is there? It's never been enough for me to know the keys of joy if I can't share them with sincere kids like yourselves."

Ephraim looked quickly around him as if he were looking for hidden cameras. "And the town of Niederbipp isn't paying you a bunch of money to do this?"

Hildegard laughed. "Heavens no. I do this because I'm a junkie."

"A junkie, huh?" Ephraim asked, thinking she was certainly too old to be tweaking on drugs.

"A *joy* junkie. I didn't understand it until I was in my mid-forties, after I'd learned that there's great happiness to be found in the very act of sharing the truths of joy."

"Okay, so, great, I see how that works for you..." Ephraim said, looking like he was choosing his words carefully, "but we've got jobs. We've got bills to pay and dreams to chase."

Hildegard nodded as if she were waiting patiently for the rest of his protest.

"How the heck are we supposed to fit one more thing into our lives? I mean, I obviously can't speak for Genevieve, but I already work sixty hours a week, plus I try to get to the gym, and make an attempt at a social life, and then there's my commute, and trying find time to sleep. I like the idea of joy, I just don't know when or where I'm ever going to fit it in."

"You almost make it sound like you believe joy has to function independently of the rest of your life."

The statement seemed to surprise him.

She shook her head, tapping the tip of her cane down on the cobblestones at her feet. "Few of us have the time to devote our hours exclusively to joy."

"But I thought you..."

"Joy, if it's to have much power to do any good at all, can't simply be a hat you put on when you've got a little time or are feeling particularly magnanimous. It has to live in our heart and become a way of living… an attitude you carry with you everywhere you go, almost a sixth sense which has the potential to influence and transform every interaction into something of substance and meaning."

Ephraim's eyes brightened. "So this right here," he said, motioning with his hands to the space between them, "this is joy?"

She nodded. "True connection is a beautiful source of joy. Wherever there is truth, there is joy. Wherever there is anything shared in the spirit of love, there is joy."

He nodded slowly. "So, it doesn't have to take a whole bunch of extra time?"

"No, but it does require making your time count, that you share something of yourself, that you allow yourself to be vulnerable in an effort to create real connections."

"That sounds like everything on the farm," Genevieve mused.

"That's because the farm was founded on the principles of joy. Joy is somehow tied to everything you kids do up there."

"No, that kind of makes sense now," Ephraim started. "So when are Pops and Ruby going to tell us the other two keys."

"The way you kids were learning those first few weeks this summer, I would have thought you'd have them all figured out by now," Hildegard admitted.

"Are you saying we're behind schedule?" asked Genevieve.

"No, as far as I know there is no schedule. But to see kids with three keys before the end of the first month is very rare. What happened? Why'd it all stop?"

Genevieve shook her head. "I felt like we were figuring things out really well, but…I guess I was afraid to ask."

"Why?"

"Because I wasn't sure I wanted to know."

Hildegard nodded. "You closed the door."

"Excuse me?"

"Truth, and its companion, Wisdom, are funny that way. If you open the door to them, they'll come and enjoy spending time with you. But they're sensitive guests. They tend to leave when interest wanes, when they're forced to compete with lesser things, or have to struggle for your attention or sincerity. And when the door closes due to any variety of busy-ness, it often requires a sincere invitation to make them feel welcome and tempted to stay."

"So, what does that invitation look like?" Ephraim asked.

"It generally looks like a question."

"What kind of question?"

"A good one, sincere and thoughtful."

"Okay, I've got one. What are the last two keys?"

Hildegard rolled her eyes and shook her head.

"What's wrong with that question? It's direct and sincere, just like you said."

"It may be direct, yes, but there's no soul searching involved, no honest quest for vision, no sincere effort to understand."

"Okay, what would a better question be?" Ephraim asked, slightly more humbly than before.

"How about, 'Why did I come here this summer'"?

"That's easy. I came here because I wanted to find out what I was missing." Ephraim replied.

"And what have you learned so far?"

Ephraim glanced at Genevieve, looking uncertain. "Well, I've learned the keys of joy."

"*Have you?*"

He looked surprised by the question. "Well, I know what they are, and I'm trying to learn how they work."

Hildegard closed her eyes and took a deep breath. When she spoke again her eyes remained closed. "You kids started out faster than any group of campers I've ever witnessed in the eighty years I've been watching kids come and go from Harmony Hill. You discovered those first keys quickly and were curious and interested in seeking wisdom and experience and understanding. And then, from my perspective, outside looking in, it seems you got comfortable and complacent. You stopped asking questions and seeking answers and wisdom. Instead, as far as I've observed, you turned your attention to making money. I watched as you came and went from the hardware store and the craft shop, too anxious to get back to your widgets to even notice the people the universe placed along your path. You returned to your nets."

"Our nets?" Genevieve replied.

Hildegard nodded. "It's a common tale, and one we all must be aware of. It refers to the fishermen of Galilee, the early apostles of Christ. After answering a greater call and walking with Jesus, sharing His light and hope and witnessing His miracles, they returned to their nets after the Lord was crucified. After all the good they'd seen and done, after all the good they heard and said, they went back to what they knew, back to what was comfortable, back to what came easy. We all have a tendency to return to our nets—to our old ways—if we are not mindful of the new light we've received.

"But we were doing it for the farm," Genevieve protested. "We were doing it to support Pops and Ruby. Don't we get credit for service—for charity?"

"Charity is a tricky thing. It can become all about you if you're not careful."

"But…that's ridiculous," Genevieve said.

"Is it?"

"Yes! We were working to support the farm."

"I wasn't aware that the farm needed support."

"Of course it does," Genevieve responded before the question had time to ruminate in her mind. "There's no such thing as a free…"

"Tell me," she said, cutting her off as she turned to Ephraim. "How much did it cost you to come here this summer?"

"Uh, actually cost me…like out of pocket?"

"Yes."

"Well, besides getting myself here, I guess…nothing."

She nodded. "Nothing. Have you ever stopped to consider why that is? In exchange for five short months of your life, you're given a bed to sleep in and food to eat. And in return, if you're diligent and thoughtful, you're given the secrets of the universe—secrets that most of the world has forgotten or never knew—secrets that have the ability to change *everything* for you and bring you all the happiness you desire. But instead of focusing on those rare truths that can set you free, you've traded your time and energy for what you know best—chasing money. You returned to your nets. And in the process, your progress has been impeded. The reasons you are here have been clouded and eclipsed by irrational fears and distractions."

"Irrational fears? What about the taxes? What about keeping gas in the truck and the lights on? What about keeping the farm going for future generations?" Genevieve protested.

"Have Lorenzo and Ruby ever once expressed even one of those concerns to you?"

They thought for a moment before Ephraim shook his head.

"There's a reason for that. Lorenzo and Ruby learned long ago that you cannot run a farm on fear. The simple truth is that you couldn't squeeze even one drop of nourishment or sustenance from all the fear in the world. Fear may protect you from doing stupid things, yes. But most fear slowly suffocates you by stealing away your time and your energy and ultimately robbing you of love, and of power, and of all reason."

"So, what's the point of the farm stand if we don't use it make money?" Genevieve asked.

"There's a fine balance that exists in all things. Sure, we all need to eat. But if we eat too much, we suffer. We all need to breathe, but even breathing too much can cause us to hyperventilate and pass out. And yes, we all need to work, but working beyond what is needful just to pad our bank accounts or fill our garages with toys...I'm quite sure that if you honestly weigh it against all that you lose in the process, it will only equal a net loss in the joy department.

"The balance on the farm was designed centuries ago. If you'll meet your daily work with an honest heart and keep your wants in check, all your needs will be met. If you diligently work the garden and the orchard with reverence for God and the earth, the earth will pour forth her bounty and abundance, and provide not only for your needs, but enough to share. The earth, the trees, the animals—there is a balance that must be maintained in order for joy to be present. Lose the balance, lose the joy."

Ephraim turned to Genevieve as if he were checking to see if she was hearing all of this too.

"If you don't mind me saying," Hildegard continued, "your generation is in trouble because you've forgotten the principle of moderation. You live your life on the extremes; you take more than you need; you hold onto more than you can reasonably carry; you give back only what you believe you can spare; and in your effort to suck more than your share of the marrow out of life, you're choking on the bones. Instead of searching to restore balance, you've paid far too much admiration to that ridiculous Jones family—whoever they are—as people worth keeping up with. You spend money you don't have to impress people you don't like. You make love to people you don't love. You give away all that is precious and hoard all that is cheap and lifeless. And then you can't figure our why you're depressed and stressed and unhappy."

Genevieve shook her head slowly. "So, what's a girl supposed to do to find her way out of that mess?"

Hildegard smiled soberly. "I've been asked that question many times by campers just like you over the years."

"So, you make it a habit of accosting people like us?" Ephraim asked with a broad grin.

"Only when I see stagnation where I once saw hope and growth. You're far from the first group of campers to lose their concentration on the keys of joy in their pursuit of money or other distractions, and I'm certain you won't be the last."

"So...do you work with Pops and Ruby then?" Ephraim asked.

Hildegard smiled. "Let's just say we're on the same team. It takes a village, you know. I decided many years ago, shortly after I learned the keys of joy for myself, that I could not simply be a bystander. I'm a German and a Jew, therefore I'm both blunt and nosey. It didn't even take practice to get to the point where I could walk up to strangers and invite them—with all the tact of a feathery two-by-four—to wake up."

She chuckled softly. "Life is short, children. There's a time and a season for everything, and you mustn't forget why you're here for this short season. I learned long ago, and have learned it many times since, that if you miss the joy of any season, you really miss it all. Too many, in their efforts to get ahead, find themselves in a lonely place with everything that money can buy, but with cold, empty hearts."

Ephraim nodded slowly. "The keys of joy...do you believe they're the antidote to cold, empty hearts?"

Hildegard shook her head. "I *know* they are. Anything less than the keys of joy, no matter how spectacularly bedazzled it may appear, is a counterfeit to joy, a cheap alternative that can never last."

"Why haven't Pops and Ruby said anything about this?" Genevieve asked.

"Haven't they?"

"I don't think so," Genevieve responded, suddenly uncertain.

"I thought you said they've taught you the keys of reverence, hope and charity?"

"Yes, that's right."

"Then you have not sought to understand them."

Ephraim shook his head. "We've wasted a whole month, haven't we?"

"It's only a waste if you learn nothing from it," replied Hildegard.

"And we have learned *something*," Genevieve protested. "We picked up some good lessons about charity along the way with Ned and Nora, right?"

He nodded. "But Ruby was trying to bring us back into balance right after we all lost our minds with those stupid ornaments?"

"Hey, those ornaments put a lot of money in the farm's coffers," Genevieve replied.

"Yeah, but at what cost? A whole month!"

"And you'll lose much more if you're not mindful of your purpose," Hildegard replied.

"So how do we keep on track? How do we regain our balance?" Ephraim queried.

"You ask questions like that everyday. Good questions. Hard questions. Questions that make you think and stretch and seek for truth and answers. You stay conscious and sober and apply all the light you know to every choice and every decision of any consequence. And when more light comes, you apply that light. You stay humble and hungry, anxious to gather truth and to share it with anyone who'll listen. And you never forget that you are a child of the Creator of the entire universe who is anxious to share His abundance of wisdom and mercy and joy with all who'll reverence Him and His endless creations. And you remember that love is the only gold and joy is ultimately the only treasure worth collecting because it's the only treasure you can take with you. You do that, and balance and joy will be your companions. You forget any one of these things and balance and joy will always remain temporary and elusive."

Genevieve pursed her lips and slowly shook her head.

"You disagree, dear?"

"No, I can't disagree because in my heart, it feels like truth. But you do know that everything you've said runs contrary to basically every common philosophy of the world we live in?"

"Of course it does," she responded, unapologetically. "Of course it does." She leaned forward on her cane and stood before turning to face them. "The longer you live, if you'll remain an honest seeker of truth, you'll undoubtedly find that common philosophies rarely offer much to sink your teeth into, and never a saving grace. Now, if you'll excuse me, I've got an appointment."

"Down by the river?" Genevieve asked

The old woman nodded, lifting the tip of her cane to the level of the Ephraim's belly. Surprised by her sudden threat of unprovoked violence he quickly moved to the side to avoid being poked by her cane. But the cane kept moving, stopping at the back of the bench, and it quickly became clear that she meant them no harm.

"If it's wisdom you seek, and you seek it with a sincere heart, truth will never be far from you, and the writing will always be on the wall, waiting for you to discover it."

They turned to look at the faded carving which Ephraim had been resting his back against, unaware. Though the stone was worn from more than three centuries of wear, Genevieve recognized it immediately. She ran her thumb over the faded carving before turning to Hildegard, but the old woman had gone, already ten paces up Hauptstrasse.

CHAPTER 120

Symbols and Keys

With an eye made quiet by the power of harmony, and the deep power of joy, we see into the life of things.
—William Wordsworth

"Do you know what this is?" Ephraim asked, turning his body to allow himself to fully take in the faded carving.

"I think I do, though I don't know if I've ever seen it in this format."

"The same symbol is in the library," Ephraim reported.

"You've been to the library?"

"Uh, yeah, so have you. You were just in there the other night," he responded as if he were wondering if she'd bumped her head.

"Oh, you mean the library at the big house?"

"Yeah, where else?"

"I, well…never mind. You think there's one of these in *our* library?"

"Yeah, I just saw it the other morning when I was on kitchen duty with Holly."

"Really? Where is it?"

"It's hanging in the window."

"What?"

"Yeah, it's made out of stained glass." He pointed to the barely discernible heart in the center of the carving. "The one in the library has yellow and orange flames coming out of it. That's what caught my attention the other day—those bright colors in the glass."

Genevieve shook her head. "The writing's on the wall."

"That seems to be a common theme around here, doesn't it?"

Genevieve shook her head again. "I've sat on this bench at least a few times in the last two months, but I missed it."

He nodded, but looked uncertain. *"Remind me what we've missed."*

"The answers! They've been here the whole time; here and probably on every bench around town and the farm. Matt and I discovered the symbols weeks ago, but…man, we've wasted a lot of time." She stood, stepping back from the bench to look at the conglomerate of symbols layered upon each other. "It's been there all along, and we've been wasting our time with those stupid ornaments."

He stood next to her. "I feel like I'm missing something."

"You and me both."

"What is this supposed to mean?"

She shook her head, looking over her shoulder in the direction Hildegard had wandered. "Come on," she said, turning on her heel.

They were nearly jogging before they reached the pudding mold museum.

"Are you looking for that old lady?" he asked.

"Do you see her?"

"No."

She paused to catch her breath when she reached the bicycles, scanning the crowd for Hildegard.

"Where are we going?" Ephraim asked as she reached for the handlebars of her bike, kicked the kickstand, and began pushing the old tank uphill.

"We've only got three months left," she said as she stepped through the frame and sat down on the saddle.

He followed, catching up as they peddled past the dental office, turning left past the bus platform where they'd all met for the first time two months earlier.

"Are you okay?" he asked, obviously winded.

"Yeah, just wondering how we're going to catch up."

He laughed. "I'm pretty sure riding our bikes like bats out of hell isn't going to make time go backwards."

She forced a smile, recognizing he was right. There was nothing she or anyone else could do to restore the time they'd lost as they'd been wrapped up tight in the thick of thin things. An old bench on a shady patch of grass on the side of the road drew her attention and she coasted to a stop in front of it.

"You need a break already," he teased.

"I just want to check something." She parked the bike and quickly approached the bench, not stopping until she'd walked around to the backside.

She rubbed her thumb over the top of the wooden leg in the same place she and Matt had discovered the symbols on the bench near the phone booth at the top of Harmony Hill.

"Are you sure you're okay?" Ephraim asked as she squatted at the side of the bench, stooping to take a closer look.

She nodded when she found what she was looking for, moving on to the other leg where she quickly found another symbol. "We've wasted a lot of time."

"Yeah, you said that before. Tell me about all of this."

She forced a smile, sitting down on the bench as she shook her head. "I didn't even bring my journal."

"Uh, you're wanting to journal right now?"

"Have you got a better idea?"

He sat down on the opposite end of the bench, looking befuddled. "I feel like I'm missing something big."

"We all are. We've been wanting to learn the last two keys, but we've all lost our minds on those stupid ornaments, and Ned and Nora, and… it was right here waiting for us all along. We stopped asking questions. We stopped trying to figure it out. The puzzle pieces have been right in front of us the whole time, waiting for us to put them together and make sense of all of this."

He nodded slowly, but was obviously still confused. "You think that symbol on the bench by the fountain…and in the library…are you saying they're symbols of the keys of joy?"

"Yes!"

"And that's what you were looking for on this bench?"

Genevieve nodded.

Ephraim jumped to his feet, turning his attention quickly to the tops of the bench's legs where Genevieve had been looking. "Hey, there's something here," he said.

She nodded without turning around.

"And there's another here," he said, pointing to the top of the other leg. He squatted to take a closer look and noticed the small heart with flames carved into the backrest. He looked up, his eyes wide. "You've known about this for weeks?"

"Yeah, well, Matt and I discovered them a while ago, but I don't really know what they mean. We…got busy with other things and… forgot about them."

"And you said Matt knows about them too?"

"Yeah, why?"

He turned and looked again at the flaming heart. "I don't think Matt gave up."

"What do you mean?"

"I didn't put it together until just now, but I saw him sketching in his journal a few nights ago. He was sketching one of these," he said, pointing at the heart.

"Really?"

"Yeah, I'm sure of it. I thought it was kind of weird for a dude to be drawing hearts, but yeah, he's definitely been working on something."

Genevieve took a deep breath and nodded. "Good for him. Do you know anything about the Ebenezer behind the milk barn?"

"The what?"

"You know, that tall stack of rocks by the bench?"

Ephraim looked confused.

"Come on," she said, getting to her feet. "We can't waste any more time."

On their way back to Harmony Hill, Genevieve shared with Ephraim all that she knew about both the symbols on the benches and what they'd learned about the Ebenezer. She was surprised that Ephraim knew about none of it, but then she remembered that her understanding had been substantially enhanced by reading Thomas's book. She'd been curious. She and Matt had asked questions. But the questions had ended, and the learning had stopped. By the time they reached the summit, Genevieve was determined to not let anything else get in her way of getting back on track to understanding the keys of joy.

But getting back on track was not as easy as wishing it so. From the top of the drive they could see that Patrick O'Brien's Land Rover was still parked in front of the big house. Not wishing to either tangle with him, nor explain to Ephraim her aversion to the photographer, she kept on riding until they coasted into the shade of the tree near the Cartwright's corral. The yellow pony was rolling on its back, kicking up dust in the afternoon breeze.

When the pony stood, Genevieve noticed something different about the horse. It had been weeks since she'd visited this neighboring farm, and sometime since her last visit the wild horse had acquired a halter on its head. It wasn't a bridle. Having seen the stallion's strength and destructive ability, she doubted he'd be ready for a bridle. But even a halter suggested that David, the Amish horseman, had made some serious progress, daring to get close enough to equip the horse with this dark leather halter.

She pulled a handful of crabgrass from under her feet and approached the pipe fence, whistling softly to get the horse's attention. He stared at her for a long moment before looking from side to side as if he were looking for signs of an ambush. Then, with graceful strides, he approached the grass held in her outstretched hand. He stopped a few feet from her, his big, black eyes watching her closely as he slowly closed the gap. Not removing his eyes from her, he first nibbled, then chomped on the verdant grass. Ephraim, having watched this, stooped and gathered up a hearty handful of grass and offered it to the stallion through the fence. But though the offering was the same and the presentation equal, the horse refused it.

Ephraim dangled the grass for a moment, trying to encourage the horse, but he could not be persuaded to even look Ephraim's way. Frustrated, he let the grass fall to the ground as the horse continued to stare at Genevieve. She stooped and gathered another handful of grass, and again the horse came close, eating the grass directly from her hands.

Not wanting to be bested, Ephraim gathered up a large, bounteous bouquet of grass, offering it to the yellow horse in a graceful presentation. But again, he was ignored by the horse who only had eyes for Genevieve. Seeing Ephraim was frustrated, she took a handful from him and offered it to the horse. Again, without losing his gaze on Genevieve, the stallion took and ate from the same grass Ephraim had just offered him.

She'd never considered herself a horse whisperer. Since the time she was a child and had given up on riding lessons after only a few visits to the stables, fear of the large, unpredictable animals had kept her away. But this was somehow different. This was somehow magical. As she stared into the big, dark eyes of this majestic animal there was an unmistakable connection.

"I'm ready to go back to the farm," Ephraim said.

"Do you think that's a good idea?" she asked, trying not to panic.

"Why wouldn't it be?"

"I don't know if that photographer would be too keen about discovering that the gifts he bought for Ruby were purchased from her own farm stand."

Ephraim laughed. "Good point. What are we supposed to do for the rest of the day?"

"I don't know. Do you think he's staying for dinner?"

"I hope not. We've got stuff to do, right?"

Genevieve nodded. "We could take a closer look at the bench by the phone booth, that way we'd know when he leaves."

He looked confused. "There's a bench by the phone booth?"

"Seriously?" she asked, turning back to the bikes.

"What? I've been too busy making ornaments and mobiles to spend time looking at benches."

She shook her head as she mounted her bike. "We really have wasted a lot of time."

They backtracked to the summit and she led the way as they walked their bikes past the phone booth and over the narrow path to the bench that overlooked the Niederbipp valley.

"How did I miss this?" Ephraim asked, taking in the majestic view.

"I think we've all missed a lot of things." She laid her bike down in the tall grass and took a seat on the edge of the bench.

"And this bench—this has the same symbols as the one in town?" he asked, turning to face it.

"See for yourself." She leaned back, turning to point to the symbol at the top of the leg.

He knelt on the bench to take a closer look. "An X?"

"I don't think so. Look closer."

"Oh, yeah, there's an ellipse at the top of the X, and another one at the bottom." He moved to the opposite leg. "And this…it looks like a… lamp post with hanging flowerpots."

"Matt and I thought it looked like one of those old time balance scales."

"Yeah, I can see that. What are the other symbols?"

"Well, you already know the flaming heart, right? And under the seat…if I remember right there's an anchor, and then on the stabilizing bar between the legs…"

Ephraim walked around to the backside and knelt on the ground, bending over even further until the side of his head was parallel to the ground. "It's a circle…a circle with a plus sign in the middle. And there's the anchor," he said, turning his attention to the bottom of the seat.

He stood and brushed off his knees. "So what does this all mean?"

"Other than the fact that whoever built all the benches around here must've wanted their more curious visitors to ask questions…I don't know."

"That's all you've got?"

"Really? Do you have any more?"

"Well, no, but I just found out about it today. You've known about it for weeks. Surely you must have come up with something."

"We *have* been a little bit busy," she responded impatiently. "But, Matt and I did chat about the heart being a symbol of charity."

"I could see that."

"It seemed the most logical to us. We only know the three keys, of course, but which symbols do you think represent hope and reverence?"

He sat down on the bench, visualizing the other four symbols. Holding out his left hand, he tried to remember what he'd learned. Reverence is the thumb, right?"

Genevieve nodded.

"Charity is the pinky, and hope, that's the middle finger. So if charity is the backrest…what if hope is…hope is the anchor, right? And if hope and charity run parallel to each other, it might make sense for reverence to also run parallel to the other two, right?"

He got up and returned to the back of the bench, kneeling again in the dirt. "What if that plus sign is actually a cross? And the circle...that's also a spiritual symbol, right?" he asked, sounding excited.

She slipped from the bench and knelt in front, noticing for the first time how the narrow piece of wood that spanned the distance between the two legs actually passed through them, ending on the other sides with what looked fancy pegs passing through each end.

"This is actually a brilliant design," Ephraim offered, sounding again like an engineer as he wiggled the peg on the outside of the leg until it came loose.

"Did you break it?"

"No," he said, sliding the peg back into place and tapping it down with the heel of his hand. "I didn't see this earlier, but this board actually holds the whole bench together."

"What? How?"

He moved to the opposite end of the bench and removed the peg on that end. "These pegs are called keys," he said, straightening up and handing the peg to her. She took it in her fingers, examining its weathered, grey surface. She was surprised to find that it was not square or round, but rather wedge-shaped, tapering from one inch down to less than a half inch over the course of its three-inch-long length.

"It almost looks like a dissembled clothes pin," she said, handing it back to him. "What does it do?"

"Have a seat and I'll show you."

She sat down as he stood behind her. Placing his hands on the backboard, he wiggled the bench, the wag quickly becoming more profound as the bench listed from side to side. He stopped after a moment and slid the key back into its slot, tapping it down with the butt of his hand.

"Try it now," he said, looking up.

She tried to move the bench from side the side, but the motion that had happened before was no longer possible. The bench, recently rickety and infirm, was now solid and secure.

"That little piece of wood made that big of a difference?" she asked, shocked.

"No, that piece of wood only locked in the support. It's called a keyed mortise and tenon joint."

She laughed. "You don't have to make stuff up just to look smart."

"No, really. It is."

"How do you know?"

"I probably took my wood shop class in junior high a little too seriously, but it was a major contributor to me becoming an engineer. My teacher, Mr. Schneider, was this old Swiss woodworker who'd retired from a long career in cabinetry and decided he'd rather keep working than have to spend all day with his grouchy wife."

"Seriously?!"

"Yep, and his goal was to pass on all the old ways before he died. He promised us all that if we ever sold out and bought IKEA furniture rather than building our own, he'd come back and haunt us. These keyed mortise and tenon joints were Mr. Schneider's magnum opus."

"And did you learn how to make them?"

"Pfff. I was in the seventh grade. I could hardly tie my shoe. I made plenty of attempts, but they were never anywhere as tight as his."

"So, what's the point of teaching something to seventh graders that's so difficult?"

"I wondered the same thing, but even if you fail trying something difficult, you still can learn lots of great lessons."

"And what did you learn?"

"Discipline. Determination. Patience with myself and my materials, and the importance of keeping my tools sharp. He inspired us to do our best work—always. It's a shame, but they don't even teach wood shop in most junior highs any more."

She shrugged. "We're the IKEA generation. Following those instructions is hard enough."

"Okay, but what would an IKEA bench look like if it was left out in the weather like these benches?"

Genevieve laughed. "Good point. So tell me why is this joint important?"

"Like I said, it keeps this bench solid and steady. The keyed mortise and tenon joint doesn't use nails or glue. It's just those keys that keep it tight. If those keys remain in place, this bench could last at least a generation."

"And it's really called a *keyed* mortimer tension joint?"

He smiled. "Close. You got the keyed part right, but it's actually *mortise and tenon*."

"I've heard it both ways," she lied. It's kind of interesting though, isn't it?"

"Which part?"

"Well, considering that this bench has been tagged with symbols of the keys of joy, it's just…"

"Thoughtful," he replied, finishing her sentence.

"Yeah, thoughtful."

He sat down on the bench, looking out at the beauty all around them. "What did Pops say about reverence—about how it's tied to the thumb?"

"Uh, something about how, like the thumb, it makes all the other keys—or fingers—more useful."

Ephraim smiled but shook his head. "The tenon—the circle with the cross—that's got to symbolize reverence, doesn't it?"

She nodded slowly. "It's the thumb of the bench, isn't it?"

"Yeah. We've missed a lot, haven't we?"

"You mean like pretty much everything?"

He nodded. "Do you think we should tell the others?"

"I was just thinking the same thing. We're going to need all of us if we're ever going to catch up."

CHAPTER 121

Trailing Clouds of Glory

*You can never get enough of what you don't need,
because what you don't need won't satisfy you.*
—Dallin H. Oaks

The sound of crunching gravel alerted Genevieve and Ephraim to an approaching car, but they couldn't tell from which direction. They stood and walked back toward the phone booth, hugging the shrubbery and grasses as they approached the road, trying to stay hidden and avoid contact with the photographer. But they didn't need to worry. Patrick was distracted by the satellite phone held between his ear and shoulder as he rounded the corner onto the old road and zoomed off without even slowing down to take in the incredible view.

They found the rest of the campers on the front porch of the big house, looking worn and tired. They listened to their stories of the day, how several of the ladies had attempted to charm the handsome photographer only to discover around lunchtime that he'd gone and gotten himself married in the six weeks since his last visit. The men shared what details they'd been able to glean of his honeymoon in Tuscany, visiting several medieval towns on an olive and wine tour for two. It all sounded romantic, but Genevieve was over it, and before she get any further distracted, she hijacked the conversation, sharing with them all that they'd learned from their conversation with Hildegard, as well as the symbols they'd discovered and deciphered on the benches.

When James and Rachael had to leave to make dinner, the entire group went with them, carrying on the conversation in the kitchen so no one would have to miss out. Pops and Ruby, catching wind of the conversation, excused themselves to set the table and allow the conversation to continue without interruption.

The things Genevieve and Ephraim had learned from Hildegard about the keys had been revelatory, but they admitted being surprised by her calling them out for losing their focus on the more important reasons for them being at the farm this summer. The old woman's pointed rebuke felt equally difficult for many of the others to hear, and the conversation continued around the dinner table as they ate grilled cheese sandwiches and several bottles of fruit.

For their part, Pops and Ruby remained largely silent until questions arose that only they could answer. And it was here that they all learned that they were far from the first set of campers to fall prey to the false gods of free enterprise, losing their minds and their time in the pursuit of unnecessary money. Many of the campers were slow to accept this summary of their activities, echoing Genevieve's earlier rebuttal about *doing it all for the farm.* But the debate was calmly extinguished when, with kindness and patience, both Pops and Ruby informed them that the farm had always provided enough to cover the needs of those who came here as well as those who kept it going.

This mentality was an epic shift for all the campers, and a warm discussion carried them through dinner, clean up, and onto the porch. Before breaking for evening chores a question was posed by Genevieve for each of them to consider while they finished their work: *how much is enough*? It gave each of them pause as they took care of evening milking, checked on the animals, and brought in the laundry.

The discussion continued when they all gathered again to the porch, each of them anxious to share what they'd been thinking about. So many of the *needs* that each of the campers believed they had were slowly peeled away, one by one, until they recognized what *need* really was: food, water, shelter, love. Those four basics covered the *needs*. And to that list, they added something meaningful to do and something to look forward to as essentials of a happy life. Six items. But, as Rachael observed, if water and food were placed in the same category there were really only five. Five essentials of a happy life! It was so much simpler than any of them had imagined or the way most of them had lived. And yet they recognized from their two months of simplified life since coming to the farm that life was better, richer, fuller, and more meaningful than the lives they'd each left behind. There was time to think, time to talk, time to serve and worship and rest. There was no racing from big thing to big thing. Stress—except for the stress they'd created for themselves with the ornaments, and the looming stress they each felt at returning to the real world in three months—was lower than any of them had felt in years. Admittedly, no one was getting rich. No one was scrimping and saving for a lavish vacation. And thanks to Ruby's requirements of no credit card debt for acceptance into the program, no one was worried about looming clouds of bills. It was a simple life, but one which had allowed each of them—until the ornament explosion—to remember, or experience for the first time in many years, what was truly important.

But they also collectively recognized that much had been lost over the last six weeks as their focus had shifted to keeping up with the demand of the ornaments and seeking for other ways to make more money. The realization that none of their extra efforts over those weeks had been necessary for the farm to survive left each of them pensive as they considered the many alternative uses of their time. This sense of time being ill-spent only grew as Genevieve shared with them what Hildegard had shared that afternoon about focusing on the real reason they'd come to the farm in the first place. They'd missed the point. They'd traded their time and energy for something that was both distracting and unnecessary. And they'd lost their minds and a whole month in the process.

But James, after listening to these conclusions, asked them to take another look. Yes, the ornaments had been distracting and superfluous, but not *all* their time and efforts had been lost there. He reminded them of the good that had come from the ornaments, how they'd bonded as a team—coming back to a place of relative harmony after harmony had been lost. And he reminded them how they'd been able to share money, time and friendship with Ned and Nora. Had that not been productive time? And what of the friendships with each other and their customers that had been forged and strengthened in those busy weeks? His argument had merit, and they all accepted his truth, recognizing that in spite of the distraction, the ornaments had indeed given them a chance to learn the virtues and brotherly love which they reckoned had to be somehow associated with the key of charity.

Genevieve and Ephraim shared with the group what they'd learned from Hildegard about charity, that it could, if not watched carefully, be turned into something that was all about them rather than true magnanimity. And with that revelation came the guilty admissions from many of the campers that helping Ned and Nora had given them an unwarranted sense of moral superiority. But despite their possible selfish reasons for doing so in the beginning, they had in fact helped Ned and Nora. They'd sacrificed time, effort and selfish comforts to helping strangers, turning perceived enemies into friends.

The discussion offered a release valve to bottled-up emotions regarding the elderly couple. The transition from self-centered commerce, to cut-throat competition, to slow understanding, and ultimately to friendship had given them all a lot to think about. But when Greg asked why Pops and Ruby had allowed them to go so far down a path that had consumed so much time and energy and distracted them from their real purpose for being there, their answer offered even more food for thought.

All choices, they explained, had consequences. How one used one's time, considered one's challenges and accepted truth, how quickly one turned back when finding one's self on the road to a destination one didn't really want to visit, and how one dealt with disappointments, delays, and inevitable discouragements determined much of one's peace and ultimately his happiness.

The campers took comfort as Pops and Ruby shared the fact that they'd never had a group of campers what had not temporarily lost their focus—if not their minds—on why they were there. Some groups, Ruby reported, had lost more than ten weeks in the process of finding their way out of their own heads and back to their purposes for being there. Other groups had been a little faster, rediscovering their purpose relatively quickly, but often having to learn the same lessons again and again as they were distracted by tangents, detours, and perceived shortcuts. Ruby reported that every group of campers had eventually come back around only after thoughtfully focusing on the bigger picture and their reasons for being there. After noting that balance and focus were obviously difficult to maintain, she admitted that the singular way by which she knew it could be accomplished was with the continual exercise of all the keys of joy.

Crystal protested that with only three of the five keys having been identified, they were at a distinct disadvantage. But Ephraim countered her argument with the things he'd learned from Hildegard, that one could not exercise the keys they already knew without working subconsciously on the last two. Living up to the light they'd already received, he suggested, was perhaps more important than discovering the last two keys. He illustrated his argument with what he had learned that afternoon with Genevieve at the bench at the top of Harmony Hill. How, for example, the tenon under the bench, representing reverence, kept the whole bench from slowly being wiggled apart by offering tension created by the two keys that locked the tenon tightly in place.

Pops and Ruby seemed pleased by the discovery and the conversation Ephraim and Genevieve's findings prompted. Matt joined in with what he'd discovered weeks earlier, excusing himself to get his journal before opening its pages to the things he'd discovered at the benches as well as the Ebenezer behind the cowshed. The talk of the five symbols drew the family into the library, where, in the evening's fading light, Ephraim pointed out the stained glass conglomerate of the five symbols.

While the rest of the campers were focused on the glass window, Holly was distracted by a small painting she'd seen before but never really looked at, hanging on the wallpapered wall next to the large picture window. Hung in a gilded frame, the painting almost looked like something that had been borrowed from a cathedral or a shrine. It pictured a pleasant-faced Jesus, dressed in a red robe and a blue shawl, pointing to his chest where an oversized heart, encircled with a thorny band, was crowned with flames.

Calling the others' attention to the artwork, they each acknowledged that they'd seen the painting but had never really *seen* it. Pops and Ruby, who had found a comfy spot on a the soft, leather loveseat, watched silently as the campers began connecting the dots. With the help of Genevieve and Ephraim who'd had the advantage of a little time to think about it, they offered their speculation that the flaming heart in both the painting and the window represented charity, and could be found also on the back rests of the benches.

"The writing, as we've said many times before, has always been on the wall," Ruby said as she leaned forward, watching the campers' minds begin to click.

A second painting, hanging on the opposite side of the window, drew their attention to the rather dimly lit corner. Also in a gilded frame, this one was a painting of dark, blustery clouds hanging over harbor where several sailboats of various sizes were battened down and ready to ride out the coming storm. A sunbeam broke through the foreboding clouds, shining on the boats, while the rest of the picture was slowly being cloaked in a growing darkness.

While the rest of campers debated what if anything the painting might have to do with the keys of joy, Matt slipped away to the bookshelves, pulled out an old, leather-bound book and flipped through the pages.

"I think I have something here," he said after a moment, interrupting the debate. Without his reading glasses, he held the book at arms length and read the words once the others had quieted down. "This hope is a strong and trustworthy anchor for our souls. It leads us through the curtain into God's inner sanctuary. Jesus has already gone in there for us. He has become our eternal High Priest in the order of Melchizedek."

"Whoa, what's that?" asked Josh.

Matt held the book up so they all could read its cover: The Holy Bible.

"And you just happened to have that scripture memorized?" Josh asked incredulously.

Matt laughed. "I wish I was that good. No, I read the writing on the wall," he said, nodding to the painting.

Holly returned to the painting where she pointed to the small, brass label that nearly disappeared into the gilded frame. "Was that Hebrews 6: 19-20?"

Matt nodded.

"Can you read that again?" Sonja asked.

He nodded, but passed the book to Crystal who read the words with younger eyes. "This hope is a strong and trustworthy anchor for our souls. It leads us through the curtain into God's inner sanctuary. Jesus has already gone in there for us. He has become our eternal High Priest in the order of Melchizedek."

"Christ is the anchor of hope," Holly mused as Crystal finished.

Ephraim turned to the stained glass window. "So, charity and hope," he said, pointing to the heart and the anchor. "On the bench at the top of the hill, we think that circle with the plus sign might symbolize reverence," he said, pointing to the top symbol in the conglomerate.

They all looked around the room, searching high and low for any representation of the symbol. Bookshelves lined the other walls, leaving no room for artwork. Pops and Ruby sat silently waiting as the search continued. And then, without warning, soft yellow light illuminated the dim room, driving out all the darkness with its warm, amber hues. They turned to the beautiful drum-shaped pendant, hanging about ten inches from the ceiling. Its round, flat bottom was divided by two perpendicular iron rods, dividing the circle into four equal quadrants. The side of the cylinder was also divided into sections by iron slats and rods in a simple yet elegant mission style. Eight smaller circles with perpendicular rods were unmistakably present and evenly distributed around the lateral edge, and translucent yellow-veined mica was attached within the framework, generously bathing the room in artificial sunlight.

"Found it," Susan said, flipping the light switch near the doorway off and on again.

"Was all of this really here all along?" Greg asked.

Ruby smiled. "We get asked that every year, but yep, everything you've just discovered has been here longer than we have, waiting for you to discover them."

"So, are the other two keys here, too?" Ephraim asked.

"Yes, like Mom said, waiting for you to discover them," Pops admitted. "You kids had us worried for a bit."

"Why?" asked Holly

"You'd broken most of the speed records in those first couple of weeks, plowing the fields and learning three keys before many groups ever learn one. But then it all came to a screeching halt."

"It was those stupid ornaments," James declared.

Pops nodded. "If it wasn't those it would have been something else. It always is. Some years its chocolate chip cookies, or homemade soaps, or even wire-wrapped rocks turned into bangles. They're all great ideas."

"But those stupid ornaments have sucked our brains out of our heads through our noses," Josh offered.

Pops chuckled. "They kind of did, didn't they?"

"So why did you let us make them? You even taught us how!" said Sonja.

"Yes, I did."

"But why? Why did you purposely give us something to make that you knew would keep us from doing anything else."

"I don't recall ever teaching you anything that would keep you from choosing to do anything else, *or suck your brains through your noses*. I taught you a skill, something I thought you might enjoy and give you a chance to work on together as you learned to love each other and work your way through the keys of joy."

"But, didn't you imply we needed to do these to make a bunch of money for the farm?" Crystal asked.

"If I did, inadvertently, forgive me," Pops said. "Making money has never been what this farm is all about."

"But…we lost…like four weeks," Rachael protested.

"They're only lost if you learn nothing from them," Ruby replied.

"But why didn't you stop us? Why didn't you say something?" asked Spencer.

"We did. Many times. But you kids were so distracted that you didn't want to hear any of it"

"Okay, but something this important..." Matt said, "...wouldn't it have been better to bring us back to why we were here rather than let us waste all that time?"

Pops smiled, turning to Ruby. "Do you remember asking the same question, fifty-seven summer ago?"

"Yes," she replied. "Our distraction was knitted caps, remember?"

"How could I forget?"

"You know how to knit, too?" Spencer asked, looking at Pops.

"Only hats, and only with a hoop. It's not rocket science. The twelve of us must have knitted a couple hundred hats before we wised up and remembered why we'd come. But we lost a few good weeks there, thinking we had to save the farm."

"It's such a silly thing, right?" Ruby replied. "You kids are sitting in the middle of a farm that has been self-sustaining for hundreds of years. You learned that in your paperwork before you even got here, and yet, every year, kids just like you, and some even smarter, spend weeks if not months, stressing out, trying to fix something that's not even broken."

"But...why?" Holly asked. "Why do we do that?"

"After watching it for the past fifty-seven years, I think it must be human nature to freak out when you're spending your time doing work that's different than you're used to."

"Hildegard called it returning to your nets," Genevieve said.

"Nets? What does that mean?" asked Greg.

Genevieve glanced at Ephraim before answering. "She said it had something to do with the first apostles who went back to fishing after Jesus was killed. She said they forgot that they were supposed to be busy doing something different...something more meaningful."

Pops nodded. "We're all susceptible to feelings of panic. And panic rarely leads to our best decisions. On top of that, we're all prone to experience bouts of imbalance, disharmony and failure in the moderation department. Some, particularly many from your generation, in an effort to keep up with the Joneses and increase their status, slash and burn any notion of moderation they may have once had."

"I represent that remark," James admitted.

Many of the others nodded.

"So how do we come back to sanity?" Susan asked.

"You learn what's most important, and you don't let yourself or anyone else steamroller you into believing your priorities are misplaced," responded Ruby. "There isn't an individual, a marriage, or a family in this world that wouldn't benefit from that simple truth."

"But…" Susan started and stammered. "How…what do you do if you realize your priorities are all off."

"Yeah," Holly agreed, "And how do you get a new set of priorities that are worth defending?"

Many of the other campers nodded.

Ruby smiled. "The keys of joy weren't just designed to be pretty decorations," she said, pointing to the pictures on the wall and the light above them. "When you live your life with reverence for God and all His creations, you see differently than you would if you were bumbling about in the haze of your own pride and selfishness. There is hope. There is light. There is the promised reality of seeing, if you will, His unquenchable and unconditional love for you."

"C.S. Lewis once said," Pops interjected, "I believe in Christianity as I believe that the Sun has risen, not only because I see it, but because by it, I see everything else.'"

"Are you trying to make Christians out of us?" Josh responded, pointing to the light above them.

Pops shook his head. "Mom and I learned long ago that was far above our pay grade. One of the great beauties of faith is that we each get to decide what it means for us, how we'll embrace it, and how we'll allow it to direct our lives. These shelves are filled with the musings of wise men and women from throughout the ages. You can find within the pages of these books the religious philosophies of all of the world's great religions. There is beauty and light found in everyone of them, but Mom and I each independently recognized during our first summer on the farm that beauty and a little light is not enough."

"What does that mean?" asked Josh.

"We were both raised in Christian households, but neither of us truly became believers until we came to this farm and learned for ourselves that light has many degrees of brightness and glory, and grace that has the power to redeem has but one true source."

"I think we've all felt that light and hope and grace here," Matt said as all of the campers nodded. "But how do we take all of that with us when we leave?"

"That's a very common question with a very important answer," Ruby admitted. "Tonight, each of you have three keys, but where are they?"

The campers looked at each other blankly.

"Are they here in this room?" Ruby asked. "Are they found on the back of the benches, or in that window, or in these paintings and the lamp above us?"

Many of the campers shook their heads, but didn't answer verbally. The rest of them looked uncertain.

"Your question, Matt," Ruby continued, "'How do you take this with you when you leave?'—it's a question I hope that you'll each ask yourselves every day for the next three months. And when you're home, and married, and you find yourself in the thick of raising kids, and when you're old and tired and life is weighing heavy on your souls, I hope that's a question you'll continue to ask yourself every single day.

"The answer is probably far more simple than you might imagine. It's the reason we wait to plant the garden until you kids arrive each year. To plant a garden is to exercise hope. It teaches, if one is open to it, reverence for the earth and ultimately for the God who set all this in motion. A garden teaches us the need for patience, care and discipline. In every good seed is the potential for a miracle. But how that seed is planted and cared for will determine what that miracle looks like and how it will benefit humankind.

"The keys of joy are little more than seeds of true principles. Leave them alone and they'll do nothing for you. Plant them in your brain, and they'll certainly sprout, but normally only superficially, and remain incapable of yielding much fruit. If you want the greatest yield and desire the greatest miracle, the only acceptable soil for those seeds is in the rich, fertile soil of a meek and humble heart."

"Is that the reason for the heart being at the center of the combined symbols?" Holly asked, pointing to the stained glass window.

"That's a fine observation, and it certainly could be understood that way," Pops responded, "but perhaps the better way of understanding that heart in the middle of the symbols is that charity, which, in its finest definition, is the love of God—it centers all things, creating balance and grace that could never exist on the fringes or the extremes. And when we do our best to align our hearts with God's love—charity—we tend to focus on what matters most. Like a refiner's fire, the nonessential and unimportant things fade away, leaving behind what is pure and most true—our best selves."

"So, once again, everything comes back to God," Josh observed.

"If we're lucky, yes, it does," Ruby acknowledged.

"'Our birth is but a sleep and a forgetting: the Soul that rises with us, our life's Star, hath had elsewhere its setting, and cometh from afar: not in entire forgetfulness, and not in utter nakedness, but trailing clouds of glory to do we come from God who is our home[1]," Pops recited.

"My mom used to say that all the time," Greg replied.

Ruby nodded. "Your mother committed that to memory right here in this very room, forty-something years ago."

"Where does it come from?" Spencer asked.

"That's Wordsworth, isn't it?" Matt asked.

"Very good," Pops replied. "It's from his ode, Intimation of Immortality from Recollections of Early Childhood."

"How did you know that?" Susan asked, turning to Matt.

1. Arthur Quiller-Couch, ed, 1919. The Oxford Book of English Verse: 1250-1900, Ode: *Intimation of Immortality From Recollections of Early Childhood*; William Wordsworth.

He looked uncomfortable. "I, uh…I saw those words carved into a stone, twenty years ago in England."

"Twenty years ago…and you just happened to remember them?" Holly asked.

"Apparently they left an impression," he responded, looking embarrassed.

"You didn't happen to be in The Lake District, did you?" Ruby asked.

Matt nodded. "I visited the Wordsworth estate on a jaunt through Europe right after college."

"Is it as lovely as pictures make it appear?"

"Even better," he said, smiling. "The stone I spoke of, it was actually on the ground beneath a…*bench*…not far from Wordsworth's writing shed in the woods. I sat on that bench and read those words at my feet, and for the first time in years, I wanted to believe."

"Why? What made you want to believe?" Pops queried.

Matt was pensive for a moment. "Because his words…they felt so far away from the cynicism I'd grown accustomed to. I felt like they were true…like they were a window into another world…a better world."

Pops nodded. "I felt the same way the first time I heard them, right here in this room, fifty-seven years ago."

"Can you say them again?" Sonja asked.

"Sure. 'Our birth is but a sleep and a forgetting: the Soul that rises with us, our life's Star, hath had elsewhere its setting, and cometh from afar: not in entire forgetfulness, and not in utter nakedness, but trailing clouds of glory to do we come from God who is our home'."

"But trailing clouds of glory…*do we come from God who is our home*," Susan repeated thoughtfully. "If only all truths were so simple."

"If they're not, it's only because we're not ready to hear them," Ruby suggested. "Most of us are our own biggest roadblocks to accepting truth and gaining understanding."

"Tell me about it," Greg responded, shaking his head. "My dad used to say I was my own worst enemy. I hated hearing that, but it was true."

"So, how do we get out of that cycle?" Crystal asked. "How do we stop being our own worst enemy and actually progress?"

"That's an important question, and probably one we all must ask, in one form or another, before truth can penetrate our thick heads and our traditional ways of doing things, and open new doors and windows for us," Pops suggested. "There are few of us who don't spend at least some time during our formative years wandering through the desert of criticism where all truths are offensive to us."

James laughed. "Yeah, like basically all the teenage years, and most of college, and...okay, maybe I still have some of that left," he admitted.

Ruby nodded. "It's not uncommon for remnants of the desert to stick around for decades."

"So...if you find yourself either subconsciously or purposefully holding onto those remnants, how do you stop?" Crystal asked, humbly.

"You have to come to a point where you're more interested in the light than either darkness or apathy," Ruby answered, pointing to the light above them. "And when you reach that point—that place of sincere desire and real intent, sometimes called a holy longing, you have to be willing to lay down your weapons of war and seek solely for the peaceable things of God."

"So, basically...like living according to the keys of joy?" Greg asked.

She nodded. "Jesus taught that the kingdom of God is within."

"I've heard that before, but I've never understood it," Matt admitted.

"Yes, it can be a tough one to understand," Ruby acknowledged, "I may not have it right, but I believe it means that it's only by tuning our hearts to the things of God that we can hope to find peace and joy in this world, and the hope of even better things in the next. It seems sometimes like all the world is searching for a different, easier way to peace and joy, but in my ninety-four years, I've never known anyone who's chosen any number of shortcuts and found much more than a dead end. In that same time, we've known loads of folks who've entered in through the straight gate, set their course on the narrow way, and found all that they're looking for and more."

"So, you basically *are* trying to make Christians out of us," Josh joked.

"If it's joy, peace, and hope you're after, we don't know of any alternative path that can provide it all in ample portions," Pops responded. "But we've never asked anyone to take our word for it. Take it out. Try it on. You'll never get any pressure from us. The entire purpose of this farm, since the very beginning, was to share true principles and allow each camper to do with them what you will."

"And what about the last two keys?" James asked.

Ruby smiled. "They've been in front of you all along. And when the time is right, and your desire to know them exceeds your desire to be distracted by lesser things, you will wonder how you ever missed them."

CHAPTER 122

The Shift

You have to say no to a lot of good things in order to be able to say yes to a lot of great things.
−Aunt Ann

It was unanimously decided that night before any of them left the library that enough time had been wasted on less important things. The conversation had awakened each of them to the reality that there was a higher purpose for them being here, one that certainly did not include Santa ornaments, no matter how cute or how popular they were at the farm stand.

They collectively decided they would, as time permitted, finish painting the remaining ornaments that had already been carved, but they would not carve any more. Nor would they spend any more time doing anything that might distract them from their purpose, which they now recognized was to gain a more solid understanding of the keys of joy. With the three keys they'd already received, most of them recognized they already had enough of a challenge to keep them busy for months if not years. But there was more knowledge and understanding to be gained and only three short months of unobstructed time to obtain it.

The shift that began that evening created something of a seismic change over the course of the next week. Collectively, there was a real and deliberate return to the pace and effort they'd all experienced in their first couple of weeks. But with the benefit of experience and an awareness of the shortness of time, conversations became more meaningful, efforts were more spirited, and minutes became more valuable. There was still plenty of time for fun, but even leisure time and games on the front porch at the end of the day were accompanied with richer conversation and a renewed and developed sense of honesty and thoughtful openness.

To better understand the three keys they already knew, it became a common practice whenever they were together for meals or during afternoon breaks to explore aspects of each of the different keys. And with this came an ever-growing awareness of how the keys worked together. The humility required for honest reverence, for example, also supported the key of charity. And gratitude, a critical pillar of charity, also supported hope while offering important structure and definition to reverence. They soon found as they discussed these things together that any virtue or admirable quality they could think of could be easily incorporated into and offer a better understanding of these three keys.

Before the end of the next week, it was clear to each of them that many of life's most simple beauties and virtues had been largely neglected, forgotten, or set aside in the endless pursuit of far lesser things.

While money and the accumulation of wealth and status had consumed most of their time and efforts prior to coming to the farm, they each recognized that they'd systematically starved themselves of nearly all of the simple and transcendent meaning that was found here in abundance. This revelation was not easy for any of them to swallow, as it called into question their education, their lifestyles and their priorities. But the more time they had to consider the ramifications of this alternative way of living and thinking, the more hope they had in the possibility of these keys providing a more solid foundation for building a brighter future.

Pops and Ruby seemed pleased by the return to progress, but they continued to offer both subtle recommendations to each of the campers that a little time spent on the thinking benches might offer additional insights. It was not until several of them stumbled upon Ruby and Pops enjoying time on the benches however, both alone and with each other, that more of them began seeking out opportunity to enjoy the quiet reflection the benches provided.

It didn't happen all at once, and both the timing of their own breakthroughs and the overall experience proved to be different for each of them. But over the next few weeks, something big changed for each of them as they deliberately placed themselves in quiet, still places, sincerely seeking answers, light and insight.

For most of them, this stillness was difficult at first. It was new and often a challenging task to tame what Holly referred to as *the monkey mind*. Her limited experience with yoga and mindfulness classes in college made her the resident guru as she offered small clues and insights to each of them as they practiced being still. At meals and other gatherings, they began sharing their growing understanding until each of them had experienced the unique peace that came from what Ruby referred to as the Quaker practice of *expectant waiting*. For many, this practice offered a more comfortable structure and purpose to their efforts on the benches than just quietly sitting. Expectant waiting, she taught, encouraged them to purposefully begin each stillness exercise with sincere questions, prayer if it felt comfortable, an open mind and heart, an honest desire to learn whatever the universe had to share, and an earnest intention to implement whatever true answers came.

With this new direction and insight, the practice of stillness evolved rather quickly into a richer, more beneficial experience for everyone. Some learned that answers flowed through the tips of their pens as they wrote in their journals. Others mentioned being filled with a calm and peaceful aura that offered a richer perspective and a window into their purpose for being there and thoughts for their future. Each of them noted experiencing a foreign yet somehow familiar sense of wonder and reverence, turning even the most cynical and skeptical among them into more hopeful, believing creatures. While each of them later admitted their initial fears and awkwardness with silence, through the open sharing of their experiences they each came to the recognition that fear had only served to hamper or halt the flow of inspiration which the universe now seemed eager to share.

For many of them, the lifting of these roadblocks provided a cathartic release to weighty emotional baggage, making room for many insights and answers to lifelong questions and struggles. But they also came to the realization that there was more to allowing the doors of understanding to swing open than just letting go of unwanted clutter. Sunday Sermons and the conversations they inspired brought each of them to the humble recognition that they were incapable of fulfilling the measure of their creation on their own. For those who'd grown up with a religious or spiritual foundation, this truth was somewhat easier to swallow. But each of them recognized how shame, spiritual apathy, cynicism and pride had clouded their eyes to the reality of both their limitations and their unbounded potential. And the light and hope that came from their personal practices of stillness further opened their hearts to the reality of the love of God and the hope that came through exercising the key of reverence.

For those campers who'd grown up with some form of spiritual practice, this truth proved easier to reconcile than for those whose upbringing and outlook had been void of spiritual possibilities. But they also discovered there were no hard and fast rules. James, for example, had grown up going to Sunday school, but had developed an aversion in his early teens to all things that required vulnerability. As they worked together, sharing answers and discovering resolutions to many of the challenges and the questions they shared, they soon recognized that for each of them there remained a very real and intimate impediment which hampered their personal, independent progress.

At times like these, Ruby and Pops were quick to share anecdotes from their vast library of fifty-seven years on Harmony Hill. These stories confirmed to each of the campers that they were normal people struggling to find answers to normal, even common problems. But it was also comforting to recognize that for each challenge that kept them from fully accepting the keys of joy there were answers that seemed to be custom-made and available to every individual.

In the sharing of these stories, they collectively came to the conclusion that it wasn't necessarily the complexity of the problem, challenge, or question that kept an individual from discovering an answer or solution. Without patience, discipline and fortitude to press on when the path became challenging, it was far easier to simply adopt a cynical or indifferent approach, or give up on it all together. They each knew this was the easier route; they'd all taken it, either from time to time or as a general rule. But with this acknowledgment came the reality that the easier route had availed them nothing, driving them only deeper into the desert of criticism.

Equipped with this knowledge, their discussions and councils continued to evolve in enlightening directions. When they recognized the waste of bandwidth that cynicism had been in their past, they collectively agreed to clip its leaden wings and vanquish it from their lives, thoughts and habits. This course did much to help chip away at their personal weaknesses and unhelpful attitudes, but before too long it became clear once again that despite all their efforts and positive conversation, there remained in each of their backpacks at least one indissoluble stone.

To their surprise, much of Thomas's sermon the following Sunday offered insights which only a few of the campers had ever honestly given space to consider: the need for a savior. Beginning with Saint Augustine's famous quote from his early years, 'Grant me chastity and self-control, but please not yet,' Thomas briefly spoke of the transition that turned sinner to saint as Augustine discovered for himself that the happiness he sought could not be found in the things of the world or the appetites of the flesh. And it was during this time of enlightenment that Augustine recorded his truth, 'You have made us for yourself, O Lord, and our hearts are restless until they rest in you.[1]'"

Thomas turned next to Blaise Pascal, the seventeenth century French Catholic theologian and philosopher who said in his *Pensees*:

"What else does this craving, and this helplessness proclaim but that there was once in man a true happiness, of which all that now remains is the empty print and trace? This he tries in vain to fill with everything around him, seeking in things that are not there the help he cannot find in those that are, though none can help, since this infinite abyss can be filled only with an infinite and immutable object; in other words by God himself.[2]"

In addition to the wise words of others, Thomas shared a window into his own personal awakening of the reality that he was a spiritual being having a mortal experience rather than the other way around. Much of that awakening had taken place there in Niederbipp, where he had been marooned on the banks of the river, had been taken in by a magnanimous potter, and had spent the last few decades learning the reality of God's love through the humble practice of what he came to know as the keys of joy.

Later that afternoon, while discussing Thomas's sermon, Matt recalled the C.S. Lewis quote he'd read in the dining hall many weeks earlier about God being unable to provide happiness and peace apart from himself. As Matt finished reading the quote once again, there were grumblings about the time that had been wasted since its first reading. But before the lamentation could escalate to much more than a whine, Ruby

SEE PLEASANTLY RUBY PAGE 881 —

1. Confessions, 8, 7, 17
2. Blaise Pascal, Pensées VII(425)

shut it down by suggesting that looking back or dwelling on lost hours had never once provided any true seeker with even the smallest hint of either hope or peace. Instead, she warned, misery, discontent and loneliness had been the unfortunate companions of every soul who had ever neglected the light of the present day by dwelling in darkness of the previous night.

Reminding them that they were eternal beings, trailing clouds of glory, she emphatically recapitulated that the only part of their existence that could still be nobly shaped was their present and their future.

Excusing herself to the library, Ruby returned a moment later with a dog-eared, hardback copy of C.S. Lewis's *Mere Christianity*. In the evening's golden light, she read of the words that had initiated a mighty change in her own life:

"Fallen man is not simply an imperfect creature who needs improvement: he is a rebel who must lay down his arms. Laying down your arms, surrendering, saying you are sorry, realising that you have been on the wrong track and getting ready to start life over again from the ground floor—that is the only way out of our 'hole.' This process of surrender—this movement full speed astern—is what Christians call repentance."[3]

Ruby shared the abbreviated story of Lewis's transition from atheist to Christian apologist that he outlined in his book *Surprised by Joy*. She went on to explained how his clarion words gave her the desire and fortitude to sincerely ask, seek, knock and discover truths that allowed her to transition from a cynic and a skeptic to developing an attitude of reverence which eventually led to faith during the first summer she'd spent here. That faith, she admitted, though it had been questioned and challenged over the years, had continued to grow as she consciously chose reverence and faith over skepticism and doubt. And with that reverence and the exercise of her faith, her eyes had been opened to the miracles all around her.

The choices Ruby presented that evening, clear and unambiguous, were surprising in their simplicity. On one hand there was skepticism,

3. C.S. Lewis, Mere Christianity (1952; repr., San Francisco: Harper San Francisco, 2001), 56.

cynicism, pride and indifference. On the other there was gratitude, reverence, hope, redemption, charity, miracles, answers, understanding, awakening, inspiration, kindness, mercy, and joy.

When presented in this manner, it was clear to all of the campers that they had nothing to lose in choosing to live by the keys of joy, and everything to gain. It felt like an obvious no-brainer. And yet, somehow, it was a choice that required thought and deliberateness. It required, as Lewis had suggested, the laying down of arms and the emptying of arsenals accumulated over a lifetime and guarded behind fences, gates and barricades.

The promises were great, but the commitment was large. If Pops and Ruby's choice to take over the farm were any indication of the extent of the lifestyle changes that may be required, was it worth the cost? From everything the campers had seen, they had no reason to doubt their hosts' happiness and satisfaction by observing the life they led. But nothing was free. And though it seemed unlikely that none of them would be required to give up their vacations, jobs or dreams as Ruby and Pops had done for the past fifty-seven years, it would inevitably require untold adjustments to patterns, attitudes and the borders of historically guarded comfort zones.

Was it worth it? That was the question they realized they each needed to ask themselves. From all they'd seen here on the farm and in the lives of the people of Niederbipp, a commitment to live by the keys of joy was no casual commitment, one that could be donned like a article of clothing when it was easy or attractive, and removed when the going got tough or was otherwise unappealing or unpopular. It called for sincerity, and heart, and action.

It didn't take long in their discussions and contemplations to come around to the realization that the same argument could be had for marriage. It, too, in the best case scenario, was a serious, lifelong commitment that demanded much but promised a substantial return. It, too, called for the sacrifice of one's will and the expansion of one's comfort zone. It, too, narrowed the range of outside possibilities and charged those who bought in to enthusiastically provide for its defense, development, and support.

This direction of thought and conversation seemed to please Pops and Ruby a great deal. As they explained one morning at breakfast, the choice to live one's life by the keys of joy could only enlarge the possibilities of happiness and success in marriage. And a strong and happy marriage could only enhance one's growth and engagement with the keys of joy.

When James challenged the implied generalization that marriages based on something less or different than the keys of joy were any less happy or successful, Ruby turned the onus back on him to find a marriage that could not be improved by the three keys they'd already learned. When a quick review of Ruby's argument among the campers resulted in most of them siding with her, even James acknowledged how a better understanding of the key of charity alone would go far in improving any marriage.

It was a small thing, this acknowledgement, but it was far from insignificant. There was something about it that brought about another shift as their discussions quickly turned from simply understanding what the keys were to figuring out how they might be applied and incorporated not only into their lives, but into their current relationships and their future marriages. Somehow this small shift opened new potential, changing the keys from interesting ideas to inspiring and practical possibilities. The keys became real!

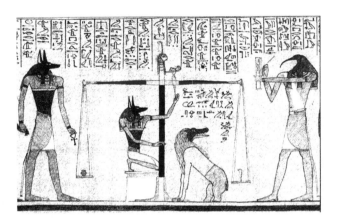

CHAPTER 123

Center of Gravity

Many people have ideas on how others should change;
few people have ideas on how they should change.
— Leo Tolstoy

Over the course of the next few days, Ruby conducted individual interviews with each of the campers in the library. As the campers shared their experience with each other afterward, they were surprised to discover that the only consistent questions Ruby asked across every interview were related to each individual's experience with putting the keys of joy to work in their lives.

Speculation quickly arose of the possibility of learning the long-awaited second or fourth keys. Anticipation grew with each interview, and on the evening of the last interview, the campers gathered on the front porch with a united hope that the time had finally arrived.

The conversation quickly fell silent as Susan and Ruby exited the library and made their way out onto the front porch. Ruby sat down next to Pops and looked around at their expectant faces with a look of childlike mischievousness.

"You kids look like a cackle of hungry hyenas, ready for dinner," she said with a pleasant laugh. "Will there be ice cream tonight to feed these famished varmints, Pops?"

"I don't think they're hungry for that sort of thing tonight, Mom. You do know it's been more than a month since they put their heads back on straight and remembered why they're here, right?"

"A full month? Are you sure?" she teased.

"That's what they tell me. I doubted it myself—time's been going so quickly—but it seems it might be time to share the next key."

"Hmmm," she responded, pursing her lips as she looked into their hopeful and expectant faces. "I will say it's been fun watching you kids figure this out. It never gets old, watching campers begin to move the magic of the keys from their brains to their hearts."

"And it's always great when we witness that change taking place with this much time left in the summer," Pops replied. "You kids have shared the good fortune of being able to get your gears working together much faster than many groups have."

"I can think of only one group who beat 'em," Ruby confirmed. "But then they had two kids of alumni that year. It's hardly a fair comparison."

Pops nodded. "After fifty-six years, it feels like we finally got it right. You kids are about as different as they come—a truly mixed bag of nuts—but look what you've accomplished together! The garden's never looked better; the meals—for the most part—are edible if not delicious.

Nothing's been burned to the ground, and we're actually up two bicycles thanks to you kids making friends with Ned and Nora, God rest their souls."

"And don't forget to mention that the cows are giving more milk," Ruby interjected, "and we've already filled two hundred quarts of fruits and vegetables, all before the pears have even come on. Thanks to you kids and your hard work, there's already enough money in the coffers to cover the taxes for this year, and a give us head start on next year."

"Will there be a next...?" Holly started, but didn't finish as the rest of the campers looked at her incredulously.

"It's a fair question," Ruby said, holding up her wrinkled hands. "The only answer we have for you is that we don't have an answer, at least not yet."

"But you still feel it's important to bottle the fruit and make the cheese?" Spencer asked.

Ruby nodded, patting Pops's knee. "I'd rather go down with a pantry full of fresh preserves than lookin' like I'd given up early. Besides, you kids signed up for the whole package, not some shaved down version of the whole enchilada. I may be dying, but I ain't dead yet. As far as I can see, there's still way too much to live for to turn in early and miss out on the grand finale. Besides, I don't think there's one of you here who'd be willing to cash your chips in early and miss out on the jackpot."

"I don't know if I like the gambling metaphor," James protested.

"Oh, James," she responded with a sigh. "Haven't you discovered it's all a gamble?"

He looked surprised.

She nodded. "You bet five months of blood, sweat and tears to come here this summer. You all did. Bet it all, hoping it'd turn out in your favor. In the process you picked up a few good keys to help you make the most of the rest of your life, if you choose to put them to work—and choose to keep doing the work so they'll keep them working for you. It's easy here with the twelve of you, united in your efforts and sharing a common goal. But you'll all be leaving in a couple of months, heading home to the *real world* as I've heard each of you call it. And it won't be so clear where you're headed. You won't have each other to bounce ideas off of during three meals a day and evenings like this on the porch. You'll have to decide if you'll keep the ante going or drop out and walk away. It's all a gamble, but one we hope you'll keep making, keep giving your heart to, keep throwing your back into.

"If you learn anything here this summer, I hope it's this: that life is what you put into it. You want love? You gotta give love and live in a way that makes room for love and welcomes love. You want to live your life in joy? Well, joy has rules, and joy certainly doesn't come easy or cheap. You want anything worth having in life, you gotta be willing to give whatever it takes to attract it to you. There's a balance that exists in all things. Remember that. It takes practice and discipline to always give at least as much as you take."

"There are far too many in this world who are net consumers of love and happiness," Pops interjected. "You can't be one of those and expect your life to end well and happy. You gotta be a net producer, everyday, always putting in more than what's required, more than you'll cash out with at the end of the day. And you'll run into lots of folks whose efforts and contributions to life lack integrity, hoping to sneak by with the minimum effort, and often far less. But don't you dare let them keep you from giving it your all."

"That hardly seems fair," James murmured.

"Nope, you're quite right. It never has been fair, and it never will be. And any time you spend moaning about that is sure to be wasted time. Do your part to fix it if you can, but know that even without lawyers, justice eventually will take care of itself, and karma always catches up. Meanwhile, you've got your own work to do. Important work. Work that matters far more than pointing fingers or whining about fairness. And that work is gonna take time—probably the rest of your lives if you do it right. Of course, if you work on it every day you'll develop some proficiency at it before long. But unless you keep working at it, keep striving for better everyday, the balance will be lost and you'll have a heck of time getting it back."

"So, balance—is that one of the keys of joy?" Matt asked.

"No," Ruby responded. "But it's part of all of them."

Matt nodded thoughtfully. "I can see how that applies, but the balance scales…isn't that the symbol on the benches and in the stained glass window in the library?"

"And there's that balance thingy on the shelf in the library, too," Crystal replied.

"Are you talking about that old brass scale? The one on the top shelf with the eagle on top?" Sonja asked.

Crystal nodded. "I've also been thinking that balance was for sure one of the keys."

"I saw that scale a few weeks ago and wondered if it might have something to do with the keys of joy," Sonja admitted.

"It has quite a lot to do with the keys of joy," Ruby admitted. "Please, Sonja, will you bring it out here for us to examine a little closer."

Sonja quickly obliged, returning a moment later and setting down the brass scales on the table in the middle of their gathering before taking her place again on a wicker loveseat.

"Balance, as has been suggested, plays a critical role in each of the keys, but the use of this symbol to represent one of the keys of joy was a deliberate choice made at least hundreds of years ago."

"Scales like that have probably been around for at least a few thousand years, right?" Josh asked.

"At least," Ruby confirmed. "They became a critical tool in many trades and professions, especially once standard, universal weights were created by the Romans, a few thousand years ago. Scales like this are still used today in many places across the globe."

"They're based on the same principle as the mobile," Ephraim pointed out.

"Indeed they are," Pops confirmed. "Because the law of gravity is a universal principle and works the same throughout the world, that which weighs four pounds in North America will weigh four pounds in Australia or Europe or Asia. And the balance scale, designed presumably by ancient engineers, relies on the fulcrum, or the center of gravity, to find the exact place where the balance of gravity is created by equal weight resting on either end of the beam."

Pops pulled a few coins from his pocket, placing a penny on the left pan. The beam immediately tipped, the left pan dropping an inch beneath the pan on the right. He placed another penny in the right pan and the pans quickly returned to equilibrium.

"So, if this key is all about balance, but it's not balance, what it the key called?" Genevieve asked.

Ruby smiled. "We thought you'd never ask?"

All of the campers protested, as both Pops and Ruby raised their hands, broad smiles across their faces.

"It was mentioned some time ago that you could not work on reverence, charity and hope without also working on the last two keys," Ruby reminded them. "All things in order. All things in order," she repeated as the protest quieted. "We've watched it every year, and it was the same for us our first summer here. Timing is everything in developing an understanding and appreciation for each of the keys. Milk before meat. Foundations before walls. Plowing, sowing and a whole lot of nurturing must proceed the harvest. We know it's been difficult to wait, but the waiting is also a critical part of the learning, giving each of you time to think, discover, and develop an appetite for additional light and knowledge."

"Yes, in a world that's increasingly swept up in the rolling plague of impatience and immediate gratification, the slow and methodical learning of these things can be torture," Pops admitted. "But the growth and acceptance of most good and true things has never been dependent on external schedules or popular opinion. Foundations, if they are to serve their purpose, must be squared, set, and solidified before anything worth building can be built upon them."

"So, again, it all comes back to the writing on the wall," Sonja mused. "'Except the Lord build the house, they labour in vain that build it.'"

Ruby nodded. "Before the first matchmakers began inviting campers to this farm, the fundamentals of what we've shared with you were outlined using the keys of joy as their foundation. Those keys, if you missed it so far, are supported by scripture and are the fundamental building blocks of the gospel of Jesus Christ. Thousands of successful marriages have since been built using the same principles at their foundations. There are, of course, endless other foundations upon which one can build a life and a marriage, but as we've told you from the beginning, we believe the foundation we have shared with you—reverence, hope and charity—offers the greatest possibility of happiness and success."

"So what then is the purpose of the last two keys?" Josh asked.

"To fortify and strengthen the individual and family as they grow," Pops responded.

"So…if we're sticking with the building metaphor, the last who keys could be kind of like a buttresses?" Ephraim suggested.

"Precisely," said Pops.

"Wait, a what?" asked Crystal.

"A buttress." Ephraim repeated. "It's basically a support that helps to keep a structure straight, like those over there," he said, pointing to the corner of the house where stones had been cemented together forming a squatty corner, making the base wider than the top.

"Is that like a *flying* buttress?" Genevieve asked. "I saw those in Paris, at the Notre Dame Cathedral, before it burned down."

Ephraim nodded. "They serve the same purpose—to keep the walls straight and strong, especially when stained glass windows are involved, even under the heavy weight of a cathedral's roof," Ephraim explained.

"I don't know what difference it makes if the fire just rips through and destroys it all anyway," Crystal replied.

"Buttresses aren't built to prevent fires," Ephraim responded. "And in the case of Notre Dame, they actually did their job exactly as designed—the roof burned and fell in, but the walls remained standing. Even with the intense stress of the fire, the buttresses helped to maintain the integrity of the walls."

Ruby smiled, looking pleased. "Thank you, Ephraim, for the engineering lesson. It's actually a beautiful metaphor for both marriage and life in general. Challenges will arise. Hardships will occur. And storms will inevitably come. But if your foundation is solid, and you've built buttresses to support your growth along the way, the calamities will not prevail, and the structure will survive and endure to be mended and repaired."

"I watched my parents' marriage and my family crash and burn," James responded. "I've been wracking my brain trying to figure out what key or principle could have prevented any of that from happening."

"And what have you come up with?" Ruby asked.

"Oh, quite a few things actually—unselfishness, integrity, sobriety, fidelity, discretion, temperance."

Ruby nodded. "Very good, James. And if you were to unite all of those things under one big tent, what would you call it?"

James thought for a moment. "I'd probably call it self-discipline."

Ruby laughed. "Ladies and gentleman, I give you the fourth key of joy," she said, pointing to the brass scales, "Self-discipline."

CHAPTER 124

Quartus Clavis

Most powerful is he who has himself in his own power.
— Seneca

Self-discipline?" Genevieve repeated before she could stop herself, sounding almost bothered.

"Actually, that makes a lot of sense," Matt suggested.

"Does it?" Genevieve asked. "Self-discipline could mean so many things for so many different people."

"I think that might be the point," Spencer responded. "Of all the keys so far, this is obviously the most pointed and personal."

"Yeah, I agree," Josh admitted. "It actually reminds of something my track coach used to always say: that until we've learned how to master ourselves we'll remain subject to outside forces and at war with our better selves. I'm sure I didn't appreciate that truth when he said it, but over the last few years I've become convinced that he's right."

"I like that," Rachael admitted. "The keys of joy—the keys of liberty—I don't know if you can have either joy or liberty without learning how to be the boss of your best self. I feel like I've struggled with self-discipline my whole life."

"Don't we all?" Susan responded.

"Yes, most of us do in one aspect or another, and a struggle in one area of self-discipline very often infects the self-discipline in other areas. But fortunately, the same is true on the positive side of the spectrum as well—when we conquer our lesser selves by neutralizing our weaknesses, and work on turning them into strengths, we are liberated," Ruby said pointing to the eagle at the top of the scales. "Until we—as Rachael so aptly put it—decide to become the boss of our best selves, we cannot enjoy the fullness of either joy or liberty. Self-discipline has meaningful applications to every aspect of our lives—spiritual, financial, emotional, sexual, physical…every aspect of who we are can be improved and enhanced as we harness the powers of agency with the bridle of self-discipline."

"Bridle…you mean like for horses?" Greg asked.

"Exactly," Pops responded. "You kids have been around horses enough in the past couple of months to understand the metaphor. It's nearly impossible to get a horse to do what you'd like him to do without first putting a bridle on his head and a bit in his mouth. Without it, he's little more than wild bronco—incapable of being much use to mankind, and prone to all manner of aggression, distraction, and even destruction."

"Like that stallion down the road on the neighboring farm," Genevieve offered.

Pops nodded. "Mom and I were there the day they unloaded him out of the trailer he'd nearly destroyed on his way here. We heard him coming from half-way up Harmony Hill; sounded like the collision of a hurricane and a freight train. I'd guess he has at least a dozen generations of wildness in him. Those types don't tame easily."

"But they can be tamed?" Susan asked.

"Sure, with the right tools—training, hard work, and patience—all things can fulfill the measure of their creation," Pops replied.

"This feels like a collision of metaphors," James said. "Horses, bridles, buttresses, scales. I'm not sure where one starts and the other ends."

"There is no end to metaphors for self-discipline," Ruby responded. "As soon as you come to an understanding of one there will be another to understand, and more waiting in the wings."

Rachael shook her head, looking overwhelmed.

"You disagree, dear?" Ruby asked.

"I don't know, I guess I was just hoping for an easier answer. Why couldn't the key be… learning how to whistle, or maybe learning a new musical instrument. Those things could bring you joy, right?"

Ruby smiled. "Yes, but they, too, require self-discipline and practice to eventually master, don't they?"

"Okay, but how far do you really have to go with this?" Spencer asked.

Pops laughed. "I'm pretty sure that's not the right question."

"Why not?"

"Because you might as well be asking what's the minimum you could get away with. That kind of attitude might work when you're a teenager, but it doesn't bode very well for a responsible adult, a spouse, or a parent. Nobody want to be married to someone who's goal is mediocrity."

Many of the campers chuckled at the sentiment.

"But this could take pretty much take forever," Spencer argued.

"That's pretty much the point," Ruby said unapologetically. "If you hope to ever master yourself, there can be no end to self-discipline."

"I'm reminded of a quote from the Buddha I saw written on the wall of a train station in Tibet a couple of years ago," Matt offered. "It said something like, 'Before Enlightenment—chop wood, carry water. After Enlightenment—chop wood, carry water.'"

Ruby smiled and nodded. "In the end, all enlightenment comes down to better knowing yourself and learning how to bridle your own soul for higher purposes. And there is perhaps no better way to reach that enlightenment than through the life-long practice of self-discipline."

"But where do you even start?" asked Spencer. "I've got so many things to work on that I don't know if I'll ever dig out of the hole I'm in."

"Funny, you didn't strike me as one who struggled with confidence in your abilities when you first arrived here," Ruby responded.

"Yeah, well…" He laughed. "It must be something in the water that's brought me low. I think we've all felt it."

Many of the campers nodded.

"We hear this every summer," Pops replied, "kids with normally generous egos coming to a knowledge of their own weaknesses and fallibility. It can be troubling in the beginning as important adjustments are made to egos. But hang on. I have yet to meet anyone who's given up the onus of ego or the burden sin without feeling like he has a new-found ability to fly."

Spencer nodded. "Yeah, I've already felt some of that. Is there more to come?"

Ruby smiled. "Spencer, if you'll stick with it, what's to come is exponentially bigger and better than anything you're willing to leave behind. You've only but dipped your finger in sea of magic."

"So, do you mind if I ask you a question about the scales?" Rachael asked.

"Please do," Ruby encouraged.

"The eagle on top…isn't that a symbol of liberty?"

"Yes, very good."

"And what about the scales themselves?" Greg asked. "Doesn't that have something to do with the law?" he asked, turning to James and Susan.

Susan nodded. "I think you're probably referring to Lady Justice who's often portrayed blindfolded, holding a set of scales in one hand and a sword in the other."

"It's old symbolism, dating back to the Greek or the Romans, I believe," James confirmed. "She's interested in blind justice—thus the blindfold—trying to be impartial to wealth or status as she weighs truth and error, and is always ready to mete out justice."

"That doesn't sound like there's a direct connection to self-discipline," Greg suggested. "Even in the paperwork we got before we came here we were encouraged to come into this with our eyes and hearts wide open."

"Lady Justice is a beautiful symbol," Ruby acknowledged, "but it's her scales that we try to focus on here. They offer the same sensibility to you as they do to her as you do your best to distinguish truth from error."

"And what about the words at the base of the stand?" Holly asked. "Is that Spanish?"

"Close, but it's actually Latin," said Ruby.

They all leaned forward to read the words that few of them had noticed before.

TRADE NON QUOD VIS MAXIME QUOD VIS NUNC.

"Anyone know Latin?" Greg asked after mumbling through the first few words.

They all turned to Matt who shook his head.

"It's an important phrase I hope you'll all remember," Ruby said.

"We heard one young man from a few summers ago tattooed it on the back of his hand so he'd never forget it," Pops said.

"We'd much prefer it if you imprinted it on your heart than your skin," Ruby suggested. "But it's our job to teach you truth. You each get to decide what you'll do with it. The phrase is quite simple, but how you live it will make a whole lot of difference in the level of joy you'll walk with everyday. The translation is, 'Trade not what you desire most for what you desire now.'"

"So, like…I want to fit into my bikini, but I also want to eat a box of creamsicles?" Rachael asked as the campers laughed.

"Or I want to save money for a wedding ring, but I also want to go to buy the new Play Station?" Josh added to the moans of many of the men and the mocking guffaws of all of the women.

"Or what about, I want to improve my relationship with God, but I also want to sleep in on Sundays and hang out at the bar," Sonja suggested.

"Or, since no one's saying it, I want to go into my marriage without regrets, but I also have sexual needs that are itching to be fulfilled with anyone with a pulse," Ruby said. "That's one we hear in one variation or another every year."

The campers look at each other, beginning to recognize the depth and breadth of the this key.

"I've never really thought about it these terms, but looking at it like this…self-discipline is basically always an uphill climb, isn't it?" Susan asked.

"So much for living for the moment!" Spencer muttered.

"That really depends," Ruby responded.

"Really?" asked Spencer, looking surprised.

"Sure. It's important to live in the moment, to be present and aware and thoughtful. But people tend to get into trouble and lose their way, if not their souls, when they live as if this moment were the only moment."

"Tell me about it," Greg replied, shaking his head. "Believe me, it looks even stupider when you live your life as if every moment were your last moment! Then all the stupid ideas win out over the good ones, and sobriety takes a backseat to passion and impulse. I lived too many years by the mantra: if it feels good, do it. It's a dead end. It always stops feeling good eventually, and then you have to take more of what you don't need to numb your senses and make it feel good again. There's no end to that lie."

"I don't believe anyone is immune to the siren call of folly," Pops responded, consolingly, laying his hand on Greg's shoulder. "The trick is to recognize that the highway to hell always ends badly. Whether you ride it for a mile or for a lifetime, it's only self-discipline and love that can get you off it and point you back to the humble path of joy."

Greg nodded. "But I'm still struggling to forget all that folly and move on."

"Shame and regret are indeed powerful destabilizers," Ruby responded.

"You're not kidding!"

"No. In order to overcome both shame and regret we must first recognize their common root," Ruby added.

Greg looked puzzled.

"Fear, Greg," Ruby continued. "Fear is at the root of all things that hold us back from healing and progressing. It blocks out the sun and makes us feel unworthy, unloved, and worst of all—unloveable. The one path out of the pits of misery and regret is exercising hope and love—love for self, love for mankind, and ultimately both the love *for* God, and accepting the love *of* God. Peace and joy, as I'm sure you've already learned, can never be found by wallowing in self-flagellation, or dwelling on the folly of our youth. We mustn't forget that these, too, can be weapons of war that can separate us from God's love.

"Most of the kids who apply to spend the summer here have been humbled enough by the consequences of their choices that they are willing to look at things differently than they have in the past. I'll admit that we look for signs of humility in the applications, and encourage those who aren't quite there yet to consider the ramifications of meekness before applying again."

"*Meekness*?" Josh asked, surprised. "I can't imagine that being a very common trait, at least not anymore. It seems like that requirement would eliminate most applicants, wouldn't it?"

"Yes, it does," Ruby admitted. "But we learned decades ago that it's nearly impossible to influence the course of those who lack humility or are prone to self-destructive decisions until they've decided for themselves that light may have more to offer them than the path of least resistance and the traps of carnal gratification. With any luck, we are able to sort through the hundreds of applicants and choose the ones who are ready and eager to progress into the next refining processes of marriage and family."

"I know I didn't appreciate it at the time I received my first rejection letter...or my second," Greg admitted, "But I was ready by the time my acceptance letter finally came."

Ruby smiled, nodding. "Timing is everything, and all good things—if you'll continually seek and pursue them—will come in their own due time."

"And self-discipline..." Matt said thoughtfully, "Is that also one of the things you look for when you decide who you'll accept?"

Ruby nodded. "If you haven't at least begun to learn how to govern yourself by the time you're in your mid-twenties, there's not a lot we can do for you in five short months to prepare you for the most important decision you'll ever make in your life."

"So why did you think I was finally ready?" Greg asked.

Ruby turned and smiled at Pops before turning to face Greg. "We were impressed that you stuck with it, Greg."

"That's right," Pops admitted. "There aren't a lot of kids who stick with it after being asked to work on a few things and apply again, and even fewer who receive two letters like that and still press on. It showed us that you were both humble and teachable, and hungry enough to make sincere strides toward a happy life."

"I know I was really angry and discouraged when I got my rejection letter," Crystal said. "I fumed for a couple of weeks before I decided to take an honest look at your suggestions."

Ruby nodded. "But do you see the wisdom in waiting now?"

"Yeah, I do, but I don't see how your standards are equally applied to everyone."

"Tell us what you mean," Ruby urged.

"You encouraged me to get out of debt before applying again, which I did by working two and sometimes three jobs. But then I got here and found out both Susan and James are still paying off their student loans. Why was my debt any different than theirs?"

"There are many different kinds of debt, and I don't like any of them," Ruby admitted. "Debt can be and often is a major point of contention in marriage. We encourage all applicants to be debt-free, but I absolutely require that applicants rid themselves of all credit card debt before I'll accept them."

"Is that because of the interest?" Matt asked. "I was curious about that myself. I'd been lazy about paying off the last of my student loans because the interest was so low. But I can imagine that the high interest on credit card debt could be difficult to handle."

"Things have changed an awful lot in the nearly six decades Pops and I have spent on this farm. There was no such thing as credit cards when we came here, and we've never had a reason to own one. Sure, the convenience is attractive, but we've never been able to understand how making money easier to spend is good for anyone.

"To answer your question, Crystal, I'll give you a hint—credit card debt—and many other kinds of debt—generally have everything to do with self-discipline. Questions about debt had never been part of our application until about 30 years ago when we began noticing that some of our campers were receiving forwarded credit card bills here at the farm, and they were then stressing out about how they were going to pay them. It was a major distraction, and it kept kids from focusing on the things they needed to be working on.

"You're talking about Jennie Larkin?" Pops asked, a wry smile on his face.

Ruby nodded. "Debt is usually a far easier hole to fall into than it is to climb out of. We never made it a point to ask about debt until Jennie opened our eyes to the problem."

"Did she have more debt than I did?" Crystal asked.

Ruby nodded. "We didn't discover until our second interview—after several credit card bills had been forwarded to the mailbox at the top of the hill—that Jennie had come to the farm with the hopes of meeting a wealthy man who would marry her and accept her debts which had grown to be more than her annual salary."

"Ouch! What did you do with *her*?" Spencer asked. "I hope you didn't arrange a marriage before her fiancé could learn the truth."

Ruby shook her head. "No, I would never do that. When I learned of Jennie's financial baggage I refused to help her find a husband until she had paid her debt in full. After her summer on the farm, it took her nearly four years and the application of more self-discipline than she'd ever known, but she was able to pay off her debts, and eventually find a practical husband who appreciated her ability to live modestly and stick to a budget. She's written two books about the merits of thrift and freeing one's self from the bondage of debt. You'll find them in our library on the Personal Finance shelf. Self-discipline, I might add, is a major theme in each of her books."

"It all comes back to balance," Pops added. "If your life is out of balance in any one way, it's unlikely you'll find balance in any other aspect of you life; and financial imbalance is generally a major contributor to many other imbalances."

Many of the campers nodded.

"Getting out of debt—living without debt...it all sounds good in theory, but unless you make a ton of money, I'm not sure how practical it is," said Ephraim.

"Tell us what you mean," Pops probed.

"I don't know how the rest of you were raised, but my parents have lived with credit card debt their whole lives. I carried a balance on my cards until I heard paying it off was a requirement to participate here. I just can't imagine maintaining that during marriage and for the rest of my life. I've got a buddy who's still paying for his wife's wedding ring and their honeymoon, three years later."

"And how does that affect the happiness level of his marriage?" Ruby asked.

Ephraim shrugged. "It can't be good if he complains about it to me, right?"

"And what if you need a new car, or your washing machine breaks, or your whole family is going to Disneyland and you don't have the cash to pay for it. What's wrong with putting that on a credit card?" asked Crystal.

"Disneyland? Really?" James responded, looking incredulous. "You'd go into debt for Disneyland?"

"To be able to spend time with my sisters and their families, yes, I would."

"I'm actually glad this came up now," Ruby spoke up, interrupting a potential argument before it could get started. "Such questions give us all a good glimpse into the lives of everyday families across the world. Paying for Disneyland would definitely be considered a first world issue, but there's not a family in the world that doesn't have to make financial decisions on a regular, if not a daily basis. Many of these decisions have the ability to create hard feelings among couples, and difficult financial situations for families, potentially for many years. Most families in the first world require at least one car. Yes, washing machines break down from time to time, usually at the most inopportune times. And most folks enjoy taking a break from the hustle and bustle of the regularly scheduled program to enjoy time away with friends and family. But how are you supposed to meet all of those needs while also maintaining a sense of financial self-discipline?"

The campers looked around at each other, waiting for a good answer, but no one spoke up.

"We'll give you a hint," Pops said. "You can't do it alone."

"So, maybe you need to talk to your banker?" Holly suggested, looking and sounding quite uncertain.

"It many cases, that could be helpful," Ruby responded. "Banks can be great partners in securing loans or consolidating unexpected debts. But I think what Pops is getting at is that once you're married, most financial decisions are no longer yours alone to make."

"Oh, right, like your husband or wife should be part of those decisions." Holly suggested.

Ruby nodded. "That may seem self-evident to many, but depending on how you grew up and what your experience has been since coming of age, making a unified decision with your spouse may require a major shift in how you do things, even a shift of self-discipline and deeply embedded habits and beliefs."

"Uh, what if you don't have the patience for people who have dumb ideas about how to spend their money?" James asked.

"Then you better get some patience—and some tact—or your marriage is going to be very tough," Ruby responded.

"But in all seriousness," Matt said, "how are you supposed to come to a consensus if you're diametrically opposed about a big financial decision of, say, you want to buy an Audi and your wife wants a minivan."

"What woman would ever seriously want a minivan?" Holly challenged, drawing the laughter of all of the women, including Ruby.

"Okay, but you know what I'm saying, right?" Matt continued with a deferential smile.

"Judging from what we've learned about balance, it seems like it would be best to find a compromise of some sort—like maybe a Subaru wagon," Sonja suggested.

"Very good," Ruby responded. "Ugly arguments and divisive interactions are avoided everyday by compromise, and self-discipline can go a long way to keep such interactions civil. But there are few things that can cause normally affable interactions to go south faster than throwing money into the equation."

"Oh boy! There's an understatement. In my family, you even mention money, and you basically sign up for all hell breaking loose, and calling each other terrible names before retreating to separate corners of the house where you try to ignore each other for as long as possible, or until the other person gives up or gives in," Crystal replied.

"Is that the way you'd like to be treated?" Ruby asked, looking alarmed.

"Well, no, but I've seen it work quite effectively for my mom. She usually got her way."

"Maybe, but certainly at the expense of love, understanding, and joy," Ruby responded.

Crystal exhaled loudly as she nodded solemnly.

"Mom and I learned many years ago that it's much better to come to the realization that you made a bad decision after you made that decision together than it is to have someone to blame for that bad decision."

"You're not suggesting that life's somehow better if everyone's wrong, are you?" Sonja asked.

"Sometimes, actually, yes, I am suggesting that."

They all turned to look at Pops, surprised by what he'd just said.

"If you're both wrong together there exists an opportunity to learn together," Pops explained. "Balance remains. Hope remains. Without balance and hope there is strife and disharmony. Without harmony, walls are built, chasms are formed, feelings are hurt and families are threatened. But if love and harmony prevail, it's likely that the next decision you make together will be better, and the one after that, and the one after that."

"Okay, that's all well and good, but how do you find harmony when your spouse makes foolish decisions and is dragging you down with her?" asked James.

Ruby turned and looked at Pops, waiting for him to answer.

"We received two helpful bits of advice on our wedding day that I've never forgotten," Pops said, sitting up a little taller. "The first is to never argue over anything that's more than two weeks old. And the second: it's usually far more enjoyable to be married and at peace than it is to be right. The purpose and blessings of both practices are to keep love flowing. We've discovered for ourselves that each of these gems of wisdom have deeply embedded ties to self-discipline. Mom and I have done our best to remember and review them every time things get difficult."

"*Do things still get difficult?*" Holly asked, looking surprised.

"Oh, far less than they used to," Ruby replied. "We both came to our marriage with habits, quirks, and preferences, as each of you will. You figure a lot of things out over the course of fifty-seven years, especially if you have the keys of joy to help you soften your corners and edges, and to help you unite in a common work. At this point, I'm just grateful to have had someone like Pops who's loved me in spite of my quirks and has treated me like the queen of the farm."

"When you get to be married to an angel-queen for fifty-seven years, gratitude is really all there's left to feel," Pops admitted.

CHAPTER 125

Fruits in Their Season

You will never have a greater or lesser dominion than that over yourself...
the height of a man's success is gauged by his self-mastery;
the depth of his failure by his self-abandonment.
...And this law is the expression of eternal justice.
He who cannot establish dominion over himself
will have no dominion over others."
— Leonardo da Vinci

The evening's discussion and the identification of self-discipline as the fourth key invited lots of thought and conversation the following day. By that afternoon, after bottling fifteen jars of stewed tomatoes and six jars of raspberry jam, a rather lengthy list of details and attributes of self-discipline had been compiled by Holly who took it upon herself to sift through the chatter and find the nuggets. Anxious to share this list with Ephraim and Rachael who were working the farm stand, they all rode their bikes to the bottom of the hill.

They found Ephraim and Rachael, equally inspired by the previous evening's discussion, working on their own list. Before they left the farm stand that evening, the list had grown to well over fifty items, and each of them had identified both personal strengths and personal weaknesses that needed work.

They were surprised to find Thomas riding his bike along the highway, heading south, as they approached the junction to Harmony Hill. They were even more surprised when they learned he was headed their way at the request of Ruby and Pops who'd summoned him to dinner.

He pedaled with them, even challenging them to see who could pedal the furthest before the inevitable dismount where the walking and pushing would begin. He surprised them all by keeping up with the leader, Spencer, until the very end, losing the contest by only a dozen steep feet of asphalt, which he quickly made up for on foot when Spencer was too winded and nauseated to care.

They all walked together the rest of the way, the campers joyfully announcing that they'd finally learned another key, even sharing with the old priest some the virtues and habits that had found a place on their lists of all things they felt necessary to both obtain and maintain this key of self-discipline. Thomas appeared impressed, sharing a few from his own list that he was still working on.

After dinner and evening chores, they gathered back on the porch where Ruby announced that the evening's activities would resume in the orchard. She invited each of them to help carry either the fixings for s'mores or roasting sticks and follow her and Pops along the narrow path to the orchard.

They'd all been this way before, but not often. Several of them, in their explorations of the farm, had discovered the bench that offered a commanding view of the beautiful rows of trees and the valley below. And all of them had visited the orchard on several occasions to pick apricots and cherries for the farm stand, the table, and the cellar. According to Sonja's most recent progress report, some of the peaches were getting closer to being ripe, but the pears and apples still had a ways to go.

But it wasn't fruit they were after tonight. And instead of stopping at the bench that overlooked the orchard, Ruby led the gang down a terraced berm and into the rows of fruit trees. The rich, sweet aroma of mouldering fruit wafted about as the walked past the apricot and cherry trees, their branches much lighter now that their fruits had all been picked or fallen to the ground. Wandering through row after row of trees, Ruby led them on until they came to a fire pit, encircled by a bench made of logs and graying, weathered boards. A huge, haphazardly-stacked pile of branches, looking much like a gigantic bird's nest, stood over eight feet tall adjacent the circle.

"Mom and I always look forward to this annual bonfire," Pops said after he'd helped Ruby step over the bench. They stood in the center, encouraging the campers to find a seat.

"Despite the beauty of this setting, this will be the only time this summer that we'll gather together here as a family," Ruby offered. "We encourage you, however, to come here on your own from time to time to consider the things we have to share with you tonight. Like everything else on the farm, this evening's activities have ties to the keys of joy as well as many of the other lessons and themes we have shared with you or hope to share with you."

Pops nodded. "We're grateful you kids have finally arrived at this point and learned the fourth key of joy. The timing of this bonfire varies from year to year, depending on when we reach this point. Like Mom said—and I'm sure you've all noticed by now—the keys of joy are tied to everything on the farm. You may have already noticed that the surface of the benches on which you sit are carved or inscribed with the musings and reflections of many generations of campers, who, like yourselves, came to the farm in search of a better life."

He paused as the campers turned to look at the boards beneath the backsides, seeing for the first time what they had missed at first glance.

"The writing's on the wall," Sonja mused aloud.

"Yes, or in this case, under your butts," Ruby responded with a smile. "In case you missed it, this circular bench is symbolically made up of five boards, each of them serving as a reminder of the five keys. You will find written and carved over the surfaces of these benches many things that might surprise you—things you may not have ever considered a tie to the keys of joy. But as you come here to learn and to contemplate your own journey and understanding of the keys you already know and the one you have yet to learn, we invite you to share the wisdom and understanding that flows through you. You may write, scratch, carve or even burn—within reason—anything onto the surface of these benches which you hope to share with those who will follow you."

"That being said," Pops interjected, "we hope you'll recognize this place as a place of reverence and reflection and take your time here seriously."

"How long have these benches been here?" Holly asked, rubbing her fingers over the carved surface of the thick board on which she sat.

"We're not sure. These benches were here before we arrived," Pops answered. "But to our knowledge, there have been benches here on the same spot since the first matchmakers planted the first trees in this orchard, three hundred years ago."

"So, is there a symbolic tie between the orchard and the keys?" Matt asked.

"Yes," Ruby responded with a broad smile. "We'd like you to discover your own connections, but to set you on the right track, we'd like to present to you a visual aid." She pointed to the adjacent mounded tangle of branches. "In order to keep the trees in this orchard healthy, they are trimmed and pruned every fall. You too will have a chance to help with the pruning at the end of September when the last of the fruits have all been picked. This tangle of limbs are last year's cuttings. And the fruits you'll enjoy this year have last year's pruning to thank, in part, for their success, just as the success of next year's fruits will depend upon your work. You, too, will set aside the branches of this years's trimming for next year's fire.

"Why didn't last year's campers just finish the job they started?" James asked, nodding to the oversized pile.

Pops nodded. "Does anyone have an answer for James?"

"Uh, is it because green wood doesn't burn?" Ephraim asked.

"That's right," Pops affirmed "Practically speaking, it would have been pointless for last year's crew to try to rush things along when it takes at least several months for wood to dry to the point it will burn without smoking everyone out. But symbolically speaking, there are myriad lessons to learn from this pile of trimmings. We'll share only one and leave the rest for you to discover on your own. As this pile will be consumed tonight, we encourage you to remember it during future visits."

"Pops and I learned our first summer on the farm, and many times since, that the best lessons are the ones that are revealed to you when you find yourself in quiet places like this one, asking and seeking for answers. The carvings on these benches are the lessons and answers that have come to others. Like last year's branches that will fuel our fire this evening, we encourage you to use these carvings to kindle your own fire of self-reflection and self-mastery."

Ruby turned and pointed to Josh. "You will find a beautiful truth carved just beneath your pockets. Would you please read it to us?"

He smiled, turning to kneel on the ground where he could better examine the carving which spanned at least twenty inches. "The... unexplained leaf...is not worth...lifting?" He looked up and turned around, looking confused. "That doesn't sound right. What do leaves have to do with anything?"

"It sounds like last winter's snow has worn away some of the meaning behind that one," Pops suggested, smiling. "It might be better understood as *'The unexamined life is not worth living.'* It's a quote from Socrates, and one that is certainly as true today as it was when he spoke it in Athens 2,500 years ago. We learn and grow and get better only as we develop within us a desire to become our best selves, work through our struggles and challenges, and cut from our lives all that is unnecessary and burdensome."

"So..." Ephraim said, fading out before he even got started. He looked lost for a moment before finding his voice again. "Based on that quote from Socrates, why is the key self-discipline rather than self-mastery?"

"That's a great question," Pops admitted. "Thomas, would you like to answer that one?"

Thomas nodded, glancing around the circle into each of the camper's faces. "There is great virtue that comes from mastering one's self—in learning how to set aside our natural tendencies that lead to selfishness and egos run amuck. Both self-mastery and self-discipline require the exercise of our best selves, but in my mind the difference between the two lies in our reasons to put forth the effort. It's a fine and noble thing to become the master of one's self. And in my humble opinion, self-mastery is an essential part of self-discipline. But self-discipline ultimately requires another, more elevated level of understanding. It requires a connection to the divine—to a God who elevates us with His grace and mercy, and who helps us recognize the seeds of our own divinity."

"You mean like a disciple?" Holly asked.

"Exactly! A disciple is one who follows another for the purpose of gaining wisdom and understanding. A person can obviously gain much by learning to master himself. But a disciple of God has no ceiling or limit to how far he might rise in virtue, understanding and grace. We all must answer to ourselves as we learn to master the natural man or woman within us. But for those who commit to living by the keys of joy, we all will learn—as our understanding grows—that our bigger interests and concerns must be how we'll answer to God. Where self-mastery may elevate you to become the best man or woman you can be, self-discipline encourages you in the endless, eternal pursuit of following the one, true Master."

He stopped for a moment to look into the faces of each of the campers. "I don't often share my story, but something compels me to share it now. Like Ruby and Lorenzo, I'm a transplant to Niederbipp. I was born the youngest of seven children, the bonus child in a large, traditional Irish Catholic family. And before I was even born, my mother gave my soul to Jesus, which, I understood from the time I was very young, meant I had little choice but to become a priest.

"I never remember having any arguments against it, so I grew up serving as an altar boy. I attended seminary where I worked for four years on mastering myself before I became a priest and took a job in a small parish, about eighteen miles upriver. To make a long story a little more palatable, my assignment there was not a good fit. And so one Sunday morning before I'd even finished a year of service in my parish, I was gagged and hogtied by my congregants, tossed into the bottom of a leaky rowboat, and sent downriver. I washed up that evening on the banks of town not far from your farm stand."

"I hope you got yourself a good attorney and went back and pressed charges," James said.

Thomas shook his head. "That was more than fifty years ago, and I've never been back."

"Why not? I could think of at least a handful of possible suits you could file against the town and the individuals responsible."

Thomas chuckled. "I'll keep that in mind, though I'm sure the statute of limitations has long since expired, and most of the congregants are most certainly dead. No, instead of placing blame for what happened on anyone else, I decided I would accept responsibility for myself, and my life has been much different than it might have been otherwise. Without a reason to go back, I decided to reinvent myself here in Niederbipp as a part-time plumber and a part-time baker and a part-time librarian, spending the rest of my time serving God in a way I hope will still make my mother proud."

"So, you're not *really* a priest anymore," Sonja asked

Thomas shook his head. "I still embrace the standards of a priest, and do my best to minister wherever I go. But my understanding of self-discipline has expanded and grown, helping me learn to embrace all truths and love all of God's children. I don't know if life ever works out exactly the way either you or your parents plan it, but I've discovered that if we're hungry for truth, and flexible enough to roll with the punches—as well as the more compassionate nudges from the hand of Providence—great and beautiful blessings will be waiting around every corner, and new friends will be found in the faces of all people. I learned some degree of self-mastery in my youth, and much more at the seminary. But the understanding I've gained over the past fifty-plus years through learning and exercising the keys of joy has given my life a balance and peace I never knew before."

"But, wait," Crystal interrupted. "You were a priest. How is what you're doing now any more balanced or disciplined than before?"

Thomas nodded. "There comes a time for all of us when we must choose for ourselves the course we will travel—and the many choices we will make along the way. When you grow up in a structured environment, surrounded by rules and dogma, many of those decisions are made for you. That's not necessarily a bad thing, but it's different than making those decisions consciously. My parents pointed me in a positive direction, and the church swept me along, giving me plenty of encouragement. But I don't know if I truly understood or consciously chose the path I was on until I landed in Niederbipp, humbled and bruised. It was at that point that I knew I needed to discover for myself which of all the paths was right for me."

"You didn't feel like you needed to know that before?" Josh asked.

Thomas shrugged. "When the teaching is comfortable and the

sailing is smooth, few of us have any need to rock the boat. More often than not it's only when our boat springs a leak and is headed for the rocks that the big questions arise. For some, the leaky boat comes early. For others, the leak comes much later. But whether it comes early or late, a leaky boat is quickly filled with existential questions. And the answers that come in times of desperation often feel very different than those answers that come when the boat is tight and the wind is steady and from behind. Learning is often much more meaningful when the threat of drowning is real. At times like those, we are hungry for answers and anxious to learn all we can. But when things get better and the crisis is over, our hunger for answers is too often sated, and we get lazy and careless and forget our need for a more consistent connection to the God who not only created the seas, but is also most capable of calming them."

"Do you believe He calms all seas?" Rachael asked.

Thomas nodded thoughtfully. "Not always in the time we feel is best, but always in the time He knows will be best for us. I know from personal experience that His timing can sometimes feel infuriating and leave us feeling doubtful of either His love or mercy. It may take many years to receive the wisdom and understanding we desire. But if we practice faith, the storms will pass and the sun will rise, and all will be well. All questions will have their answers, all heartache will be soothed, and all that is broken will be mended."

"But how can you believe everything will work out if there's so much that's wrong with the world?" Susan asked. "Doesn't it make you question everything?"

"There was a time that I did question everything, and there are still plenty of days when my number of questions seem bigger than my number of answers. Faith, I suppose, is different for everyone, and there will always be those who set it all aside as the fruitless musings of feeble minds. But seeing what I've seen, and maybe more importantly, having felt what I've felt, and having experienced all that I've experienced, I've learned that it's really more fruitful to question my questions than to question my faith. Perhaps some of you are familiar with Pascal's Wager?"

Most of the campers shook their heads.

"Blaise Pascal, if you'll remember from my sermon a few weeks back, was a seventeenth-century man of both science and theology who posed an argument that still feels relevant today. His take was that humans must wager with their lives that God either exists, or He doesn't. If He does not exist, believers have lost very little—mostly small pleasures or perhaps a few luxuries they sacrificed for their faith while still having lived a good, clean life. But if God *does* exist, Pascal suggests, believers have, quite literally, everything to gain."

"Is that argument enough for you?" Susan asked, looking sincere.

"If you're asking me if the argument alone is enough to keep me going for the next twenty to thirty years, the answer would have to be no."

Many of the campers looked confused.

"As I said, faith is different for everyone. Some may be able to take their faith and put it under a glass dome, maybe place it on the mantle for all the see and admire. And if anyone asks if they have faith, they can point right to it."

A couple of the campers chortled at this illustration.

"For me, my faith has always required more than a one-time declaration of belief. I like to think of my faith as something more like these trees. It requires sunlight and nurturing with study, and service, and gathering with others to share strength and love and experience.

"Faith, without works, is dead," Spencer spoke softly. "My mother used to tell me that all the time."

Thomas nodded. "And scripture would agree with her. Anything that's living and growing and becoming something more or better requires work, and sweat, and action. If there are any exceptions, I haven't discovered them yet. But faith-filled works encourage us with the nudges of unseen hands and invite God's grace and spirit into our hearts, minds and lives. And in quiet places like the benches scattered across this farm, the small, delicious fruits of faith whisper forth in the form of answers, guidance and inspiration."

"I don't suppose Mr. Pascal said anything about the virtues of instant gratification?" Spencer asked.

Thomas smiled. "Only in an era of microwaves and Netflix has the world celebrated the concept of instant gratification." He stood, and stepping outside of the circled bench, walked to the nearest tree. Stooping underneath, beyond the reach of sunlight, he plucked a hard, green, fuzzy fruit before walking back to the circle and handing it to Spencer.

"What's this?" he asked, taking it in his hands.

"It's a peach. Go ahead, take a bite."

Spencer looked at it closer. "Uh, no thanks. It doesn't look like a peach. And it's hard."

"Yes, and it's certainly bitter, but that doesn't change the fact that it's still a peach—one that will now never reach maturity or have any hope of sweetness." He sat back down on the bench, leaving the fruit in Spencer's hand. "Instant gratification may move things along at a more pleasurable pace, but that pleasure will rarely be as sweet or share the same promise of reward as patience and self-discipline."

Spencer nodded slowly.

"Choosing if and how we care about either self-mastery or self-discipline is a river we all must learn to navigate on our way to adulthood. Many teens and young adults, who upon feeling liberated by age and opportunity, choose to throw off the guidelines and burn down the guardrails put up by their parents and others to protect them from the rapids and the falls. Some choose instead to sow their wild oats and paddle their canoes while eating and drinking and making themselves merry, without even a thought of what might be around the next bend. But sooner or later, most of us come to the true and unavoidable conclusion that regardless of our belief in laws, commandments and standards, the consequences of ignoring them don't care if you believe in them or not. And one way or another, we all learn those consequences know our numbers and where to find us, and where it hurts the most to exact their toll."

Spencer nodded knowingly, looking at the tiny, useless fruit in his hands. "I...I hadn't put that together."

"Oh, why should you? You're still young and sporty," Thomas chided. "There's still plenty of time for fun. What have you got to lose? All the cool kids are doing it!"

Spencer shook his head, but smiled. "That sounds awfully familiar."

"Sure it does. Fortunately for each of us there's a difference between our lives and the fruit in your hand there. If you haven't discovered it yet, let me assure you that there are both forces of light and forces of darkness in this crazy world of ours. The light will offer hope and truth and love, while its opposing force offers fear, hopelessness, and despair. And somewhere in the middle there's a vast and ever-growing, stagnant pool of apathy and indifference. It feels as if an increasing number of people are choosing to bob about in the apathetic marinade, hoping somehow to stay neutral rather than offend their companions. This may be the greatest lie that's ever been told, and yet it's being told millions of times everyday around the world—the lie that neutrality is safe, that's it's politically correct and unoffensive. And in the process billions of people are forgetting that they are children of light—that they're made of light—that they've been created to be fueled by light."

He paused for a moment, letting his words sink in as he looked into each of their faces.

"The difference between Spencer's fruit and each of you is that you have the ability, through the love and grace of God, to return to His tree of life, reconnect with its life-giving truths and virtues, and fully ripen in maturity and understanding. And at the heart of that ripened fruit lies a seed that cannot only create a new tree that can offer shade and fruit for those who follow, it can create an entire orchard, spreading its hope and goodness far beyond even your biggest dreams."

"It almost sounds like you're talking about...family." Greg suggested.

"Yes, but not just family alone." He pointed to another tree, this one covered with small apples. "The apples on that tree may all look alike, but if you you'll follow the branches on which they grow to the trunk, you'll find something you might not expect."

They all turned to look.

"It almost looks like bark is different on the branches than on the trunk," Sonja observed.

"But look," Rachael said, pointing. "The bark on each of the main branches is also a little bit different."

"Very good. There are least four varieties of apples on that tree."

"How do you know?" Genevieve asked.

"For many years now, in the early spring, I've been coming up to help Lorenzo and Ruby graft different varieties onto the old rootstocks. And as we've worked, I've listened to whispers on the wind as they've tried to teach me some the subtle lessons of the farm. There are great things to be learned here as you contemplate the value of roots and the stretch and flexibility of branches. You'll learn later this fall that trees have to be pruned and trimmed in order to maintain both their shape, and a healthy vibrancy. But you can also learn from the pile of branches over there, that in order to be vibrant and productive, they need to maintain contact with the trunk and the roots."

Josh nodded, turning to the pile of limbs and branches. "So, if these have to be connected to the roots in order to be productive, why do you chop them off and burn them?"

Thomas smiled, turning to Lorenzo for the answer.

"The longer you work with nature, the more you begin to recognize that there's an order to all things on God's green earth. Your question is a common one, and so a few decades ago, as an experiment, we began letting one apple tree in the far corner of the orchard go without its annual pruning."

"What does it look like now?" Sonja asked.

"Well, it's hard to miss as its the tallest tree in the orchard by at least ten feet."

"You almost sound like that's a bad thing?" James responded.

"It is if you're growing apples. If left to their own devices, fruit trees tend to forget that the purpose of their existence is to produce fruit, and they just become wild ol' trees, turning all of their energy into wood, their branches quickly becoming tangled and growing every which way."

"But it still produces apples, right?" Genevieve asked.

"Hardly. Most of the apples are bitter and mealy and never grow much bigger than a golfball. If it weren't for the lessons kids learn from that tree every year, I would have worked it over years ago," Pops reported.

"Worked it over? Does that mean cut it down and burn it?" Holly asked.

Pops shook his head. "No, if you treat a tree right, it can last for a hundred years. If you let it grow wild, it will attract disease and a number of other problems before it dies an early death, rarely longer than fifty years. There are trees—or at least trunks and rootstocks here in the orchard that are probably close to two hundred years old. Like this one over here with the four varieties growing out of a single trunk, you can graft young branches onto older roots."

"And that actually works?" Susan asked.

"Like a charm. Of course it needs a little finesse and some watchful care, but if done right, both the roots and the branches are strengthened and encouraged."

"It's a symbiotic relationship that's not unlike what happens every summer here on the farm," Ruby added. "You kids bring your youthful vim and vigor to the farm with you, jumpstarting our old bones, and we in turn provide the tried and true roots that will hopefully give you kids a head start in your marriages and family lives. It's a win-win."

"And there are few things that provide a greater chance for success in life and marriage than the key of self-discipline," Pops said, bringing it back around.

"If that's true, why did we wait till now to discuss it? We could've been working on this months ago," James whined.

Ruby smiled but shook her head. "James, what would you have done if we'd marched you kids down here the first evening you arrived and told you it was about time you got working on yourself?"

James sat silent for a moment, thinking. "I probably wouldn't have been very happy?"

"Why not?"

"Because…no one likes to be told how broken they are by someone they don't know."

"I don't doubt that's true, but I think you could have left off the last few words of your answer and it would still be true."

He thought for a moment, nodding. "No one likes to be told they're broken."

Ruby shook her head. "And yet we *all* are in our own special way. It's one of the few universal truths. The words that have been carved into these benches by the hundreds of campers who came before you attest to the fact that each of us is an unfinished mess who can become better and stronger through the application of self-discipline. Pops and I are happy to offer you suggestions on starting points if you've not yet identified a weakness you'd prefer to be a strength, or a hurdle you're struggling to clear. But we encourage you to examine your life and identify your own. This space, we hope, will provide you all with a lot to think about.

"That's right, Pops confirmed. "For many campers, this has become one of the most transformative areas of the farm as they've come to recognize kindred spirits in the messages left behind by others. It's a place where many have discovered they're not alone in either their weakness or their desires for something better."

"But tonight there are s'mores," Ruby said.

"Before the work?" asked Pops.

"Oh, I almost forgot. Why don't I get the fire going while you and Thomas train the kids how to guard the bank?"

"Sounds like a plan."

CHAPTER 126

Preemptive Banking

*Though no one can go back and make a brand new start,
anyone can start from now and make a brand new ending.*
—Marcus Aurelius

G uard the bank?" Spencer asked, as the campers followed Pops and Thomas through several rows of trees to a large, organized pile of yellow bamboo rods, about four to seven feet long, most of them about an inch in diameter.

"Yep, I forget now who started calling it that, but somehow it stuck," Pops said as the campers circled the pile of smooth sticks . "Do any of you remember from your summer camp days what this is called?" he asked, pointing to the sticks.

"Um, that wouldn't happen to be a rick-a-bamboo, would it?" Genevieve asked, trying to keep a straight face.

"As a matter of fact it is, Princess Pat!"

"Wait, *what*?" Spencer asked.

"You mean you don't know?" Holly asked, smiling playfully.

Spencer lifted one eyebrow. "A rig of bamboo?"

Holly laughed. "No, a rick-a-bamboo."

"What the difference?"

"Oh, if you don't know, we probably can't tell you," she said, winking at Genevieve.

"Oh, I don't know," Crystal said. "I think Spencer would like it, and it's been a million years since I last sang it."

"Then I'd say you're way overdue," Thomas said with goofy grin. "Why don't you show him how it's done?"

Crystal smiled at Holly and Genevieve, who each returned her smile. Sonja, Susan and Rachael, not wanting to be left out of the fun, moved next to the other ladies, huddling for a moment to whisper their plans before turning around with their fists on their hips like a group of cheerleaders about to start a cheer.

"Okay, you boys, repeat after me," Genevieve shouted.

The men glanced at each other bemusedly, but quickly returned their attention to Genevieve who led out loudly.

"The Princess Pat." She paused for the women to holler their refrain as the men tried to make sense of what was happening, only a few of them repeating the words.

"Lived in a tree." This time they all followed along, including Pops and Thomas, even mimicking the goofy dance moves and hand motions that Genevieve and the other women were doing.

"She sailed across
the seven seas.
She sailed across,
the channel too,
and she took with her
a rick-a-bamboo."

Before the first verse was even through, the women were all laughing and the men were wondering what was happening. But the song continued through all four verses and the choruses, leaving everyone laughing at the goofiness of it all.

"Where in the world did that come from, and how do you all know it?" Ephraim asked.

"It's a camp song," Crystal responded. "I used to sing it in Girl Scouts."

"Me, too," said Susan.

"Just to clarify and bring us all back to the present, no one should ever mistake a rick-a-bamboo for a rig of bamboo," Pops said, picking up one of the straight bamboo poles.

The campers turned their attention away from the momentary silliness and back to Pops and the bamboo poles.

"On the far south end of the farm where the ground was a little swampy from a spring, Mom and I planted a single bamboo shoot nearly fifty years ago. That single plant has become quite prolific, turning into a small, rather invasive forest. We try to keep it trimmed back so it doesn't get out of control, but we found many years ago that the bamboo makes great limb supporters for the fruit branches that are heavy with fruit. We'll only get started tonight, and we'll have to come back many times over the next two months to make sure the limbs have the support they need."

"So...we guard the bank with bamboo sticks?" Ephraim asked, looking confused.

Pops smiled, motioning for the campers to follow him to the nearest tree—a pear tree—whose limbs were already beginning to hang low under the weight of its growing fruit. "The lion's share of the farm's annual income comes from these trees, as you've already learned from the apricots and cherries. Every piece of fruit is valuable. The prettiest ones get sold for a premium at the farm stand. Those with minor blemishes will be bottled and stored in the cellar for next year's consumption. Even the fruit that drops early or are bruised will be juiced and the pulp fed to the pigs and the chickens. And though good pruning has its rewards in the form of large, healthy fruit, the fruit can weigh down the branches, bending and even breaking them. But a well-placed support, sometimes called around here a *banking pole*" he said, holding up the bamboo stick, "can help preserve both the tree and the fruit."

"So it's basically preemptive banking, right?" Ephraim asked.

"That's right. Some people also call it defensive farming." Pops lifted a thin branch that was hanging lower than its neighbors, six small pears growing from leafy tufts all along its length. Moving his hand along the bottom of the limb, he demonstrated how to find the center of gravity where the banking pole might offer the most support. Then, after placing the notched end against the limb, he wedged the other end of the banking pole into the soft dirt below the tree.

"These will likely need to be moved many times over the next few months to keep the fruit and the limbs off the ground. Placing these supports is best accomplished with two of you working together, focusing on the heaviest branches first. If you'll get with your partners for the day, Thomas and I will help you get the hang of it."

"How do you know when you're done?" James asked as he gathered up an armful of bamboo.

"Oh, we won't be done until all the fruit is gathered in for the season, and the poles are stacked back here in the pile for next year," Pops replied.

"Okay, but I guess what I'm asking is how many of these poles should you use for each tree."

Pops smiled. "It all depends on the weight of the fruit and the sag of the branches. Each tree will be different. Most trees will require at least a few poles. Some of the apple trees may require a dozen or more."

James turned to the pile of poles and quickly calculated how many might be needed. "What if we run out of poles?"

"Then we'll cut more," Pops said, clapping him on the shoulder. "There's plenty of bamboo, if and when we need it. I learned long ago that there's no sense in worrying about hypothetical problems when most of them never materialize, and those that do are generally quite easily solved."

Under the direction of Pops and Thomas, the six teams fanned out across the orchard. They quickly discovered that several other piles of bamboo poles were distributed around the orchard, many of these marked with faded inscriptions that had been carved or scratched into their otherwise smooth surfaces. They worked until the light had faded into darkness, but they were only able to reach a quarter of the trees before Pops called them together. They walked back up the gently sloping hillside to the fire pit where they were welcomed by Ruby's glowing face, smiling as she tended the blazing fire. The pile of branches was now only half as high as it had been, and a thick bed of coals burned bright within the ring of rocks.

"How'd it go?" she asked, as the campers found their seats around the pentagonal bench.

"I believe we'll make farmers out of these kids yet," Pops said, handing a giant bag of marshmallows to Holly.

The collection of sharpened roasting sticks leaned against the bench and Ruby invited each of the men to take one. But before any of them could get started roasting their marshmallows, she explained they would not be making them for themselves. Instead, each of the men would be roasting marshmallows and building s'mores for their work partner of the day. This announcement was met with some concern from the women, two of whom protested, vocally expressing their dislike of both burnt and ash-encrusted marshmallows.

But before any additional protests could be lodged, Ruby explained that as soon as the men were done creating their edible masterpieces for the ladies, the ladies would have their turn to create s'mores for the men. This addendum put an abrupt and obvious end to some of the men's juvenile and rowdy attitudes. Instead, with poise and good behavior, they skewered their marshmallows and silently circled the pit, scouting out the best coals. As the women watched on, a hush fell over the men as they concentrated all of their senses on this one job.

Pops, upon finding that his eyes were having trouble focusing, knelt in the dirt, getting himself closer to both the coals and his marshmallow. Fearing his positioning might offer him a strategic advantage, one by one, each of the men stooped and knelt on the ground, slowly rotating the end of their roasting sticks.

Spencer's browning marshmallow was off to an early lead when it suddenly burst into flames. Amidst the howls and yelps from the ladies, he quickly blew out the flame, localizing the scorch to only a small area. Distracted by Spencer's blooper, Ephraim momentarily glanced away, accidentally dipping his marshmallow into a depression of ash and coals as the women vacillated between chuckles and chides.

Before long all of the men had produced respectable specimens somewhere on an amber-to-sepia spectrum. While the six male campers were ready to assemble their s'mores, Pops stayed on his knees, patiently continuing to coax a little more color from the glowing coals. After another two minutes, he stood, and the other men, assuming he was done, quickly assembled their s'mores and handed them to their partners.

But to everyone's surprise, Pops was not done. Instead of sandwiching his marshmallow between the graham crackers and chocolate as the others had, he carefully moved the unassembled s'more to the fire's side, setting the crackers on a rock before carefully spacing the two flat rectangles of chocolate to allow for a more even melt.

As the lady campers ate their s'mores, they silently watched as the radiant heat slowly softened the chocolate on Pops's cracker. Meanwhile, Pops had returned the marshmallow to its optimum hovering height over the coals, continuing the slow rotisserie action as the golden morsel almost seemed to plump up, its edges becoming somehow even softer and rounder.

After another two minutes as all of the campers looked on, Pops gracefully assembled the most perfectly succulent s'more any of them had ever seen, presenting it to Ruby with a deep bow.

The campers exploded into a raucous ovation as Pops smiled and bowed again; then they all turned to Ruby who took a bite of the perfect s'more. Gooey marshmallow and melted chocolate oozed out from between the crispy crackers but slowed their crawl before the stickier components could reach her hand. Ruby closed her eyes, the reflection of both the coals and the starlight dancing on her glasses as she chewed, moaning quietly with delight. They all watched on as she continued the ecstasy of her enjoyment, licking her fingers as she finished.

"If that's the last s'more I ever get to eat in this life, it will be enough to keep me going through all eternity," she said as she opened her eyes. The campers once again erupted in applause as the women took their turns with the roasting sticks.

Inspired by Pops's graceful performance, the women attempted to exhibit a similar air of gracefulness. All of them followed Pops's example, placing their graham crackers on the rocks around the coals and pre-melting the chocolate. They were all nearing completion when Ruby surprised them and held her marshmallow right next to the hottest coals until it burst into flames. Reflexively, Sonja tried to blow it out, but Ruby stopped her, lifting the marshmallow high above their heads like a torch to keep any others from tying to extinguish the bright yellow flame.

Shocked, all of the campers watched as the flame petered out on it own, leaving a crispy, formless clump of char at the end of her stick. But without missing a beat and acting as if this behavior was totally normal, Ruby stooped and swept up the two covers of Pop's s'more, fluidly dislodging the charred clump between them. Then, with a grace equal only to Pops's performance, she turned and presented her burnt offering with a deep and dignified bow.

Pops smiled, and graciously thanked her, reaching for her hand and kissing it gently before biting into the blackened treat.

"If this is the last s'more I ever eat, I hope you will all bear witness that never has there been a s'more that was enjoyed more completely than this one, here, tonight."

When the men had each consumed their s'mores with varying degrees of contentment, the coals were stoked with more of last year's branches, and the flames and sparks rose high into the night sky as the campers watched on, entranced by the fire's primitive magic. And in that enchanting space, the conversation was warm and nourishing as they shared and laughed and joked around like a group of comrades who'd been friends for much, much longer than just three short months. Before any of them were ready to be done, the last of the wood had turned to coals, and the coals had grown dim, fading to ash.

Without artificial light, they made their way slowly back to the bunkhouses, oohing and aahing over the display of fireflies which lit their way through the woods, offering additional magic of their own. Not ready to be done nor end the fond sense of camaraderie, the campers walked Pops and Ruby to the big house before walking Thomas and his bicycle to the top of the drive.

Though the moon had not yet risen, the sky sparkled with a hundred billion stars. They huddled together, watching the headlight on Thomas's bike wind its way halfway down Harmony Hill before disappearing beyond their view.

"Can we do this again tomorrow?" James asked, surprising everyone.

"I don't think so," Genevieve responded, draping her arms over the shoulders of two campers close to her, unsure, in the darkness, who they were. But the gesture of friendship and goodwill spread and they were soon standing in a circle, this ragtag group of friends, enjoying a wholly unique sense of true connection.

"Well, if we can't do this, can we do something like this?" James persisted.

"I guess that's entirely up to us, isn't it?" Genevieve replied.

"I'm in," Josh offered, leading the chorus of affirmative voices.

"What's going to happen to this place?" Holly asked, her voice obviously filled with concern. "I can't imagine this being...the end... when Ruby..." She faded off, unable to say more.

"I wondered the same thing tonight when she was talking about that being her last s'more ever," Sonja admitted, her words also softened with concern.

"What if it didn't have to end?" Ephraim asked.

"What do you mean?" asked Crystal.

"Well, what if...what if we could find another matchmaker to take her place? Then more people could come...maybe...maybe even our own kids could come if they needed help figuring life out."

"Yeah, but who would do this?" Susan asked. "This is a *huge* commitment, and with so many moving parts, it feels like it could all blow up any time without warning."

"And yet it's been going for 300 years," Matt reminded them.

"Yeah, but could it keep going without people like Ruby and Pops running it?" Ephraim asked. "They obviously love this place and are totally committed to it—and to each other. I don't know anybody who'd be willing to set aside their lives and dreams and try to make this work. What would motivate someone to do that?"

The group sat silent for a moment as they considered the question.

"Insanity?" James suggested, laughing as he did.

"The only answer I've been able to come up with is love, which, as I understand it, may actually be a form of insanity," Genevieve admitted, laughing out loud.

The others joined her in the laughter for a moment, but it quickly died down.

"I think Genevieve should do it," Crystal said.

"I was just thinking the same thing," Holly seconded. "Actually, I've been thinking about it for a couple of months now."

"I'll vote for her!" Josh added.

"Me too! That totally makes sense," said Ephraim.

"No, it doesn't!" Genevieve spoke, exasperated. "Guys, I'm a writer. I don't know the first thing about dating or matchmaking or running a farm."

"Well, neither did Ruby. She was a school teacher, right? And she was on her way to being an old maid when she came here," Rachael said. "I doubt she would've known much about dating, and for sure not much about matchmaking. And I'm pretty sure she didn't have any farming experience."

"Aren't we all basically farmers-in-training?" Greg asked. "By the time the summer's over, won't we all have a pretty good idea of what we're doing?"

"I think you're all nuts," Genevieve said. "There's no way I could do any of this without help."

"Are you suggesting there's no way you could do this without a husband?" asked Susan.

Genevieve laughed. "Let me rephrase that—I think there's no way I could do it, period."

"I think you're a lot stronger than you think you are," Rachael responded. "I think you could do it, no problem."

"Uh, thanks for the vote of confidence, but making me the next matchmaker is the surest way to make it fall apart. I'm not good at any of this. I don't like animals, and I don't like dealing with difficult personalities, and I don't know the first thing about love and all of its complications."

"You could have fooled us," Josh responded.

"*Us?*" questioned Genevieve.

"Okay, we'll admit it," Susan responded after a nervous moment that seemed to be shared by all the campers. "We've been talking."

"Who's we?"

"All of us," Susan replied. "Ever since Ruby told us this would be her last summer, we've been talking about how someone needs to keep this going, and we've all come to the same conclusion. You're the only one of us that makes any sense to carry on Ruby's legacy. Don't you see it?"

"Uhhh, *no, I really don't see it.*"

"Sure you do!" James responded. "I don't say this lightly, but you're a natural. I mean, okay, you're still a bit rough around the edges, but that's nothing the eleven of us couldn't help you smooth out by the end of the summer."

Many of the campers laughed.

"Think about it, Genevieve," Matt encouraged. "This obviously isn't a decision that you should make lightly, or tonight, but you need to know there are eleven of us in this circle who believe in you—and believe you *can* do this."

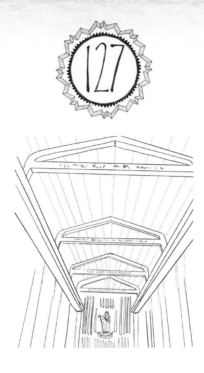

CHAPTER 127

Motes and Beams

Above all, trust in the slow work of God. Only God could say what
this new spirit gradually forming within you will be. Give our Lord
the benefit of believing that His hand is leading you, and accept the
anxiety of feeling yourself in suspense and incomplete.
—Pierre Teilhard de Chardin

S leep came quickly for Genevieve, and for the first time in three
months it was deep and full of pleasant dreams, none of which
she remembered when the rooster welcomed the new day. Rising before

the others, she walked to the sink and splashed water on her face before undoing the still-damp braid she'd bound her hair up in after her shower the night before.

Despite the shampoo and conditioner, the light scent of the evening's bonfire still clung to her wavy locks. She held her hair to her nose, breathing it in deeply, remembering the evening, Thomas's chat, the s'mores, the gathering at the top of the hill where the rest of the campers had made the suggestion that she take over the role of matchmaker and continue Ruby's legacy. Had it been any earlier, the suggestion would have certainly been too much. She wasn't ready to admit it to any of the campers, but she couldn't deny that something had changed sometime over the course of the last month.

There was no single event she could pinpoint, nor had there been a subtle whittling away of her resistance to even the thought of it. She looked up at the note Holly had taped to the mirror during their second week here and read it again even though she'd long since committed it to memory:

Write it on your heart that today is the best day of the year!

So much had changed since the first day she'd cursed that note, and so much more since she'd cursed the farm and everything and everyone on it. It was different now, and she couldn't deny that it had been different for several weeks. Though the first two weeks of the summer had passed at a snail's pace, these last eleven weeks had flown by faster than the express train in the New York Subway. With only eight weeks left now, there was already a piece of her heart that was fluttering a little differently than the rest, as if it were fluctuating between wanting to race through the finish line, and pumping the brakes in what she knew was a feeble attempt to slow things down.

The idea of taking over for Ruby, though still completely overwhelming and impractical, somehow felt intriguing. She still didn't understand why Ruby would choose her. The talk of her "sass" and "chutzpa" might reasonably account for some of it—heaven knew she'd been born with an ample share of both. But things were different now in that respect, too. It had been weeks since she'd yelled and cussed, at least a week since she'd even felt the need. The old Genevieve would be worried that she was losing her edge, but as she looked at it now, that edge had come with the high price of alienating friends and the accumulation of foes.

With everyone working together, the Sunday chores went smoothly, and they were all on their way to church well ahead of schedule, twelve campers on bikes, nearly keeping up with Pops and Ruby in the old pickup.

Arriving at church early, they had their pick of the pews, and for the first time that summer, they sat together, packing one of the long central pews, only three rows from the front. The organ prelude music filled the simple, sparsely unadorned hall with peaceful strains, and many of the campers closed their eyes, enjoying the pleasure that only a well-played Bach organ sonata could provide.

The chapel was full when Genevieve opened her eyes again, as they all stood to sing a rousing opening hymn about sunshine and the love of Jesus, filling the warm space with a joyfully jubilant and refreshing spirit. An invocation was offered by the florist who'd given the sermon many weeks earlier, then Thomas surprised many in the congregation by welcoming the very pregnant Amy Kimball to the lectern to deliver the morning's sermon.

Amy stood from the front pew, walking confidently to the lectern. She took a deep breath and smiled generously at the congregation as she exhaled. "You may think it a cruel and unusual punishment to ask a woman in her final week of pregnancy to stand before a congregation like this and share the contents of my heart. I'd like to first publicly exonerate Thomas. I am here today not because he asked me to be, but because knowing my life soon would be changing in dramatic ways, I wanted to share some of the contents of my heart with all of you."

She paused to look into the faces of the capacity crowd before beginning again. "Thank you for being here. Thank you for your prayers and support in our behalf. And thank you in advance for listening to the hormonal ramblings of a woman who has been waiting her whole life to become a mother.

"Gratitude is a common theme in the sermons that are delivered here each week. We all have much to be grateful for. Jake and I, as he mentioned in his sermon several weeks ago, are transplants to Niederbipp, though my roots from my father's side run deep in this town. Most of you probably know I'm an Eckstein. My great-great…I forget how many greats—grandfather and his sons help lay the foundations and set the cornerstones of most of the older buildings in this town, including this chapel. I'm grateful for that heritage, and I'm grateful for the responsibility that connection to this town has instilled in me. It's made me want to do more to honor that legacy by doing my part to preserve and perpetuate the faith and convictions of those who've gone before me.

"I remember a sermon by George Hagen, given from this pulpit many years ago. Some of you old-timers will remember that George was the youngest son of the last blacksmith of Niederbipp. He passed away not long after he delivered that sermon, but his words have lived on in my heart and have been the topic of many meaningful discussions between Jake and myself over the ensuing years.

"You may recall that George brought with him that day a long metal chain which he draped up and over this lectern, leaving lengths on the floor on either side. As I recall, the chain had been created by his relative, one of the town's early blacksmiths, who'd forged the links a couple of centuries earlier for use in the lumber trade. I remember George identifying one link, somewhere in the middle, as the link which his father had told him represented George in a long line of men and women who had come before him and those who would follow after him.

"Tied to both the past and the future—as all of us are—George shared how his father had taught him from the time he was a child to honor the strength of those who'd given him his name, but also to recognize the responsibility he had to future generations.

"He then shared the story his grandfather had told him of a barge that had run aground during a storm up on Lake Erie. An investigation into the cause of the wreck found that the vessel, heavily laden with cargo, had been unable to outrun the storm and return to the harbor. Instead, its captain had turned the ship's nose into the storm and dropped the anchor, hoping to ride it out. But as the wind howled and the waves crashed, no one noticed that they were adrift until it was too late. The stern crashed into the rocks, the hulls filled up with water, and the cargo was lost.

"As I recall from George's story, the cause of the wreck was one broken link on the anchor chain. *Just one broken link!*"

Amy looked out into the congregation and shook her head. "I don't know if it's the fact that I'm about to give birth to a new, innocent life, or if my emotions are constantly threatening to snap, but this story has been on my mind a lot over the last couple of months. I recognize that we will be introducing our son to a world that's probably full of as many distractions and challenges as have ever existed in the history of humanity. As much as we've consciously tried to avoid allowing fear to influence our attitudes and outlooks, Jake and I are both nervous. Even in a town like Niederbipp where we have each of you as examples and friends, we've recognized more than ever how our own faith and hope will be critical in raising our son.

"The anchor of hope that our faith has provided us has already proven to be a critical source of stability in the storms we've encountered through our miscarriages. I...we...we've wondered many times how people who live without either hope or faith carry on through difficult times and circumstances. We've found ourselves being continually grateful for that anchor, and have recognized the importance of keeping our ties to that anchor strong and secure."

Amy continued with the theme of the faithful link and the chain as she expressed gratitude to the community that had supported them as artists, but also in their faith. She spoke of the strength both she and Jake had drawn from interactions, conversations and valued relationships over the last eight years, and how they'd learned to love and serve from watching their neighbors and through identifying faithful characteristics they'd attempted to adopt and make their own. And she shared with the congregation how their recent prayers had included expressions of gratitude for a loving and supportive community in which they had to raise their son and, hopefully, other children.

As Amy spoke, Genevieve turned to her fellow campers on either side of her, recognizing in each of their faces a longing for the kind of community Amy was describing. What had seemed like such a quirky, backwater town at first was actually much different than Genevieve could have imagined. As she looked around the congregation, she was embarrassed at the way she'd written off the whole town as ignorant simpletons. She felt squeamish when off to her right side, she recognized the young waitress she'd berated at the restaurant her first evening in Niederbipp. She'd been a beast, a difficult and unpleasant person to be around, a person she now knew would certainly have been rejected had she gone through the normal process of coming to the farm on Harmony Hill.

She leaned forward, looking down the aisle where Ruby sat, hand in hand, with her gentleman-farmer-of-a-husband. For more than five-and-a-half decades they'd been welcoming young people to the farm, presumably helping them in the same way they had each of this year's campers to recognize their strengths and identify their weaknesses. With patience, kindness and love, they'd inspired change, the softening of rough edges, and the building of faith as they taught the keys of joy in word and in deed. These were the same people she'd come here to mock and expose as frauds. And in return they'd given her nothing but love and encouragement. Not only that, they'd seen something in her that had somehow convinced them that she had whatever it took to carry on their work and legacy.

The whole idea of it still made her stomach knot up, but she couldn't ignore that the seed of possibility that had fallen into her heart many weeks earlier had somehow sprouted and was already sending out both roots and branches. Despite all her reluctance and even active efforts against it, this growing bit of possibility remained, becoming ever more impossible to ignore.

She closed her eyes, fighting with the voices within her. Part of her still wanted to scream, run away, and be done with this backwater town and all of its people. But in that same breath, she felt a different voice whispering in a deeply penetrating tone, drowning out her natural cynicism with something far more holistic, filled with innumerable possibilities.

Startled by what she was feeling, she looked up into the rafters high above her head. These whitewashed timbers had certainly been there every week since the beginning, but she had never noticed them. And there was something else she'd missed: some indecipherable detail painted in a shiny white paint over the matte white face of the beams.

Trying not to draw attention to herself, she turned and looked behind her to the three other beams that spanned the width of the hall. Including the one beam in front her and the one directly over her head, there were a total of five beams. She turned her head back around, looking up at the beam in front of her that hung almost parallel to the front of the pipe organ whose pipes rose at least fifteen above the floor.

Nestled among the pipes on the second level of the organ was a nearly life-sized wooden statue of Jesus. She'd seen this before. It was hard to miss. But as she looked at it now, she realized she had never truly seen it, her normal place on the back row not providing anywhere near the same access to the details. The statue's right arm held a curved shepherd's staff, his left hand holding the feet of the lamb draped over his neck. The statue, natural in color to match the wood of the organ, was much different than the icons she'd seen in the handful of churches and cathedrals she'd visited over the years. There was no blood or signs of suffering and death that she'd seen in other sculptural depictions of Jesus. Instead, there was a serene and loving face, and the simple portrayal of a gentle and concerned shepherd.

Genevieve looked into the statue's face, its eyes looking out into the congregation, not at any one person, but at everyone, inclusively. She didn't see it at first—it would be so easy to miss since it was nearly the same color as the wood it was carved into—but there, carved into smooth space between the statue's shoulders was the undeniable outline of a heart with flames rising from it.

Amazed at yet one more thing she'd missed, she looked up in the direction the good shepherd's staff was pointing. Squinting, she tried to decipher the barely visible characters, realizing they were letters and words. Though the shadows made it difficult to discern them on either end of the beam, the words in the middle made the message clear enough:

...KNOW THAT I AM...

Of course, she thought to herself. What else would it say? She turned her head back around, noticing there were words painted on each of the beams, though they were equally difficult to discern, especially while trying not to be disruptive during a sermon.

"Are you okay?" Ephraim whispered.

"Yeah, yeah, sorry. Just distracted," she whispered back.

Genevieve turned around and tried to focus on Amy's closing words, and she was glad she did. As she spoke, Genevieve saw Amy for the first time as a complete woman. It had been so easy to remember her as the gawky, young freshman from so many years ago, but even at nearly nine months pregnant, she was now filled to overflowing with beauty and grace that ran deep. In a few short days she'd be a mother. *A mother!* As she watched and listened to her old roommate, she recognized that the faith which had sustained her had also caused her to radiate an undeniable glow from somewhere deep within.

The jealousy and envy which had so soured Genevieve toward Amy during that first, awkward year of college had vanished, making room for something much better. As Amy took her seat and the congregation rose again to sing, Genevieve now recognized that she wanted what Amy had here. But it was something much more than just envy or jealousy. She didn't want Amy's life. But she recognized within herself a deep, elemental hunger for something very similar. There was no longer room for any hard feelings toward the girl she'd once referred to as 'Perfect Amy.' That girl was gone—grown into a woman who remained light years ahead of her both in her confidence and her natural poise and grace. And as she thought of her now, there was nothing left but admiration.

At the close of the benediction, Genevieve did something she'd seen others do, but had never done herself: she stood, excused herself as she squeezed past the other campers, and walked into the growing gathering at the front of the chapel where congregants waited their turn to greet Amy.

As she waited, Genevieve rehearsed in her mind what she might say from the long list of words of admiration she felt for Amy. But by the time she stood before Amy, those thoughtful words had evaporated. Instead she took Amy's hands in hers, looked into her eyes, and genuinely thanked her for her message. No more was needed. The simple expression, sincerely uttered, instantaneously melted away any remaining hard feelings, leaving only goodwill between them. Amy pulled Genevieve in for a hug, and when she let go, both women had tears in their eyes. Genevieve nodded, saying nothing more as she moved to the side to make room for Amy's other admirers.

Genevieve was halfway down the aisle when she remembered the words painted on the foremost beam. She turned to see them, the light now reflecting across all of them making them easier to read:

BE STILL AND KNOW THAT I AM GOD.

From this vantage point, she could almost read the words on the second beam as well, these, too, reflecting the light pouring in from the front doors and the tall leaded glass windows on either side. She moved further back down the aisle, then shuffled between the empty pews until she stood directly in the center of the middle benches. Here the words could be clearly read.

ASK, SEEK, KNOCK, RECEIVE.

She sat down, looking up at the words above her. For the first time since coming to the farm, the idea of prayer did not feel daunting or scary. She wanted to know. If this was to be her lot, she knew she *needed* to know.

It had been years since she'd prayed on her own, years since she'd even felt the desire. It wasn't that she doubted the existence of God. It was more that she just didn't know how prayer would fit into her life. Being raised without religion and with a father who was proud and unwilling to give anyone but good fortune and his own skills at business any credit for his success, she'd never known a real reason to need a god. And she couldn't remember a time when she believed God had any interest in her, at least not in a recognizable way.

She had plenty of questions, but they all still felt too uncomfortable to share, even with the other campers with whom she'd already shared most everything. She reckoned she'd gotten close to prayer a couple of times on those quiet afternoon and evening visits to the benches. In the process of practicing stillness or *expectant waiting*, she often felt a gentle and calming presence around her. Was that God? There'd been talk of those peaceful feelings, among the campers and others, being some manifestation of the Holy Spirit, but she didn't know for sure what to believe or why it was relevant. The only thing she knew for sure was that she had a very big decision to make.

Since that night, more than two and-a-half months ago when Ruby had offered her the top job and she'd read Julia's letter almost encouraging her to accept it, the thought of it had never been far from her. She'd found herself many times paying close attention to how things were being done in case she would need to reproduce it at some time in the future. So much of it felt completely overwhelming. But there were also many things that felt right, even doable—but not alone.

Trying not to allow herself to become stressed by too many questions, she tried to focus on the one main question. If she were to accept Ruby's offer, everything would change: her residence, her travel, her day-to-day activities, her writing, her focus, her purpose...all of it, everything. It felt so big, so beyond what was reasonable, so daunting in basically every way. So why couldn't she simply say no?

She'd seen first-hand the magic of the farm, but unlike the smoke-and-mirrors brand of magic, this was something altogether different. It was real. She'd watched people change, many in dramatic and significant ways. Spencer was no longer the self-centered, swaggering, ego-maniac. He was quiet and thoughtful and kind. Crystal's rough edges and her sharp, combative tongue had been significantly softened, making her pleasant, even fun to be around. Even James, the bull-headed brute who'd been prone to daily outbursts and ugliness had been tamed into something far more congenial.

But as she watched Amy and Jake interacting with those who'd crowded the front of the chapel to chat with them, Genevieve recognized how much she herself had changed in just the last three months. She'd learned to consider the effect of her words before she uttered them. She was no longer primarily interested in the sensational fads and trends— heaven knew there was nothing of that here. But she recognized how her focus had changed from the shallow, flighty, outward appearances to looking deeper into what made a person tick, understanding their hopes and aspirations, and watching how they navigated through their fears and challenges. In the process of watching all of this she'd discovered that people were far more complicated and three-dimensional than she'd ever imagined. But on the flip side, she'd also discovered that there were far more commonalities and shared foibles, which, if properly understood, had the potential to unite all humanity.

And then there were the keys of joy, those precepts and principles which had the power, if sincerely applied, to change the world. She couldn't think of any of the world's most pressing problems that would not be positively altered if more people would only choose to live by them. War, human trafficking, corruption, intolerance, hate, greed, indifference, poverty, extremism, excess, debauchery...every one of them, she knew, would be tempered if not completely eradicated through the widespread application and practice of the keys of joy—even if people only knew four of them.

But how could the keys have any power to do any widespread good with only twelve people learning them each summer? She'd heard that others, like the Parkins, were sharing them as well, but even if there were a couple hundred people learning them each summer, could it ever be enough to create real change?

Genevieve sat back, looking up again at the words painted on the beams above her. The writing was on the wall, or in this case, the ceiling. She had to admit that Julia's idea of using the magazine to help share the secrets of Niederbipp with a broader audience, as grand and audacious as it was, had merit. If not by those means, how? If not now, when? If not Genevieve, who would be the voice that would introduce the world to an alternative, more positive course of action?

As she thought about it, remembering what she'd learned about the historicity of the keys, she recognized that there was nothing new about this way of living. It was not the alternative path. In fact, it was the original path, a path that could lead people to happiness and even harmony. But it was a path that had been largely disregarded and corrupted. In its purity, it offered no one an opportunity to get ahead of his neighbor. There was no room for those who wanted power or domination. This was a path of peace, of equality, of shared opportunities. It was a path of love and compassion and charity and hope. And it was a path that encouraged its travelers to harness both their individual gifts and their weaknesses, and to put them to work in the cause of the greater good. And unlike communism or authoritarianism, it didn't demand compliance or obedience, but rather *invited* people to bring their best selves and unite in something far more powerful and harmonious than they could ever create on their own. It was, in every sense, Protopians.

"Is everything okay?" Matt asked, standing next to her, following her gaze to the beams up above.

She turned to look at him, smiling. "I've never been better, actually."

Matt looked at her for a moment, before turning his eyes back to the beam. "There's something up there, isn't there?"

"Yes, there is. There's definitely something up there." She stood and smiled at Matt. "I need to go."

"Where?"

"I have an appointment."

He looked at her closely before nodding thoughtfully. "Do you need some company?"

"I think I need to do this one alone," she said solemnly.

"Got it." He looked disappointed.

"But if you want," she continued, "I know of a bench where you can wait your turn."

CHAPTER 128

The Burning Bush

Remain true to yourself, but move ever upward toward greater consciousness and greater love! At the summit you will find yourselves united with all those who, from every direction, have made the same ascent. For everything that rises must converge.
-Pierre Teilhard de Chardin

It had been more than a month since Genevieve and Matt had followed Hildegard out of town and down to the river bottoms. The wildflowers welcomed her as she walked along the path to the tree

Hildegard had referred to as her second temple. The sounds of insects and birds mingled with the gentle purr of the river, creating an ethereal sense of tranquility.

She parted the draping branches, and finding the space unoccupied, entered into the sacred chamber. She paused just inside, watching the reflections of the sunlight off the river dance like silver coins on the thick canopy above her. She walked to the limb and sat down, making herself comfortable as she listened to the sound of her own heart beating softly in her ears. She was alive. And she was here for answers—answers she wanted—answers she knew she needed—answers she knew had the power to change her life forever.

She looked up at the instructions that had been carved into the limb in front of her, tracing each letter with her fingers as she did her best to still her anxious heart and mind. She wanted to know if this was where she was supposed to be. There were hundreds of other questions, but somehow she knew that if she could get an answer to this one, everything else would work out. Is this where she was supposed to be? Is this the place where she should dedicate the best years of her life? It was a big question, a huge question, a heavy question, a question with enormous ramifications for herself and potentially so many more.

Finally feeling herself slip into that place of calm she'd discovered on the benches on the farm, she closed her eyes, and for the first time in her life she asked God a sincere question: Should she accept Ruby's offer? But even as her question passed through her mind, it somehow changed into something very different: Was there any good reason why she should not accept Ruby's invitation?

The words that came almost implied that she'd already made the decision to accept Ruby's offer and simply needed to know that it was right. Did she already know the answer? In so many ways, she knew that she already did. The door had been opened for her. The path was clearly drawn. She just needed to know.

She took a deep breath and asked again, and before the words could pass through her mind, a warm rush washed over her. Starting at the top her head and flowing through her like a warm, electrified current, it felt like it filled her body up to overflowing with an all-consuming sense of joy and peace and love. But this wasn't the kind of peace that felt sleepy or languid. Instead it felt invigorating and empowering, leaving her with a glowing desire to go, and do, and be. It felt right. More than anything ever had, it felt right! The hundreds of questions that still remained were no longer hindrances, their power to confuse swept to the wayside by a greater power—the power of hope.

She took a deep breath, filling her lungs with this hope and light. She stayed for another few minutes, basking in the light which made her feel as if all things were possible. *She knew.* She knew! And with that revelation came another beautiful piece of knowledge: she was loved. Some being beyond her view knew her, knew her question, knew the best path for her.

As her eyes filled with tears, an image flashed in her mind. It was the statue of the shepherd, nestled among the organ pipes, his staff in one hand, a lost-and-found sheep in the other. He'd found her. Here, in Hildegard's temple, on a river in the middle of nowhere, He had found her. She wept, struggling to breathe as the now familiar warmth swept over her again, filling her once more with the same empowering, ennobling sense of peace. She knew!

She stayed, ready for more if more was to come, but already filled with all that she needed. It was enough. It was enough.

She stood and watched the light dance again among the branches above her. And then, with more confidence than she'd ever felt, she walked to the other side of the canopy and parted the veil of hanging branches.

"You look as though you've seen a burning bush," Hildegard said, looking up into her face from her seat on the bench.

Genevieve smiled, unsure of what to say as she glanced at Matt sitting next to her, his face full of anticipation. "This is a special place," she managed to say, the last word getting hung up in her throat.

Hildegard reached out, taking hold of Genevieve's hand and

squeezing it softly. "I'm glad you like it. Mr. Matthew, here, was kind enough to escort me to my appointment," she said, leaning on her cane to help lift herself from her seat. "It's a beautiful day for two lovebirds like you to be out enjoying the glories of God."

Genevieve smiled. "That's very nice of you to say so, but I'm sure Mr. Matthew is far too smart to get tangled up with a girl like me."

Hildegard turned and looked at Matt. "Last time, I heard it was the other way around."

"That's the way I remember it, too," Matt said. "It's nice of you to think I'd ever be compatible with such a lovely woman—nice to me, that is, but not so nice to Genevieve."

"Oh, you kids! Don't you see it?" she asked, shaking her head.

Genevieve and Matt looked at each other and smiled.

"Look, I'm old. I've got nothing to lose so I'm just gonna say it. You kids would be foolish to not entertain the possibility of turning your friendship into something far more permanent. I've been around a long time, and I'll tell you friendships like yours don't come around that often. When they do, you know they've been touched by the hand of God. Of course all friendships that are touched by the hand of God can't possibly turn into a marriage, but those that do tend to make the strongest marriages. I know I'm just an opinionated old bag, but as I told you before, I've been watching you two. And I'm not just blowing off hot air in saying you both should open your hearts a little wider and make room for love to grow between you."

Matt glanced again at Genevieve, finding it impossible not to smile.

"Like I've told you before, I'm a Jewish German. I'm blunt and honest and generally impatient. What can I say? It comes with the genes. Now, if you'll excuse me, I'm late for my appointment."

She lifted the tip of her cane and swept aside the hanging branches, walking into her temple without another word.

"Sorry, that was probably really awkward for you," Matt said.

Genevieve nodded slightly before shaking her head. "Actually, no, it wasn't so bad. You?"

Her response seemed to surprise him, and he paused for a moment to review the conversation.

"Your silence might be more awkward than anything *she* said," Genevieve admitted.

"Sorry, I...I guess I'm just trying to understand why it wasn't awkward. Not that I get sucked into conversations like this on a regular basis, but maybe this was the least awkward conversation I've had about...relationships in a long time."

Genevieve nodded. "I was thinking the same thing, even though it was totally blunt, right?"

Matt laughed. "Maybe that's been my problem all along."

"What? Truth and vulnerability?"

"In so many words."

Genevieve nodded thoughtfully as she walked away from the tree, looping her arm through Matt's and continuing to walk back to main path, turning back toward town. "So...what if none of that protectionism and stonewalling that we've been practicing our whole lives is necessary?"

He raised an eyebrow. "Really?"

"Yeah!" she replied emphatically. "What if it's all just a fortress of fear—a big, fat lie we've been telling ourselves for way too many years."

Matt thought for a moment as they continued to walk, side by side, her arm still looped through his. "I can't tell if you're speaking of all relationships, or just...whatever this...is. If I didn't know better I'd say you were suggesting that our lives could be better if we weren't so... guarded."

She nodded slowly. "Isn't that the way it feels? What are we protecting ourselves from, anyway?"

"Well, you can't just go up to someone and say something crazy like, 'Hey, you strike me as really cool person. I'd love to get to know you better.'"

Genevieve thought about it for a moment. "Why not?"

"Because where's the mystery in that? Where's the potential for misunderstanding? What would you do with all of the time you normally spend guessing what the other person is thinking, or trying to figure out where you stand?"

She chuckled. "Yeah, that way really sucks. What if you could just lay it all out there, like an open book, and not hold anything back?"

Matt considered her question for a moment. "I think that would be absolutely frightening and wonderful and liberating and horrifying—all at the same time!"

"So, why don't we live that way?"

"You mean besides the fact that it would require the surgical removal of all of our fears of having our hearts chewed up, spit out and stomped on?"

"So...it's all about fear then?" Genevieve asked with a playful smile.

He nodded after a moment. "It's basically ruled my entire life."

"Oh, really? Your *entire* life? Sounds like a major exaggeration if you ask me."

"Why do you say that?"

"Matt, you've traveled the world! What could you possibly be afraid of?"

"Well, maybe my fear is more localized...maybe it's only the parts that include conversations with women."

She thought for a moment before shaking her head. "We've had some really great conversations that at least seem to have been honest and candid."

"Yeah, okay, but that's different."

"How?"

"We're friends. We're safe. We agreed to be honest with each other. You needed a microphone for that little voice in your heart...and I needed someone I could trust."

"A yin for a yang," she mused.

Matt smiled. "I'm flattered, honestly, but aren't you forgetting something?"

She looked confused. "What am I forgetting?"

"Really? I'll give you a hint: It starts with fourteen years!"

She laughed. "I can't believe you're still hung up on that?"

He looked surprised. "I thought *you* were hung up on that."

"Was I?"

"Yeah! You said so yourself."

"When?"

"A couple of times. From the very beginning."

She stopped walking, realizing where they were. Dropping his arm, she skittered to the edge of the embankment, nearly disappearing down the steep earthen stairway that had been cut into the bank before she turned back. "What if it's not that big of a deal?" she asked before turning and scrambling down the rest of the stairs.

"Excuse me!?!" Matt asked, almost laughing as he looked down at her.

She shrugged. "What if Hildegard's right?"

He laughed "I can't tell if you're serious." He scrambled down the terraced bank, quickly catching up.

"Your pants are still dry, aren't they?"

He chuckled, remembering their earlier awkward conversation they'd had with the old woman. "Last I checked."

"Then what's the problem?"

"Genevieve, look at you. You're young and sassy and have your whole life in front of you. I'll be almost sixty by the time you're my age. You don't want to get tangled up with an old guy like me."

"Can I just say you're a terrible salesman!"

"Maybe, but think about it. I already have to wear reading glasses, and I'm balding on the crown of my head, and…I want kids."

She looped her arm through his again and led him out further across the stoney river bottom to the swing which hung close to the water's edge. She sat down on the worn wooden seat and walked backwards before jumping aboard, swinging out above the rounded rocks.

"What do kids have to do with it?" She asked after she'd pumped a couple of times, the swing going higher with each exertion.

Matt moved behind her, pushing her so she wouldn't have to pump. "You've already said a couple of times you're afraid of kids."

"That's totally true. I am. But that doesn't mean I don't ever want them...maybe."

He laughed. "What does that mean?"

"Look, no woman in her right mind would ever seriously attempt to raise kids in New York. It's gotta be one of the least kid-friendly places in the world. It would be a nightmare with strollers and subways and all the crazies. Plus, I had a career that I loved. And I don't have a husband, and I'm not even thirty yet, and I've never had the time to consider parenting, until now."

"*Until now?*"

She shook her head, trying not to smile as he moved around her side so he could see her face. "Maybe it wouldn't be such a terrible idea. I mean...eventually, right? With the right person. I don't know, Matt. It's a lot to think about. I feel like my whole world has been turned upside down. I'm not going back to my job. I'm reinventing myself. I've kind of got a lot on my plate right now."

"You're not going back to your job?" he asked, looking confused.

She shook her head, dragging her feet across the gravel to stop herself. "You're the first to know, and I'd appreciate it if you could hold it in confidence for now, but I've decided to accept Ruby's offer."

"What?!?" he asked, looking well beyond surprised. "When?"

"Just now. That's why I came down here, to the tree. I needed to make sure it was right."

"Wow! And I guess you feel like it is?"

"Yes...I, Matt, I've never felt anything like this before. As totally insane as it looks, it's right. This is where I'm supposed to be."

He nodded. "I know."

"What?"

"Genevieve, I've known this was where you were supposed to be since that night we chatted about it the creamery."

"Why didn't you say something?"

He shrugged. "I knew it had to be your decision. It's a big one. But I've been hoping all along that you'd do this."

Genevieve nodded thoughtfully. "Why? Why were you hoping I'd do it?"

He shifted nervously, looking uncomfortable. "There's something here, Genevieve. Something that the whole world needs. Look what's happened to us—to all of us this summer. We're at least a million miles from where we were when we got here three months ago. The world needs this kind of hope. It's great that twelve lucky souls get to experience this every summer, but with your platform...just think how many people you could reach...how many people could learn about the keys of joy."

"Matt, I don't even know if I'm a writer anymore. I've got nothing for this article and less than two months to come up with 10,000 words."

"It'll come."

"How can you be so sure?"

"Because this is where you're supposed to be. Proceed as way opens."

"What?"

"That's what Hildegard shared with me on our way down here. I guess it's an old Quaker proverb."

"Say it again."

"Proceed as way opens."

She nodded thoughtfully. "I like it. Did she say anything about it?"

"Yeah, have you ever heard the scripture where Jesus said something like, 'I am the way, the truth, and the life?'"[1]

She nodded. "That sounds vaguely familiar."

"Yeah, as Hildegard said, if Jesus is the way, and He's willing to open a path for us, it falls on us to move our feet—or our hearts—or both—in the direction He has made available to us."

Genevieve nodded slowly, remembering once again her earlier interaction with the statue at the chapel, His staff, the sheep draped

---

1. John 14:6

over his shoulders, and the kindness in his face. "I guess that's where reverence comes in, right?"

"I suggested the same thing, but Hildegard said that all sincere reverence eventually leads to faith, and sincere faith eventually leads to knowledge. But you have to start somewhere, right? You have to ask, seek, and knock so you can be ready to receive."

"You saw them? The words in the chapel?"

"Not before I found you looking up at it. Did you notice there are words written on both sides of all of those beams?"

"Really? What do they say?"

"I don't know, the light wasn't quite right to see them all, and I had to catch up to you and warn Hildegard that you were already down here."

Genevieve shook her head. "We've missed a lot, haven't we?"

"Yeah, I'm glad we still have some time before the summer's over."

"How are we going to fit it all in? I don't have a clue how to put a harness on a horse, and I really haven't been paying very close attention to the cheesemaking and bottling, and I'm sure at least a million other things."

"Proceed as way opens."

"Matt, I don't think you understand. I have all my regular chores, and learning how to do all the extra stuff, and trying to figure out how to come up with 10,000 words."

He nodded. "Proceed as way opens."

She shook her head, but smiled. "You think it's all just going to magically fall into place?"

"Hasn't it so far?"

She took a deep breath, slowly recognizing that he was right. "Proceed as way opens," she said softly.

"Besides, I'll be around, just down the hill if you get yourself into a pickle. I'll help you every chance I get."

"Is that all?" she asked, looking disappointed.

"I...I guess that's entirely up to you."

"No, it's not."

"No?"

"No. I don't want you to be *just be down the hill!*"

"Why not?"

"Because…it's so…*geographically undesirab*le." She shook her head, looking thoughtful. "Yeah, you—that far away—that doesn't really work for me at all. What if…heaven forbid, the cow has a baby, or the summer recruits stage a mutiny, or the washing machine breaks down. I'd have to walk all the way up to the phone booth, and you might be busy with a patient, and then you might not be able to help me until the end of the day."

"Yeah, but I'd come as soon as I could—depending on business."

She thought for a moment. "Yeah, that won't work at all. Niederbipp is way too far away from the farm."

He laughed. "Genevieve, it's like a fifteen minute bike ride."

"That's at least thirteen minutes too far away."

He laughed out loud.

"I'm serious! Who would be a megaphone for the voice in my heart if you're not there whenever I need to hear something important?"

Matt shook his head. "I don't think you need me as your megaphone any more."

"Why would you say that?"

"You've figured it out…you learned how to listen to that little voice in your heart." He smiled. "My work here is done."

"Matt, you don't get it. I'm not ready to be done with you, and two more months is not going to change that."

"What are you saying?"

"Matt…," she shook her head. "Okay, look, *I need you.* I can't do this without you and there's no…" She took a deep breath and stood from the swing, moving closer to him. "In the interest of honesty and full disclosure and absolute vulnerability, I'm just gonna say it…there's no one I'd rather do this with. There's no one who gets me like you do, who can tell me I'm ridiculous and irrational and insane and get away with it. Can't you see that you need to be a part of this, too?"

Matt looked away, smiling but shaking his head. "Genevieve, look, you're talking about really big things here. I appreciate your honesty, and I'm flattered that you'd even consider me—truly, I am. But I really think you need more time to think about what you're suggesting."

"I don't want any more time to think about this. I'm ready to talk about this now!"

He looked at her for a moment before shaking his head. "This is crazy," he said, almost a whisper.

"Isn't this why you came here?"

He smiled. "Yeah, this *is* why I came here."

"Am I not what you want?"

The question seemed to shock both of them and somewhere deep within him, he responded with a primal reaction that felt like the only natural thing to do. He closed the gap between them and wrapped his arms tightly around her.

They held each other for what felt like minutes, saying nothing, but saying everything that needed to be said. There was nothing more they could give each other now. With two months left, and regular chore rotations with all of the other campers, they couldn't make this awkward and threaten the harmony that had been created over the last three months. It would have to wait. They both knew it. It was going to be tough, but they had each other. *They had each other*!

Neither of them wanted to be the first to let go, but when they finally did, Matt took Genevieve's hand in his, and together they walked back into town to find Pops and Ruby.

To Be continued in Gracefully Ruby!

ABOUT THE AUTHOR

God. Family. Art. Stories. With his head, heart, and hands, Ben Behunin tries to bring his passions together to make the world a little more kind, thoughtful, and beautiful. A potter by day and a writer by night—and whenever he can get away with it, Ben maintains a studio just inches away from his home in Salt Lake City, Utah. He and his wife, Lynnette, are the happy parents of two teens, Isaac and Eve.

Information about studio visits and the Behunin's semi-annual home tours is available at www.potterboy.com.